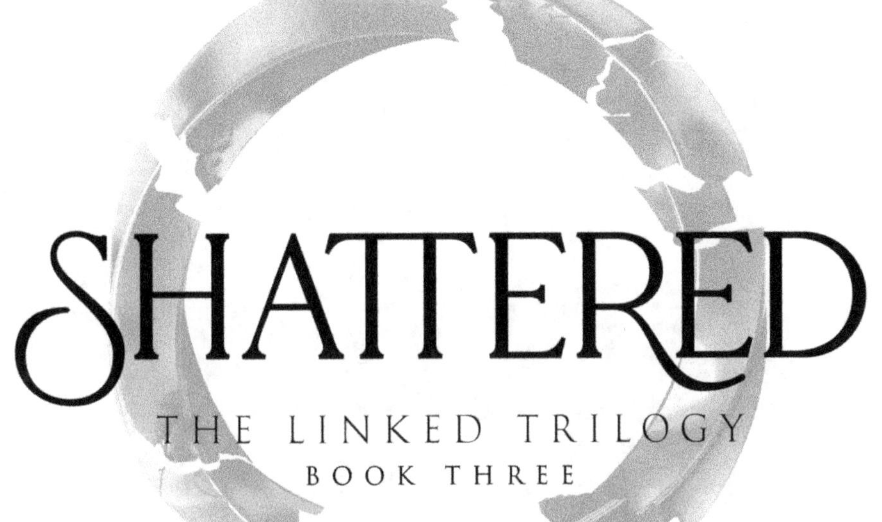

SHATTERED

THE LINKED TRILOGY
BOOK THREE

CASSIE
SWINDON

ISBN for hardcover: 978-1-7373469-4-4

Cover Design by Christian Bentulan

Interior Formatting by Jennifer Laslie

SHATTERED

Kyra Kozelski

Darkness is gnawing at my soul. The shadows swallow me a little more each day. But someone needs to destroy Elana Elidi. And I may be the only one who can. There's a spell to stop this whole mess. But it requires a sacrifice from my true love. The problem is—who does my heart belong to—Jay or Isaac?

Also by Cassie Swindon

LINKED TRILOGY

Scorched

Severed

Shattered

GOLDEN CHAINS TRILOGY

Break the Stone

Hunt the Storm

Stop the Clock

Dedicated to:

Anna Cackler and her froughtin' bunnies.

ACKNOWLEDGMENTS

Developmental editor: Kirsty McQuarrie at Let's Get Proofed

Copy line editors: Kirsty McQuarrie at Let's Get Proofed and Kelly George at Polished Proofreading

Proofreading: Kelly George at Polished Proofreading

Trilogy Covers: Christian Bentulan at Covers by Christian

Interior Design: Jennifer Leslie

Beta Readers: Aubree Anderson, Ana Maria Tufescu, Paula Lloyd, Michelle Richardson, Arceli Friage, Aimee Harrison

Map Designer: Adriana Pausenwein

Character Illustration Artist: Claudia Hopkins

Short Story Covers: Anna Cackler

This shout-out goes to all the first responders, health care workers, therapists, and you-name-it professionals all battling against Covid. I was fortunate enough to only have a mild case while drafting this book (but of course, symptoms started on my birthday of all days.) After struggling through the symptoms, I was grateful for the opportunity to receive medicine and have virtual appointments with doctors. Many of my family members are in the healthcare field, and they all deserve a standing ovation for their dedication and hard work during the pandemic.

TRIGGER WARNINGS

Recommended for age 18+ due to profanity, violence, sexual content, and other sensitive topics that could potentially trigger the reader.

Read at your own discretion.

I

KYRA

Dark desire danced in the shadows between us, teasing me to the point of insanity. From across the crowded room, his eyes pinned me flat against the wall. I dropped my gaze and allowed the intoxicating music to take control as I swayed toward him. I forgot about the responsibilities weighing on my shoulders and the devious gray tattoo hiding under my skirt.

The bass thumped sensually, and I rocked my hips back and forth to the beat. Dim lights cast a faded beam onto Jay's dark, thick hair, then over his stern face, and finally over his sculpted arms that would soon claim me. He wrapped me into his chest, holding me close, and our hearts rammed together as one. Some days, his devotion felt like a dream, but this was as real as the Magik coursing through me.

Unable to hold back for a second longer, my hands found the hem of Jay's shirt, and I slid my hands up his firm, sweaty abdomen. In one quick peek, I savored the view of the upper curve of his green Möbius circle arching out from the top of his jeans. If only I could kiss it again.

Jay's sweet smile turned wicked, testing the limits. I'd been stuck in this safe house for weeks, but I hadn't even kissed him. Weeks of torture. I breathed Jay in and relished his woody scent, full of life. My heeled boots gifted me a few extra inches, almost allowing me to reach his plump, full lips. What I'd give to feel his mouth on mine once more. Just once. Maybe I'd tie his shoelaces together.

"Enjoying yourself, Petal?" Jay's smirk made everyone else in the room vanish. He rolled up his sleeves, the white fabric contrasting against his darker skin.

I licked my lips while staring at his. "Well, it *is* my birthday, after all."

Suddenly, a second, firm body pressed against my back, and a large hand grabbed my waist from behind.

"What birthday gift would you like, love?" Isaac whispered in my ear, devilish venom oozing from each word like a luxurious promise.

My breath hitched. I knew what I wanted for my birthday, but that didn't mean I could ask for it. Neither man would agree, even if it were for only one night. My chest churned with the craving taking hold of me.

Isaac's chin brushed the top of my head, and I turned around to face him while Jay caressed up and down my spine. All three of us swayed to the beat. Craning my neck to meet Isaac's radiant blue eyes, I studied the devious look plastered on his face.

A fan from the corner blew his white tee up, showing his washboard stomach and the blue-ish gray tattoo. Our Link was severed weeks ago, but I could still hear some of his witty remarks in my mind.

The fan blew again, enveloping me in Isaac's crisp scent, like laundry detergent and a spring breeze on a starry night. It was too bad I hadn't stepped outdoors in weeks to breathe in any fresh air. Isaac had become my connection to the sky and what lay beyond this safe house.

A group of women clinked their glasses together, tipped their heads back, and swallowed their alcohol. Sandwiched between the two men, my heart rate tripled, and desire tormented my Circle, surging with raw power. I couldn't lose control, not in front of all these society members. The outer world might have been falling apart, but we were all letting loose for one night—my birthday.

Bass thrummed violently, conquering my senses until all my rational thoughts were scattered into pieces on the floor. The sounds reminded me of my days as a drummer in a band. It felt like so much time had been stolen. Within the mass of writhing bodies, someone bumped into my side.

"I got you a gift, love," Isaac said over the blaring music as he eased a mini drumstick hairpin, curved at the bottom, into my heap of hair. He pressed against me again. I needed his chest. Needed his arms. Needed his lips.

But whose? Jay's or Isaac's?

My skin tingled, and my body scorched from within. Desperate. This destructive game the three of us had been playing had built up to an unsustainable pressure, ready to erupt. My body was on the verge of exploding. My four tattoos begged me for release. I was so fucking desperate. I wasn't strong enough to keep resisting them. I wanted them both. I loved both—no—I couldn't love them both.

A glance around the room confirmed that no one's eyes were on us. I grabbed Jay's hand and guided him between my legs.

His eyebrows knit together. "I can't, Petal. Nilson is *right* here."

I gulped and nodded, wishing his hand was where my skin yearned for his touch.

"Such a tease, love," Isaac whispered.

I arched my back and turned my neck. Isaac's blue eyes seared a deep, passionate hole through me. I knew he didn't need my words to know what I wanted. But I wouldn't let his lips meet mine—not in front of Jadox. I wouldn't taste his cotton candy and tequila drink. I wouldn't explore Isaac with urgency.

Both men supported me as we continued dancing. Jay caressed teasingly. One of his fingers trailed up the side of each vertebra. My skin flushed, and my muscles eased into his touch. The music beat faster, faster, matching the intensity of my heartbeat. I had to stop this. I couldn't lead them both on. But…feeling their bodies pressed against mine was *so* damn good.

I pulsed my hips, coaxing for more. "Please," I begged. "Please, Jay, just kiss me."

Isaac froze. His body turned rigid, and his hips stopped completely. The sadness on his face as I met Jay's eyes again wiped away all ecstasy. A breeze from a nearby fan whipped between us, and, for that moment, it felt like an entire tropical storm separated Isaac and me.

The music was suddenly suffocating as both men's eyes were trained on me. What the Flames was I doing?

I flattened my skirt and pushed them both away. Darting down the hall and further from the music, the crashing sounds from my birthday party turned into a low hum in only seconds. The safe house hallway was lined with doors leading to the conference room, the group kitchen, the weapons room, and the sleeping quarters, just to name a few. I fumbled in the darkness, hoping the two of them wouldn't follow me. That was if they'd even want to.

Finally, when I closed a door behind me, a deep sigh parted my lips. Stealing a moment, I slowed my panting breaths and flipped the lock on the door handle. The faint, old lights winked like stars on the ceiling, so I summoned fire to my fingertips as a much-needed torch.

Light burst and illuminated the near-empty room. Bunkbeds belonging to the Aurum Orbis Society members lined one wall with backpacks draped from their corners, each fully stocked with emergency necessities. I headed to the one bed that wasn't made; mine, of course. My boots made the floor creak, so I treaded lighter so as not to wake Chocolate, sleeping at the foot of the bed.

I slumped onto my mattress with a heavy groan. The sounds of the party still *tap, tap, tapped* in my ears.

Phantom feelings of Jay's hands on me flattened me against my pillows. Ghostly sensations of Isaac's lips on mine lured my fingers down my stomach. I grabbed a pillow. The soft cotton was glorious against my skin, but I shoved my face against the fluffiness and screamed and screamed and screamed. My life was falling apart.

For the last few weeks, something else was forming in place of my soul as if tendrils of ashes were shedding from my skin, exposing a monster that lingered deep below. As each day crept by, the gray tattoo was turning me rotten. I was becoming the darkness between branches, the shadow in the corners. These wicked truths of my identity peeled away the version of a girl trapped by fear for years. Now, infected with evil from the inside out, I wasn't the same girl I used to be. She was gone. Something had changed deep within me.

I stopped screaming and lowered the pillow when my throat turned raw and scratchy. Two pitiful brown eyes stared at me.

"Hi, Chocolate. Sorry I woke you." I sighed, with all the weight of the world sagging down on my shoulders.

Her floppy tongue, hanging out the side of her mouth, gave my knee a quick lick before she circled and lay by my feet again.

Defeated, I sunk back into the mattress, staring at the wooden slats above me. I touched the mini hairpin Isaac had stuck in my ponytail. He was sweet to think of me, but the gift reminded me that I only had two weeks left until his deadline to decide who I wanted. Isaac or Jay? My fists curled into balls. The pressure was killing me. How was I supposed to know which man I truly loved?

"Enjoying your birthday? You look like absolute sunshine, sis." Caspian walked in through the outside door that I'd forgotten to lock.

"Why are we wasting resources on this party, Cas?" I got to my feet and connected Chocolate's leash to her collar. "We should've used this booze money for weapons."

Caspian sauntered through the room, drenched in shadows from the moonlight. "It may be our last celebration for a while, Kyra. Might as well enjoy one more night. I know I've been busy. Why do you look like Lady Death?"

I sighed again, letting all the weight on my chest fall away. "How do I know who is right for me?"

He nodded and sat on one of the empty bunks. "Well, they both could be chosen to pose on the front of a men's fitness magazine, so they have that in common."

I snorted and laughed at the same time. "Yeah, that's about the only thing."

Jay was as stubborn as me, protective, nurturing, and sacrificial, yet Isaac was cunning, dedicated, hilarious, and so charming.

"It wasn't fair that Isaac gave me an ultimatum."

"Or maybe he's the smart one." Caspian traced his long scar. "You've been stringing them both along for weeks."

"I know." I dropped my head in my hands. "Goddess, I know."

He rose and placed a hand on my back. "Ky, the world is literally at war."

"Don't make fun of me. Not right now."

He wrapped me in a hug. "Well, if you'd just let me finish for once, you'd know that I was going to say the world is literally at war, but I know what it feels like to have your heart in pieces. Your struggle is just as real as the battle between the society and Elana's army. I'll be here no matter what, no matter who you decide."

I eased into my brother's chest, letting him hold my weight.

"And if you want my opinion, just choose the guy I can beat at surfing."

I laughed again and wiped away the free-falling tears. "Thanks, Cas."

"No problem. But I do need to make a call." Slowly, he moved toward the door.

"At midnight?"

"Well, it may or may not be about Narelle's choice of pajamas or lack of them."

I threw a pillow at him. "Ew, gross. Get out of here. I don't want to hear that about my little brother."

Chocolate whined and pulled me toward the door. According to the society's rules, I wasn't allowed outside the Aurella Fortress. But no one else was around to take care of our pup. There was no chance I was going back to ask for Jay or Isaac to help. Plus, surely, there was no way that Elana's forces knew that the crumbling castle at the edge of Vayu's border was a massive safe house.

"You need to go out, girl?" I asked.

Her feet pranced in that little happy-puppy way. Each time she stepped toward the door, one of the joints in her knees clicked. I should take the time to ask Jay Chocolate's age. How had I never asked before? Probably because I was too wrapped up in learning who I belonged to in this life that any topic not completely about my fate was completely off-limits to my stupid brain. Chocolate dragged me to the back door.

I unlatched the seven locks and punched in the code. The metal door slowly nudged open, and I heaved against it with my shoulders to inch it further, then squeezed through the opening. Leaving it a sliver open, I stepped into the night fog.

I hadn't known how much I longed to leave those concrete walls until now. Relief washed over me as the sounds of nature sang. Crickets chirped, owls hooted, and ventus shrieked, harmonizing in a melody that blessed my soul.

I craned my neck to the ancient arrow-slit holes at the top of the castle. The stark contrast to the skyscrapers across the courtyard was breathtaking.

Despite the soothing ballad of Vayu's forest, the silent moon loomed over us as a steady reminder of Gemm's last prophecy. Her words rang in my head again and again.

"On the full Teal Moon, one man will lay down his life for love."

I gulped and squeezed my eyes shut, praying to the goddess above that she was wrong. I only had two weeks left to find a way to prevent that fate. It wasn't fair. I had worked too hard to keep them both alive, and we had all sacrificed so much. Maybe if I had never picked either of them, then neither man would be doomed to this fate.

Tears pooled behind my eyes. "You won't win," I whispered up at the moon, but she only smiled down in return.

Following Chocolate's tug, I lumbered through the tall grass toward the abandoned skyscrapers of Vayu. Trying to claw myself out of the fog, I contemplated Gemm's other words for the hundredth time.

One of them became cursed and was trudging toward death.

I shook my head in frustration and shot a random burst of fire at one of the buildings. "No! I won't let them die. I won't." Flames shot through a window, and glass shattered, cascading over the sidewalk.

The peaceful sounds surrounding me dropped to silence.

"I'm sorry, critters. I didn't mean to scare you."

Chocolate barked and tugged hard, her leash slipping from my hand as she darted into one of the shadowy buildings.

"Chocolate! Hey. Come back!" I sprinted over the fallen glass through the quiet streets. Too quiet.

When I reached the threshold of a door, a strange feeling warped my tattoos. I rolled the hem of my skirt down and stared at the gray tattoo on my hip, which now resembled a toxic mist. *Shit.*

"Chocolate?" I whispered and tiptoed forward into the building. The sensation of icy wings fluttered against my steel, solid heart, sending a warning.

"Hello, Kyra," said a familiar yet unexpected voice. "We have a lot to catch up on."

"This isn't possible." I held my breath.

"Anything is possible, but whatever you do, don't take another step closer."

2

JADOX

Sweat was dripping off me as I searched for Kyra in the bunkhouse. In defiance against the society's only rule for her, she had disappeared. Her intoxicating scent flooded the bunkroom and led straight to the back door. I rushed forward and reached to twist the handle, but the door was already open a splinter. Shit. I could forgive her for being unsure about me, and I could forgive her for jumping into action without talking to me first, but I could never forgive her if she had gotten herself captured by Elana's army.

It simply wasn't an option.

Outside, the smell of rain lingered in the air. The moment the wind hit my cheeks, it carried away the last of Kyra's scent into the inky sky. I crouched and brushed a fingertip over the mushy earth. Only one set of boot prints led towards the city with pawprints alongside them.

Ahead, streetlights flickered over an abandoned alley like a beacon, projecting an overwhelming sense of dread. With every urgent step, worry clamped down on my gut.

Something wasn't right.

"Kyra?" My boots crunched over dead leaves as I approached the closest building. Most of the windows were shattered, and glass covered the sidewalk.

I sniffed the muggy air again and sucked in the sinister energy of the alley. Sharp letters spelling the store's name, *Rob's Mart,* hung crookedly above the doorway, shadowed by the flickering lights. When the wind blew, the sign creaked back and forth from one nail. Back and forth. *Creak. Creak*. Gooseflesh covered my arms, and a shiver crept up my spine.

I stepped forward into the unknown.

"Kyra? Are you in here?" I whispered. Damn, I should've brought another weapon–just in case.

Kyra's voice met my ears from inside the desolate shop. She spoke softly and slowly to someone. Who else was there? I peered around empty crates, and upside-down vegetable stands. Power thrummed through my Circle, and I held out both hands, Magik rushing to my fingertips: my true weapon.

Moonbeams sliced through the far window and shone off Kyra's long, thick, golden hair. A strange vibe sent chills along my spine. She sat on the dusty floor, legs crossed with Chocolate's chin laying on her. I breathed out a deep sigh and let my heart rate calm. Everything was okay; she was safe. First, I spotted her heeled boots coated in mud. Then my gaze raked over her smooth legs up to the black skirt. My heart pounded at the memory of her soft skin when we were on the dance floor less than an hour ago and how badly she wanted me to touch her. Each day, I longed for her touch, smile, warmth, and jokes. But ever since our Link was severed, part of me had felt misplaced.

The red haze cleared to show her white shirt, covered with a ridiculous plastic sash that read *Birthday Girl* across her torso. And finally, her crimson lipstick glittered through the steam. I'd give anything to kiss her again, but she had set boundaries until she'd made her choice. There was no way I could share her. What was going through her mind these days?

Just as I was about to call her and tease her for having a full conversation with my dog, she spoke again.

"I don't know who to choose."

For once, I was glad we weren't Linked, so I didn't have to suffer through her turmoil of emotions for Nilson. I'd wait patiently for her choice, but that didn't mean it was easy dealing with her hesitancy between the two of us. I'd never tell Kyra how agonizing it was when my memories came crashing back, mixed with all the interactions I had witnessed between her and Isaac. I knew she hadn't simply forgotten about me, yet, at the same time…no, I wouldn't pin her as the bad guy. Kyra wasn't my villain, but I still wanted to be her first choice—with certainty. Mid-thought, Kyra's next words cemented me to the spot.

"Hallie, how can I find the answers?" Kyra asked.

My chest tightened as I scanned the room fast. Her sister? Impossible. She couldn't be alive. I saw her die myself. A bullet had torn through her sister on a rooftop not far from here.

After a quick sweep confirming the room didn't hold anyone else, I processed the options. Maybe this was Kyra's way of grieving. Lots of people spoke out loud to themselves or loved ones. She probably just needed privacy and wanted to connect with her sister on her birthday. There was nothing wrong with that.

Her life had been chaotic ever since she made that fateful wish. She never had the chance to mourn her sister or mother. Now that the immediate danger had subsided, her heart, body, and mind must finally be accepting their deaths. What kind of support would she want? I just wished she would've told me where she had headed tonight so I didn't have to worry about her safety. Elana Elidi's soldiers might find our hideout any day.

I stepped out from the shadows, and Kyra turned fast with both hands afire, aimed at me.

"Who's there?" Her voice cracked like embers in a campfire, and she shot a burst of red steam into the space between us, blocking her from view. It smelled like gasoline fumes, a smell I'd only experienced in historical museums.

I jumped back with both hands raised. "Woah, Kyra, it's just me."

The red steam shifted into devilish shapes until it started to lift.

When the red cloud finally dissolved and rose over her head, I gasped and took a huge step backward. Instead of her amber eyes glowing, as usual, onyx irises had taken their place. Her gaze was soulless, empty, carved out, and entirely black. I didn't dare breathe or move.

What the fuck?

She tilted her head to the side while slowly patting Chocolate's head. "Jay, me and Hallie were just talking about you. Come join us." A crooked smile crept up her cheeks, and my heart just about stopped. This wasn't Kyra. This wasn't my Petal.

Terrified of making any sudden movements, I crossed the room at a snail's pace. Chocolate's tail thumped happily as if nothing was wrong. Weren't dogs supposed to have a sixth sense of darkness? Kyra patted the floor beside her without taking those obsidian eyes off me. Haunting, unnatural eyes.

Another shudder threatened to rip through me, but I held it back, using all my energy not to spook her. One wrong move might push the thing possessing her to lash out. As a child, I had heard Gemm tell a story about spirits, but it was only supposed to be a fairytale.

I gulped down what felt like a pile of stones and carefully sat beside her. The healing spell was at the tip of my tongue, but I didn't want to scare her. Instead, I silently chanted *Terra angakok. Terra angakok,* again and again, praying to the Divinity above that it would save her from whatever monster bewitched her body. It didn't work. Kyra stared at me like an empty shell.

My heart rammed chaotically against my chest. I needed help. Reinforcements. Where was fuckin' Nilson when she actually needed him? Maybe if I distracted her, it'd break the stupor.

"Kyra? Tell me about the first time you played the drums," I said quietly.

A wave of hesitancy flashed across her features, smoothing her face for only a moment. But then, the commanding darkness overpowered it again. "Hallie was there with me, weren't you?" She turned her head straight and stared at a pile of empty bins.

Terror seized my soul, and I didn't move a single muscle. What the Flames was I supposed to do? If I touched her, would she snap out of the trance? Had someone cursed her? Why were her eyes the color of death? Sweat dripped down my back, and time ceased to exist.

"Hallie wants me to buy Landon a puppy." She stroked Chocolate's head again and again. "Maybe Landon will pick a lab too." The sweetness of her voice had an actual scent; it was like ice cream dipped in poison and spider webs.

"Kyra, I think we should go to bed and —"

"No!" she bellowed, making Chocolate jolt out of her embrace. "It's my birthday, and I can do whatever I want! I don't have to go to sleep. I don't have to choose one of you! I don't have to save anyone."

I clenched my fists into balls by my side, then released them. Clenched. Released. There was a fundamental wrongness in the air. Gemm had never taught me how to deal with dark Magik as a child. This wasn't something I had ever trained for. It was time for a new approach.

"Kyra, I don't see Hallie. No one is there," I pleaded, hearing the uncertainty in my voice.

She laughed, but the sound was foreign to my ears, veiled in jagged, harsh edges. "Of course, she is. Hallie, don't let him tease you? What did you say...oh, yes, of course, I love that you shaved your head, sis. It looks great."

If I knocked her unconscious and carried her inside, maybe Narelle or Caspian would have a solution. Or we could call Gemm. But there was no chance I'd leave her here alone to search for them.

"What if I die soon?" Kyra asked, her tone sweeter than Gemm's scrumptious pies.

"What?"

Her gaze latched onto all my fears. That fraudulent smile returned, slithering up her face and claiming it. I had to stop this. Whatever controlled Kyra was taking another piece of her with every passing moment.

"Do you remember when you died, Jay?" She started twirling her hair like a schoolgirl.

Shaking, I covered her hand with mine, stopping her compulsive movement. Her fingers were ice-cold to the touch. I placed her hand on my chest, right over my pounding heart. "Kyra, you don't have to worry about death. We'll both live a long and happy life. Now, come back to me, Petal. I need you."

She pulled her hand away, but those hollow eyes stayed fixated on me. "I think I understand what Gemm said now."

"What...what are you talking about?" I asked slowly.

"Weeks ago...." Her voice turned fragile and impossibly softer. "Gemm had another prophecy, she said, *'after the Links severed, one of them became cursed and was slowly trudging toward death.'* It's me. I'm cursed."

Panic lodged into my stomach, curling it into knots. I inched closer and held both my hands on her cheeks. A lost soul glared back, but I refused to believe my Kyra was gone.

"You're not cursed, Kyra. We all have darkness inside us, but it will not break you. All the gifts we each hold could also be twisted into curses. That heaviness you feel doesn't have to destroy your light."

"You're the wisest, cutest little puppet."

Deep down, I could feel her essence under the cement below us, crawling through the soil. How could I bring her back? Unsure of the best choice, I hovered my lips over hers and searched her face for danger. Her gaze was vacant, an endless hole, but she wouldn't hurt me.

"I'm going to kiss you now," I said. "Come back to me, Petal."

A quick spark of gold flashed in her eyes, pushing through the cavity for only a moment, then disappeared again. I couldn't risk losing her. I pressed my lips to hers, and the room faded away.

After only a pause, she came back. Her energy returned to the room in a flurry. I kissed her harder, desperate to show my devotion. We melded like lava and stone, forming a new shape altogether to fossilize for eternity.

Kyra tasted like pineapple and coconut, and her passionate desire reminded me of a summer night under the stars. Her hands grabbed my neck, hungry for more. Kyra's fiery spirit meshed with mine. She rooted me in this life. I wanted to be tangled in a knot so messy that there'd be no hope of unraveling from each other.

A soft bite on my lip snapped me out of the frenzy as she slowly pulled away. I locked onto her eyes—amber once again.

"Hey there, Petal." I traced circles over her wrist. "You came back to me."

Kyra laughed, the sound music to my ears. "It's only been two weeks, Jay. You need to work on your patience."

I rolled my lips and studied her face, unsure if she was joking. "Kyra, do you remember walking out here?"

She glanced around the dark store. "Sure, Chocolate needed to go for a walk. Wait, where is she?" She snapped her fingers. "Chocolate?"

My pup frolicked over hesitantly and sniffed Kyra's boot before jumping on her lap. Kyra fell back against my chest, and I soaked in the scent of her shampoo. I'd give anything to simply sink into this moment, but there was too much at stake.

"Kyra, do you remember talking to anyone by those boxes?"

Mid-smile, she attacked Chocolate's forehead with mini kisses. "Huh? What do you mean?"

She had no idea what had just happened. Shit. My teeth ground together as I watched her rub Chocolate's belly. The last thing I wanted to do was increase her stress, but it was necessary to find the answers.

"Kyra, did Gemm tell you a prophecy you've kept from me?"

With that, her attention snapped back to me. "How…how do you know about that?"

"You just told me a few minutes ago."

"I did?" She scrunched up her lip and leaned back on both palms. "Maybe I drank too much earlier. Um, remind me, I said what exactly?"

"How about you tell me what Gemm said." She was hiding something. Tightness squeezed my chest again.

"Well, if I already told you, there's nothing else to talk about." She stood and brushed off the dust from her skirt.

"Why won't you look at me?"

Kyra began walking through the store, but I reached forward and laced her fingers with mine. "*Please* don't hold anything back from me."

Her head dropped. "I don't want to hurt you, Jay."

With one finger, I lifted her chin. "You know how you're my roots...."

"Even if they're covered in thorns." She smiled, and this time it reflected in her eyes. "Gnarled, twisted, and rough."

"Exactly." I pressed my lips to her forehead.

Kyra sighed, but instead of defeat, it seemed like a river of relief washed off her shoulders. "Gemm said, after the Links severed, *one of them became cursed and was slowly trudging toward death.* And also, *that on the full Teal Moon, one man will lay down his life for love.*" Kyra shook her head fiercely. "But I won't let that happen, Jay. You'll be okay."

"One of them became cursed...." I repeated.

"I'll make sure the curse stays away from you, I swear. And if it happens, I'll cure you. I promise, Jay."

"And one man will lay down his life," I whispered, contemplating why and when. I loved her with all my heart. Did Gemm see a future in which I sacrificed my life to save Kyra? Or did it have a different meaning altogether? Gemm's prophecies weren't always what they seemed. Wind whipped through the door, and Kyra shivered.

"Come on, let's get you warm."

"I'm fine. I'm made of fire." Kyra rolled her eyes and blasted a small flame from all five fingertips. "But, please do me a favor and don't tell anyone else about Gemm's prophecy, at least not until I can figure out a plan."

I took a deep breath, letting it out as I answered, "That's only about two weeks away."

"I know, but tonight is my birthday, and I want to dance again and just forget about everything."

"Happy birthday, Kyra." I kissed her forehead. "I got you something." Reaching into my pocket, I pulled out a solar pod.

Her smile lit up the darkness. "Wow! Jay, where did you find one?" She quickly inserted the music device behind her ear and started tapping her watch to sync the programming.

"It was Alaska's idea actually." I stared at the shadows of the wall, wondering where my sister had run off to this time.

"Well, thank you, Jay. It's perfect. How many songs does it hold?"

"Unlimited."

Her smile fixed all the brokenness of Lodesa and turned the world right again.

"Come on, Narelle swore she'd take a shot with me."

Kyra dragged me through a mud puddle toward the Aurella Fortress. The castle's crumbling walls loomed under the moonlight, and the ancient castle seemed to take us back in time, but time was something we didn't have.

I hated prophecies. We were wrong about the first one. Kyra was never supposed to Link with Isaac or me but with her long-lost brother. What did this new prophecy mean? Fear gripped my power and coiled it tight. My mind fractured down the middle like a violent quake had ruptured it.

Kyra strutted ahead into our safe house. She flung off her muddy shoes and marched straight to the hallway in only her socks.

"Kyra, wait." I stormed after her, wincing from the music, increasing in volume with every step.

"Catch me, soldier." She smiled over her shoulder, daring me to play, and jogged down the hallway to the beat of the bass that rattled the whole fortress.

Back at the party, twice as many Ordulls were asleep on the couches compared to when I had left. Isaac Nilson's gaze snapped up the moment we entered. Goddess, I wish that man never existed. If she picked him, I'd be completely devastated. Maybe that would be how I laid down my life for her, so she could be happy with him.

At least Kyra was safe and smiling again. I'd do anything to keep her that way. But for one night, I needed to relax and leave the problems for tomorrow.

"Here, man." Nilson nudged my shoulder and handed over a beer.

I cracked it open and chugged half the can.

"Woah, slow down, big guy." Nilson chuckled.

"Why are you talking to me? We aren't friends."

"Such a charmer." He sipped his can and smirked behind the aluminum as Kyra pulled Narelle to the dance floor. "She's a handful, huh? Keeps us on our toes."

"Kyra is losing herself, Nilson."

"Naw, look, she's happy." He pointed to the dance floor, where Kyra rolled her hips against Narelle. "She's letting loose."

"No, something is very wrong."

"What do you mean? Like, you can *feel* it?" Nilson's eyes snapped to mine, worried. "Through the Link? Did it come back?"

I shook my head. "No, but can't you see it in her? She's...different."

"I think you've had one too many beers, man. Or maybe your time working for Elana has damaged you."

He was probably right. Agonizing memories as Elana's brainwashed soldier came back, full of my torturous actions toward innocent prisoners. Images of caged Mystiers from all tribes— thin, dirty, pale, and broken—still haunted my nights.

Kyra glanced at me from the dance floor. Passion like that couldn't be faked. The past few weeks trapped in this fortress had been rough; I needed to get out of here. We had plenty of time to form a plan, yet Caspian and the Aurum Orbis Society leaders refused to let us leave. Enough was enough. Tomorrow, I'd ask Kyra to join me and set out to rescue the prisoners. The question was whether she was ready to say goodbye to Nilson.

"See, Griffin." Nilson pointed. "Our girl is happy."

Tension clamped on my throat. "Our?"

Nilson winked. "Well, for now. She'll pick soon enough."

My fists clenched into tight balls. "You sound so confident."

His gaze dropped to my chest, where the corners of the word *MINE* peeked out from my shirt. "Kyra *needs* someone confident to rely on."

"You don't know anything about her or what she needs."

Nilson shrugged. "I know she'll agree to dance with me."

A snort erupted from my throat. "I doubt it."

He pushed his beer against my chest. "Watch this."

3

KYRA

Narelle ground her ass against my stomach, and we moved like a wave. Music blared to the point of pain, vibrating through my bones. I undulated faster as the bass pulsed. My cheeks heated, and sweat formed on my forehead. Through the mass of waving arms all reaching toward the ceiling, I caught Isaac's gray eyes.

I pressed a single fingertip to my mouth as the phantom feeling of his lips on mine returned. He didn't smirk this time but pushed through the crowd with a devilish look saved only for me. What was he thinking?

The women in the room partied like they'd all had the same premonition about this night being their last chance to celebrate. If we were eventually successful in bringing back all males, then they'd have more dance partners. As if dancing truly mattered.

Narelle tapped my shoulder and yelled something about Caspian. I followed her finger to the corner of the room where my brother had sunk into a couch. Over the last few weeks, I'd watched him like a hawk and learned my brother's trademark movements and tendencies. He always twirled a straw clockwise in each drink three times before taking a sip. He never sat with his back to an exit. Our chats revealed that Caspian loved action movies, sailing, water-skiing, and walking barefoot. I also learned that even though an elder couple took him under their wing in Cydon, he had been independent most of his life, coming and going from their house without rules or discipline.

Caspian was a self-made man, and my heart cartwheeled in pride for what he had accomplished.

I nodded to Narelle before she pranced away, leaving me alone in a crowded room—although not for long.

Isaac reached my side and confidently held out his hand. Jay's eyes were trained on me, but I pretended not to notice. The tension within my Circle immediately doubled. I had to at least give Isaac a chance. His hand dwarfed mine when he twirled me into his chest, gluing our bodies together. I looked up, and the adoring look on his face was too much, too soon.

Hastily, I turned and bumped against his front until Isaac's unmistakable arousal pressed against me. Every inch of my skin tingled.

As if he could sense my thoughts, Isaac's hands wrapped around my waist, guiding my movements against him. The beat entranced me into a hypnotic ecstasy. Holy Divinity, I missed this sense of living free and careless. That was the gift Isaac always provided me—vibrancy. We were alike in that way, both possessing the longing to take life by the horns. But then, why was I delaying my decisions and showing hesitancy at every turn?

The heat of Isaac against my back was so alluring that I remembered the erotic dreams I kept having about him thrusting inside me. I gulped and guided his hands to my tattoo. His long arms reached easily as he traced little circles under my shirt. I arched my neck back and met his gaze again. The hunger in his eyes was undeniable, but just as he licked his lips, I froze. His face held a hint of something I couldn't describe—something that wasn't meant to belong to me.

Isaac stopped dancing too and mouthed, "Are you okay?"

I cupped my ear with one hand and leaned in. "Can we talk?"

He nodded and grabbed my hand, leading me away from the dance floor. The song eventually faded into white noise the further he pulled me down the hallway. When he swept me into the bunkroom and shut the door, my feet immediately hollered from fatigue. I groaned and sat on the edge of my bed.

"Here, let me," Isaac whispered as he kneeled in front of me and his fingers caressed my sore foot. I moaned so loudly it coaxed a bright smile to his face. "Now, don't be doing that too loudly, or there'll be talk tomorrow," he said.

I nudged him playfully, then watched his talented fingers work as he switched to my other foot. The tenderness with which he moved showed a skill of experience. I wondered how many times he had done that with Wes' mom in the past. How often did Isaac think of his ex?

"Are you having a good birthday?" He kissed my ankle, then continued the glorious rubbing.

"I'm not sure. It's been a weird time."

"I think all of Lodesa would agree that the last few months have been anything but ordinary."

"Hey, Isaac?"

"Yes, my love?" My eyes flew to his full lips, which curled wickedly.

"Why don't you hate me for Rajitha's death?"

He stopped massaging and closed his eyes for just a moment. That told me what I needed to know. He still grieved her loss. When we were Linked, it changed the dynamic of everything. Now that he was free from my intrusive thoughts, he must have had the last few weeks to truly process a future life of raising Wes without Rajitha—as a single father.

He climbed onto the mattress and faced me. "I could never hate you," he said, then brushed a strand of hair behind my ear.

"I feel like you're holding something back. Like there's a needle just under your skin wanting to push its way through, but you won't let it."

"You're starting to sound like Griffin with your metaphors," Isaac took my hand and traced shapes on my inner wrist, making my breath hitch. "What do you mean?"

"I can feel your anger, Isaac. Maybe you don't know it's there. But there's bitterness just under the surface, ready to pounce like a ticking time bomb. It's slow and quiet, but it's there."

"I'm not bitter. I love you." But his eyes dropped to our hands when he said it.

My fingers skimmed the blue veins from his hand to his elbow. "Why, though? Why do you love me?"

His jaw dropped a little, and he looked up again. "Have you asked Griffin the same question?"

"This isn't about him. It's about us. Why do you love me?"

"You know why. You make me smile, and our energies vibe. Something about us just flows, and we both have a passion for life."

I wasn't sure how I felt about his answer. It felt too...shallow. "Aren't those things that someone else could give you? Why does it have to be me specifically?"

His brows pinched, and he frowned. "What are you doing, Kyra? Are you *trying* to push me away?"

"No, I'm trying to understand *us*. Didn't Rajitha give you those same feelings? If she were here right now, would you choose her over me?"

"Hey, that's not fair, she and I had a history, and she's not here, so it's not relevant." Isaac stood and faced where Chocolate slept on the floor. "And if we're not talking about Griffin, then we're also not talking about Rajitha."

"But—"

"What else do you *want* from me?" He clasped both hands behind his head. "I left Wes with Gemm for you. I'm telling you how I feel, but you won't accept it. I'm trying to fight for you, love."

"Maybe I don't want anyone to *fight* for me."

He paused. "Then what do you want?"

"Time."

He ran a hand through his hair and pulled it loose, so the tips dangled at his shoulders. "I won't change my request, love. Wes comes first, no matter what, so I need an answer about us in two weeks. That's my limit."

I laid a hand gently on his chest. "I can't give myself to anyone yet if I don't accept and understand who I am, both my light and my darkness. I still have to come to terms with my own shit. And right now, there's some sort of shadow inside me. It's overbearing, Isaac. I can feel it haunting me."

"What do you mean?"

"Well, for one thing, everyone looks at me like I'm fragile now, like there's something wrong with me. Even Jay looks at me differently."

"Ah, well, if you're looking for advice about another dude, then I've already been pushed to the friend zone."

I scooted closer to him on the mattress and laid my head against his arm. "No, that's not it. I want you in my life."

"As a friend?"

"I...I don't know yet."

We sat in silence, except for the intermittent sounds of Chocolate's snores and the far-off vibrations of the bass from the dance room. I concentrated on Isaac's steady heartbeat and how my head shifted up and down slowly in unison with his every breath.

Suddenly, he slapped his knee and stood, making me fall to my side on the bed. "I have something to show you," he said. "It might make you feel better."

My gaze dropped to the zipper of his jeans. "Um, if it's your precious goods, I told you."

One of his eyebrows rose like a mountain peak. "If you're thinking about me naked, then maybe I'm not out of the picture quite yet." He smiled. "Hey, don't you roll your eyes at me."

"Fine. What do you have to show me?" I asked.

He glanced quickly over his shoulder to the doorway, then extended both hands out, palms up. "After our Link severed, I gained a new power."

"What?" I bolted up, my head barely missing the bunk above me as I shot to my feet.

"I've been meaning to show you, but we haven't had any alone time." His eyes narrowed, and both his lips rolled together in concentration. After a few seconds, a green gas flowed out of his palms and hovered above his hands. "Stand back."

I stared, completely entranced. A strange magnetic force pulled me closer to him as I reached out to touch it. But the green vapor vanished as fast as it had appeared.

Heart pounding, my gaze snapped to his. "What was that?"

"I think it's a poisonous gas, but it doesn't affect me. I wanted you to understand that we all have our shadow side, love. This poison is mine, and you have yours. But we can still move forward together instead of dealing with it alone."

I stared at his fingertips. Conflicting thoughts raged through me. On the one hand, it seemed like we were both taking this too lightly. Yet, something pulled me to know more. "Do it again," I whispered.

"Okay, but just for a second, I don't know enough about it yet."

Green gas rose from his hands again and lifted higher. A pressure in my tattoos urged me to leap forward. I inhaled a deep breath and tasted malice in the air, swallowing it down in elation. The gas filled my soul with renewed strength and power, completing me. I needed more.

"Again!" I demanded, gaping at his fingertips.

But Isaac lunged back, almost tripping. An expression I'd never witnessed on him covered his face as he asked, "Kyra? Do you feel okay? What's wrong?"

"Huh? I'm fine. That's amazing. Show me again."

"You aren't fine! Your eyes changed. They're all messed up!"

Chocolate growled. She bared her teeth at Isaac.

"What are you talking about? No, they're not. Now, give me more of that!"

Isaac scrambled back, but I couldn't look away from his hands. For some reason, his voice sounded shaky when he said, "No, Kyra, we need a healer. I need to get Griffin."

"No, I just need that green stuff. Now!"

An obsessive yearning prodded my Circles, and Magik sprung to life. Flames exploded from my fingertips. I felt like fuckin' dynamite, capable of anything. With a flick of my wrist, the floor cracked below our feet. Isaac yelled out and grabbed the post of a bunk bed as the floor opened and split between his feet. Roots thrust out from the cement and pinned him to the wall. His body slammed, and a hard grunt exploded from his lips.

"Give me *more*!"

"No. Look at me, look up, look at me!" His voice sounded frantic for some strange reason.

Finally, I lifted my gaze and met his terror-filled eyes. Why was this man looking at me like I was crazy? With my chest heaving, I reached for his fingertips. An all-consuming desire stretched through my veins and pounded in my blood. I needed that elixir. Blondie Puppet had what I needed.

His face slowly turned red, and I noticed the roots obeying my commands were strangling him.

That wouldn't do. I needed Blondie alive to access his elixir. Before I could release the roots, a fierce gust of wind shoved me back, knocking me to the floor. My head smacked against the base of a bunk bed, and the room spun. Faint footsteps clonked from the other side of the bunkroom door, and I smiled.

A door slammed against the wall, and a man with hair darker than oil and a face sharper than stone appeared. His white shirt was rolled up to his elbows, and his worried look betrayed his tough exterior. Did he have an elixir for me too? I licked my lips and crawled toward him.

More toys to play with. I loved dear puppets.

"Nilson? What's going on?" This puppet sounded so lusciously distraught.

"Griffin! She's fucked up. Look at her eyes. Heal her!"

More footsteps.

"Oh, shit! Not again...Kyra...I'm going to touch you now."

A heavy hand pressed against my back and pushed me to the ground. My face scrunched against the floor as Tough Puppet restrained my hands behind my back and tied roots around my wrists.

He rolled me to my side and stepped back while rubbing his black beard.

"Shit, shit, shit." He paced back and forth, his boots clomping in front of my face.

"Hello, Mister Muscles. Have you come to play?" I grinned and bit my lip. "I can play with both of you, but first, I need more of Blondie's elixir."

Tough Puppet's eyes darkened, and he darted across the room and shoved Blondie against the wall. I giggled and savored the euphoric warmth running through my system. The little puppets didn't know that these roots around my wrists were useless. But I could still enjoy a little show first. I had time. So much time.

"What did you give her, Nilson?" Tough Puppet pushed his arm against Blondie's neck.

"I-I didn't…I-I swear," Blondie stammered, sounding completely heartbroken. How tragic.

A tree trunk crashed through the back window and flew between me and the two ridiculous puppets.

"Stay back, Kyra!" Tough Puppet yelled as if I'd follow any of his pointless instructions.

Wind howled through the open window, and all the sheets on the bunks billowed like a parachute. Another spurt of giggles overtook me. This show was nonsense and was taking too long. They needed to give me more elixir before I showed them what damage truly meant.

A mini tornado pushed Tough Puppet away from Blondie. How absolutely hilarious.

"Griffin, stop! I'm on your side. She needs our help."

I easily snapped the roots apart and rose to my feet. The four-legged creature barked at me in the corner and attacked. It chomped down on my arm, but I threw it off, and it rammed into a bunk's post. Hard.

Tough Puppet's eyes widened in horror. He raised both hands and started to speak, but I was done.

I raised both hands toward the open window and smiled. *"Dehano huc, Ashes. Dehano huc!"*

"What's that mean?" Blondie backed away further, eyeing the door. "Griffin, how do we stop her?"

"I see them all, Puppet," I whispered with a smile.

"Who do you see?" Tough Puppet asked.

"Thousands and thousands of boys, young and old, dark and light, waiting in the light. They wait for me to release them, but I think I'd rather use them as dolls. Toys are more fun, don't you agree?"

My tattoos surged with power as I awaited the beast I had just summoned. She'd arrive any moment. In the distance, I could already hear her giant wings flapping in the dark sky. A creature of the night. My jugosaur. My Ashes.

"I need to kiss her." Tough Puppet braced himself against the side of a bunk as my wind roared through the open window.

"What? This isn't a fuckin fairytale!" Blondie yelled.

I laughed. He was right. This was my nightmare; they were doomed when they stepped inside. My Ashes was close. I had taught it to her when I was four years old, back when we were best friends.

"Trust me—I have to kiss her!" Tough Puppet tried to step forward into the cyclone ravaging the room. "Help me, Nilson! Try to stop her wind power so I can get to her."

"So you *do* want to play? Come here, and I'll give you a kiss that'll haunt you for eternity." I licked my lips and held out my hands. The elixir's manic taste lingered on my tongue, and I wanted to share it with this delicious man.

An unseen force wrestled with my wind power and decreased its strength. Tough Puppet stepped closer, terror written all over his features. Fear was priceless. I relished it.

"Petal, come back to me." Tough Puppet sucked in a breath with concern in his pitiful eyes and reached behind my neck.

The warmth of his hand on mine sent a thrill of craving in my core. I planted my mouth on his and devoured the puppet completely. Maybe I could own them both. Blondie would supply my elixir for eternity, and Tough Puppet would be my plaything. I continually ravished him with kisses like he was my last meal until strange images flashed in my mind.

. . .

A man with a dog helping me on a roof.

A man teasing me in a treehouse.

This man helping me in a cave.

This man dipping in a lake with me—naked.

His lips.

His love.

His essence.

Jadox.

Jay!

I gasped and pulled away, my heart slamming against my ribs as I locked on his brown eyes.

"Jay? What happened?" My legs shook, and my knees buckled.

I almost fell to the floor, but Jay swiped me into his arms and carried me to my cot. He stepped over piles of tossed backpacks, broken beds, splintered wood, and Chocolate's whining body.

"Jay!" I gasped. "Something happened to Chocolate." I tried to wiggle out of his arms, but he grasped me tighter.

When I looked up to meet his eyes, frantic and worried about his pup, a lone tear slid down his cheek. "Kyra. It'll be okay. I've got you."

Every muscle in my body burned with exhaustion.

"What should we do?" Isaac panted from across the ramshackle of a room, trepidation lining every word.

"Isaac? What's wrong? What happened?" I pleaded and looked from Jay back to him.

Jay cleared his throat. "Go get Caspian and Narelle. Hurry."

Isaac rushed out of the door while Jay slid a hand over my forehead as if to check my temperature.

"What's wrong with Chocolate? Why is the room a mess? You're scaring me."

Jay's stern look didn't shift into calm for even an instant. "We need to get you in an ice bath, Kyra. You're burning up."

I shivered but pushed my chest against his. Jay must be losing his mind; except for near fainting, I felt fine. But he started to tug down my pants for the bath.

"Kyra!" He inhaled sharply and pressed a finger to my tattoos. "How long has this tattoo been gray?"

"Hmm?" My eyelids drooped, fatigue overtaking everything.

"This gray tattoo, how long has it been there?" The rigidity of his sounds made me nervous.

"Since the night we severed."

"Why, Petal?" His jaw clenched tight. "*Why* didn't you tell me?"

As I was about to answer, an enormous screech pierced my ears. Jay fell to his knees, almost dropping me. He screamed, and both shoulders rose to his ears as if to cover them. A giant roar exploded, and the entire wall erupted in flames, then fell to the ground in a pile of ashes. Terror claimed my entire body.

In the midnight darkness, a dragonesque creature towered over us and roared fire again, scorching a tree to a pile of ashes.

"What the fuck is that?" Jay bellowed.

4

KYRA

The creature's bone-chilling screech drowned out my screams as Jay yelled, "Is that a fuckin' jugosaur?"

The creature was massive. I'd only heard legends of the infamous jugosaur, but the sharp, curved fangs the size of my entire body surpassed any expectation. Jay shielded me by wedging me between him and what was leftover of a bunk bed.

Brilliant red scales shimmered like rubies under the moonlight, and when the jugosaur tossed its head around, the horns slashed through a high branch. It sliced clean in half and dropped with a heavy thud in front of the remains of our safe house wall. Every muscle clenched, and I reached deep within to call Magik to life. My fire felt weak, far, and hesitant. Ahead, embers sparked near a pile of ashes, matching the jugosaur's wild yellow eyes. It crouched into an attack position and clawed the dirt. That simple movement formed a trench at least six feet deep—a fuckin grave. Crap!

Its sudden roar shook the ground, and Jay swayed to the side. I steadied him from behind, terrified of what the animal might do. My heart rammed almost painfully. Smoke was billowing from its nostrils as it glared at us, ready to pounce.

Jay reached back blindly and shoved me further into the corner. “Stay back!”

Narelle and Isaac burst through the door, and relief washed through me that Isaac was unharmed—for now. His eyes widened at the magnificent jugosaur bellowing and swiping its claws frantically in the dirt.

He rushed forward to Jay’s side and yelled, “Whatever you do, don’t let its tail touch you!”

Both men pointed their hands forward, Magik at the ready. I wanted to fight by their sides, but no power hummed in my core. Something had entirely drained me, and that scared me more than the fire-breathing beast threatening to destroy us all. In fact, why hadn’t she burned us to a crisp already? Why wasn’t she charging? I tilted my head. Why did she feel so familiar?

“She’s not angry,” Jay said.

His biceps flexed, and he summoned at least fifty giant trees to form a tight circle around the jugosaur. She lifted both front legs and stomped them to pieces while shrieking loudly, then paced in front of the rubble. She wasn’t advancing at all.

From across the room, Isaac lifted his hands at the same time that Narelle brought a swirl of water to her fingertips.

“Wait! Wait.” With both hands in the air, I jumped between them and the jugosaur. “I don’t think she’s here to hurt us.”

Tentatively, I stepped closer to the giant.

“Kyra! Get back here.” Isaac launched to grab my wrist, but Jay slapped his hand away.

“Don’t touch her again, Nilson.” Jay sounded pissed, but I couldn’t focus on why as he continued, “Why are you even here? I told you to get Caspian.”

“I couldn’t find him.”

Their annoying bickering was like nails on a hoverboard, so I tuned them out and tiptoed over debris. My hand stretched out in invitation like I always did when giving Chocolate a treat. The jugosaur bowed her head to me and sniffed the air.

“I remember you,” I whispered.

The jugosaur blinked, her long eyelashes resembling peacock feathers. Soft smoke twirled from the corners of her mouth, and I reached out further.

"Kyra, no!" Isaac's voice grew louder behind me, and two sets of footsteps sprinted closer. "Don't!"

My fingertips brushed against the scales, sharp at the corners and smooth as metal in the middle. Absolutely fascinating.

"Her name is Ashes," I whispered to no one specifically but felt the crazed energy thundering behind me from both my men.

"I don't think it's going to hurt her," Jay said.

He was right. I smiled; he always had a connection with nature. Ashes leaned into my touch like she had been deprived of physical contact for years.

"I remember you from—" but before I could finish, Isaac rammed into me, knocking me over.

"Kyra, run!" Isaac yelled and reached out to the sky. Clouds crept, quickly masking the stars above, and a drizzle started sprinkling in a light mist. "I've got this. Go. Hurry!"

I shook my head. I had no enemies here. Ashes would never hurt me. She was mine.

"Isaac, she won't hurt—"

But he wasn't listening. Lightning splintered the sky like toxic veins. Then, green fumes poured out from his fingertips.

"Isaac, it's okay, she—" I stepped forward and sucked in a breath of the green gas. Something snapped inside me like a rubber band busting.

A heaviness clamped down on my toes and crawled up my legs, cementing me to the spot. Everything turned to lead, and I had to work hard to gather air. The green fog changing shapes in front of me was the most glorious thing I'd ever seen, tasted, or even heard. Its shifting shadows sang like a siren from a deep darkness I didn't know existed, and something pulled at my soul. Yanked. My chest heaved up and down. Something was *very* wrong, but I couldn't move because it was also so, so right.

"Isaac!" I reached toward him, needing to feel grounded, but instead of his solid shoulders, the green gas twirled over my fingertips.

"Nilson, stop!" Jay finally arrived at my side, but I had no strength to stand upright. He lifted me straight and stared into my eyes. "Kyra, talk to me about Hallie."

I couldn't focus on Jay's question because the green gas rose to Ashes' nostrils. Ashes roared and rose on two hind legs. Her claws swiped at the air, and her yellow eyes rolled to the back of her head. She fell to the side without a fight, crushing a row of bushes.

"Is she…is she dead?" A tightness in my chest bore down so strongly that I still had to work to breathe.

"No, I can feel her spirit still," Jay said as he held me tight. "Kyra, look at me. What's my name?"

"What?" I half-laughed, but nothing felt funny. "Jay, why would you ask me that?"

When Isaac turned toward us, a few more green swirls of gas twisted between his fingertips, and I sprung forward desperately. I sucked it in, letting it fill my lugs. I needed more. More

But someone swept me into their arms and pulled me away, then said, "Stay the fuck away, Nilson. You're doing this to her!"

"Doing *what* to me?" I giggled at the suddenly entertaining thought of lighting the entire forest on fire. Everything needed to burn.

Vayu should burn. The Aurella Fortress should burn. The Aurum Orbis Society should fuckin' burn. All of the Ordulls too. Tension knotted in my core, and I reached over the man's wide sculpted shoulders and pointed at Blondie. I shot fire straight at his perfect face, angelic nose, gorgeous bone structure, and gray eyes. Maybe he should fuckin' burn too. It'd be fun to watch him writhe in pain.

Blondie stood like a statue and pushed both palms against his temples. His face was made for epic comedy, the way it twisted in agony and disbelief. He dodged just in time and finally stopped chasing us.

I laughed as Tough Puppet sprinted further into the forest. "I wanna ride you a different way, Puppet!"

He didn't respond, making this far less enjoyable. Once alone, he set me down by a tree stub and kneeled in front of me, rubbing my hands with his. "Kyra, you grew up in Andersonville and have a nephew named Landon. When you were little, you had a cat named Kit, and you used to let it lick yogurt off your finger."

I giggled and ran a hand through his thick, silky raven hair. It was so scrumptiously soft that I could sleep in his hair. Maybe if I cut it all off, I could braid the strands together and twist them with mine. That way, I'd always have a part of this puppet with me. First, I'd have to wake up poor Ashes and ride her back to the Land of Nothing. Oniskel would be so happy to see us again. She'd probably throw a coming-home party and invite all the other Elidians.

I'd blissfully burn through every city and town we'd fly over on the way back. Fire. Flames. Heat. Death. My fire was meant to consume this world.

"Kyra, look at me." He spoke funny, like a captain giving orders to soldiers.

I whispered softly in his ear, "Crack goes the night when the moon sucks all the light." I giggled and licked his ear. "No need to hunt 'cause I'll corrupt you with my cunt."

This adorable puppet didn't understand at all. It was time to play. Play, play, play. Play all day.

"No, no, Kyra, please remember. You love drumming and worked at an ice cream shop through high school to buy your first set of drums. You formed your first band junior year, remember? Please remember. You told me the first time you stepped on stage felt like your destiny."

"So, you don't want my cunt?" I smiled and rubbed my finger up his edible jawline.

Footsteps swished in squishy mud to my right, and Tough Puppet's tantalizing gaze snapped over to the distraction.

"It's me...Caspian," a new voice said. A stranger, younger than Tough Puppet, stepped out of the drizzle and under the tree's protection. His brown hair dripped onto his blue tunic that stuck to his broad chest, covered in the unmistakable scent of salt and sand.

"Caspian, I need you to Link with her. We can't wait any longer."

"I'm not rushing into anything."

"My healing powers don't work on ₵sµwi Magik, but maybe the Link will help her." Tough Puppet squeezed an emerald necklace in his hand.

"₵sµwi? Why are you talking about dark Magik?" When the man with the long scar met my gaze, he jumped back. "Holy Divinity, what's *wrong* with my sister?"

I tried to ignore the tunes in my head and sang, "I have dark corners of my mind that you would never discover."

"Who are you?" Caspian asked.

"I am the heat in hatred, the—"

"Bring Kyra back!" Caspian yelled.

"I don't want to." I crossed my arms over my chest. "This mind has so many voids ready to be filled with shadows and my songs."

"When she snaps out of this, please don't tell her, but my kiss brings her back."

"You're joking, right?"

"No, watch."

Tough Puppet pressed his devastating mouth against mine. Those lips were meant for romance novels. I could dream in this kiss, live in his kiss, die in this kiss.

Wait, how did Jay and I get into a forest? I shook my head, making it throb.

I blinked and met Jay's concerned look. I glanced around at the darkness. "Jay? How did we get out here?"

Caspian kneeled next to him and said, "Kyra, something's happening to you. A spirit is taking over your mind."

I laughed, but when I looked between him and Jay, a shudder crept up my spine. "You're serious?"

Jay's hand hovered over my waist. "Can we show him your new tattoo?"

"You know about that?"

He nodded softly. The only thing daring to make a sound was the rain increasing in force.

I reached to my waist, feeling my hands tremble, and rolled down my skirt. I had the greenish-brown Draven Circle, my original Gold Circle, and the blueish Vayuian Circle, but the new gray one looped with them. An empty spot remained—leaving space for one more tattoo to complete a five-circled ring.

"Shit." Caspian ran a hand through his messy hair. "Have you ever heard of anything like this, Griffin?"

"No."

"What's wrong with me?" I searched their faces. "Why did you say a spirit is in me?"

"Kyra, you've been acting very different for the last few hours."

"I…how?" When I looked out, each rain droplet froze, suspended in the air like a thousand tiny marbles. Isaac must be having a fit if this is how the weather presented itself.

Jay tucked a loose strand of my hair behind my ear. "You don't remember anything?"

"I remember dancing with Narelle and wanting to kiss…." I looked around for Isaac. "Where's Isaac?"

"He can't come near you anymore," Jay said.

I jumped up straight, nearly knocking my head on a low branch. "What? Why?"

"Because he has some new toxic gas enhancement that seems to affect you."

"Toxic gas?" I pressed against my temples, where a migraine drilled into my skull.

"Maybe it's finally time for us to Link," Caspian said, "to keep you safe."

I shook my head and held a hand out as a shield. "No, I won't put you through that. You've been through enough."

Caspian rubbed his scar, his only nervous tell, then stopped halfway down. "Ky, do you know how I got this scar?"

"No, I didn't want to ask."

"On a stormy night, under the sea, I was swimming around Cydon's village to ensure everyone was safely inside their homes. I heard a whimper and followed the sound to a shadowy cavern under a reef. A figure was thrashing, and as I moved closer, it became obvious that a siren was caught in a fishing net. Even though they're a dangerous species, I tried to free her, but she clawed open my face in fear."

I clutched my heart. "Caspian, I'm so sorry."

"I'm not done, have a little patience to get to the good part, sis." He smiled gently. "I eventually managed to calm down the siren by singing to her. We worked together to untangle her from the ropes, and she sped away."

"Without a thank you?"

"That's not what matters," Caspian sighed.

"So, the moral of the story is you want me to accept your help without giving you another scar?"

"No, it's that not all scars are evidence of pain or turmoil. Some marks are simply welcomed reminders of courage and strength. I don't blame you anymore for when the waves took me away as a child, but you hold onto the fear that you will hurt me somehow, and that burden is your own scar. Change the story and make that mark on our history a story of your strength of finding your place in this world despite your rough childhood. You said after I disappeared that the man who raised you was abusive."

I nodded.

"So change the narrative. You survived. You're strong, Ky. Embrace your marks."

Contemplating his words, I started marching back toward the fortress, feeling a little steadier on my feet. Maybe he was right. I had always twisted the events in my life as negative circumstances, placing me as the victim. But I could just as easily rewrite my own perspective.

In the distance, a large mound caught my attention, and I stopped short, squinting. "What is that?"

"That would be a jugosaur," Jay said plainly. "Apparently, this giant dragon creature is the spirit's friend."

My heart hammered, and the forest faded in and out. "What?" I crouched down to the ground, my butt balancing on my heels. "How is this possible? What is happening to me? None of this makes any sense. Jay, I'm scared."

He crouched too and stroked a hand over my back. "We'll figure it out, but I think you need to stay away from Nilson."

My teeth started chattering, and pressure pushed on my chest. "That's not possible, he's…he's my…."

Jay dropped his head. "Okay, I won't push you to do anything you don't want to."

Caspian pulled me upright. "Ky, what if our Link is the only thing that saves you? Please."

"Maybe I don't need to be saved."

Jay's jaw clenched tighter.

"I'm not the Golden One. I'm the Cursed One. I only bring destruction, pain, hurt, and death. Maybe I'm the problem."

"Kyra, Link for Landon," Jay said softly. "Your nephew needs you."

"He's happy and safe with Gemm. He doesn't need me anymore."

"Then do it for *me*. Kyra, please, just say the spell. Link with Caspian."

"For you?"

Jay gently stroked the side of my cheek. "I can't…I can't let anything happen to you. I can't live without you."

I paused and studied his face. What did that mean? On a range of desperate-commit-suicide-without-me types of love to heartbreak-if-I-ever-left-him love, where did he fall? I felt the same. A day without him in my life or by my side didn't feel right.

"There has to be another way to keep a spirit away than Linking," I pleaded.

"Should we try to cut the cursed tattoo out of her?" Caspian huffed. "I'm great with a dagger."

I sighed and fixed my gaze on my brother's blue eyes. "This is what you want?"

"Yes, I think we should Link. Gemm's prophecy said we were always meant to anyways." He smiled weakly, which altered the shape of his long scar. "I know you're worried about the pain from severing, but let's just promise to never sever, okay? We'll be Linked for our entire lives."

"Forever?" I asked, hesitancy creeping through my words.

"Forever."

"Okay, fine, I'll do it. But I can't remember any spells for some reason. It's like I've been sucked dry."

"I do." Isaac's voice came from across the clearing.

"Back off!" Jay yelled.

"Don't worry, I won't use the poison again. It's *Atuyasdodi promitto."*

But as he spoke and the breath left Issacs's lungs, I could hear a song from the poison seeping out of him. Its energy was just as mouthwatering as before. A change was manifesting inside me, and this time, I welcomed it.

"Jay..." My heart sped again, threatening to explode. I didn't want the spirit to return. I didn't want to disappear. "Jay, it's happening."

His eyes grew wide, and he grabbed my hand, touching it to Caspian's. "Say it!"

"Atuyasdodi promitto. Atuyasdodi promitto," Caspian chanted.

The wind changed direction and blew my hair across my face. For a moment, all I saw was gold and fire and lava and a volcano and.... "No, I won't Link," a high-pitched voice that wasn't my own came from my body. Terror trapped me in a cage of my own bones.

"Kyra, you can do it," Jay pleaded, rushing out his words. "Say it with Caspian. You can do it."

I couldn't rely on my Magik for strength this time because it had abandoned me. So I squeezed my eyes shut and focused on a rhythm from a song I had learned long ago. An image appeared of a male's calloused, large hands banging a beat on a rock, then waiting for me to imitate. When I stuck out my hands, they were tiny—the size of a toddler. I followed his movements with pride, then peeked up to meet the man's eyes. Brent. My father. He had taught me a song once. So long ago. Courage and resistance coursed through me, and I gripped Caspian's hands tighter. I wouldn't let a demon take over my mind, body, or soul. Not today or ever. I'd fight against it.

"Atuyasdodi promitto," I chanted weakly. *"Atuyasdodi promitto."*

The Link crashed into me with full force. Caspian's memories hurtled at me like a deadly tsunami, full of passion and energy. They pulled me into his past, a world I had never imagined since I always thought my brother had died.

Drip. Drip. Drip. Trickle. Water drizzles into my mouth, my ears, and my nose. Every inch of my skin absorbs it. Water leaks into my soul and seeps into my heart. Drip. Drip. Thump. Thump. My heartbeat turns into the ebbing and flowing of a tide. A reef. A boat. The rush of a river swells and crashes against the bank. Drip. Splash. Water consumes me.

Cold water meets his—my— skin and strengthens me the deeper I swim. Dolphins rub against my side, chirping joyfully. Learning at a young age that I could hold my breath underwater for miles. Years sweep by, and my skills grow stronger, but I have no family to call my own. I lock eyes with a beautiful girl and know my heart is meant for her 'til the end of time, even though she ignores me. Cydian villagers nominate me as their leader, despite not knowing where I came from. A demon whispers a secret in my ear that a prophecy has been made in my name and that my sister is alive. The first time I meet Kyra's amber eyes at the lighthouse, relief washes over me like a tsunami. She is my home. My family.

I snapped out of the strange hallucination. And just like that, I knew my Link with my brother was complete. A different sensation scorched my stomach from the inside, and this time, I didn't know what I'd see when I checked my hip.

5

KYRA

When I opened my eyes, my brother was smiling warmly at me. His essence wrapped around us like a comfortable cocoon. Home.

"You have some interesting memories, Ky."

"Shut up," I teased and checked for the new turquoise Möbius Circle that looped between the cursed gray one and Draven's tattoo. All five were now connected. I stared in awe as each glowed, wondering what this meant and if any Mystier had ever been like me in the past. More importantly, what did the gray Circle mean, and how could I get rid of it?

Caspian reached his hand out and tried to capture the rainfall in his open palms. His thoughts rang through our new bond.

Well, dear sister, lovely weather we're having.

The sound of someone else's voice in my mind again was a strangely welcoming sensation.

Caspian looked upward at the unnatural clouds swirling above us. The power of water rushed through me. I stretched my hand toward the thousands of dripping branches above, and each little pearl droplet flew at me. Under my command, they merged, growing larger in the blink of an eye. Water was supposed to be fire's nemesis, yet nothing felt unnatural about the liquid washing through me.

Caspian smiled again and pointed up. The giant ball of water lifted and bounced in the air like a rubber ball. He hovered the enormous, still-growing bubble directly over Isaac's head. Then my brother gestured for me to pop it.

"You wouldn't dare." Isaac frowned, but before he could move, Caspian snapped his fingers. The bubble popped and cascaded water over Isaac's already wet man bun.

I couldn't help but smile as Caspian chuckled and spoke through our new Link.

Serves him right for sending us that monsoon.

I wanted to respond, but too many emotions bombarded me like dodgeballs, catapulting from all directions. Was the prophecy finally complete now that I had Linked with my brother? Everything felt so intense. And Jay needed to stop looking at me like I was a piece of porcelain on the verge of shattering.

"Goddess above, Kyra, did I do that?" Jay's finger brushed a patch of new bruises on my arm.

"Um, yeah, when you shielded me from Ashes. But I'm okay."

"Shit, I'm so sorry." He ran a hand through his hair, spraying water in all directions.

"You didn't mean to." I swept my gaze around at the rummage of bricks near Ashes' still-unconscious body. "Okay, so first things first, is Chocolate okay?"

"Yeah, Chocolate's fine." Jay absent-mindedly rubbed the emerald hanging from his neck. "I think I gained a new power when we severed. Sometimes, I can sense animals' emotions. It wasn't making sense to me until tonight, but that's how I knew the jugosaur wasn't here to hurt us."

It seemed like the three of us added a power when we severed. That wasn't something I had expected in the least. Chocolate limped out from under a bunk and licked Jay's hand. Jay's mouth moved silently, and I knew the healing spell was pouring into Chocolate's body. After a moment, she sprang away toward Ashes, sniffing the sopping grass by her claws.

I followed Jay into the bunkhouse, where several wide-eyed Ordulls were now examining the carnage of their safe house. With every step I made toward the group, they all moved further away, including Isaac. When I met his eyes, he dropped his head and shuffled his feet. My heart raced. This wasn't good. I needed to figure out what the Flames was going on with this gray tattoo.

I leaned against the crumbled wall remains as the navy sky showed a sliver of maroon with the rising sun.

"I guess we need a new plan." I surveyed the wreckage and landed on Narelle, who was ringing out her hair into a puddle.

Isaac straightened and spoke to the group of Ordulls. "Let's all get cleaned up. Grab a snack, get some rest, and meet in the conference room in six hours for lunch."

The Ordulls nodded and scrambled around, pulling pieces of wood and brick off their backpacks. One ran out of the room, probably to alert the others who might still have been dancing without any idea what had occurred out here.

Caspian walked over to his wife and hugged her. I was jealous of the way they melded together with such ease. Their years of a trusting relationship had built a foundation that couldn't be toppled. I needed that. But with who? Had my parents had a solid marriage before Elana stole Brent away? It wasn't like I had great role models who had shown me what a lasting relationship looked like.

Caspian, do you remember anything about our childhood together?

Not much.

So, he wouldn't know if Brent had been in our lives for a short while when we were younger.

We need to free Brent from Elana.

I agree, Ky, but we need a detailed plan. Give me the morning to think about it.

This time, Caspian glanced over Narelle's shoulder and met my gaze. His radiant blue eyes resembled the deep sea and all the life thriving under the waters. While Isaac was picking up broken glass, he accidentally bumped into Caspian. In a quick flash, Caspian's eyes switched to obsidian, wicked and devouring. My heart leaped out of my chest, and I tapped Jay on the shoulder hard and fast.

"Jay, Jay!"

"What?" He spun around. "What is it?"

When I pointed to Caspian, his eyes had already reverted to ocean blue, sparkling like beautiful scales. Completely normal.

I wrapped my shaking arms over my chest and said, "Never mind," but a dark shiver rattled my spine. I must have imagined his eyes changing color. There was no way it was possible.

Caspian walked toward me. For a split second, irrational fear coursed through me, and my muscles clenched. But that was absurd. He was my brother, my flesh and blood.

"Why do you want to free Brent before anything else?" Caspian asked.

"Well, *no one* should be a prisoner, and maybe our father knows more about how I managed to wish all males away and how to return them."

I knew Narelle wouldn't want Caspian to go with me to free Brent. For the last few weeks, all she could talk about was creating a relief program for all the Cydian villagers. They had to evacuate their homes and were trying to rebuild their community elsewhere. Caspian was their leader and belonged by her side.

But now that we were Linked, I felt a strong claim on him. We belonged together, too, and needed to stay close. Would I ask both Jay and Isaac to help or just one? My gaze seesawed between the two men across the room. One was my source of release, and the other was my roots anchoring me to what was real. Which did I truly want to stand by my side? Could I love either of them enough while still trying to accept myself?

My focus magnetized to Isaac's wet shirt that clung to his chest. He tore it off and dropped it into a soggy mess. My cheeks flushed warm just as Jay cleared his throat. My gaze whipped to meet his but quickly lowered to Jay's lips.

"Did you hear me?" Caspian asked.

"Hmm?"

"The Soul Stealer, Oniskel, is the last sister of the other two demons. Just like them, she can answer one question—for a price."

"Divinities, above, no way!" I shook my head. "I don't want to do that again. Plus, nothing good came from Surh-Sig or Moroka. Zeph and Paola are both dead because of them. We need to free Brent. He'll know the answers—"

"Kyra, let's talk about this," Jay interrupted. "Brent is already dying from Elana stealing all his energy. Now, she needs one of you two as a replacement to continue living. If we go to your father, we'll be walking into a trap." He grabbed my arms and massaged hypnotizing circles on my inner wrists. "If Brent dies, Elana will follow soon after, without any life source to rely on. Nothing else can sustain a one-hundred-year-old in a thirty-five-year-old body. Once Elana is dead, we won't have to worry about her eliminating the rest of the Ordulls, so that problem will naturally be solved for us."

"But Elana has three of the necklaces. Their power alone might be enough to keep her alive for a while."

"Well, do you want us to march into her domain *with* the fourth necklace?" Jay stopped as his eyebrows scrunched tight. "If we're caught, we'd be handing over the last piece of the puzzle."

"Dangerous or not, I'm going," Isaac interjected. "I must get my Vayu Crystal back to rebuild my city…even if I have to go alone."

"No, Isaac, I'll go with you," I said.

Jay shook his head fiercely. "No! I can't let you risk everything again, Kyra. Please, let's think of something else."

"Run? Hide?" I huffed. "Should we go build a little cabin by ourselves in the woods and never be seen by anyone again? I know that's your dream, eventually, but I can't stand by and do nothing when this…." I spread my arms wide and yelled, "*This* constant destruction is my fault."

Ashes stirred from the volume of my yelling and stretched. Her mighty spiked tail whipped against a tree, slicing it in half. The loud crunch echoed in my ears as it smashed into the ground.

Jay's watch beeped, and a light flashed. He groaned and held up one finger. "Wait one sec."

After he pushed a few buttons, and his eyes flickered across the bottom of the screen, reading the contents, the muscles in his jaw clearly tightened.

"What's wrong?" I moved toward him and wrapped a hand around Jay's curled bicep.

Isaac's expression winkled into a mess, so I lurched away from Jay. I needed to make up my fuckin' mind and stop torturing them—and myself. It wasn't like I was trying to lead them on; both men truly had a place deep in my heart. Every fiber of my being wanted to touch Jay and comfort him from whatever bad news he had just received, but that wouldn't be fair to Isaac.

"It's Alaska." Jay projected an image on one of the remaining walls of the fortress. Alaska's scowl shadowed her face despite the sunrise shining through the gaps in the trees.

In the image, Alaska stood in a dark room full of cages. With both hands on her hips, I squinted at the background. Dozens of thin arms reached out from the cage bars in the murky room.

"Jadox," Alaska spoke defiantly. "*You* did this. You put these prisoners here, beat them, and caged them."

His body went rigid next to mine.

"You have three days to meet me in the Land of Nothing with the emerald."

"What's the Land of Nothing?" I asked, my eyes darting between the three men in the room—the three most important men in my life.

Caspian stood close to my side, the strength of our Link pulling us closer. Isaac and Jay both stood tight as a knot. We formed a triangle of sharp corners with no easy access to a midpoint.

"It's the land of lava," Jay divulged. "A death trap."

Alaska continued, "After the third moon passes if I still don't possess the emerald, one prisoner will be electrocuted daily until there's no one left." She paused and lowered her chin. "You did this, brother. Blame yourself. Just like I blame *you* for taking Paola away from me. You have three days. Come alone."

My heart spasmed in my chest. No, no, no. This was all wrong. I knew Alaska had gone to the president's headquarters weeks ago but as a spy. This wasn't our plan. She was supposed to be finding a way into The Crooked Chateau so we could infiltrate Elana's base easier.

"Fuck!" Jay mashed his hands into his thick hair. "This is a disaster! I need to get Alaska out of there now."

"We should split up," Isaac deadpanned. "Some of us can meet Alaska, and some can free the prisoners…."

Caspian nudged my side and grinned.

Your two boys are about to fight over you, Ky.

No, they're not.

Isaac stepped toward Jay, taking up half the room with his stance. "I can go with Kyra and Caspian to The Crooked Chateau, and you two..." Isaac pointed to Jay and Narelle. "You two can go—"

"No, I won't separate from Kyra again." Jay closed the distance between himself and Isaac and glared.

"Well, you can't go to where Elana is because she wants to jump your bones and make a litter of Golden baby monsters." Isaac's smile conveyed his self-proclaimed victory.

Jay's veins bulged in his forehead

"I hate this! Stop fighting." I kicked a bunch of broken pieces of wood. "I get a vote too."

"Ky, I think there's ₾sμwi coursing through our veins," Caspian cleared his throat. "When we Linked, I could feel darkness trying to pull me under. I don't think we're the best ones to lead right now."

"I *knew* we shouldn't have Linked. I'm only going to hurt you," I said.

"Wait, this might be a good thing." Caspian passed me a bottle of water from his pack. "I think Elana has the same ₾sμwi Magik within her. If we can learn to understand it, we can defeat her."

"How can we learn to understand it?" I shut out the immediate protests from Jay and Isaac in the background.

Caspian's expression shifted, for just a moment, changing shapes like the fluidity of water itself.

We use the ₾sμwi*…and experiment...slowly.*

Caspian, I can't see that being a good idea.

"I think we can get rid of cursed ₾sμwi by getting the other three necklaces back," Isaac's voice finally jerked me out of my trance, and he continued, "Maybe we can do it all. We can save Alaska, get all three necklaces, free Brent, defeat Elana, and bring back the rest of the males."

It's only possible through the ₵sμwi, Ky.

I begrudgingly agreed with Caspian, even though it felt dangerous. During our voyage, Caspian and I could try to slip into the dark Magik to learn about the curse upon us.

What my boyfriends didn't know wouldn't kill them. Hopefully.

6

ISAAC

I stood in front of the crowded room of Ordulls, who filled the dining benches. Kyra and Griffin stood side by side in the back—a bit too close for my liking. A thousand emotions attacked me, but I had a new job. Apparently, these Ordulls designated me the point man on whatever fiasco we were about to endure. Maybe I wasn't their worst option—at least they weren't looking to Griffin for answers. In fact, by having the strongest Magik in this room, she should be leading this group. I waved for her to join me, but she shook her head.

Through the windows, afternoon sunlight illuminated Kyra's golden hair. I tried to meet her eyes, hoping to Divinity above they were still amber instead of the undead-black like before, but she was mid-conversation with Griffin. What I'd give to be a fly on the wall to eavesdrop. I had never missed the Link as much as this very moment.

I took a few moments to calm my racing nerves by focusing on the technique that had always worked in the past: concentrating on details I knew no one else could see. There was a small heart etched into the side of the wooden table, probably decades old by now. On someone's lunch tray, a ladybug sat atop a strawberry, and the shoelaces of someone in the back row were coming loose, nearly untied. But my strategy wasn't working this time.

All eyes were trained on me. I clasped both hands behind my back, hoping the green mist stayed away. It had never impacted a fellow Mystier until Kyra's reaction last night. Now, I wasn't sure if it would be toxic to Ordulls too. Over the last few weeks, my control over it had grown stronger the more I practiced. It responded to my commands as I experimented with plants, bugs, and the occasional chipmunk. All animalistic creatures would pass out immediately, just like the jugosaur. Why was Kyra the only human to succumb to it like a drug? There were too many questions—again. The women in the Aurum Orbis Society leaned toward each other, whispering in hushed anticipation. They all wore matching spandex that changed colors according to their surroundings.

"What are we going to do with that dragon thing when it wakes up?" one woman yelled.

"Where did Alaska go?" another jumped in, and the others nodded their support.

"How long can we stay here without a back wall to the bunkhouse? The army will find us in no time," another hollered.

Mumbling exploded into a joint agreement that we had to leave this fortress quickly.

I cleared my throat, and the chatter immediately ceased—good, I had their undivided attention.

I rubbed my cheeks, the stubble scratching my palms. Every little thought seeping through my brain was trying to convince me that Kyra and I were supposed to retrieve the three necklaces from Elana. But I didn't have a good reason why. Elana would now have an entire army guarding the crystal, ruby, and pearl. It wouldn't be an easy task. But we had to succeed.

There was no chance I'd let the other half of Ordulls be wiped from this planet. Plus, Wes would never fully understand his hybrid nature and where he came from if he lived in a land of purebred Mystiers.

"We need to split up into teams to accomplish our goals. I feel that the highest priority is to obtain the three necklaces first," I said to the crowded room.

"We disagree." Another Ordull stood, and the others quickly joined her. "We need to free the prisoners, then kill the president."

One group all raised their fists in the air and whooped in unison.

"Ladies, please sit down."

They sat. Immediately. Maybe they didn't agree with my first plan, but some of them still gaped at me like I was a god. Maybe the extra pushups I'd been doing were becoming noticeable?

A smile lit my face as I smoothed out my tone, "Ladies, I'm not sure how many of you have been informed, but President Syvonne Stirk isn't an Ordull like you. She possesses Magik of her own and has a golden Circle."

One teenager gasped and pointed at Kyra. "Then what is *she* still doing here? If they're alike, then *this* one will eventually turn on us."

Thanks to my stupid enhanced vision, I picked up Griffin's slightest shift in front of Kyra as his forearms tensed, ready for action. That man would be my downfall, but at least he'd sacrifice himself to keep her safe.

"Mr. Nilson..." another young girl said while batting her lashes ridiculously.

"Just call me Isaac," I sighed and leaned back against a table, feeling like a professor in a room full of eager sorority girls.

"Isaac," she said. "We don't care about Magikal necklaces."

"Well, that guy back there does," I said while quickly pointing across the room to Griffin. "He is in possession of the emerald right now. He's super approachable and would love to hear everyone's ideas."

Griffin's face screwed into gnarled, frustrated wrinkles. Instead of the calm soldier I'd come to expect, he stormed out the back, leaving the door to squeak on its hinges. The following stiffening silence lingered in the air as I wondered whether Kyra would follow him.

"Listen, everyone. You *should* care about the necklaces," Kyra finally spoke up and squeezed between the narrow aisles to my side.

My heart thumped vigorously as she approached. The intense lust feeding my body was almost hypnotic.

Kyra climbed onto the front table. "Listen up. I know everything sucks right now, but Ordulls and Mystiers need to continue working together."

"Why?"

Kyra scrunched up her nose and glanced to where Griffin had been standing, now, only an empty space. She was clearly looking for permission for something. I hated that she didn't seek me out in this silent conversation. But I also didn't want to be someone who controlled her every move. She could do whatever she wanted and didn't need my approval.

With a few clicks of a watch, Kyra projected an image of Alaska onto the back wall. The sunlight flares cast strange lighting on the image, but I doubted any of the others could zoom in on the shadowy figure of Surh-Sig's skeleton form distorted in the background of the image anyway.

So, Alaska was in the same location as a demon. *Great.*

The room watched Alaska speak in the video, saying, "Elana wants the fourth necklace to eliminate the remaining Ordulls."

Shocked gasps echoed throughout the dining room.

"And I'll be the one to gladly rip the emerald from my brother's dead body and hand it over," Alaska said, then the video abruptly turned off.

A blonde girl in the back started crying, then an explosion of comments soared like fireworks from the group.

"What are we going to do?"

"We need to protect the emerald."

"No, we need to bury or destroy the emerald."

"What about Alaska? We need to save her from the person brainwashing her."

"Wait, why don't we make a fake necklace and hand it over?"

Conversations burst into chaos again until I whistled and stood on the table beside Kyra. My pinky brushed against hers, causing my entire being to call out to her. Power thrummed in my Circle, begging to be used. But we were no longer Linked telepathically. Where Kyra's teasing jests used to be was now just a void, slowly filling with toxic gas.

"As I said, we need to split up to accomplish all of our goals," I said.

I sensed a change in the wind and glanced out the window, where the beams of cracked wood and smashed bricks piled high in the dirt. I set my sights on a brief movement between the trees. Squinting, I leaned forward and finally understood what caught my attention. Before I could yell a warning, a blood-curdling screech ripped apart my eardrums. I covered my ears as Kyra leaped off the table and zig-zagged through the crowd.

"Kyra, wait!" I ran after her.

"Ashes needs me!" Kyra yelled over her shoulder.

My legs burned from dancing all night at her birthday party and the chaos of the night, but I still caught up. It didn't matter though. Before I could grab her, Kyra ran outside, and sunlight splashed across her entire front.

The jugosaur stood in front of a row of trees. Her radiant red scales reflected the bright rays and sent them like lasers back into the clouds—an obvious signal any enemy could easily track.

Kyra raced to Ashes and placed her hand on the giant clawed paw. "What's wrong, girl?"

"She's scared," Griffin said as he stepped out from the tree's shadows, holding two backpacks. "And I can smell an incoming threat. We need to leave. NOW."

"I'll send a message to Caspian," Kyra said with a subtle far-off shift in her eyes.

It was the first time I had seen her purposefully communicate with Caspian through the Link. A jolt of jealousy ripped through me and shredded my insides to pieces. I wanted to be the one she relied on, the one she told her secrets to and trusted above anyone else. She was going through so much; eventually, it'd all catch up with her. When the intensity finally slowed, Kyra would have a lot to process. Everyone grieved differently, but she had recently lost both her sister and mom. Then lost both her Links. I wanted to be there to support her.

"Okay, Caspian knows we're leaving." She tapped Ashes' side, and the monstrous creature dipped low and stuck out her leg as a ramp. Kyra climbed fast; no one but me would guess she was afraid of heights. Well, maybe Griffin knew. She grabbed Griffin's hand and pulled him up. "Come on."

My heart caved in on itself. She had grabbed Griffin's hand. *Griffin's*. Not mine. I stood frozen, watching them climb the rough scales a bit at a time. She left me behind. Kyra's foot slipped halfway up, and I lunged forward to catch her if she fell. But I was too late. Griffin gripped her under her arm and wedged her between him and the scales. I couldn't breathe. This was it. She didn't need me. Kyra was choosing him for her adventure, for her life. At least it hadn't taken her too long. A thousand sharp needles prickled me in phantom pain, but the tightness in my chest was real.

I turned slowly toward the fortress to form my own plan when Kyra yelled from atop Ashes' back. "Hurry up, Isaac, she really wants to take off."

Was I hearing her right?

At that exact moment, the flirtatious Ordull from inside rushed outside and met my eyes. "Narelle is leading a group of us to the Cydian prisoners. Are you coming?" she asked.

I glanced back and forth between the blonde and Kyra, who was firmly supported atop the beast with Griffin's hands around her thin waist. A severe wind whipped through the trees, but I swore to myself I wouldn't create another mood-induced storm.

"Isaac, let's go!" Kyra waved in earnest. "Don't make me climb down to get you!"

Without addressing the new girl, I sped toward Ashes' leg and ascended her side toward Kyra. Her scales were slippery, making me fumble halfway. Just as I was about to fall, a strong hand latched onto my wrist and yanked me up the rest of the way. Griffin. Again. Of course, just another way for him to show off to Kyra and save the day. I couldn't wait for a chance to pummel him. Just once.

The height on top of Ashes back was much higher than I expected. I scooted my way to Kyra's side to check on her nerves. "You okay?"

She trembled slightly but nodded. "Can you sit in front of me so I can have something to hold onto?"

"I can *always* give you something to hold onto, love." I tried to keep the airiness in my jokes, but Griffin's glare cut through me.

"If your poisonous gas affects her at all, I'll gladly push you off this jugosaur," he said.

"Noted."

I tensed at the thought of his crotch pushing against Kyra's ass the whole ride, but I settled into my spot. Over my shoulder, I whispered, "Are you sure you want me to—"

Before I could finish, Ashes lifted straight up, both mighty wings flapping so fiercely that we dipped and jostled like a rollercoaster ride as we rose higher. Kyra clutched onto my waist. I squeezed my calves against the hard scales and leaned low. For the first time in two weeks, I didn't care if we ever retrieved the Vayu Crystal again or rebuilt my city because Kyra's warm body against mine, paired with my love of flying, were what I currently needed. Except she was sandwiched between another man and me. All three of us were on a voyage to… to…. "Where are we going, love?"

"The Land of Nothing!" she yelled over the roar of Ashes' wings and wrapped her hands around my waist.

7

KYRA

A warm hand tapped my thigh, and I opened my eyes. I pulled my forehead away from its spot against Isaac's back and wiped the drool from my cheek. The music pod Jay had gifted me played soft symphony music in my ear until I powered it off.

"We're almost there, Petal," Jay whispered from behind me.

I tried to stretch, but every leg muscle screamed from the hours riding atop Ashes' solid back. The wind whipping at my face didn't even bother me anymore.

Are you all still okay?

I checked in on my brother through the Link. He updated me quickly about the attack on the fortress and that everyone on our team had survived.

We found three safe house options, so we've split the society into segments.

Okay, keep me updated.

Oh, and Ky, don't look at the hundreds of jagged rocks below.

Thanks for that, turd.

You're very welcome.

This time, when I glanced over Ashes' side carefully, the ocean was gone, and now only brown and red splotches were far–inconceivably far below. My muscles tensed, and both men wiggled closer, sandwiching me tight.

"You said there's lava in The Land of Nothing, right?" I somehow managed to ask, despite my exploding heart rate from the terrorizing heights.

I felt Jay nod as his face brushed against my hair. "Mhm, and volcanoes."

"That must be why my Circle is flaring."

We dove lower into the barren land painted in red and black. An unfamiliar tree glowed crimson as if it had grown from centuries of spilled blood that drenched the soil and stained it forever. Isaac was unusually quiet in front, and I wondered if he had fallen asleep sitting up.

Is The Land of Nothing my next luxurious vacation spot?

I laughed at Caspian's remark through our bond.

Only if you want the world's worst sunburn and heat stroke.

His chuckle rumbled deep in my soul, and I relished in the comfort of the sound. Home. Linking with my brother finally felt like I had a place where I truly belonged. It was supposed to be him all along. Maybe they were right, and Linking with Caspian had calmed the dark Magik inside me for now. Fingers crossed.

My tattoo zipped with excited energy at the lava boiling beneath us, but I studied the endless unhospitable land.

"Where did Alaska say to meet?"

"Click the top right button on my watch," Jay whispered, his baritone voice like a lullaby to calm my nerves.

With his arms still wrapped around my waist, I pushed his watch, read the most recent message from Alaska, and answered my own question, "We need to land at the southern point of Bukti volcano. This map says it's that tall one over there."

Ashes didn't even need to be directed or steered. She shifted her outstretched wings just a tad and angled to where I had pointed.

"Isaac, what do you see?"

"Oh, *now* you want to talk to me?" His shoulders went rigid.

"Excuse me?"

"You two made a plan about Alaska during the flight without asking me."

"Oh, um, what do you think we should do?"

"It's a little late for that, love." Isaac's voice was as sharp as a knife. "But I disagree with Griffin; I don't think Alaska is still on our side."

I leaned back against Jay's chest to give Isaac some space. Of course, he'd be in a sour mood after straddling such a monstrous flying creature, especially when he missed riding his venti.

Ashes swerved to the right, and I braced my arms around Isaac's stomach, making him grunt in response.

"Sorry." I squeezed him tighter. "And I'm sorry for not asking you last night."

"I guess I can manage to forgive you, love." Isaac's charming tone returned in an instant.

A tingling sensation spread down my neck at the sound of his deep voice that always turned my bones to water.

"I see two people down there. Who did Alaska bring?" Isaac asked.

"Where? I don't see anyone."

The further we dipped, the more sweat rolled down my back. Heat enveloped us like an exotic tomb, but I savored the burning energy at my fingertips.

"There, see them now?" Isaac pointed to a single spot where red bubbles didn't boil over the hard volcanic rock.

Alaska tossed her long black hair behind her shoulders and glared up as we landed. The striking woman beside her had an auburn pixie haircut that framed her face beautifully. Freckles spotted her cheeks, making her look younger, even though she was probably the same age as Isaac, twenty-nine or thirty. Her bright blue eyes held the potential for a warm friendship that I didn't realize I was missing. Isaac slid off the side when Ashes touched down and squatted, rubbing his crotch entertainingly.

"Goddess above, that was awful." He picked at his pants.

The new woman hopped forward and kissed Isaac straight on the lips. My heart stopped, but the expected feeling of jealousy wasn't hammering into me; something else took its place. Her tongue flicked against Isaac's mouth, but his whole body went rigid in shock before he came to his senses and pushed her away.

"What the Flames are you doing?" Isaac straightened. "And who are you?"

"I've always wanted to know what it felt like to kiss Vayu's most popular bachelor," the stranger said.

His cheeks flushed slightly. "That wasn't my best work."

A whip of wind power lashed inside me, sending my feelings into a twisted, chaotic mess, but I just stood there, unsure of what to say or do. Seeing Isaac kiss someone else was a punch to the gut but also, in a strange way, felt relieving. Why? What did that mean? Time was running out to make my choice. I could envision both men in my future. But there was only one I couldn't imagine ever saying goodbye to—my anchor. Maybe I had already made up my mind, after all.

"We don't have time to mess around, come on," Alaska said as she ignored her brother and marched away.

"Wait!" I scooted down Ashes on my butt, and Isaac caught me at the bottom. "Wait, Alaska, hold on."

"We can't stay out here in the open!" Alaska said.

Jay thumped off my jugosaur last and jogged passed me to his sister. "Alaska, we need to talk."

"Not here. Oniskel will feel your arrival soon," said the stranger, "I have a safe place, y'all."

I crossed my arms, unsure whether I wanted her to be a friend or a foe. "Who are you?"

"My name's Dezlian, and I'm the leader of Elidi." Fire shot from her fingertips, and she burned a hole through the volcano's wall, which led us into a dark cave. "Follow me."

Elidian. Their leader. Which must mean.... "Wait, are we related?" I asked.

"Yeah, probably second cousins, twice removed or something." She smiled as warm as pie. "Come on."

"What about Ashes?"

"This is her home. She'll probably find her nest and rest," Dezlian said.

When all five of us were tucked into the cave, a sharp feeling pricked my tattoos, and I knew immediately that it wasn't good news. Ȼsµwi Magik coursed through me as if its energy fed off the darkness of the volcano's heart. I longed to taste Isaac's elixir, taking a step toward him and licking my lips. Maybe if I could get him alone and seduce him, he'd let me have a drink.

"Kyra?" Jay's voice grounded me in an instant.

Breathing hard, I swallowed nervously, "Do...do we have to stay in there long?" I stuttered.

Dezlian shot me a quick look of judgment. "You aren't comfortable? I thought you'd thrive in the heat."

"Um, it's hard to explain." I pressed a hand to my five looped Circles.

As the others started chatting about the emerald around Jay's neck, Caspian's words vibrated through our Link.

You okay, Ky? I felt that.

Yeah, I'm okay. I hate that this Ȼsµwi affects you too.

Let's just check in with each other every few hours.

Before I could respond, an argument ripped my attention away. "I hate you! I hate you!" Alaska was shoving her big brother, twice her size, against the volcano's wall. Her fists punched his chest, and Jay took the full brunt force, allowing her to release all her tension.

Her hits and screams finally eased until Alaska sobbed in his arms, face buried in his shirt. Jay ran a hand through Alaska's hair and held her close. His brown eyes met mine, and the utter despair shattered my soul. I knew he'd blame himself for her grief over losing Paola. But for now, I needed answers about whether Alaska was planning to murder the man I loved. Because whether she was his kin or not, I'd protect Jay against any threat with everything I had. The fire sizzled at my fingertips as I stepped forward.

Dezlian blocked my momentum and nodded in the opposite direction. "Let's give them a minute."

"I'm not going to leave her with Jay if she's planning to kill him for the emerald."

Dezlian laughed. "You haven't spent much time with Alaska, eh? He's the sun her life revolves around."

"How do you know Alaska?" Isaac crossed his arms. "Why are you with her?"

"Alaska asked for my help to...well, she could use some extra hands," Dezlian's peppy words were layered in sugar. "But that doesn't mean you have to. Elidi is on the other side of this tunnel. It can be your safe haven."

"I thought the remaining Elidians were nomads."

Dezlian smiled. "Well, I'm glad our rumor worked. We spread that story to keep this place secret. You can walk straight through and stay in the safety of our village, or...we have a proposition."

"Is it dangerous?" I asked.

"It's necessary." Dezlian moved closer to Isaac, and a wave of some undefined emotion roiled through me again.

It couldn't be nausea. What exactly was triggering this response? To distract myself, I focused on the faint sound of magma far below, a soothing hum that slowed my heart rate. Jay approached with his arm wrapped around Alaska's shoulders. Her blotchy face and red eyes couldn't hide the fierceness of her features when she stated plainly, "We have a way to defeat Elana."

Jay dropped his arm and stepped toward me. Isaac casually stuck his foot out, and Jay tripped over it, sending him straight into my arms. Jay's blood pumping with adrenaline was the last thing we needed when emotions ran high.

"Watch it, Nilson!" Jay roared.

Isaac just shrugged. "Wasn't me."

"Divinity, Isaac, if you have something to say, just say it. You've been sulking ever since we left the fortress. Stop acting childish."

After his beautiful gray eyes met mine, he bowed low. "Fine. Griffin, would you kindly forgive me if I apologized for tripping you?"

"No," Jay snapped.

"Good, because I wasn't going to."

Jay lunged forward and grabbed Isaac's shirt by the collar, pinning him against the wall. "What's your problem?"

Isaac lifted both hands and grinned. “Nothing. I’m not the one assaulting anyone.”

“Boys!” Alaska yelled. “Now is not the time to puff out your chests for Kyra. If she were smart, she wouldn’t pick either of you.”

Jay released Isaac, and both their shoulders sagged like they were being disciplined by Gemm.

“Now, listen up, or we won’t even give you two a chance to join us.” Alaska opened her satchel and pulled out the ancient Unetlo Book.

The Ꮳsμwi Magik within me desperately reached for it, and the word “*mine*” repeated in my head in a foreign voice.

“Gather around, and don’t interrupt me until I’m done. I’m still going to take Draven’s Emerald to Elana.” Alaska opened the animal hide cover and flipped through the thick pages until she stopped at a bookmark.

“No, you’re not—” I started.

“I said, no interruptions. I know my brother puts you on a pedestal. But to me, you’re careless and don’t think before acting,” Alaska said while Jay silently handed over the emerald to his sister. “Anyways, the videos I made and sent you were just to convince Elana that I was on her side. Those prisoners need me, and I promised I’d try to help them escape. It was the truth when I said Elana would electrocute them in three days. So, I need this emerald to transport more than one prisoner to safety at a time. Elana would only be strong enough to eliminate all the Ordull women for a few weeks longer because Brent is hanging on by a thread, so when he dies, she will need you or Caspian as a replacement. As long as you two stay away from her, she’ll eventually weaken and, hopefully, die in an excruciatingly painful way.”

A lump formed in my chest. My father was dying, and I couldn’t do anything about it. Just like I couldn’t save mom from the car or Hallie from that bullet. Guilt crawled under my skin and buried deep.

We’ll save him, Ky. It’ll be okay.

Caspian’s calm assurance through our Link gave me hope—even if it was false hope.

"I planned to kill Moroka," Alaska continued. "But Brent convinced me we need the Blood Maiden alive. He thinks the only way to control ᏣsᏌwi and bring back the males is to change the demon sisters back to their original forms."

Isaac snorted. "And how exactly will someone do the impossible?"

"Did everyone ignore the 'no interruptions' rule?" Alaska chastised as she pointed to a page in the Unetlo Book, its corner smeared with a black substance. "There's a spell to revert a demon, but three items are needed when the spell is cast."

"What are the items?" I asked.

"A vial of lava from the center of Bukti Volcano, which is why we met here, a piece of the demon's body—"

"Absolutely not." Jay snapped the Unetlo book shut. "Kyra, please don't go near those demons again."

Isaac grabbed the book from his hands and handed it to me. "Let Kyra decide for herself."

"Stop speaking for her!" Jay yelled, shaking some of the stalagmites in the corner of the cave.

"You just did the same damn thing!" Isaac roared.

Silence.

Rage spewed through my Circle. I wasn't someone to own. Before I had a chance to pin them with my fire, a gust of wind blew into the cave's opening with embers floating among it. With Isaac's hands guiding the momentum, the wind lifted Jay from the ground and hovered his entire six-foot-two mass above us.

Jay wobbled mid-air like an ice skater trying not to slip. "Let me down."

"Not until you apologize to Kyra," Isaac snarled.

"You first." Jay clenched his fists.

Oh shit, I knew that look. I leaped back and pushed Alaska and Dezlian against the wall.

Alaska cleared her throat. "I wasn't done, stupid boys. The third item is we also need proof of a sacrifice from Kyra's true love. There are three demons, so that means three sacrifices."

Everyone silenced, and Isaac lowered Jay back to the ground.

"Who is her true love?" Isaac asked, something akin to hope in his eyes.

Alaska shrugged. A crack formed in the floor and tore apart, exposing a deep crater. Lava began bubbling to the surface. "You'll figure it out while I go help the prisoners," she said and shoved the emerald into her pocket. "Keep my brother alive, or I'll…please, just don't let anything happen to him."

"I won't." Yet every bit of me currently wanted to feed both these men to the Blood Maiden herself for their atrocious caveman behavior. I had to keep my idiotic men from killing each other first.

"*Enough*!" I shouted. "Neither of you is making my decision, and you're both morons."

"Sweet and sexy morons, though, right?" Isaac winked.

I grunted and faced Dezlian. "Okay, I'll do it. I'll get all three items. Show me where to start."

"I'm sorry I got carried away." Jay stood by my side. "I'd like to come with you if you're okay with that."

"Oh, *now* he's a gentleman." Isaac hopped around the exploding lava, rising with every second.

We didn't have enough time to discuss it further. "You're both coming. But Dezlian is in charge."

"There's one thing you should know," she said while guiding us to a hidden path inside the cavern, "when you're under the volcano, a spell will strip you of any natural Magik. It's Oniskel's way of protecting herself against the Elidians. Once you get out of the tunnel on the other side, it'll return."

"Great, we just have to be on the lookout for anything *unnatural*." I meant it as a joke, but Jay and Isaac's faces drew lines of concern as they glanced back and forth at each other, then at me.

Shit, was ₵sµwi unnatural? Would it be stronger once we entered that tunnel? Should I warn Dezlian of the darkness possessing me? No, everything would be fine. It had to be.

8

KYRA

The temperature somehow grew hot and cold simultaneously as we marched under the volcano. The heat of the magma and lava overwhelmed my Magik in excitement. Yet, when we stepped out of the sunlight, a deathly chill wrapped its claws around my neck and warned me to turn back.

Dezlian led us with a torch at her fingertips. I was completely entranced by the first Elidian I'd met other than Elana. The glow of her flames cast shadows against the cave wall that shifted like monsters stalking us in silence.

Are you writing a novel in your head, sis? Are monsters stalking you? How very entertaining.

Shouldn't you be busy saving the world, Cas?

I thought that was your job.

I couldn't hold back a smile at my brother's words, but it didn't last long when I remembered how much was at stake. Landon's sweet mop of curls and sparkling eyes flashed in my memory. Too many lives counted on my success. I hadn't even had time to check in on Landon recently, and guilt gnawed at me for asking Gemm to care for him and Wes even longer than we expected. The old lady was obviously experienced but deserved a break from two energetic boys.

Hopefully, after all this mess was sorted out, thousands of other children would be returned to our world. I wished Landon was standing in front of me at this very moment. Instead, I only had Jay's backside to stare at. Tilting my head, I stifled a laugh. I guess his ass wasn't the worst view.

"What's so funny?" Isaac studied me and brushed his hand against mine.

"Nothing."

Slowly, I moved my hand away. Isaac's gaze darted to mine, noticing my small retreat. Hurt blazed over his face for only a moment. Just like that, reality struck that it was far more painful to consider Jay not in my life than the risk of hurting Isaac. In no world could I lose Jay because true love was worth the discomfort of saying goodbye to another.

"I changed my mind," Isaac said softly.

Shit, even without the Link, this man seemed to read my mind. I slowed my pace so Jay couldn't eavesdrop and asked, "About what?"

"I'm kind of glad our Link severed."

I agreed, but all the same, his admission felt like a coiled serpent strangling my neck. Hopefully, Isaac didn't sense the sadness in my tone when I asked, "Because you didn't like my jokes in your head all day long?"

"No...because when you choose, I'll know it'll be who you truly want, who you can't live without."

"Isaac—"

He held one hand up. "Don't. Not yet. Let's just get through one thing at a time."

I rolled my lips. Isaac deserved a love I couldn't give him, and it wasn't fair to string him along. His shoulder sagged as we walked, pulling at my heartstrings. I fought every urge to reach out and comfort him.

"This is where I leave y'all." Dezlian stopped at a dead end.

"You're not coming with us?" I asked.

"No, the Elidians need me in case you don't make it out of this volcano."

"Oh, that's reassuring." Isaac's sarcasm rolled off his tongue.

Dezlian pushed her shoulder against a boulder, but it wouldn't budge. "Can you two help me?"

Isaac and Jay went to her side, and all three of them shoved the boulder, faces strained and veins bulging. The giant rock finally inched over, leaving a gap with a faint red light glowing through a fog.

Dezlian handed over a satchel with the Unetlo Book of spells tucked inside. "There are three vials in here for you to collect the lava. Follow the path to the pool inside, but whatever you do, don't step off the path."

Jay pushed buttons on his watch, but nothing showed up. He shook his head and handed his watch over to Dezlian. "Alaska plans to send me a message soon, but there's no service here. If I don't come out on the other side, I don't want her to find out until she's safely back with you, so sign my name to messages until you see her in person."

Dezlian nodded and wrapped the watch around her wrist. "Remember, first: lava. Second: a piece of Oniskel. And third: proof of love."

Isaac snorted at that last bit, and my cheeks flushed. Maybe it'd be better to set Isaac free now....

"Isaac, we should—" I started.

He ignored me and stepped forward, disappearing into the red fog. Jay followed, leaving me with Dezlian. A bundle of nerves fluttered deep in my stomach at what we were about to face. "Thanks for helping us."

"Of course."

"How will we find Oniskel?"

"She lives here under Bukti volcano." Dezlian stared through the fog. "Can I ask you something, Kyra?"

"Sure."

"If Isaac...if Isaac's the one your heart belongs to, then whatever sacrifice he has to make, can you try not to have it be a big one?"

Sorrow clamped down on my heartstrings because this felt real, the first step of a goodbye that I didn't want. "I don't think, um, you probably don't have anything to worry about, Dez."

She blew out a tiny sigh and turned away quickly without another word. I tightened the strap on my satchel and merged into the red mist. The second the thick fog brushed against my cheeks, a tingle poked at my Circle. When I felt the darkness approaching this time, I welcomed it because I'd need every ounce of strength possible, even if it was help from the unnatural ₾sµwi. What scared me was I had no recollection of what happened when the darkness fully took over. Who would I become if I fully let it in?

"Jay?...Isaac? How can we stay on the path if we can't see anything? My fire won't light."

"Take my hand." Isaac's large hand groped my side until his fingers laced with mine.

But I still couldn't see his face. Blood-red steam encompassed us like a tomb.

"Jay?"

"I'm here." His steady voice purred, and his hand melded with my other one.

Isaac led us for what could have been minutes, hours, or days down the path. Time ceased to exist when all my thoughts were wrestling with how to tell Isaac where my heart truly lay. The very thought of hurting him felt like a jugosaur stomping on my skull. What if this was my last time holding Isaac's hand? What if I regretted my decision in a decade? What if he never wanted to speak to me again? I never wanted to lose him as a friend.

Isaac stopped our momentum suddenly. My chest slammed into his back, and Jay almost smacked into my side.

"I think we're here," Isaac said.

"Where?"

But then I heard the faint bubbling and popping of my boots. I pulled out the glass bottle and knelt, hovering my hand over the burning heat rising slowly.

"Let's hurry, love—I mean, Kyra—I have a bad feeling about this," Isaac mumbled.

As I reached toward the lava to scoop some out into the three vials, a burning drop splattered on my skin and scalded my wrist. I screamed and recoiled, falling back on my ass.

"Kyra? What happened?" Jay was by my side in an instant.

"I burned my skin. Apparently, I'm not immune to heat in here."

"Damn it. I can't heal you, either. We have to hurry and get out."

"No, I'll be okay. Let me try again."

Like a wicked nightmare, a hand emerged from the pool of lava and slapped the vial away. I gasped and crawled back. Thankfully, the vial didn't shatter but merely rolled along the harsh, solid rock floor. Despite being unable to see my other surroundings, a porcelain face resembling a doll appeared from the lava. When she opened her mouth, an eerie siren's voice rang from between her sharp fangs.

With my emotions spinning like a wild fan, that addictive energy started knocking on my soul. Overwhelming feelings and memories hit me like a storm. My steps stuttered, and my heart rammed harder. And just like that, I merged with whatever being was tackling my spirit. Strange memories suddenly charged me.

Faint silhouetted figures hunch over a campfire.

A baby jugosaur stretching out of its mother's womb all sticky and red.

Smiles and laughter greet me as a striking woman with red hair down to her ankles greets a crowd.

The siren song grew louder. I glanced but then realized the melody was coming from my own mouth. I clutched my throat, feeling the vibrations as the song continued.

If you want what you seek,
There's a simple game to play.
Be my guest and take a peek,
But hurry, I don't have all day.

"Fuck, Nilson, did you know she changed?"

"No! How would I know? I can't see her eyes."

I licked my lips. Both men sounded devastatingly delicious.

"Kyra!" One of them smacked my face. "Kyra, come back to me."

But whether he was Blondie or the other Puppet didn't matter. I waved my hand, and the red fog formed detailed images on the walls. The first was an image of a woman making cookies in her farmhouse. So grotesquely tragic.

"Rajitha!" Blondie shouted and ran toward the wall, only to run smack into it.

Tough Puppet wrapped his arms around me and held me back, but there was no reason to fight against him. I was exactly where I was meant to be as I sang again.

If you want what you seek,
There's a simple game to play.
What makes you strong? What makes you weak?
Answer now, or he will pay.

"Who will pay?" one asked.

"Little Blondie," I snickered.

"Are you trying to torture me, Kyra?" Blondie yelled as his hands were buried in his hair. "What does that mean?"

His frustration was evident in the green swirls of elixir jetting out of his fingertips. I only needed to push him a little further so I could suck in the tasty drug. I cast the red smoke against the wall and showed Blondie his son's empty bed on the night of The Scorch when all worthless Ordull men vanished. And soon, we'd get rid of the women too.

"Nilson, it's a riddle!" Griffin held me tight. "I think if you answer it, the siren will let us collect the lava and move on."

Two red images painted on the wall showed Isaac's past, but he said, "I don't understand the answer."

From within the steam, small toes emerged, dangling. Then knees and boy shorts. A rope was tied around a small waist. Then the rest of the child dropped, only feet above the lava. He wiggled and squealed. If they didn't solve my riddle fast enough, my siren friends would have dinner early tonight.

"*Wes*!" Blondie's voice echoed against the walls.

"Kyra, look at me. Come back to me. We need you." Tough Puppet begged. It was adorable. I could run my finger over his full lips and make him beg in other ways too. I smiled. He was cute when distressed. I started singing again.

The answer to the riddle you must speak,
Or the darkness within will cause decay.
The little boy's future frankly looks bleak,
Confessing your fear is the only way.

"Forgive me, Petal, but I have to do this again." Tough Puppet turned me and lowered his gorgeous face to mine. His lips claimed me —rich, violent, and possessive. The kiss was long and hotblooded, thoroughly and shamelessly ours. Never did I want to pull away, but suddenly, I flinched. I gasped for air and stared at a burn mark on my skin, then into Jay's dark eyes.

"Jay? What—"

Looking up at him confirmed his was the only face I'd ever truly need. We were two bodies, but we were one soul.

Ky! Ky! Are you okay?

Caspian's terrified pleas streamed through our Link, but I had no energy to respond as I sagged into Jay's arms. I glanced up and covered my mouth with both hands. My heart exploded when I saw Wes dangling and terrified above the lava. Frantic drumming pounded my heart. His wide eyes cried a river into the lava below him. I had no idea if Wes was an illusion or real, but I wasn't about to leave it up for debate.

"Wes! Wes, I'm coming. Hold on!" I leaped toward Wes, hoping to swing him close to the bank so Isaac could grab him, but Jay pulled me into his chest. The devastation on Isaac's face obliterated any rational thought I had.

"I'll get you down, Wes. It's okay." Isaac's voice shook more than a quake.

Wes mumbled something through the gag stuck in his mouth as he writhed and swung in the rope.

"Isaac! The song, it's a riddle, Isaac. What's your biggest fear?"

Wes dropped another foot, and lava sprayed onto his sneakers. He screamed through the gag, and his tears soaked his cheeks.

"Stop, okay, okay." Isaac raised both hands to the cavern ceiling. "I was afraid of a future without Rajitha. I'm scared of a future without a woman I love." His voice turned desperate. "And I'm terrified of a future without you, Kyra."

Immediately, the images disappeared from the cave walls, and Wes flew straight up and into the darkness. His squeals faded away until only the bubbling lava stole back my focus.

"Wait, come back!" Isaac jumped up and down, reaching for the tall cavern ceiling like a madman.

"Hurry, Kyra, fill the vials with lava!" Jay commanded.

The bottle's narrow opening gave me no choice but to dip my hand a few inches in the nightmarish lava. I bit the inside of my cheek, expecting pain, but none came. I filled all three, then Jay shoved the topper into the vials and tightened them.

"Wes!" Isaac screeched again and again. "Wes!"

A siren slid out from the side of the pool and latched onto Isaac's ankle. I grabbed the drumstick hairpin from my ponytail and gauged it into her eye. Something about that felt very right. She screeched and fell back. I tugged Isaac away toward the tunnel.

"No—I can't leave Wes!" Isaac yanked away from me.

"He's not here, Isaac." Bats dove from above and flapped chaotically passed my head.

"Wes!"

My heart was shattering at the sound of the desperation in his call. I never should've brought Isaac in here. I had to fix this. He twisted, tripped, fell off the path into the fog, and disappeared.

"Isaac!" I screamed, my head spinning.

Three more sirens crept out of the water, hissing and crawling toward us. I stared at one, but Jay swept me into his arms and jumped over one siren.

"No, we can't leave Isaac here." I punched his back over and over. "Put me down, Jay. I have to get him."

"No."

I kicked and punched and slammed and screamed. "Jadox Griffin, if you make me leave Isaac, I'll never forgive you."

He slid me down and begged, "Please stay here," and then rushed into the fog. I tapped a neurotic beat on my thigh, listening to the hisses and claw sounds within the mist.

"Jay?"

I'd count down from ten, then go after him.

Ten.

Violent shrills and cackles echoed in the cave. My body tensed.

Nine.

Lava gurgled and whirred, making all the hairs on my arms stand straight up.

Eight. Seven. Six.

"Jay!?"

Five. Four.

A wet, hard, loud thump bumped off the ground. Sweat dripped down my back.

Three.

A spine-chilling, sinister scream was razor-sharp against the cavern walls.

Two.

I held my breath as the sound of nails sliding over rock pierced my ears.

9
JADOX

I flopped Nilson's unconscious body over my shoulder. His long arms draped over my back and thumped against my sweat-soaked shirt. Lava splattered on my pants. The heat burnt a hole through the fabric and singed my skin, but I bit my lip to prevent crying out. There was no need to scare Kyra. Her nervous calls from the other side of the red mist only motivated me to move faster. Sweat dripped down my neck as I hauled Nilson's heavy ass out of the nightmarish cavern.

The hot steam stung my eyes. It smelled of burning rubber and toxic fumes mixed into a deadly concoction. Kyra yelled my name once more as I stumbled through the fog, coughing and gagging with each step.

"Jay!" Kyra's voice cracked. Her hands wrapped around me, only to find I was carrying Nilson as she patted his body up and down. "Is Isaac okay?"

"I don't know," I pushed out the words between breaths. "We need…to move…from the mist…before I can set him down." I sucked in thick, hot air. "But…I can't see."

She grabbed a fistful of the bottom of my shirt and pulled me through the pitch-dark tunnel. I'd give anything for her torch abilities to return. Each step forward felt like a gamble with death. The volcanic ground ahead of us could drop down to a ravine or crater at any moment. And since she was leading, Kyra would be the first to fall.

"Kyra, stop. Let me go first."

"No." She coughed. "You're carrying him."

My chest twisted tight. Was she offering to put herself in danger first to protect Nilson or me? I shook my head and shifted his two hundred pounds. He groaned for a moment.

"Is he alive?"

"Yeah, he's alive." I cringed from her obvious eagerness and focused on taking just one more step forward. And then another. Another.

"Does he need to be healed?" Her voice was hesitant in this darkness, like a whisper within the cracks of the walls.

"I can't heal anyone down here. My powers have been stripped, remember?"

Nilson's dead weight made my knees wobble with every step. There was no way I'd be able to carry him much further. Before long, the smell of the lava and mist behind us finally faded, and I only inhaled the muggy, earthy scent of the damp stalagmites.

"I'm gonna…set him down…here," I grunted out the words as I heaved Nilson over my shoulder and onto the ground.

We were a pretzel of three bodies and limbs grasping in the darkness. My leg bumped into Kyra. She immediately helped me slowly lower him. When she softly slapped his cheeks and shook him, Nilson released a soft snore but didn't wake.

"Damn it," Kyra whispered.

I collapsed to the rock, body shaking, heart hammering, and adrenaline slowly dissipating. "Can I…have water?"

"Oh yeah, hold on." Her hair swooshed by my face, and through the mist, my eyes adjusted to see snippets of her silhouette outlined by a faint orange light. A backpack zipped open, and plastic crinkled. Kyra accidentally groped my chest as she searched for my hands and said, "Oh, there you are," then placed a warm bottle of water and a protein bar in them.

"Thank you."

Her head rested against my shoulder as we ate in silence. The much-needed water glided down my throat in glorified gulps, and I chomped at the chewy granola. Each swallow felt like eating a boulder of unanswered questions. How would we find Oniskel? Was an Elidi village truly on the other side of this volcano? Would Kyra even choose me, or was Nilson the one claiming her heart? A hundred other questions rushed through my mind as I finished my snack and rested my head against the hard cavern wall, completely spent.

"Do you think he's just sleeping?" Kyra shifted against me, and I breathed in her coconut shampoo scent.

"Yeah, he's okay," I whispered without any clear idea if I was speaking the truth or a lie, but needing to keep her calm until we found a way out of this volcano. Ancient legends had told stories of strange creatures lurking in The Land of Nothing, and I had no interest in meeting any today.

"We need to keep moving," Kyra said.

"Okay."

"But we can't leave him here."

"Okay."

"Do you have any other words to say?" she asked.

"No."

"Caspian and Narelle are okay," Kyra whispered. "They're assembling a team right now."

I crumpled up the bar wrapper and shoved it into my pocket. "I thought Magik didn't work in here."

"I can hear Caspian in spurts," she said.

"How?"

"I was thinking about it. Dezlian said *natural* Magik. Maybe Links aren't natural."

"Hmm, that's interesting." I rubbed my eyes which still stung. "So, ₾sµwi probably isn't natural either."

Kyra wrapped one hand around my bicep like I was her security blanket as she admitted, "I'm not sure that ₾sµwi is entirely a bad thing, though. Something deep down inside the darkness is calling to me like it knows me."

My nails pressed into my palms, no doubt creating little crescent shapes. This was bad news. Very bad.

Kyra scooted closer. "Maybe I'm only made of darkness."

"Cursed or not, Kyra, I'm here and always will be. You can't get rid of me."

A beat of silence passed. Then another. Kyra shifted, and, at first, I thought she was about to pull away to check on Nilson, but instead, she straddled me in the darkness. I froze, my heart pumping wildly.

"Jay?" Her voice came out fragile, too vulnerable.

"Yes, Petal." I didn't need to see her face to know her facial expressions.

"I feel like I'm breaking apart and just trying to keep my pieces together." She leaned forward, and her lips gently trailed my neck up to my ear.

I tried to hold my breath but relented by curling my fists into balls, then releasing, curling, then releasing.

"Am I a demon?" she asked.

"Most demons don't straddle laps," I managed to mumble.

"Oh, but some do?"

"Some."

"And you know from experience?"

"Well, if you need to know—"

"Kiss me," she commanded, her voice still gentle, still herself.

It didn't matter if I was blinded by the mist or not. My heart led me straight to where I needed to be. I kissed along the line of her jaw up to her lips. She tasted of strength, heat, and the sun at its brightest moment. My body ached to fully belong to Kyra.

"Pick me," I whispered against her skin.

"What?"

My breathing hitched, and all our problems faded as her mouth explored.

"Jay?" she asked into my skin. "What did you say?"

"Nothing, Petal."

"You swear you'd still love me, even if this ₾sµwi Magik stays forever?"

"Only if you kiss me again."

Her fingers slid under my shirt and caressed over the jagged "*MINE*" brand she had seared into my chest. At this point, I didn't mind it anymore. Instead of her lips meeting mine again, Kyra whispered, "I want only you. This. Us. Forever."

"Only me?"

"Only you, Jay."

A slow smile rose on my face, and the fear holding me back shattered into a thousand pieces. My hands found her waist, and I pulled her closer. Chest against chest. Lips against lips. Her breath was mine. Mine was hers. I'd give her anything: the stars, the ocean, every leaf in the forest, every snowflake and flower. She could have every breath in my body until the end of time.

"Jay, it's always been you," she whispered between kisses. "I'm sorry that—"

"There's nothing to apologize for, Petal. Just promise me, promise me you're sure."

"I promise. I'm very sure." Her hands were buried in my hair, desperate to be closer.

"Thank all the Divinities above."

My tongue explored tentatively at first, like it was our first kiss. It felt like I knew her soul better than my own heart. She was my roots, and I'd never let our relationship sever again.

"Hey." The tip of her nose rubbed against mine. "We probably should stop…in case he wakes up."

I peeked over but still could barely see Nilson's sleeping body. Hopefully, he'd wake up soon. I didn't want to ask the one question weighing on my mind, but it'd forever be lingering if I didn't ask now.

"Why did you choose me?" I stroked her cheek in the darkness.

"Because you're mine, and I'm yours. Isaac is…he's refreshing and keeps me on my toes. He's alluring and entrancing and sexy—"

I cleared my throat.

"Not as sexy as you, of course."

"Of course," I repeated and let my fingertips wander to her collarbone.

"Listen, I'm serious." She shivered at my touch. "Isaac and I could work if I wanted. But I could imagine a life without him. I could imagine saying goodbye to Isaac and surviving that. Jay, I can't see a future without you. There's no point in living if you and I aren't together. If I can't share myself with you, if I can't kiss you good morning or steal all your hoodies, then what's the purpose?"

I chuckled and tugged her in closer. "I love you, Miss Kyra Kozelski."

"I can't wait to spend an eternity with you, Mister Jadox Griffin." With her words, my entire world stopped spinning. "And, call me Kyra Elidi. I should embrace who I am eventually, the good and the bad."

"Well, then…" I brushed my lips against her cheeks, forehead, and temple. "I love you, Kyra Elidi, and I always will, even on days when you steal my hoodie." I tugged at the drumstick hairpin. "Will you keep this hairpin from Nilson?"

"Yeah, he's still a friend," she said.

"Okay."

"And I'll tell him my decision when he wakes up—as long as he's stable," Kyra said.

"Okay."

"Do you have anything to say other than okay?"

"Nope."

"Well, I do. I'm worried about Gemm's prophecy." Kyra rubbed my thigh softly in little circles. "She said a man will lay down his life for love. Don't do that for me. No matter what, it's not worth it."

I smiled. "Yes, ma'am."

"I'm serious." She slapped my leg.

"I know." I pulled her in close, relishing in simply touching her again.

"It's not a joke, Jay."

"I'm not laughing."

Kyra slid off my lap and zipped up her backpack. After she blew out a big puff of air, she asked, "Do you think *this* will work?"

"What do you mean? You and me?"

"No, we'll be fine." She grabbed my hand. "I mean everything: returning the males, keeping the Ordull women safe, freeing the prisoners, defeating Elana, using the spell. It's all so complicated."

I reached into the darkness and slowly massaged her shoulders, letting her tension ease into my fingers. "Well, we already got the three vials of lava. And now, I know who your heart belongs to. I just need to sacrifice something as proof."

Kyra blew out a deep breath. "What does that mean, though?"

Unease wrapped around my neck like a boa constrictor. "I'm trying not to think about it too much."

"Then let's focus on finding Oniskel. We need a piece of her to revert her to her original form. Does that mean like a tooth, hangnail, or strand of hair?"

"Let's just find her first," I said.

She stood. "Right, I'll let you do the tracking, soldier. How big is this volcano?"

"Well, the size doesn't matter if we have to stay on this path. Don't fall because I won't be able to lug both you and Nilson over my shoulder." I nudged his useless body with my boot, but he only snorted.

"Maybe sleeping beauty needs a princess to wake him from his slumber," she said.

Silence.

"I was just joking, Jay," she said.

My stomach turned as my body repelled the thought I was about to voice, "Actually, you should try it. My kiss seemed to snap you out of the trance earlier. Maybe he needs the same."

"What?" Kyra half-laughed, a forced sound that wasn't pleasant at all.

"Sometimes, love is needed to break a curse."

"I care for him, but I'm not *in* love with him."

"If he's in love with *you*, it might work. It doesn't hurt to try."

"Yeah, it could, it could hurt you. I made you a promise, Jay."

I leaned forward and took both her hands in mine. "Kyra, I trust you. Think of it as a goodbye kiss, a bit of closure."

"This is the *only* time I'll try this. And then, my lips belong to you for the rest of our lives," she sounded nervous again.

"Deal."

She kneeled to the ground, and I turned, grimacing, wishing I couldn't hear anything for the next few seconds. But the soft brush of her lips on Nilson's was the same to me as a murder of crows diving in an attack or the violent screams of the Blood Maiden's victims. Maybe Isaac would never awake again, and I wouldn't have to deal with the following conflict.

Then Kyra's unnatural moan hit my ears, and jealousy clawed up my spine.

"Um, Kyra...."

"Oh, Puppet, why won't you wake?" Kyra's voice was stolen again by the devilish spirit put on this planet to utterly destroy me. "I'm ready to play. Come taste me."

"Fuck!"

"Yes, please." She laughed.

"Petal?"

"Yes, branch?" The demonic cackle echoed off the walls with the ear-splitting volume ripping open my spine.

Dread pumped through my blood. How often would she turn into this other spirit?

"We need fire!" she bellowed deeply.

Impossible fire blazed from her hands, and I caught a glimpse of the onyx eyes leering at me, sucking out my hope. My traitorous eyes dipped to her lips, covered in a thin minty-green layer like lipstick. Isaac's poison had still seeped into her. If I kissed her now, would she revert to Kyra, or would the poison affect me too? I couldn't risk falling unconscious because Kyra might be trapped in the monster's soul for good. My temples pulsed when she started to sing.

Little toy, little boy, time to play with me,

Quiet creatures of the night come out and roam free.
Little toy, little boy, drop down to one knee,
Because you search for the dark door and I hold the key.

"What's the dark door?" I asked.

"You seek Oniskel, my sister, my love, my friend."

"Yes, where is she?"

"First, drop to your knees to please." She started rolling down her yoga pants, showing all five tattoos, the gray one glowing fiercely and deadly.

To please? This demon expected me to…fuck no.

As if she understood my refusal, the spirit's mouth opened wide in the blink of an eye, and she screamed words of an ancient language I'd never heard. Skittering sounds echoed down the tunnel closer. Louder. A scent similar to rats grew stronger. My heart galloped in my chest, on overdrive.

"Drop down to one knee," she ordered, "and worship me."

Suddenly, a herd of glow-in-the-dark cat-like creatures dropped from the ceiling onto Nilson's prone body and tore into his shirt with fierce claws.

"Get back!" I swiped an arm at them and received a dozen slashes through my skin.

The spirit in Kyra grinned wide, an outlandish and terrifying sight, and then repeated, "Drop down to one knee."

Instead, I threw her over my shoulder.

"Weeee! Ride number one, you will lavish ride number two." She giggled. "Get your tickets for a soldier ride at the ticket booth, ladies."

Even though Kyra wasn't herself, I wouldn't let anything hurt her. I kicked at the cats, and they all hissed in response as they tried to attack from all angles. I shielded Kyra's body. Unable to scoop up Nilson, I grabbed his wrist and pulled, then dug my heels into the ground. I tried to run, but vicious cats jumped on my head. Jumped on my shoes. My neck, slicing my skin.

I screamed. I pulled Nilson. I steadied Kyra on my shoulder. Blood trickled down my arms. Cats hissed. I heaved. He was too heavy.

The ₾sµwi spirit in Kyra laughed and laughed, then repeated, "Drop down to one knee for you to search for the dark door, and I hold the key."

"I'll do anything you want. Just bring Kyra back to me." I quickly dropped Nilson's hand to the ground, slid Kyra off my shoulder, and kneeled in front of her.

"Anything?" She smiled, shadows storming through her eyes.

"Anything. What do you want?"

IO

JADOX

On my knees, I hesitated, searching the spirit's expression for any hint of Kyra, but saw none. This was wrong. I needed to get rid of it for good. How long until it overwhelmed Kyra's body completely? What if Kyra was trapped behind a veil, watching our entire interaction?

"Dear puppet. Games are for the young, and young I will stay, so, henceforth, I will play." She giggled. "Henceforth is a funny word."

"What's the deal you want to make?"

The spirit poked my nose like I was a child and said, "Wanna play hide and seek?"

"No."

"Keep him alive, soldier. Or I'm gonna get you."

"Fine, that's fine. Now, let Kyra come back."

"You are mister not-so-fun, but the girl thinks you might be the one." Her fingertips trailed behind my ear, my sweet spot, making a shudder rush through every inch of my body.

My dick immediately hardened, and I swore under my breath.

"Mm, maybe I was wrong because you're mighty long. Do you want to play? I love to play all night and day." Her atrocious giggle racked my nerves as her hands moved down. Lower. Lower.

"Stop it. Bring Kyra back."

"Why? What's so great about *her*?" she spat out. "I can feel the Cursed One's heart. It's rotten and decayed, stubborn and wretched, impatient and cold."

"You're wrong. She's fire and strength, light and power."

The spirit finally backed up, with that ever-smirk still plastered on her face. She tilted her head, examining me from head to toe, then her eyes lingered on my crotch. She licked her lips, and I could almost read her mind.

"You said you'd give me Kyra. I don't want you. None of us want you here. Leave her alone!"

"Lies, lies, little yummy potato fries!" she sang and skipped around me.

"Kyra, please. I need you to come back!"

"No, I will lead you to my sister. Oniskel can feast on Blondie while you and I play; play all night and day."

She pushed a rock into the wall and turned it clockwise. A rumbling vibrated the ground, and the wall slid to the side, revealing a glowing gold light deep within.

"I'm not going anywhere until you bring Kyra back." I started to rise from my knees, but she pressed down on my shoulders and pushed her breasts against my face.

"Don't you even want to know my name, Draven Puppet?"

The thought hadn't even crossed my mind. Did this spirit have an actual identity? Would it help to know? Curiosity won, and I nodded. "Who are you?" I muttered between her cleavage.

"Elana Elidi's great-granddaughter." She giggled.

"No, Kyra is her great-granddaughter. Bring her back."

Hesitancy wavered in the wrinkles of her forehead for a moment, then she dropped to her knees too. Her head hung, and she leaned against the dark cavern wall.

"Kyra!" I reached forward, catching her before she fell on top of Nilson.

A soft moan slipped out of her lips as I cradled Kyra's head and angled it up. Amber eyes again. Thank the goddess. They started to glisten with tears, and one slowly rolled down her cheek. "Jay, I'm so tired."

"It's okay, I'll fix it. I'll make it right." I held her against my chest.

"How?" her voice shook, breaking me apart.

I tucked a golden strand of hair behind her ear. "Do you have any idea who or what the spirit is? Can you feel it?"

"She feels…wrong, somehow." Kyra hesitated. "I remember more this time than the time before. She…I saw her touch you."

I stroked Kyra's long hair, unsure what to say.

"Wait, what's that?" Kyra pointed to the hole in the wall that led to golden light.

"I think it's the way to Oniskel." I glanced down at Nilson, still unconscious. "Your kiss obviously didn't wake him."

"Obviously." Her nose scrunched up adorably as always. "Jay, I'm so weak. I'll stay with Isaac. You should go and get the piece of Oniskel."

"No, I won't leave you. Plus, what if Nilson wakes up and his poisonous gas changes you again."

Kyra scooted to Nilson's side and held his hand, tapping the top softly. "Isaac isn't trying to hurt me."

"Kyra—"

"Go. I'll be fine. You're the strongest of us three. I'll keep Isaac calm if he wakes up. Just, be careful, and hurry back."

I pulled a dagger out of the backpack and gripped it firmly. She was right: if I was the one to stay with Nilson, there was no way I'd be patient enough to wait for her return. Plus, Kyra was safer in the corner of a cavern than with a soul-sucking demon. Hopefully, those sinister cats wouldn't return. Sucking in a deep breath, I quickly met Kyra's eyes and memorized every inch of her face–just in case.

I reached for the emerald necklace for some much-needed support, forgetting I had given the gem to my sister. Shit. Hopefully, Alaska was safe and knew what she was doing with it.

As soon as I stepped through the threshold into the golden light, my body turned weightless. I floated like an astronaut in a simulation, unable to ground myself. My heart thudded fast, but I managed to drift to the wall and haul myself down the tunnel. The light grew brighter and had a specific scent— like honey.

I stopped; the smell was too tempting, too alluring. This could be a trap. Before I could turn around, a vacuum-like force sucked me forward. I tried to brace against the wall, but the jagged stone only scratched through my clothes. I somersaulted and flipped in the air as it pulled me closer. Faster. Stronger. More honey.

Honey. It felt like everything in my life had pointed to this exact moment, but dread dripped through me like syrupy honey as my heart beat faster still. *Thump, thump. Drip, drip.* Danger lurked in every beat like my Magik knew the threat waiting around the corner. *Thump, thump. Drip, drip.*

Finally, the vacuum sensation stopped, and I hovered above a pool of lava, sitting at the base of a steep bank. Atop it, the honey-gold light burned bright, hurting my eyes. I squinted and shielded my face.

"Oniskel?" I asked, looking at the shadowy figure ahead.

"Bow to me, boy." She wore lipstick dark enough to cover up any lies her lips whispered.

Thump, thump. Drip, drip.

Despite having minimal control over my body, I bowed, praying that this would work. Her light dimmed, revealing a tall, slender woman with skin even darker than mine and scarlet hair down to her ankles. Attached to her back were gorgeous gold butterfly wings outstretched wide. She floated above a throne with both arms extended. Transparent, golden silk hung from her curves like a toga.

Thump, thump. Drip, drip.

"Rise, boy. Why are you here?" This time, when she spoke, honey dripped out of her mouth like drool, but spiders crawled out after.

My entire body tensed in a warning. Not that it mattered because I couldn't run if I tried. Gemm had always said honesty was the best policy, so I stared at Oniskel's beady eyes and confessed, "I need a favor."

Her laugh was as sweet as a molasses cookie but had a burnt edge. "Everyone needs something. Why are you special?"

"Because I'll turn you and your sisters back to your true self."

Her wide smile flattened into a thin line. "Do not joke with me, boy. You don't even know what we once were." She glanced behind her throne into the shadows, where something shifted. Was it more of those evil cats ready to launch?

Thump, thump. Drip, drip. My heart raced faster, staring at the spiders crawling over her cheeks.

"For a thousand years, my sisters, Surh-Sig, Moroka, and I had free reign of the world. Mystiers worshipped us like goddesses and used to be grateful for our gifts. We were nymphs of the earth, sea, and sky with the gift to bless certain Mystiers with enhancements, giving them a leadership role in their tribe.

"In her outrageous tantrum, Elana vowed there and then to seek revenge. Eventually, she translated an ancient spell in the Unetlo Book that morphed my sisters and me from nymphs to *this*," she screeched, gesturing at her form.

"The emerald, crystal, and pearl necklaces confined us to isolated locations where my sisters and I could never see each other again. When *someone* took the Vayu Crystal and freed me, I came here, inside Bukti Volcano.

"I've been cursed with an appetite for souls. Do you want to be my next meal?" Her tongue licked the golden honey off her lips, and another spider wriggled out from the inside of her cheek.

Thump, thump. Drip, drip.

"I'm telling the truth: I can make you into a nymph again. I need—"

Oniskel waved away my words in the air as if they had never existed. "I know what you need—a piece of me—but it's useless. That spell won't work unless the Mystier who casts the spell possesses Ꮳsμwi Magik."

This part we hadn't known. An image of onyx eyes, victorious over Kyra's body, haunted my sights until I shook my head. "Leave that part to me."

Oniskel lowered her angelic chin, then flew down the slope. She floated directly in front of me and scanned me up and down. "I do not sense any Ꮳsμwi in you."

I gulped and swallowed. The scent of death was strong, lingering over her skin like ghastly perfume.

"I'll make a deal with you. If you pass my challenge first, I'll give you what you came here for."

Flashbacks of Kyra trembling in my arms, terrified of her future, had me agreeing instantaneously.

"Deal. What is the challenge?" I tried to step forward but was locked in an air bubble that Oniskel controlled.

She smiled, and my stomach churned. My gaze dropped to her stomach where the clear, thin silk covered her stomach. Five gray tattoos glowed menacingly beneath. Did her sisters have the same?

"You like what you see?" She bit her lip and stuck out her hip. "You haven't been bedded recently, boy?"

My gaze whipped up to her devastating smile, and my cheeks warmed.

"Let's not get distracted." She lined five bottles in a row, all floating mid-air. They reminded me of the bowls Gemm kept in her den to create potions, herbs, and mix spices.

A smart man would've stayed silent, but I cleared my throat and pointed, asking, "What do you want me to do with those?"

Oniskel's wicked grin held promises of torture when she said, "Each holds a specific scent. You will tell me what the smell is. I'll give you what you seek if you get all five correct."

It couldn't be this easy. My palms turned sweaty, and I wished I still had a functioning watch to check the time. It felt like hours or days had passed since I entered her domain. A soft, skittering sound echoed from behind her throne again, but when I checked, nothing presented itself.

"The first test." She pulled the cork off and held the bottle before my nose.

I teetered in mid-air when I leaned forward, but Oniskel still controlled my balance. She reinforced the invisible bubble between us.

I sniffed in the first bottle. "Cedar."

"Good, but there's one more ingredient—you must list all the scents."

Closing my eyes, I inhaled again. "Cedar and hesitancy."

When I opened them, her beady eyes glared. "Very good," she hissed. "Next."

I inhaled. "Gorula fur and fear."

"Yes. Next." She shoved the next under my nose. "Brass and arousal."

Oniskel grunted, and her jaw clenched tight. "Damn it!" She flipped her wrist over the fourth and then held it out. "This may be harder."

I sucked in the scent and knew the answer immediately, but my body turned to stone. The filthy scent of the prisoner girl's stench and the electric chair suffocated me entirely. How did Oniskel know about my time in The Cavity? I dug my nails into the skin on my palms. In that instant, I'd rather rip out my own decrepit heart than be forced to inhale the young prisoner's scent again.

A flood of memories drowned me in a sea of pain. The demon in front of me disappeared, leaving the only thing that mattered: my sadistic past.

I'm standing over a Mystier strapped onto a science lab table, their names all inked into my brain until my dying day. Katie Smuhb. Devin Krunt. Sammy Herns. I ignore their helpless pleas, just like all the others. I'm a torturer. A murderer. A villain. I stick another body with needles. Lila Rufiv. Killian Trudd. Thin arms reach out from metal cages, grasping at the air weakly. I ignore their cries. Wiley Nustil. Paisley Coots. I ignore each and every soul. I walk past them. Penny Jefferson. Britan Hoffer. I ignore them again and again. I'm the captor. They're in pain. Suffering. I'm worse than anyone with Ȼsμwi because I'm tearing apart their humanity. I'm the monster.

"I need an answer, soldier," Oniskel sneered, satisfaction layered in every word.

I sucked in a breath, gagging on the scent of Katie's death, remembering how light she felt in my arms when I carried her to the crematorium. "Katie Smuhb's last breath and my own agony."

"Impossible! How did you do that?" Oniskel snarled, showing her sharp teeth that matched her murderous sisters.

"Nothing's impossible."

"Last one." She shoved it over with a corrupt scowl. "Here. You'll never get it right."

Petrified of what she'd give me next, I tried to calm my racing pulse. There was no backing out. We needed a piece of Oniskel to complete the spell. Kyra *needed* me.

I leaned in and sniffed. Guilt sliced through my temple with unimaginable pressure and knocked me to my knees. It was my worst nightmare—Paola Perez's blood mixed with my sister's tears. Still hovering over the cavern's floor, I desperately reached to the earth, needing a connection to the one thing in this world that could heal me. The ground.

Tears pooled in my eyes, threatening to spill.

She created an invisible wall of air to block my access. I was hyperventilating. I pinched my nose with one hand, unwilling to breathe in the scent any longer. My world turned hazy, and I was thrown back in time to when we were all captured on the beach.

Kyra is actively scorching the "MINE" brand into my skin. It burns through my chest. Kyra sobs. Alaska screams. The Blood Maiden crawls and sinks her teeth into Paola, sucking out her blood. Crimson spots enter the corners of my vision.

Thump, thump. Drip, drip.

"I need an answer," Oniskel demanded.

How could I possibly be worthy of love after all these mistakes? Kyra would be better off without me, just like the Draven villagers were right to cast me out of my home, just like I was separated from the army. Tying myself to Kyra would be a huge mistake because I'd only cause her pain and heartbreak, just like everyone in my life.

"What's the smell?" Oniskel snarled.

"You bitch!" I gritted my teeth and writhed against the wind controlling me.

"What a clever insult, now answer." A sinful glower slithered higher on her brown cheeks.

"I won't answer. You shouldn't have access to this scent. It's not your pain to hold. You have no right!"

"Answer me!"

I choked out the words, "It's Paola Perez's blood with Alaska Griffin's tears."

Her smile swiftly fell. "How? How did you do that? You weren't supposed to win. You don't have your enhancement in my volcano."

"I haven't won." My head hung heavy. "I've only lost…again and again."

"No, you are a champion, and a deal is a deal. You can come and take a piece of me." But Oniskel flew up the steep slope to her throne. I scooped at nothing like I was swimming in the air and slowly followed. The compressed feeling in my chest was restricted in urgency. I had to get a piece of Oniskel, but before I could, she reached into the shadows and pulled out a body wrapped in electrical cords.

My mind didn't seem to register what I was seeing. Panic, denial, shock, and confusion warped into a thick wad until I finally understood that Gemm's face was staring back at me, defeated and worn. How? How had she gotten here? Prickles skittered up my spine and snaked across my scalp.

"No!" I lunged forward, only to be stopped by the bubbled wall of air containing me. I punched. Kicked. Slammed. Jabbed. Again and again to no avail. My knuckles tore open against the unseen barrier.

"On the full Teal Moon, one man will lay down his life for love." Gemm smiled sweetly.

Thump, thump. Drip, drip.

"Gemm, it's okay. I'll get you out of here."

"No, this is how it is to be. Once there was a boy who changed the world." Gemm held her hand out. "You are him, my boy. You changed my world for the better."

While looking into her wrinkled eyes, my childhood rolled in bits and pieces. Gemm was the glue that held the village together, the one who had the final say in decisions. Her hands tucked me in at night and baked me the world's most delicious bread. She was the one who encouraged me to return to Draven. My grandmother never gave up on me, always ready with open arms.

"How touching, but I'm hungry." Oniskel clutched Gemm by the neck and lifted her off the ground with one hand. She twitched as her feet dangled.

"No! No, no!" I struck against the wall. Pounded. Smashed. Useless —I was useless.

Oniskel pressed her lips to Gemm's and sucked in deeply. Gemm's wrinkled hands immediately turned gray. Oniskel sucked in again, making her skin glow brighter and her red hair grow longer. My heart splintered into a thousand pieces when the gray spread further up to Gemm's elbows, her neck, then her cheeks. Tears gushed down my face, and I choked on my own screaming.

"Stop. Stop!"

With every inhale, Oniskel grew brighter and fuller. And Gemm's eyes finally closed, her body falling limp in the demon's hands. Oniskel dropped Gemm's body to the ground in a hellish *thud,* and rage surged through my veins. If I had any Magik at my disposal, this soul sucker would die a thousand deaths.

Thump, thump. Drip, drip.

"Okay, I'm ready now." Oniskel reached through the bubble encasing me and grabbed my dagger from my hip.

She held out the hair that fell to her ankles and slashed the pointed end through it. Without a second glance, Oniskel returned the dagger through the barrier and tucked her hair into my pocket.

I could only stare at Gemm's lifeless body on the ground. She had raised me. She had loved me. She had protected me. She was Draven's elder. Our leader. My everything. And Oniskel had taken her away.

"You're welcome." The snake smile curled up Oniskel's face again. "Now, leave before I want dessert." She licked her plump lips.

I just stared at Gemm, unwilling to leave her side. If I left, no one would be by her side to interpret her endearing stories. Who would help her from the ground when she woke? She'd need her cane.

"*Go!*" Oniskel screamed, her voice making the stalagmites shake.

My entire body fought against my mind when I turned my back on Gemm laying in a heap and floated back toward Kyra in a daze.

These demons didn't deserve a chance to return to their prior selves. All three of them deserved to rot in the eternal Abyss. Death was the only future for her dark soul. But not here or now. I needed my Magik back to kill her.

Kyra didn't need to know about Oniskel's hair in my pocket or my new plan to kill the three demons instead of reverting them.

II

KYRA

I waved a piece of chocolate under Isaac's nose, hoping it'd wake him. Nothing.

"Wake up, Isaac. Come on, wake up." I clapped my hands together sharply, right next to his ears. Nothing. At least his chest continued to gently rise and fall. I took the chance to memorize Isaac's face. My pulse quickened, and I prayed to the Divinities that my remaining feelings for him would fade quickly. Though, if he slept forever, I'd never have to tell him I'd chosen Jay. The thought of Isaac's face after hearing my news filled me with immense dread.

We had been an easy choice for each other when we were Linked, serving as a distraction during our time of grief, but now, I needed to deal with reality. I needed to let him go and move on to a new future. Hopefully, he'd find the love of his life.

"Come on, Isaac, wake up," I whispered.

Neither smell nor abrupt sounds roused him. I scanned his body, feeling remorse that I'd never kiss him again.

Um, Ky, do you still love your ex?

Caspian's voice rammed through our Link. I jumped and turned, expecting to see my brother standing over us, only to catch a red glow from the lava in the distance.

He's not my ex, Caspian. We weren't ever together.

Do you love him?

He's always been my friend. And he still is.

Make sure you tell him the choice you made, Ky, right when he wakes up.

If he wakes up.

He will, sis.

I shook my head, unwilling to let my fears become a reality. Isaac deserved a long, happy, peaceful life with his son. A tightness squeezed my chest again at the memory of Wes tied up over the pool of lava. It *had* to be an illusion. There was no way he was here because that'd mean Landon was captured too. Impossible. Gemm wouldn't let anything happen to those boys.

I glimpsed behind me. What was taking Jay so long?

Should I leave Isaac and go help Jay or continue waiting? But wait for how long? I didn't know how long this tunnel was. Maybe if I sprinted to the exit and found the Elidi village on the other side, a Mystier could help.

"Wake up!" I threw my backpack onto Isaac's leg, wishing he was faking it and that his arrogant smile would return.

Eerie scratches echoed from the darkness. I crouched on my heels, shielded Isaac with my body, and tried to summon power. There was still no Magik. Wait, maybe I could call the Ꮳsµwi to help. The last time the spirit claimed my body, I was more lucid. If I could control it, maybe that would get us out of this bind.

My fists turned to tight balls as I focused on my tattoos. Nothing.

"Aaah! Come on. Something has to work!" I screamed foolishly into the tunnel, letting every horrific volcanic creature know our location.

The cursed Magik had been haunting me for weeks, and the moment I needed it, the spirit was letting me down, but I refused to give up. I traced a circle over my gray tattoo again and again and pictured Isaac's devious smile, eyes, my hands in his thick blond hair, his arms around my waist, and my lips on his neck. Nothing happened.

"Come on! Come to me!" I yelled, and a strange ping jolted my core. Ancient spells whizzed in my mind, but my enhancement of knowing spells shouldn't be working down here. Ignoring the warnings firing in my blood, I chanted, *"Tenebris agvnig. Tenebris agvnig."* I felt her lingering on the edge of my consciousness, observing, judging, and teasing.

The spirit whispered secrets and bargains in my ear, but I refused to begin talking to myself—or whoever the spirit was. I just needed her unnatural Magik.

I held both arms outstretched in the darkness, palms facing the stalagmites, and commanded, *"Tenebris agvnig. Tenebris agvnig."*

Her essence cloaked me like a heated blanket; comfortable, heavy, and mine. Energy poured into my Circle, and curiosity made me roll down the hem of my pants. The gray Circle glowed, but the blueish Vayuian Circle looped through it, started to change before my eyes, and shifted to a deadly gray.

"Shit! No! No, no, no." I tried scrubbing the gray off.

I was royally fucking up everything. If this curse truly took over, there was no chance I'd be able to fix anything. Maybe I was meant to be like Surh-Sig and Moroka, and demons didn't deserve love.

I rubbed the Vayuian tattoo, but only more power coursed through my muscles. Strength. Air. Wind. Breath. Life. Sky. I sucked it in greedily.

I knelt by Isaac, laid a hand on his chest, and chanted a spell unfamiliar to me, "*Uyetsgi waklo*."

Isaac's eyes flew open, and he gasped for air. He scrambled upright and patted his body all over. When he met my gaze, I expected a wave of relief, but he crawled backward and flattened himself against the cave wall.

"Not *you* again. Bring Kyra back."

I moved toward him slowly, with one hand out. "It's me, Isaac. I'm here."

Isaac shook his head frantically. "Even in this darkness, I can see your eyes are like midnight. Don't lie to me. Bring Kyra back."

"It's me, I promise. I can control it now."

"What have you done with Kyra? And where's Griffin, you demon?

Did you eat him?" His gaze darted around the shadows. "Well, I guess he deserved it. How'd he taste? Disgusting, right?"

A laugh caught me by surprise, but I still moved forward.

When Isaac cowered, the humor in the moment evaporated, and a shard of glass dug itself into my heart. I'd always be a monster while this spirit lived inside me—a girl full of darkness and meant to be feared.

"Listen to me, Isaac. It's me. We met in the forest. You wore a gray suit and had Tawoli with you. The first time you tried to kiss me, we were in your weird-ass feather shrine in that secret room under Aurella's fortress. You forced me to Link, and I thought it was one of the worst things to happen to me, but now I can't hear your thoughts and jokes in my head, and I miss it. I miss you. I'll always miss you now because...." Tears pooled, but I couldn't give him the wrong impression. I held them back.

Isaac's jaw dropped. Then he crawled over and placed his hands on either side of my face. "Kyra…this isn't good; your eyes—"

"I'm okay."

He leaned in, about to kiss me, but I sucked in a breath and moved back. "What are you doing?"

"Griffin said a kiss will change you back to normal."

I winced. "We need to talk," I said.

He surveyed the scene again, eyes lingering on the backpacks. "Ah, I see. So, you didn't eat Griffin then?"

"I'm afraid not." I sighed and bit my lip. "Isaac, I—"

"Wait!" He bolted to his feet. "How are we even here? The last thing I remember was Wes." His hands slammed against his temple. "We have to go save him."

I jumped up after him and reached up to his shoulders. "No, Isaac, it was dark Magik, just an illusion. He's safe with Gemm, far away from here."

Another sound scampered down the tunnel, and I braced myself for feline claws, but then solid footsteps thumped closer. My entire body tensed, and Isaac mirrored my fighting stance.

Jay stepped through the golden light, and my posture loosened. I debated running into his arms, but there was no need to make a show in front of Isaac. That wouldn't be fair. Isaac lurched forward and punched Jay square in the jaw.

Jay stumbled and hit his back into the cave wall. "What the actual fuck!?" His curled fists hovered in front of his chin like the ever-ready soldier he was.

"That's for not letting Kyra eat you!" Isaac screamed and bounced on his toes.

Jay didn't even acknowledge him with a response. He swung and missed. The momentum of his body hurdled him forward, and Isaac rammed a fist into Jay's stomach.

"Ugh!"

Jay smacked his fist into Isaac's eye, and he staggered to the side, swearing and hopping back and forth.

"Guys! Stop." Disturbing flickers of emotion flared in my Circle. Guilt. Greed. Pride. Jealousy. Denial. Emptiness. But they weren't my feelings. Whose were they?

"What's your problem, Nilson? Back off!"

"You! You're my problem. You took her from me!"

Jay's fists lowered, and his shoulders softened. "So, you told him?"

And just like that, when Isaac's pitiful eyes met mine, the rage I had for their idiotic fight sizzled to nothing.

Isaac's hand fell to his side. "Wait, seriously? You decided? You… you picked him?"

A creepy giggle echoed in my mind; *you can play with them both, puppet.*

I reached forward nervously, "Isaac, can we talk?"

Isaac's obvious torment spun like a tornado in his eyes when he ignored my request and replied, "I'm wasting time. I need to find Wes." He grabbed his backpack and turned toward the red glow from the lava pool down the tunnel.

"No." Jay jogged ahead and blocked his path. "We need to leave this volcano together. Now."

"I'm not leaving without my son," Isaac growled. "You two can go on without me; it's not like she wants me around anymore."

His tone held no resentment, only genuine sorrow, which completely ripped me to shreds.

"No, we're all leaving." Jay stiff-armed Isaac's attempt to move forward.

"Don't touch me."

A wave of wickedness, almost like sorcery, weaved a web between my core and my fingertips, desperate to be used. If I didn't release this coiled tension inside, I'd burst within moments.

"He's not this way. Wes is at the end of the tunnel, on the outside of this volcano, safe in Elidi." Jay didn't meet my eyes. In fact, Jay hadn't looked me in the eye at all. He turned and started leading us down the path we hadn't explored yet.

"Did you meet Oniskel? Did you get a piece of her?" I asked.

Ky, stop merging with the ₡sμwi. This has gone on long enough.

Caspian's voice was harsher this time, demanding and edgy.

Ignore him, Puppet. Another voice. Her voice. The spirit within.

There were too many voices. Too many messages. Too much. A scorching sensation pierced my stomach, and I knew nothing good would come if I checked what it meant. I pushed a thumb against my temple and leaned against the cave wall. Groaning sounds came from somewhere close, and I didn't realize I was making the sounds until a pair of strong hands wrapped around my waist.

"What's wrong with her?" Isaac asked.

"Don't deserve her...."

"Asshole...."

"Douchebag...."

"Shut the fuck...."

A shredding pain sliced through my temples, and I screamed, falling into someone's chest. "Voices, there are too many voices."

"Quiet, Griffin."

"I'm carrying her out of here," someone said. "Go where you want, but it's not safe that way."

Sturdy hands lifted me, and I was draped over someone's back. He started walking, fast, with purpose. Red flared brighter behind us as I softly shifted on a shoulder. I figured out it was Jay from the sound of his breathing. Weakness was stacked on my muscles, and sleep crept around the corners of my mind, but I refused. What if I woke up and the Ȼsµwi had taken me over completely? What if I lost who I was? Terror picked apart my heart, one piece at a time, until I reached out to my brother.

Cas, I can't get rid of it. Make it go away.

My second tattoo turned gray*, Ky. What's going on?*

No, no, no, what had I done? My darkness was impacting my brother. Exhaustion swept over me like a heavy fog and blocked my access to my mental bond with Caspian.

As I bounced on Jay's shoulder, I caught snippets of Isaac and Jay's conversation, not fully able to concentrate.

"What about the third item, a sacrifice from her love?"

"I *will* sacrifice…."

"If you're wrong?"

"Work together…."

Through droopy eyelids, I focused on the pools of lava growing wider like rivers by Jadox's feet. Instead of boiling pops or ripples of a current, more voices haunted me. At first, they blended, then one stuck out perfectly clearly. Caspian. But he wasn't in my head this time. His singing voice rose from the hot lava, snickering and thick with venom. How?

Our ancestor was no fool,
We were each born to be cruel.
Do not waste. You're meant to rule,
Use Ȼsµwi as your tool.

The voice was right. I didn't need to push away the cursed Magik. She was a part of me, and I was blessed to be given this gift. When I looked down, my skin was cracking and turning gray.

I relaxed into the crushing heat poisoning my heart and savored another song flowing from the magma. Brent. My father's message was next.

There's no rush to make a choice,
It's okay to keep each boy.
Listen to the ancient voice,
And use each one as your toy.

That made perfectly logical sense. Definitely. Maybe I had rushed into choosing Jay for my future when both were at my disposal. Once I was the leader of Elidi, I could summon Jay and Isaac to my bed on alternate nights, or maybe the three of us at once. Jay could feed me strawberries in a luxurious bath of scalding water, and Isaac could give me foot massages. They would be my puppets evermore.

"What's she mumbling?"

"Hurry up...."

"...That sound?"

"...Jugosaur?"

I smiled as I glided into a state of peace. Someone far away kept repeating the word "puppet" again and again until it sounded like my one true name. *Kyra Puppet. Kyra Puppet. Puppet Puppet.* I adored that voice. An image of my sweet great-grandmother surfaced with her riding on her hoverboard and serving me a spoon of syrupy honey. Ghost Elana opened her mouth, and a lullaby coaxed me into dreams.

No more time until revenge,
Scorch. Sever. Shatter. And then wedge.
Plan to push them over the edge,
With dear Kyra's authentic pledge.

I giggled, reaching my hands through Tough Puppet's thick hair.

"Stop arguing with me. You have to kiss her, Griffin."

"Not yet. She has to learn to fight this herself."

"If you don't do it, I will. Man. We have to snap her out of it."

"It won't work for you."

"What?"

"We tried when you were unconscious. Your poison leaks into her system and encourages the Ꮳsμwi."

Silence. Giggle. Silence. Giggle. *Puppets. Puppets.*

"I'm sorry, Nilson."

"Don't be." One puppet sounded so sad. "You're her cure. Just kiss her. Hurry."

In a swift movement, I swung through the air off a shoulder and landed unbalanced on my feet. Big hands found my back. A hot breath on my neck. Mm, delicious. This puppet was Dravian. And oh, so powerful.

"One, two, three tattoo. Four." I giggled and said, "I won't stop until I have more."

"Kyra, fight it. You can do this. You don't need my kiss." Brown eyes seared into mine—focused—grounding me like a root. My roots anchoring me like a plant. Deep in the earth. My center. Roots. My very source of life. Jay.

"Jay?" I dug my fingernails into his neck, hands trembling and tears prickling my eyes. Panting, I buried my head in his chest. "Jay, it's worse. I have two of them. The Vayuian tattoo is gray." I gasped desperately. "What am I supposed to do?"

12

KYRA

Jay marched away faster, and I wondered if he knew whether it was the right way or if he was guessing.

"Isaac," I said. "I can't leave you in here. Please, come with us."

"Us?" He cringed and stroked his scruff. "You really did decide then?"

I stepped forward, heart racing, wanting to avoid this conversation at all costs. "Isaac, so many pieces of you make me happy."

"But—"

I made sure to look him straight in the eyes. "But I'm in love with someone else."

Isaac sighed, "I know."

"You know?" Both relief and pain competed for the top spot in my heart. "If you know, why have you been patiently waiting?"

"Because a man doesn't want his heart shattered. Because there was a small chance that you'd change your mind. Because a tiny part of me believed you could still learn to love me. Because my feelings don't simply go away just like that," he said and snapped his fingers.

"What we had was still real to me. Please know that."

"I'm glad you decided. It makes it much easier to go after Wes now." He swung the backpack strap over his shoulder.

"What if he's not here? You could get hurt with no one to help you." A tear slid down my cheek.

"Don't cry for me, love." He wiped away the tear. "Go save the world with Griffin and be happy. Start a new life in Elidi. It's okay."

A sob exploded from my chest, releasing the guilt that had piled up like a stack of rocks. I leaned into his chest, and Isaac's arms curled around me. I never wanted to hurt him. It was the last time Isaac would hold me, the last time I'd feel his heartbeat against mine, and the last time he'd ever call me "his love." Trembling, I backed away and gazed into his deep grays, getting lost in them—for the last time.

Wiping my face on my sleeve, I forced a smile. "If you don't make it out of here in twenty-four hours, I'm sending in an entire Elidian army after you."

He half-smiled, the spark not reaching his eyes. "No, you won't. You're Golden and probably their new leader. They need someone to protect and guide them during all this chaos. I'll be okay, don't worry, just forget about me."

"I could never forget you, Isaac."

"Well, I may ask you for one favor then." He shifted his feet uncomfortably.

I glanced over my shoulder and noticed Jay's silhouette waiting in the shadows, listening to the entire conversation.

"So, we can't tear out a page from the Unetlo Book, but can I copy the memory spell into my watch?"

The passion in his eyes clouded over. Suddenly, it hit me. Isaac wanted to forget me and erase our story from the threads of time. It felt like a lightning bolt had struck me down where I stood. "Oh, but Isaac, I—"

"Please."

His glistening eyes cleaved me in two. Memories were part of what made a person, and Isaac no longer wanted me in his life—past, present, or future. I'd be gone without a trace. He snapped a picture of it quickly.

"Goodbye, Kyra." Isaac leaned forward, kissed my forehead, then disappeared into the darkness without another word.

I immediately crumbled to the ground, curling my arms around my knees. A hand softly rubbed my back. Jay slid low and pulled me into his chest. I buried my face into him, staining his shirt in tears, and let them flow until there was nothing left inside me. He stroked the side of my head gently, patiently. When I finally stopped and gained control, Jay squeezed me tighter.

"Do you want to talk about it?" he asked.

"I don't know how." I hiccupped and rubbed my eyes. "I want to be with you, Jay, and I always will."

He gulped and swept a loose strand of hair out of my face. "Do you want to be with him, too?"

"I care about him in a different way."

"How?"

"Because I let him walk away. If it were you, I'd chase you until the end of Lodesa. I'd set forests aflame, knock down mountains, and empty oceans."

Jay sighed heavily, moving my head up and down with the movement. "Okay, but please don't burn my precious forests."

I chuckled in a snot-filled mess. "Deal, now, let's get out of here."

We walked, hand in hand, for minutes or hours. I wasn't sure since my mind was fixated on the memory spell on Isaac's watch. He wouldn't know my face if I ever saw him again. And to respect his wishes, I'd have to play the part and act like a stranger.

Finally, sweat-soaked, we arrived at the end of the tunnel, where bright sunlight shone on the last few feet of the cavern's walls. A blast of fire exploded across the exit, and I shoved Jay behind me. A chirping sound peeped from outside, and I moved forward, knowing who it belonged to.

"Kyra! Wait," Jay warned.

When the sunlight hit my skin, I craned my neck to Ashes' reflective scales. She lowered her head and nudged my side with her gorgeous snout. Suddenly, Magik flowed through my veins so forcefully that I staggered back, falling into Jay's arms.

"Woah, my power is back." He hovered a hand over my skin and instantly healed the scratches from the evil cats and burns from where lava spurted up my calves.

Vigorous energy pumped through my blood, and I relished in the moment, feeling more myself than I had in weeks. I blasted a ball of flames at Ashes playfully, and she dodged it, flicking her ears back in excitement. She roared, and fire catapulted from her mouth straight at us. Laughing, I caught it and formed it into a star, then tossed it high into the air and set it off as fireworks in front of the puffy clouds.

My breath hitched as my gaze followed the streak of yellows and reds. For the first time, I noticed rock houses blending in superb camouflage within the volcanic cliffside. Along the side of the slopes, magma structures jutted out with little faces peering down at us. Hundreds of them.

Elidians stared down at me from their homes, curiosity claiming their whispers. Lava streamed down the side of the windows, pouring like a waterfall onto the roof-like canopies of other houses below. Why weren't they melting? They must be protected by Magik. Children pointed out their windows, but my enhanced hearing could only catch bits and pieces of their questions through the eruptions of the lava lake at the volcano's base. Why did this entire hidden city in the Land of Nothing hold absolutely everything?

"Who is that?"

"...Jugosaur her pet?"

"...tell Dezlian."

"...the man looks Dravian."

Ashes stepped forward and sniffed Jay protectively.

"Stay away from her tail," I said knowingly.

I searched the small faces high in the windows, hoping to recognize someone, but Brent was a prisoner of my great-grandmother, who I had to destroy to save our world, and Caspian may be in danger somewhere by now. My only family member who was still safe was Landon, but I didn't even know where Gemm was keeping him hidden and had no way of contacting them yet to check-in.

"Look out!" a child screamed from the lowest row of windows.

Loud jugosaur flapping sounds above caught my attention, and I shielded my eyes from the sun. Ashes screeched and rose, her wings outstretched and powerful. She flew away, shrieking the whole time.

"You found a way out of Bukti," a female voice said.

I gasped at her beauty. The angel-like woman shifted away from the sun's direct beams. With skin as dark as midnight and contrasting red hair flowing down to her knees, she was the epitome of seduction. Silk hung from her curves like a toga; I could even see her nipples through the fabric. Breath-taking gold butterfly wings extended wide, making her hover.

Tension radiated from Jay's stiff posture next to me. Without any warning, he summoned boulders under his command. They rolled against hot spots in the unpredictable ground, sending sparks flying at all angles. Once close enough, he hurtled them at the creature. Following Jay's instinct, I held fire at my fingertips.

"Who are you?"

"I have many names. Your people call me the Soul Sucker. Others named me the Life Stealer or Spirit Taker."

"Oniskel," I whispered and increased my flames.

She tilted her head. "Trying to threaten me, girl?"

"What do you want?"

"I was curious about the Dravian. His soul is extremely enticing, almost too pure, absolutely delicious." She licked her lips. "What do you want for him?"

"He's not available," I growled through gritted teeth.

"I'll convince you…eventually." Oniskel lifted her chin. "In the meantime, is what he said true?"

"Depends." I cast a wall of fire around us in a bubble as she circled it like a panther stalking her prey.

Jay stayed close by my side, but part of him seemed atypically frozen out of fear or rage. I couldn't tell.

"Can you make me a nymph again?" The challenging smile slithering up her face made my skin crawl.

"Yes, but the spell isn't ready." My breath came faster. "If you promise not to hurt anyone until I prepare it, I'll turn you back as soon as I can."

Oniskel floated lower, just outside my bubble of fire. She walked through it unscathed, and my heart pounded in my chest as I backed into Jay.

"I'm not waiting. Do it now," Oniskel demanded. "I've been trapped like this because of your wicked ancestor."

"I don't have everything I need yet."

Beside me, Jay stuck one hand in his pocket but still seemed cemented to the spot like he was stuck. I had never seen him unsure of how to act before, and I hoped to the goddess above that Oniskel hadn't already put him under some enchantment.

The demon glared at Jay, and spiders crept out of her mouth and wiggled down her neck. "You didn't tell her?"

Panic seized me like a fishing hook latching onto my skin and yanking me harshly. I fought the need to look at him for clarification.

"Ah, I see you keep secrets from your partner," Oniskel sneered and reached to his chest. With one long fingernail trailing down his shirt, it split the fabric straight in half like sharp scissors and exposed his sculpted pecs.

"Leave!" I stepped between them, my voice shaking. "I don't have what I need yet."

"Yes, we do." Jay quickly pulled a wad of hair out of his pocket, reached into my backpack, and pulled out one bottle of lava and the Unetlo Book. He quickly turned the page open to the transformation spell. "We have a piece of this demon and the lava."

"Yes, but you forgot the sacrifice of someone you love."

A scurry of claws scratched behind us, and I whirled around to see a pack of wild cats. Atop their backs, they carried someone wrapped in rope. A mop of blond curls made my gut curl into a wad of fury. Landon's scared gaze met mine.

"Landon!"

He whimpered through his gag.

"Let him go!" I raised a hand to strike Oniskel with fire, but she blew out the flame with a puff of air from her crimson lips.

"I'm ready to be transformed." She smiled and outstretched her arms wide. The cats dropped him to the ground and bared their fangs inches over his small body. "Hurry before my girls ravish him."

When I tried to lunge for my nephew, Oniskel stopped me with a wave of her hand. "Change me back."

"Don't hurt him! Please."

Suddenly, Jay stooped to the ground next to me, pulled out his dagger, and set his left hand on the ground. He spread out his fingers wide and hovered his knife over one.

"Kyra, get ready to say the spell!" Jay commanded.

My mind was whirling into chaos as I stared at his fingers, glanced at Landon, and looked back at Jay's determined face.

Understanding his intent, I nodded.

Jay slashed his dagger through his middle finger with one swipe and sliced it off. Blood poured out. Heart racing, I followed the spell's instructions by wrapping it in Oniskel's hair and pouring the lava on top of it.

Landon still yelled in the background, but I had to keep going.

I scanned the next line of the ancient script, smudged together, and rambled off the spell, *"Avanido muati. Avanido muati. Avanido muati."*

Tears burned my eyes and blurred my vision as I repeated it again and again despite Landon's endless screams. It wasn't working. A throbbing pulsed in my core, and dark energy gurgled intensely. Fire detonated chaotically from my hands and arched into the lava pool. Fire wasn't enough. I needed the ₾sμwi Magik.

"Avanido muati. Avanido muati. Avanido muati!" I chanted and pulled power from my corrupted Vayuian Circle. The wind whipped at my face. Darkness from within cast out in all directions, and the village was engulfed in floating balls of lava. Cats hissed and fled. Flames ignited against my fingers again, and I rose from the ground, hovering without much control.

Oniskel dropped to her knees, her eyes turning bloodshot. Her flawless dark skin wrinkled and contorted, twisting into horrifying shapes. Her mouth gaped open, but no scream emerged from her lips.

"Avanido muati. Avanido muati. Avanido muati." I screamed, feeling my energy about to explode.

An abrupt blow consumed me from the inside and ruptured. Something felt different. Something important inside of me necessary for survival had been shattered. I fell to the ground in a heap, panting and sweating, next to the trail of blood from Jay's severed finger.

"Kyra Elidi, rise."

I opened my eyes, not realizing that I had closed them to begin with, and stared at Oniskel standing in front of me. Red spots blotched my vision in the corner. I held the side of my head and tried to steady my breathing.

"Rise, Golden One." She reached a hand down to me.

I surveyed the scene quickly. Jay knelt by Landon, both alive and gawking at us silently. Jay's hand was pressed against his side where a red patch painted his shirt. He had sacrificed a finger. *A finger*. Would I have done the same? Landon blinked, then waved to me with his crooked smile, already moving on from the life-shattering moment.

I pushed off my shaky hands and stood. Oniskel smiled, her demeanor completely altered. Where wickedness used to be plastered on her face, now only softness remained. Her gold butterfly wings fluttered in the breeze like a sweet drum beat. *Flip, flip. Flip, flip.* No spiders crawled from her mouth.

"You did it, Kyra," she said.

I stepped between her and the males I loved. "Don't touch them."

"You don't need to fear me anymore." The wind nymph smiled angelically. "Come, let me show you who you truly are."

13

JADOX

I had let myself believe that Gemm's death was only a nightmarish illusion. Because it couldn't be true. Any second now, she'd be walking up to me with her whimsical smile. But when I touched Landon with my own two hands and felt his solid body under my grasp, I knew. If the boy was truly here, then Gemm was dead. Gone. Her demise wasn't a figment of cursed magic or my mind playing tricks on me. I'd never see my grandmother again. A hole opened inside my heart and grew to the size of a crater.

"I'll show you the answers," Oniskel breathed softly to Kyra, their conversation carrying from across the hot spots where lava burst and boiled.

My fists clenched like a vise. This soul-sucking demon smiling at Kyra was to blame. I reached for my emerald to use it as a shield, forgetting again that I had given it to Alaska.

"Landon, stay behind this rock, no matter what," I whispered in command and patted his shoulder. The boy didn't like being touched; it was the first time he hadn't flinched under my hand.

He nodded, and I approached Kyra. My sweaty palms clutched the dagger behind my back even though my finger-stump throbbed with pain. It was an injury I wasn't able to heal. With each step, my heart stampeded against my ribs. Oniskel reached toward Kyra's golden hair, admiring the drumstick hairpin poking out. They laughed like schoolgirls, sending a shudder up my spine. This wasn't natural. This wasn't okay.

When our hips brushed, Kyra glanced over, peace claiming her amber eyes when she said, "Oniskel is going to bring us to her lair and explain my history. She knows the answers to everything: why my tattoo is golden and why I received it late."

There was no choice but to ignore the hope Kyra clung to. I lunged forward and buried the dagger deep into Oniskel's chest. The jagged point ripped a hole through her silk robes, and her skin sliced apart. The Soul Sucker's eyes widened, and she clutched the handle with two hands.

"Jay! What have you done?!" Kyra screeched, frozen in place.

"I'm fine, it's okay—he's just being cautious." Oniskel yanked out the blade, and gold liquid poured out instead of blood.

She coughed slightly, spurting out a faster flow of gold against her obsidian skin. In a matter of moments, the liquid sealed the injury like super glue, stitching the wound together. After it healed, her hand covered the spot where not even a scar remained.

"Jay!" Kyra threw me a glare. "What were you thinking?"

"No harm. I can imagine why he's upset." She shot me a knowing look. "I have something to show you three that might make you feel better." She marched back into the tunnel under Bukti Volcano and motioned for us to follow.

"No, we're not going in there again." I grabbed Kyra's wrist. "We'll be defenseless without our powers."

"I'm a nymph again," Oniskel said matter-of-factly. "The ₾sμwi power that consumed this tunnel is gone. You should be able to use Magik inside now."

"I'm going in. You can stay here if you want." Kyra waved Landon over, who immediately skipped to her side.

Each volcanic house jutted out horizontally from the exterior ledges of the slope. A wild breeze danced through Oniskel's long hair, and they left me staring up at the Elidi villagers. How many Elidians were safely hidden in The Land of Nothing?

Whether Oniskel was a demon or a nymph, her powers weren't like ours, and I couldn't leave her alone with Kyra for a moment longer. Quick footsteps came from behind a boulder, and I turned, hoping it was an enlightened Kyra. Instead, Dezlian stepped out with her sharp pixie haircut and a ball of fire in her hands. She ran straight into me, bumping against my chest.

"Oh, sorry." Her green eyes met mine, reminding me of a cat. "Griffin?"

"Please, call me Jadox."

"Where's Isaac…I mean, Kyra?" Dezlian glanced around frantically. "The villagers sent me word that she made it out. Is everyone okay?"

"That's undetermined. Excuse me, I need to go after her."

Dezlian followed my gaze to the tunnels. "She went back inside? Why?"

"I never know. Kyra does what she wants." I threw up my hands, finally reaching the end of my limits and patience.

Storming into the darkness again, Dezlian was on my heels as she called, "Wait, was Isaac with her?"

"No, they…are done, I think."

"If you don't agree with Kyra, why are you going in after her?"

"Because she's mine to take care of." I rubbed the branded word on my chest, exposed where Oniskel had previously cut through my shirt. "Because her eyes just draw you in. And how she looks at you eases all your past mistakes because she simply accepts you as you are, the light and the dark."

Dezlian chuckled behind me.

I ground my teeth together and sniffed the air in the tunnel, realizing my powers and enhancements were present this time.

"You've got it bad." She skipped to my side.

I shot daggers at her, only feeling slightly guilty when her puppy dog eyes reminded me of Chocolate. Instead of backing down, Dezlian only increased her excitement.

"When you two get married, can you invite me to the wedding? Would you invite Isaac too? It must be hard to have an ex at a wedding though...Plus, you'll have to deal with him being in her life forever and—"

I stopped walking. "What did you just say?"

Her eyes grew to the size of saucers under the flicker of the flames she held in her hand. "Isaac and Kyra will have to be near each other forever now...and—"

"What? Why?" I held a hand up.

"Holy Flames, everyone said you were the patient one. Calm down." She eyed me for a moment too long. "Oh, I see. It must have been a while since you two...." Her intentional eyebrow raise made me roll my eyes and keep walking, following Kyra's scent.

Dezlian hopped next to me again. "So, you don't know why she and Isaac are still connected?"

"What are you talking about? Their Link severed."

"It doesn't matter; they seem fated to be in each other's lives."

"Obviously I don't know what you're talking about." I swept away a mound of rocks with the swish of my hand. "Please stop dragging out this torture and just tell me already."

"Okay, Alaska had caught me up with y'all's stories. Kyra and Isaac both have ₵sµwi changing them, right?" Before I could get a word in to clarify, Dez continued rapidly, "Isaac's new toxic gas encourages Kyra's state of darkness, increasing her abilities. They need each other. He's probably needed to calm her down too."

Her theory had my mind reeling. "No, I seem to have a *skill* that snaps her out of it."

"Oh, well, then half the problem is solved. Neither of us wants them to be dependent on each other." Dezlian's round cheeks flushed pink. "So, we need to figure out a way for Kyra not to need Isaac to survive."

"That doesn't make sense, and what do you mean, *survive?*"

"They're connected in their souls somehow," she said.

"You're wrong."

"Darkness calls to darkness," Dezlian said.

"Maybe lightness and darkness can balance each other out."

"You intend to be Kyra's light?" As we continued to walk, Dezlian gestured with one hand up and down my body. "You? Mister Grumps? No offense, but you're not quite the embodiment of radiant sunshine, Jadox. I barely know you, but you seem more like that brooding guy in the corner of a party who doesn't talk to anyone and stares too long without blinking or eating the hostess's food, and—"

"Okay, I get it. I'm not full of light. But, you have it backward. She's light, and I'm the dark. If only I could get her to accept herself the way I see her. She's fighting against herself and trying to bury what she doesn't like to see."

Dezlian snorted. "Let's just agree that we need to split Isaac and Kyra up."

"They're already split up. They said goodbye, and Nilson went searching for his son." I quickened my pace, knowing we were close, and whispered to myself, "Kyra chose me. She chose already."

"But what if Isaac returns? Do you think you and Kyra are destined for each other, or could a little intervention benefit us all?" She winked, and for the first time, I didn't have to wonder how Dezlian had governed Elidi's society for the last few years.

"I have complete faith in Kyra. I don't need to sabotage anything to know she wants to be with me." I moved toward the golden glow ahead. "Why am I even talking to you about this?"

"It's my gift." Dezlian pranced ahead.

"Wait, a gift like an enhancement? Are you of Elana Elidi's blood?"

"I have Elidi blood, Kyra's long-lost second cousin, once removed, or...something. And I may or may not be able to make people spill their hearts out to me."

Before I could ask more questions, we reached the threshold, and Kyra's scent wafted through the tunnel, stronger than ever. Dezlian had to be wrong because we were finally free of Nilson, and I didn't want him trailing around on account of his Magik calling to Kyra's.

I purposefully kicked pebbles to warn Kyra of our presence before calling out her name.

"Jay?" Her sweet button nose poked through the light and waved us in. "I'm so glad you're okay. Come on, everything's going to be fine."

Everything wasn't fine, but as I walked into Oniskel's lair, which looked nothing like I expected from a stereotypical storybook, awe struck me like a whip. A fireplace crackled with flames against the wall, and five mugs, with steam flowing out the top, sat on a high counter. Behind the counter, crooked wooden shelves were full of bottles of spiders, half-living, half-decaying. About fifty vintage clocks hung on the rock wall, sporadic and ticking at different times. Some had missing numbers. One ticked backward, counter-clockwise. One had a face on the front, and the eyes seemed alive and watching. Dust coated the tops of each, and I held in a sneeze.

In the far corner, Landon and Wes sat on the floor, flipping through the ancient Unetlo Spell Book and pointing to pictures. Dezlian left my side and joined them in hushed whispers. My shoulders dropped like a flower wilting, like I was slowly sinking into the earth. Since Wes was here too, my last shred of hope vanished instantly. Gemm was truly gone.

I glared at Oniskel in her new, brightened nymph form and asked, "How much do you remember from your time as a demon?"

Her eyes flashed with regret. Ever so slightly, she shook her head, advising me not to say anything about Gemm yet. But nothing I'd mention would be a surprise. Of course, Kyra would have suspicions that Gemm wasn't here. What convincing lie had Oniskel told Kyra in my absence?

At least Gemm had lived a long, fulfilling life. Her last words ran on repeat in my mind, "*Once there was a boy who changed the world. You are him, my boy. You have changed my world for the better.*"

I wanted to believe, but a shard of doubt wedged deep into my gut like an anchor in the deep seabed. I hadn't changed the world and definitely didn't improve Gemm's life. I had allowed her to die right in front of me. Maybe I wouldn't ever change Kyra's world for the better, either. If the Ꮳsµwi inside her resonated with Nilson, then I shouldn't stand in the way of something destined.

When Oniskel's back was turned, Kyra nudged my side. "Isn't this place awesome?"

"Not at all." I studied the spiderwebs covering every surface. "What have you two talked about?"

"She's just been apologizing for her last eighty years of sucking out souls and making us some hot chocolate. Did you know nymphs make the best cocoa—try this." Kyra pushed a mug over the wooden counter.

"No, thanks."

"After we hear her story, we need to find Isaac and Gemm. They must be worried and looking for these two."

I cringed, hoping she hadn't noticed my tension in the darkness. Unleashing information about Gemm's death now would just be selfish when Kyra was close to obtaining the answers she had been seeking.

Kyra nodded toward Wes and Landon. "I'm glad the boys are safe, but I don't think I'll ever be able to raise Landon, so I need to figure out a long-term plan with Gemm if she's willing."

Another stab straight through my heart stole my breath. I couldn't even mumble out a response about Gemm. Instead, I croaked, "Why don't you want to raise him?"

"This ₾sµwi is growing stronger. I can't subject Landon to any risk when I don't know my potential."

"We'll find a way to get rid of the curse, though."

Kyra leaned in close. "What if it's not a curse, but who I am? What if I don't want it to go away?"

My Circle sprung alert, raw with power and fear, ready for a battle. But I crushed the energy and coiled it into a ball in my core. Instead of fighting her on this, I needed her to know she was accepted, regardless of her path.

"It's your choice, Petal. Even if it's always a part of you, I'll love you."

Oniskel turned around on the other side of the counter. She rested both elbows on the wood, giving me a new view through her clear robe. I focused on keeping my attention on her dark eyes. She snapped her fingers, and images projected on her lair's wall like a movie screen.

"So, you want answers?" she asked Kyra.

"Yes."

"It all began when you were about four years old when Brent Elidi visited me…."

Kyra leaned in close. "My *father*?"

"Yes, for a specific reason."

By the looks of it, Kyra would've paid with her soul for the answers lingering on Oniskel's lips. "Why?"

14

KYRA

Tick. Tock. Tick. Tock.

The dozens of clocks in Oniskel's lair were driving me mad. None had the same beat, and the constant ticking of the moving hands made me want Oniskel to hasten her storytelling. One clock captured my attention, hypnotically ticking backward.

"We don't have much time to spend in here," Dezlian said. "I sent out a message with a raven earlier to call a meeting of the Elidian council to discuss our next step. We meet in thirty minutes."

What would their council think of me showing up? And of all people, I had the last name of Elidi–the same name as the woman who was at fault for The Fall eighty years ago. Did the villagers know that my great-grandmother was still alive and posing as Lodesa's president? Would they care that my Elidian tattoo was Golden instead of red like theirs?

"Kyra?" Jay wrapped his uninjured hand around my waist. "You okay?"

I nodded and gulped, then focused on Oniskel's dark brown eyes. We only had twenty-nine minutes, so I'd make the most of this time together.

Landon and Wes scurried over with bright eyes and climbed atop the mismatched and broken bar stools.

"My dad said the Vayu Crystal kept you captured," Wes said to Oniskel, his voice strong despite being in a volcanic "demon's" lair. "How did you escape?"

The little Vayuian was as smart as his father. The legs of Dezlian's stool scraped against the hard rock when she inched closer. "Wait, answer *my* question first. How will we find your sisters to change them back to nymphs too—"

"None of that matters," Jay interrupted. "How will we free the prisoners?"

"I'll answer some of your questions." Oniskel smiled and refilled my mug full of steaming hot cocoa.

"Kyra," Jay whispered. "Please don't drink more of that."

Landon tapped my shoulder and pulled out his laminated pictures. He pointed to a picture of Gemm and a question mark. Next to me, Jay tensed, but he didn't meet my gaze.

Sipping more hot chocolate, I let the liquid burn my throat as it slid down. I felt bad for disregarding Jay's request, but it smelled so good. Oniskel pointed to images she had cast on the wall. With a simple wave of her hand, the lair disappeared, and the scene jumped to a snowy mountain. She transported us to a mountain summit. I could feel the bitter cold against my face and Jay's presence next to me, though I could no longer hear or see him. The harsh wind stung my cheeks, and snow piled to my waist. I reached out to feel if it was fluffy or packed snow, but my hand went right through it like a specter. Atop the peak sat an empty cage coated in thick green dust.

A man climbs slowly, panting, with a hiking stick in hand and carrying a huge backpack weighing him down. He's covered head to toe in thick winter gear. The man stops, pulls his scarf down from over his mouth, and pulls the ski goggles off his eyes. Brent. My father. Twenty years younger without wrinkles or fatigue lining his face. He pulls out a book from his pocket, and the wind flaps the pages chaotically. Grunting, he finds the page he's looking for and mumbles something under his breath.

The wind stops, and an eagle's caw echoes throughout the canyon.

"Oniskel! Show yourself," my father yells. "I'm here to receive an answer to my question."

Suddenly, Oniskel's demon form appears inside the cage. Her butterfly wings are clipped, and she keeps fading in and out like a flicker on a television screen. "Others have asked questions and died trying to seek their beloved answers. What makes you think you will succeed?" Spiders crawl from her wicked mouth as she speaks.

With difficulty, in all his layers of clothing, Brent holds out the Vayu Crystal between his gloved fingers. "Because of this."

"Where did you get that?" Oniskel's brows knit together.

"It doesn't matter. My grandmother cursed and trapped you here."

Oniskel snarls. "Only a monster would cage the soul of the wind high in the skies with clipped wings and the inability to fly. The day I'm free is the day I'll spit on her grave."

"She's still alive. Elana has found a way to use her daughter, my mother, as a life source. Elana isn't aging and, instead, grows stronger each day. She's creating problems with the Ordulls. I need an answer. How can I stop her peacefully?"

"There is no peaceful solution."

"Is there a way at all?" Brent steps closer, seemingly unafraid of the demon. "You were once a nymph, you must know."

"That was two questions, Golden One." She licks her lips. "And I am no longer a nymph. The legends have a different name for me now."

"Soul Sucker," he says softly.

"Yes, that's right." She studies him with death in her eyes. Her devastating smile contrasts the joyful clouds above them. "Elana will be defeated if you give me your soul."

"No, I need to live." He shakes his head. "I have...responsibilities. There must be another way."

Her eyes narrow. "You cherish your life more than your children's future?"

"It is for my children that I need to keep my life." Brent's voice grows

louder. "I need to defeat Elana before she turns into something that can't be saved."

Snow falls on his eyelashes and the top of her long hair, but neither moves a muscle.

"Then I will empower your child for my freedom. I will give one of your children powers with the ability to defeat Elana."

He stares her down, taking a lifetime to contemplate her offer.

"What kind of powers?"

Oniskel's figure flickers again like she isn't even there at all. "You're running out of time. Put the crystal in my hand, and your child will become the most powerful Mystier in history. The child will still need to make hard choices on their path. No outcome is guaranteed."

"Which child?" Brent's voice fades, and his gaze follows the larger snowflakes.

"Which child is stronger, more capable of surviving hardships? Which can bend without breaking? Which can tolerate obstacles like no other?"

He nods, a decision already gleaming in his eyes. "My Kyra can endure anything thrown at her."

"Then I will grant Kyra the rank of a nymph."

Brent's jaw drops, and he loses control of his hiking stick. "What?"

In the vision, Oniskel shifts her silk robe and shows Brent the five gray tattoos connected in a loop. "She will not be like other Mystiers, not only because of her Golden tattoo like yours but because Kyra will eventually have the powers of a nymph. But there is no guarantee she will make the right choice. Sometimes, our choices shatter any chance of the life we wanted and turn us toward the shadows."

"Is there any other way? Kyra is too young to decide if a nymph's life is what she wants." Brent shifts. "Maybe your sisters know—"

"My sisters are not as patient as me, mortal. Moroka will suck your blood before you have the chance to explain, and Surh-Sig will only wear your skin as a cloak after she feeds off of you. You will find no bargains with them."

"Okay, I agree to your terms. Take the crystal, but I don't want any harm to come to my children." Hesitantly, Brent drops the crystal through the cage bars.

Oniskel snatches the gem. The cage immediately splits open. "We already agreed; I cannot guarantee their safety either." Her golden butterfly wings heal and stretch gloriously before she lifts into the sky and soars away.

Tick. Tock. Tick. Tock.

The next instant, I sit back on the barstool in Oniskel's lair. Jay swiveled in his chair, making it creak slightly, and took both my hands in his. Landon and Wes were both wide-eyed and silent, their hair tossed like they had endured a tornado. Dezlian opened her mouth to speak, then shut it again and stared at the clocks.

"Kyra?" he asked.

"Mhm, yes, I'm fine. Everything's fine." My heart drummed a mile a minute.

"Kyra, look at me," Jay commanded, slow and deep. "Breathe with me. In…out."

I focused on his eyes and the sound of his heart beating.

"Again, in…out. Good." He brushed a finger against my cheek. "Did you know?"

No, how was I supposed to know I was given nymph power? I shook my head while one hand found my stomach where all five tattoos thrummed with raw power, two of them gray. How many more would turn gray? Brent shouldn't have picked me. I didn't want all the responsibility of the Ordull and Mystiers' future on my shoulders. This task was made for a leader—Caspian.

Brother, are you there?

I desperately tugged at his mind through our bond.

Please answer, Caspian.

Nothing. Did Caspian know this history?

"Oniskel? What…how…" I stared at the hands of a clock. "How did Caspian get the crystal from you?"

"That's your first question? I assumed you'd want to know if another male has betrayed you, but don't worry. Your brother doesn't know this story." She smirked. "I gave Caspian my crystal when he was a tumbling toddler since I didn't need you anymore. For a while, you all lived here in Elidi."

When Oniskel touched my hand, more flashbacks bombarded my mind.

Climbing volcanic rocks with Brent. Playing fetch with Ashes near the lava pools. Holding baby Caspian in my arms as a toddler, except then, I call him Caldo, his given name.

We were a family once before Elana had stolen Brent from us. Before Caspian was swept away by the ocean waves.

"Why don't I have any of those memories?" My voice shook as Jay hugged me closer.

Oniskel shrugged. "You'll have to ask your father about that."

"I won't get the chance. He's dying by Elana's hand."

"Then you better hurry."

"I can't rush to save Brent if I don't have control of the dark Magik in me."

"You'll eventually have control. See, this is what nymph tattoos look like." On her dark skin, five looped tattoos all shone bright gold. Not one was gray. She swished the fabric up and over her waist and hip, and, for the first time, I considered that Wes and Landon shouldn't have been exposed to her transparent outfit this whole time.

"Something is very wrong with me," I murmured.

"There's nothing to fix, Kyra." Oniskel let her clothing fall loose again. "You are a nymph-in-the-making, and fire will always be your strongest. It's okay if you only have two or three golden tattoos now. You'll become stronger over time."

Brent had picked the wrong child. Oniskel had blessed the wrong one. She didn't know darkness spread through me like a plague, stronger each day. She didn't know about the two gray tattoos.

Tick. Tock. Tick. Tock.

"What do you mean I'm a nymph-in-the-making?

"If we perform the ritual to make the rest of your Circles golden, you'd become one of our sisters."

I couldn't even process that sentence but asked, "Why do you need *me* to defeat Elana? Why can't you or one of your sisters kill Elana?"

"She has defeated the three of us in the past. It has to be someone who she can't control."

There was no chance I was an equal match for Elana. "Wait, aren't you immortal?"

"Yes."

"Will I be too?" The thought scrambled my brain to mush.

"After the ritual, yes, you wouldn't age."

"No, I don't want that. I refuse. This nymph thing is wrong…it's crazy. You should've picked someone else."

"Kyra, don't fight who you are." Jay squeezed my waist, "It's okay if—"

I stood, and the stool toppled backward. "It's not okay, and I'm *not* okay. I need to be healed. Can you heal me? Can you heal *this*?" I rolled down my yoga pants to show not two but, surprisingly, three gray tattoos. The aqua Circle connecting my powers to Caspian was now stark gray.

"Goddess Above!" Oniskel hissed and flinched. "Why didn't you tell me earlier? Come with me, now." She floated out of her lair and spun around the corner.

I followed on her heels, and the others paraded behind me. Wes whispered to Landon all the possibilities of what the gray tattoos could mean, but I already knew. I was turning into a demon.

"Maybe she's a zombie…or a jugosaur in disguise…."

My nerves flared when I increased my pace to catch up to Oniskel. "Where are you taking us?"

"You need a baptism," Oniskel stated.

"A what? I'm not religious."

"It's not like that…well, it kind of is." She didn't turn but flew faster toward a faint red light at the end of the tunnel.

Jay's boots clomped quickly behind. "Kyra, when did the others turn gray?"

"I'm not sure. Sometime in the last few hours, I think, maybe that's why I can't communicate with Caspian anymore."

Wes playfully made random sounds to echo in the tunnel as he ran, then asked about his dad, but I had no answer for him. Was Isaac lost in these tunnels somewhere? Was he going mad not knowing where his son was?

The red mist ahead glowed brighter, and sweat drenched my shirt. I tore it off and threw it to the ground, feeling relieved in only my sports bra.

"Jay? I can't be a...I can't...." I pushed out the words between labored breaths. A sharp hitch cramped my side as we jogged. "I can't be a nymph."

He didn't respond. We reached the lava pool, where a dozen villagers happened to be waiting, shocked at the sight of the Soul Sucker.

"Welcome to the council meeting," Dezlian said and stepped in front of Oniskel. "I assume you want answers about why we're with the wind nymph, but for now, trust me that you're safe."

They chatted in hushed tones, and their small knot closed tighter as each counselor scanned me up and down.

"Plans have changed. I need to perform an immediate cleansing before the meeting starts." Oniskel motioned for me to swim into the lava pool as she hovered above the surface.

Tension slipped out of my body when my ankles sunk into the scalding magma and melted into the heat. I lowered further, thirsty for a gulp of the lava all around me. Energy poured into my core and ignited deep within. But when the level of the surface hit my tattoos, a burning pain throbbed over my skin. I hissed and clutched my stomach.

"It'll be better if we hurry." Oniskel leaned low and whispered in my ear, "You'll need to pick one person to support you."

Just as I was about to call Jay over, Isaac sprinted around the tunnel's corner. He stopped in his tracks. "Wes?" he panted. "Where's Wes?"

Oniskel cleared her throat. "It's time to pick someone, Kyra, tick-tock."

I glanced at the bandage wrapped around Jay's severed finger and wondered how many times he'd have to sacrifice something for me. What if the lava hurt him? If I chose someone else, it'd save Jay from further pain.

15

KYRA

Jay's eyes were trained on me, full of heat, but Isaac's attention was only on his son in the corner. My heart whispered gratitude to whichever Divinity above had kept Isaac safe.

"Dad!" Wes hopped over cracks in the volcanic rock and ran into Isaac's arms. "You're here!"

Isaac stooped low and crushed his son to his chest. "I'm here, but we need to leave. Now! All of you need to leave. There are a dozen armed Ordull soldiers on the northern side of the tunnel's entrance. They're headed this way."

One council member stepped forward, and the rest muttered multiple questions at the same time.

"How did they find us?"

"Who's leading them?"

"What do they want?"

Oniskel shook my shoulder. "Hurry, Kyra. This might be your only chance to rid of the cursed Magik."

I waved Jay over but felt Isaac's gaze bore into my back. He peeled his ripped shirt off and tossed it on the sizzling ground. In my gut, I knew Jay would be protected from the heat, but I still winced as he stepped toward the lava, recalling his boils during our last encounter in a similar grotto. The council members gathered around Isaac, gesturing wildly, their voices increasing with each passing second.

"Focus, Kyra," Oniskel whispered. "We might only have this one chance."

My attention snapped back to the moment. The blazing lava, thankfully, didn't leave a mark on Jay's skin as he waded closer. Beads of sweat glistened on his bare chest, captivating me until a stampede far off in the tunnels sent my heart rate into overdrive.

"I hear the soldiers coming," I said.

"Okay, then, hurry. Kyra, float flat on your back and, Griffin, hold her head in your hands." Oniskel rushed out her command from her hovering spot above the surface.

The lava soaked into my clothes and skin, from my heels to the base of my neck. My hair floated against Jay's stomach, and he scooped my head into his hands. Upside down, I stared into his deep brown eyes, drenched with passion and protection. But his muscles stayed clenched, and his nostrils flared. He rolled the hem of my waistline down a bit and brushed his fingertips over the three gray Circles claiming me.

Oniskel waved her hand over my stomach back and forth and said, "Close your eyes and imagine your Magik."

For a moment, anything felt possible with the pleasant heat bubbling under me.

Oniskel chanted softly, *"Aurum Shiyo. Aurum Shiyo."*

A searing jab stabbed my Circle.

"It's working. One of your tattoos is changing!" Jay's hands tightened on my skull.

"Aurum Shiyo. Aurum Shiyo," Oniskel said louder.

Footsteps thundered from the tunnels just as the intense poking in my abdomen finally stopped.

Voices echoed, hopefully, only loud enough for me to hear, meaning we still had time. "President wants the Draven soldier...."

My eyes snapped open. "They're coming for *you,* Jay."

"She's doing it!" Jay smiled. "It's shifting colors!"

Oniskel kept waving her hand over my stomach.

Jay tensed. "Wait, stop. That's not right."

"What's wrong?" I asked.

"Stop!"

My legs sank while I moved upright and looked down. Four gray tattoos glowed ominously.

Oniskel shook her head. "That's not what was supposed to happen. Let's try again."

"No, we don't have time anymore. Jay, I've got to hide you."

Oniskel glanced at the tunnel's opening. "This may be your only chance, Golden One."

"Then I'll be cursed. I don't care, as long as Elana doesn't find Jay."

Lava splashed as I treaded toward the bank.

"We have to try," Jay begged.

"I'm fine, Jay. There's nothing to worry about." But everything felt off-balance. With four gray tattoos, it felt like my powers were being pulled in a thousand different directions. A turmoil of energy swirled, but I swam faster.

The stomps from the tunnels were loud enough this time for Dezlian's attention to snap toward the entrance. I pulled myself out of the molten chamber, and thick red oozed down my clothes.

Isaac commanded the Elidian council members into defensive positions. They all had flames sparking at their fingertips.

Someone in the back said, "It's all that Golden Girl's fault. She's creating chaos for all of us."

"None of us are a fan of the Golden Girl at the moment," Isaac joined in but had a slight curve of his mouth. "She's the worst."

Well, at least he hadn't used the memory spell yet.

Dezlian summoned fire, but Isaac shook his head and pushed the boys toward her.

"Dezlian, I need someone to take care of Wes," Isaac said. "Please, take them somewhere safe."

Dezlian looked hesitant but finally nodded as she unhooked Jay's watch from her wrist and handed it back to him. Quickly, she took both boys' hands, running away toward the jagged stalagmites that hung like fangs from the ceiling.

Oniskel flew toward me and said, "Kyra, you should go. We weren't able to alter the tattoos. You're more dangerous to us if we don't know what your ₵sµwi Magik can do."

"I can help fight." My heart rammed against my chest in a deranged beat.

Jay tugged my wrist. "Come on, Petal. They've got it handled."

The soldier's shadows bounced on the tunnel's walls, and the Elidians next to me formed a shield of fire between us and the entrance.

I stared at Jay, my soldier, my protector. "But you're never one to run."

"I'll do anything to keep you safe."

"Nothing will happen to me."

"You don't know that!" he screamed. It was the loudest I'd ever heard Jay's voice. "Please, we can only deal with one thing at a time, and right now, we need to run."

I gazed at Isaac once more, meeting his eyes, but he looked away. Reluctantly, I let Jay pull me away to an exit near the back wall.

We ran, despite the yells and hollers behind us, despite the electrical zaps from the Ordull weapons and the screams and the smells of burning flesh. We fled. And I left Isaac to fend for himself. This was it—no turning back–I had made my choice.

Over the distance, the heat faded into a mild warmth and, eventually, into stagnant cool air. After a mile or so, and out of breath, our pace finally slowed into a walk as we stepped out of the tunnel and into the inky night. Jay scanned the ground for tracks and lifted his nose to the star-speckled sky. I leaned into the breeze, listening to the whispers emerging from the Elidians high in their cliffside homes. Each of the lights glowing in their windows reminded me of fireflies in summer.

"This way." Jay led the way, climbing over large rocks and helping me over the highest boulders.

"Now it makes sense why this place felt familiar, why I had seen it in my dreams," I said to Jay as some lava spurted on my knees and hissed into my skin. "I lived here for my first few years. Do you think Caspian knows?"

"Why don't you try to ask him?"

I pushed through the block between our bond and reached out.

Caspian? Are you there? Can you hear me?

A strange sensation jerked my stomach, and I checked my tattoos. The gray Cydian Circle Linking me with my brother pulsed abnormally like it had a soul of its own.

Jay sucked in a breath and brushed his fingertips over it. "Has it done that before?"

"I don't think so. Do you know of any Mystiers with gray tattoos?"

"No, Petal." He traced the green Draven Circle. "This is all new."

I couldn't shake the worry that Jay viewed me differently since Oniskel explained my possible nymph powers. I closed my eyes and breathed in deeply. The wind blew my hair, and the air power felt just as natural now as the fire flowing through my veins.

"Let's stop here." Relief coated Jay's voice.

When I turned around, Ashes' giant body rose and fell softly. One of her eyes peeked open, and her giant amber eye took us in, then rolled to the back of her head.

"We'll be safe from the battle and with Ashes watching over us. I want you to rest." Jay led me to a giant, empty nest made of soft peacock feathers.

"Only if you rest too." A large yawn followed as I lowered to the feathery bed. "I can't let anything happen to you."

"You have it backward: I can't let anything happen to *you*."

The intensity of his gaze could tear down cities. Suddenly, the reality of everything unraveled me like a ribbon. Jay kneeled by my side. Shirtless, the moonlight reflected off his muscles, painting a picture of divinity. I stared at the angry scars on his chest that spelled *MINE* in uneven, crooked gashes, then at the hand that'd forever be damaged. I had caused him so much pain and needed to make it up to him.

"I need to talk to Gemm. She needs to tell me how to prevent you from sacrificing yourself. That prophecy can't come true. I want you and only you. I want us together until my last breath, and I'm sorry for the pain I caused you while I had to learn that. But now, I'm not sure if I'm just being selfish. I've set you up for death. She said you'll lay down your life for mine on the night of the Teal Moon, but I won't let that happen. We don't have time to find an answer without Gemm."

Jay kissed my knuckles. "We can't talk to her, Petal."

"Why? Did she leave with Alaska?"

"Gemm is dead."

I choked on the very air in my lungs. I couldn't speak or breathe. I finally managed to whisper, "What? That's not possible."

"I saw it happen." He hung his head and lay next to me on the feather nest.

"How? When?"

"When I took Oniskel's hair…when she was still a demon."

"Why didn't you say something?" I wanted to shove his chest and burn down the world, but I simply tucked myself under his arm.

"It's not a surprise, Petal. Everyone close to me dies. All I ever wanted was to protect those I love. Instead, I am the cause of their pain. My parents were murdered in that alley because I foolishly begged them to take me outside of Draven as a child. I was the one who asked Gemm to watch Landon and Wes, but I shouldn't have put her in that position."

"Jay, it's not your fault. Oniskel was a demon."

Jay stared at the darkened sky. "I'd rather live a life alone than for you to be taken from this world which is why I'm going to find Alaska…alone."

"No. You can't leave me. I chose you. I'm choosing you."

"I know, Petal. But I need to choose you back."

"You can't push me away because you're hurting." My chest tightened. "That's when you need me most."

"I don't need anyone." He gulped, and his voice cracked.

"Everyone needs someone."

"Petal—" He started to tuck a strand of hair behind my ear, but I caught his wrist hard.

Shackles used to bind me to my past, but now, freedom awaited just beyond my reach. Everything I had ever wanted was in my grasp, and I wouldn't let it go. I wouldn't let Jay go.

"No. I won't accept this." A tear slid down my cheek. "Wherever you go, I'll be right beside you. If I have to, I'll let these demons destroy all of Lodesa, but I will *not* let this war separate us."

I grabbed his face with my hands and got lost in his eyes. Love was a weapon. It could be used to scorch, sever, and spill blood on our precious soil, but I'd be damned if I let it shatter us.

"I love you," I said.

"Oh, Kyra." Jay flipped my wrist over, kissing the blue trail of veins. "You are my roots, gnarled, twisted—"

"And rough…" I finished. "My very source of life."

"You're my home, Kyra."

"Then stay."

"What if—"

"Shh, stay. Just be with me."

I threaded my fingers through his hair, and his lips crashed against mine. He tasted of chocolate-caramel candy with a twist of comfort that I craved. This was it, the turning point of our relationship, the shift in my life. He was mine, and I belonged to only him. Deep down, I knew he'd never actually leave me, that those fears just needed taming once in a while.

And for the first time, I knew he'd accept me, no matter what amount of darkness ran through my blood. We had each other, and that was all that mattered.

Jay's tongue felt like silk on my flaming skin, and I relinquished all of my control. I wanted him to fully take the lead and ravish me. His thumb hooked under my clothes and slid everything off with such fluidity that I barely noticed that I was naked under him. Soft feathers from the nest fluffed against my back. His erection pushed against the fabric of his pants. I exhaled, letting go of all the tension coiling me tight. My Circle drummed with need, and I knew without looking that it was the green Draven tattoo glowing vividly in the night like a beacon of hope.

"Jay," I whispered between kisses. "Jay."

I fought against every urge to rush him, knowing this time was different. This time was a promise, a baptism of our own, washing us clean of our pasts and uniting us together for the future, whether that would be a day, a year, or a century.

Jay took his time, and I drank in the scent of his skin. He kissed the curve of my throat and the valley of my collarbone. His mouth trailed my neck and then my breast, his tongue swirling around my nipple. I moaned as he sucked and nipped. A desperate need in my core grew hotter by the second. I reached down and tugged at his pants, resisting his massive size. I stroked. Up and down. His skin was warm in my palm, twitching with need and rock-hard.

My body quivered as he positioned himself between my legs. His tip brushed against my opening, teasing, and I shifted my hips to him, but his devious smirk stole my breath. Jay pushed my hips down gently and slowly grazed the inside of my thigh with his hand. My back arched.

"Jay...."

"Relax into the feathers, Petal." He slowly pushed one finger into me. "Breathe." He slowly slid in another finger and twirled. "Breathe."

We'd waited too long to do this again. Jay's third finger dove in, and my head dropped against the feathery nest.

"I love you too," he said, his voice carnal and masculine.

My legs shook and every muscle clenched around his fingers.

"Look me in the eyes, Petal."

My gaze roved over the determined arc of his brow. Jay's passionate stare locked on mine. His sculpted chest above me was a piece of art, but the devotion in his eyes set me aflame. I didn't dare blink and wanted to memorize this moment forever.

Jay caressed my inner walls with his fingers, massaging and sending me into euphoria. All I could think of was his touch. His eyes. His smile. His love. I had completely fallen for him and never wanted to stop. My heartbeat galloped against my chest, out of control.

"I want only you," I whispered.

An animalistic grunt was like music to my ears. Jay drowned me in his kisses, our teeth clashing and our tongues wrestling. He swirled his fingers faster and faster. A wave of ecstasy barreled through and ripped me in half until I completely shattered.

Eventually, my back relaxed into the nest again. My head rolled to the side, and we smiled at each other.

"My turn," I demanded, panting. I wanted to taste him more than I'd wanted anything in my life.

"Tonight is about you." Jay chuckled.

"Then give me what I want." I winked, grabbed his ass with both hands, and nudged him over my face.

I positioned him over my mouth while lying flat on my back, hungry for his length. My lips puckered against his tip, and a low guttural moan sent a shudder through my spine. His girth filled my mouth quickly, and one hand stroked his base. Jay leaned forward and slowly thrust into my mouth. Each time, I sucked and swirled my tongue. His muscles flexed above me, and I loved watching his veins throb. His sounds alone almost made me come.

"Please, Petal."

I grabbed his ass, not letting him leave, and sucked harder, faster. His whole body shook above me, and ragged grunts exploded from his mouth.

"Ky-ra! I...Uhh! Ky-ra!"

I loved how powerful I felt in having this effect on my man.

I stopped before letting him fully release, and he slipped out of my mouth. I needed more, all of him. Panting with wild eyes, he positioned himself between my legs again.

"I'm all yours, Jay."

His cock thrust into me in one push. I cried out, and my arms locked around his neck.

He pumped in and out. "Fuck, you're so wet." Any other day, I'd match his pace, but this was different. Our clean slate started tonight.

"Jay, slow down, make love to me." I brought him closer. We were already slick with sweat, and my breathing was audible in ragged gasps.

His body was divine, glistening and doing all the work. I moaned as his every inch pushed against the inside of me.

"Oh…."

Thrust.

"My…."

Thrust.

"Fuckin…."

Thrust.

"Goddess…."

Our two worlds became one, and he almost broke me apart, again and again, stopping just before I erupted, building the tension between us to an unbearable amount. I bucked against him, and he pinned my wrists above my head. He slowly nudged me over the edge and chased my orgasm until we both shattered together under the stars.

16

JADOX

Kyra's back gently twitched against my stomach, waking me from a dreamless slumber. I shifted among the giant peacock feather nest and pulled her close to my bare chest. With the humidity as it was, there might never be a reason to ever wear clothes here. I loved her so damned much.

Relaxed, I stared at the sky. The birds in Elidi smelled different than those in Draven. With each flap of their wings, they all carried a smoky charred scent in their wake. It wasn't something I was used to. But we could still stay here for eternity, happy and tucked away in a volcanic rock den.

Eternity. Kyra might be immortal soon. What would that mean for us? When I turned forty in a decade, would she look the same as today? Kyra had said she didn't want to be a nymph, but I had to convince her otherwise. Knowing she'd be safe forever sent warmth through my core.

But would the prophecy come true? Would I sacrifice my life for Kyra soon? If the fates demanded it, of course, I'd lay down my life for her, no matter what kind of future I'd hoped for. I sighed at the thought. Eventually, I'd want Kyra to find another partner to replace me. He'd die at some point, too, leaving her to suffer more loss again and again.

Maybe that wasn't a life I'd wish for her.

Above us, Ashes yawned, and even her breath smelled like a campfire. Little sparks of fire speckled out of her mouth, matching the tangerine sunrise splattered with pink around us.

My watch finally pinged for the first time in days, and I groaned, not wanting to return to reality. The soldier side of me needed to check if those Mystiers had won against the Ordulls under Bukti. The brother in me needed to make sure Alaska was safe at The Crooked Chateau. The boyfriend in me needed to keep Kyra alive. And the Draven in me needed to free the remaining prisoners.

Yet, the man in me only wanted Kyra's lips. In sleep, she moved her ass right into my crotch. I bit my lip and rested my arm over her. Warmth. Her skin was always hot to the touch. Kyra's long hair spread like a golden puddle around her head as she rolled over. Her wonderful, sleepy eyes met mine, and I wished I could swim in them.

"Good morning, soldier." She snuggled closer and rested the top of her head under my chin.

I breathed her in, sucking in the scent of a s'mores dessert. Her toasty-warm hands pressed against my chest and trailed down my stomach. Every muscle jolted fully awake. My biceps flared, ready for action. My stomach tightened with desire, and I hardened against her skin.

"Oh my." Kyra giggled, music to my ears. "I guess it *is* a good morning." Her neck craned back, and she hovered her lips just under mine.

"How'd you sleep, Petal?"

"Surprisingly well, and you seem…*rested*." She gripped my cock, stroking torturously slow.

I sucked in a breath and let her hands claim my body.

"Kiss me, Jay."

Divinity above, she was my flower, my garden of roses, my everything. There was no chance I'd let her give up immortality. This woman deserved the world, eternity in her palms. Although right now, all I could focus on was her palms wrapped around me, worshiping me so agonizingly slow that I started thrusting my hips into her hands.

Kyra's wicked smile lifted her cheeks. "Mm, like that?"

"You have no idea." I wouldn't take my eyes off her fierce gaze for even a moment. As her hands worked me, I wanted to memorize the passion glowing from deep within.

She stopped still and bit her lip. Actually, I have an excellent idea."

I pushed into her hands again, heart rate speeding, and every inch of my skin fully alert. "Tell me all your ideas, Petal."

"I wanna play a game."

"I hope it's a naked game."

"Oh, it definitely is."

Her hands slowly moved up my cock again. Up and down. I fought the urge to squeeze my eyes shut and held in a growl.

She rolled on top of me, so I lay flat, feathers soft against my back; with a devious glint in her eyes, she said, "I will do all of your favorites as long as you don't stop talking. I want to hear how long you can speak while I please you."

"Kyra...I...ooh, damn."

Her mouth brushed against my neck and towards my ear—my sweet spot. "I'm serious. You can't stop talking, or I'll stop too."

I grabbed her ass. My breathing quickened as she licked behind my ear lobe. "Ky-ra...oh...okay, what am I supposed to talk about?"

"Anything." Her tongue swirled circles, the pressure perfect, as one hand continued to stroke me.

My cock twitched into her palm, needing more, desperate to be inside her, so I admitted, "I feel naked without my emerald necklace."

She laughed against my skin, her voice vibrating. "You *are* naked, Jay."

"Hey, don't laugh at me. You said to talk about anything."

"True, go on." Her smiling lips made their way down my chest, skimming so softly that they tickled.

Fine, you want real pillow talk?

"I think I first fell in love with you when you freed the emerald from that lagoon." My breath hitched, hypnotized by her movements.

Kyra's skin glowed under the sun. She wasn't perfect, but she was my kind of perfect. Her essence captured me entirely. Her lips owned my abs, not missing a single inch, and I used all of my effort not to let my eyes roll to the back of my head. I had to watch her; she was a queen, mastering my body.

"When you took those healing berries from Goldie…." I stopped and had to focus when Kyra's lips wrapped around my hard tip. "Mm, when you saved me from those burns, knowing the risk you took, I knew you were different… Woah!... different than anyone else."

Kyra's wet tongue tentatively tasted my cock, and my hands dug into the feathered nest, searching for purchase. Her eyes dared me to keep talking.

My chest rose and fell fast, matching the frenzied drumming of my heart. I pushed out more words, unsure if I was making any sense at all, "When we first swam together in that lake under the moonlight, I knew I wanted to kiss you, but it was too soon. I needed to make sure you trusted me first."

She moved further to my base, and my tip met the back of her throat. I gasped and held back all desire to flip her over and claim her from now until the sun set once again.

"When…mm…when I…oh, goddess…okay…fuck…when I first tried to teach you how to control your Magik, your spark refueled me. You brought me back to life…oh, wow, Petal, you have to slow down…Woah, wooooah, slow down."

She smirked, her mouth absolutely destroying my sanity. I couldn't breathe. Couldn't move.

I wouldn't last a minute longer if she kept going at this rate. And her pleasure had to come first. I tried to think of something that'd distract me.

"Jay, I said keep talking," Kyra growled.

"Uh…right…."

Kyra positioned above me, straddling my hips. I reached my hands up and traced the five tattoos under her belly button. Goddess, I loved her to the Abyss and back and always would. It didn't matter if, one day, the last Circles also turned gray; I'd still love her. Any moment without her by my side wasn't an option anymore.

With a smile, she leaned over me, chest to chest, and asked, "Are you ready for me?"

"I'm always ready for you." I swallowed my emotions and watched her lower herself onto my cock.

A deep moan shook my soul awake. I disappeared inside her, and she rode me achingly slow. Up and down, eyes fixed on me.

"Talk to me, Jay." Despite her current temptress role, her voice was layered with sugary sweetness, a tone she saved just for me.

Up. Down. She was so warm, so wet.

"Fuck…that's good…uh…I want to build a house with you."

Up. Down.

"Mmm…I want to spoil you with fresh…mmm, ahh…fresh flowers every day."

Up. Down.

"Ky-ra, damn. I want to raise children with you."

She froze, amber eyes growing wide. "You do?"

I grabbed her hips and moved her up and down on me again. "So much…I want to teach them to climb a rope ladder…and how to fish…uuuuhhh…and how to garden."

She rocked against me. "Yes, oh…fuck. Yes!"

Up. Down.

"I want that life, too," she whispered against my lips.

I thrust up into her harder, faster. She moaned and arched back, letting me take control. The mounds of her breasts blocked her face, and I wished I had a hundred hands to touch her everywhere at once.

"I want a full life with you, Jay," she moaned into the morning air. "And…raise our children together…."

Up. Down.

"Mm…and tell them how brave you are," she panted between words, "and teach them our Magik…and…tuck them in at night."

My Circle flamed hotter than it ever had, and I knew I only had a few seconds left. Panting, I begged, "Kyra, look at me."

She barely had the strength to shift as I pushed into her again and again. Pressure clamped on my core tight, and I released every bit of me into her as we slowed like an ocean wave. Her amber eyes were lit with love, and I'd never have to question what we had again.

Kyra writhed against me gently until she fell against my chest, heaving in unison. We lay down, pretzeled together, until our heavy breathing calmed.

"Wow...." she whispered.

"Definitely." I kissed her forehead.

"Well, that was a fun game," she said between shaky breaths. "We should do that again sometime."

I chuckled and swept her hair from my face, then slid my fingertips in sweeping caresses over her back. She shuddered, and I felt her shaking limbs as she steadied her breath.

Trembling, Kyra sat up, still straddling me. My heart had never felt so full.

"I saw a little waterfall over there. Want to wash up with me?" she asked.

I slapped her butt playfully. "Is it a waterfall or a lavafall?"

She snorted while gathering our clothes and shoving them in the backpack. "It's real water, but it might be hot." Her gaze scanned my sweaty chest, then lowered.

"Hey, don't look at me like that. We have things to do."

Kyra leaned in and kissed my chin. "Says who?"

I grabbed our belongings, then we walked naked, hand in hand, surrounded by monstrous volcanoes. Ashes glided through the sky, following in the air and scanning for threats. Barefoot, we avoided sharp rocks and made our way to a little pond with a small waterfall. This southern water smelled different compared to the crisp northern mountains I was used to. Soon, we'd have to put our game faces back on, but for now, I wanted to savor the last few moments of calm with Kyra until everything erupted again.

"Thank you for helping me with the baptism." She dunked her hair under and rose with glittery droplets clinging to her skin.

My gaze roved over every part of her skin. "You're welcome, and thank you for introducing me to your lovely Ashes."

She curtsied sarcastically and then splashed me from the waterfall. "No, Your Highness, thank *you* for cutting off your finger." Right after she finished, she grimaced and studied me, silently asking if she had taken the joke too far.

I only laughed and bowed. "Oh, no problem, and thank *you* for willingly leaving the cave last night so I didn't have to throw you over my shoulder like a hero."

She pulled me closer, under the falls. The water roared as it crashed into the pond at our waist. "Accept my humble thanks for… the best sex of my life, twice."

"Oh, Your Majesty…" I swept her into a kiss, inhaling her scent. "That's what I live for. Please feel free to use my services again."

"Oh, really?" She winked. "How soon will thou be prepared for round three?"

I grabbed her ass, lifted her in the air, and she wrapped her legs around my waist. Softly pinning her against a volcano's wall, I licked her neck.

"Jay!" She giggled and pretended to push me away, "Wait, stop." Her body suddenly went rigid. "Do you hear that?"

I froze and stepped away from the crashing falls. I couldn't hear anything but with one large whiff of the air, it was clear that Nilson was sprinting our way.

Quickly, I waded across the pool and set Kyra on the rocks. "Get your clothes on, Petal."

"Yes, sir, soldier." She rolled her eyes at me and fiddled with a new outfit that Dezlian had provided her within the backpack– black spandex shorts and a matching tank top.

Still dripping wet but at least clean, I buttoned up my pants. Without a shirt to wear, I simply shrugged at Kyra, who leaned forward and kissed my cheek.

"It'll be okay. We can fight whoever it is together," she said with knitted brows.

"We won't have to fight. It's Nilson."

And with that, her "ex" bound around the corner of the volcano, dripping with blood.

I held in a gasp. "Nilson? What happened?"

Suddenly, Kyra fell to her knees by my side, grasping at the air with one hand while the other pushed into her temple. "No, no, no, no!"

My heart hurt for her like coal sizzling behind my rib cage. "It's Caspian." Her eyes squeezed shut. "He finally broke through the bond."

"What'd he say?"

"I can't...it...it hurts."

17

ISAAC

Ahead of me, Kyra fell to her knees. Behind her, spurts of lava exploded into the morning sky. My arm burned. The deep gash from an Ordull fighter's blade felt just as fresh as when she had swiped at me in the caves. Ignoring the blood dripping down my skin, I dashed to Kyra's side, my anger flaring at Griffin for his obvious incompetence.

If I had been strong enough to complete the memory spell, then she'd already be erased from my life, and I wouldn't have to worry anymore. But no matter the pain I had to suffer to get over her, our time together was too precious to forget.

"What happened to her?" I roared and knelt. "What'd you do, Griffin?"

"Shut up! Just move."

A large crack split in the rocks to our left, threatening to divide our foundation. Kyra might survive the molten temperatures within, but not Griffin or me. He scooped Kyra up in his arms and pressed her against his bare chest. Why was he only half-dressed? Why were they soaked in water? Shit, I knew why. My Circle braced for the rush of emotions I wanted to bury deep.

"Isaac..." she whispered, her eyes groggy and half-opened. "Caspian...is...."

"It's okay, it'll be okay." I reached forward to hold her hand. "We need to go into the caves."

"No, I need to keep her near Ashes. She'll protect Kyra."

"No, listen to me." I yanked his shoulder, the blood on my hand smearing his skin.

"Leave us alone so I can find a way to heal her. It's the ₵sμwi. Obviously, the baptism ritual didn't get rid of it, and whenever you're around, she gets worse."

"Wait for a goddess-damned minute and listen to me." I jumped in front of Griffin. "You're needed in the cave."

"Nilson, get out of my fuckin' way!"

"It's Alaska."

Griffin finally stopped and glared. "What about her?"

"She returned with three prisoners. But teleporting that many people sucked her dry. She's dying, man."

He regripped Kyra, and his lips pulled into a straight line before he said, "Take me to her."

We jogged, ran, and sprinted between hot spots, dodging lava bursts and bubbling magma in every direction. Griffin kept my pace despite carrying one-hundred and thirty pounds of deadweight in his arms. Kyra was whimpering useless words to herself, and I had no idea if she was herself or overtaken by darkness again. If only I had a venti to fly over this horrid land.

Griffin murmured something to her under his breath. She had chosen him. It was a done deal now, and my only option was to move on. But how? How could a broken heart be repaired? It seemed impossible to glue back the pieces of my soul when they were scattered across Elidi like ashes.

Finally, we made it to the cave entrance, and Griffin halted. "What about the Ordull army?"

"Oniskel has them under her control. We had one fatality on our side, and they lost three. She's holding them prisoners until we can decide what to do next." The scrape on my arm accidentally rubbed up against the cave wall, making me hiss in pain.

Griffin moved closer and scanned my injury with the intent to heal me, but I shook my head and said, "No, you need to save all your energy for Alaska."

He looked at me in what was almost appreciation for a moment, then our footsteps thundered against the cave walls as we picked up the pace again. The red light ahead grew brighter and brighter with each step, and Kyra started mumbling in her daze. Each time I saw her, she seemed to keep getting worse. My knowledge about cursed Magik was scarce, and I knew even less about how it affected her.

"How long has my sister been back?" Griffin's fatigue began showing in the strain of his voice.

"An hour. I've been searching for you ever since." I shook my head at the sudden thought that the giant nest I ran by probably served as their bed last night.

The image of him touching Kyra sent the pain of a thousand needles through my eyes. Did she think of me? Would she ever wish it were me on top of her? Inside her? Would she ever regret her choice? I bit the inside of my cheek as my stomach turned. Considering possible scenarios was pointless– a complete waste of my time. I needed to respect her choice and move on.

What else was there to focus on as a distraction? Wes. I knew Wes was safe with Dezlian after she sent me a picture of the boys chowing down on cereal in a local Elidian's house. If he didn't need me at this very moment, then I had to concentrate on who did. The best way to serve my people and fix what Elana had done to all of us was to accept the leadership position they seemed to expect of me and do it with confidence.

Under the volcano, a cluster of Mystiers surrounded Alaska, who was sprawled on the floor. One young girl in rags sat beside her, crying and holding her hand.

Griffin slipped Kyra's drooping body into my arms without a word. He ran off as I stared at Kyra's gorgeous sleeping face. What I'd give to kiss her eyelashes once more. Tension brewed in my chest. I crouched and softly laid Kyra on the hard ground, then watched her chest rise and fall slowly. She was safe, just unconscious and not mine to care for. I had to let her go.

I left her, turned my back, and walked away. Joining the rest of the group, I stood at the edge of the circle, peeking over others' shoulders. Griffin had the emerald in his hand, and his green tattoo glowed brightly on his stomach. His eyes were squeezed shut, and he chanted the same phrase over and over. But Alaska didn't stir.

"Please, you have to save her," the tiny, dirty girl cried softly.

A second child laid a smudged hand on Alaska's forehead and nodded, "Yeah, she helped us escape. She promised she'd go back and save my brother."

Griffin didn't break his trance, just repeated the same spell, but Alaska's chest stopped rising, and a puff of air pushed out before she went completely still. A few spectators dropped their heads and turned away, already accepting the grim outcome.

The third child Alaska had teleported was only a toddler. She waddled over and lay down next to Alaska, pretending to sleep. My heart split in two. What if it was Wes who Alaska had saved? I'd owe her my life and more. These children had parents and families who cared for them. Just like Alaska had…Griffin. Damn it, Griffin needed someone by his side. And if Kyra couldn't do it right now, I'd accept the role for her. I pushed through the crowd and lowered to Griffin, putting a hand on his shoulder.

"Griffin, I think—"

"No, I won't stop. Don't ask me to stop." He pushed me away and leaned closer, forcing out the enchanted words between desperate pleas.

"Griffin, she's not—"

And then multiple gasps from behind me made me whip around. Kyra was no longer curled in a heap but upright, levitating like a ghost. Her eyes were onyx, but instead of a wicked grin, only a look of suffering smothered her lively features. She floated toward the group without a sound, and they parted for her, forming an aisle. Was it my simple touch that altered her so quickly, or was her ₾sμwi Magik taking a stronger hold?

Unnatural. She wasn't of this realm anymore. I took a step back, my heart hammering in my chest. The spirit hovered over Alaska's body, and she started chanting in a strange voice.

Griffin glanced from his sister to Kyra, back and forth. He seemed to accept the darkness that swirled within Kyra instead of trying to snap her out of it this time.

Nodding, Griffin chanted with her. The group all held hands around them, but I only backed away. Kyra didn't need me now that she had Griffin. They flourished together, and it was time to figure things out on my own. I backed further away, step by step.

From the shadows of the cave, I watched Alaska's finger twitch. Her eyes opened, and Griffin helped her sit up while steadying her back. Joyful celebrations happened right in front of me, but I felt disconnected from everyone, like I was wrapped in a fog of thoughts. I tried to tune out their smiles and hugs as Alaska stood and embraced her brother.

I needed a new purpose. Kyra was no longer mine to fight for. What did I want now—the Vayu necklace, of course. But why did it feel so emergent? I dropped my forehead into my hands and rubbed my temples hard.

Images of Vayu came crashing into me like a stormy wind. With my eyes clamped shut, I saw the kite-shaped library, the stables full of venti, the Azul skyscrapers, and my Vayuian people strolling through our pristine streets. It all clicked into place in a moment. I needed to heal what was broken by rebuilding our city.

Someone sat next to me, rubbing against my side slightly, and I didn't need to look to know it was Kyra.

"Legend has it that those who have Linked to more than one person…." Kyra said, but it wasn't her voice. "Might lose a part of themselves and become…darker."

My gaze darted up to meet hers and got lost in her obsidian eyes.

"Kyra? Do you know me?"

She fiddled with the drumstick hairpiece I had gifted her for her birthday. "That's an awkward question to ask a friend."

"A friend." I rubbed my lengthening beard and sighed.

"A friend forever." She paused. "You're meant for greater things than me, Isaac."

"That's a lousy excuse, love," I grunted. Well, at least she knew who I was.

She smiled and waved a hand over my wound, immediately healing it. Apparently, she didn't need to be Linked to Griffin anymore to hold his enhancement powers. What else could she do? Did she still have access to my weather control?

"I thought you weren't going to call me 'your love' anymore," she said.

"Well, it's a hard habit to break." I forced out a chuckle, but we both knew it was fake. "What else should I call you?"

"How about nymph?"

I froze. "What?"

"That's what Oniskel thinks I'll become."

I choked on my saliva and gaped at her, unable to process her words.

"It must be some mistake. You can't be a nymph."

"I'm not sure of a lot anymore," Kyra said, putting one hand on my thigh, staring at it for a moment, then pulling away. "Alaska is okay."

"That's good."

"Alaska said that Ordull women have started to disappear, not all at once like when I made my wish." Her voice slowly returned to normal, darkness layering the sounds receding. "But different villages and cities have reported missing women."

"We need to defeat Elana *now*." I stood.

"Are you two done discussing the statue you're creating in my honor?" Alaska strolled over, her face full of new life. "Nice eyes, Kyra. Did you eat a devil to look like that?"

"It's my new signature look. Get used to it." Kyra snorted. "How do you feel?"

"Like gorula shit." She winced and cupped her head as she sat on a bolder next to Kyra.

For a few minutes, we all stayed silent, watching the Mystiers argue about our next step. Tension was high, and no one had the best answer. So, I wanted to enjoy my last few moments of normalcy with Kyra by my side.

"I can't wait around while they argue about our plan. This is ridiculous. I'm going to The Crooked Chateau," Kyra blurted.

"Why? You'll be walking straight into Elana's hands."

"Because I have a gut feeling that Caspian is there, even though our connection seems broken," Kyra said. "I'll take Ashes if I have to."

"That'll take you too long. I'll teleport you back." Alaska frowned.

"No, you need to recover." Kyra sighed. "Plus, aren't the other demons there?"

"Yeah, Elana has trapped them again. She still wants the emerald to eliminate the rest of the women Ordulls." Alaska paused. "And she wants all *three* of you captured. You have a high price on your heads."

"Who?" Kyra faced her. "Which three."

"You, Jadox, and...Isaac."

Me? Why? A knot tightened in my chest, but I did my best, pretending not to care.

"Wait, why Isaac?" Kyra asked for me.

Alaska let her hair fall in front of her face, hiding the cringe that was evident in her next words. "I told Elana that Isaac's the last Vayuian male with enhancements, that he's an option to create...you know...Golden babies."

"How could you betray him?"

"Because I'd never bring Jadox to Elana!" Alaska yelled. "Never."

Kyra nodded. "But I need Jay to come with me." She looked up, cheeks flushed, knowing my gaze was on her. "To return Moroka and Surh-Sig into nymphs."

Of course, she'd need Griffin with her since part of the spell was a sacrifice from her love. Her love. Would I ever be able to look at her again without coming undone?

"No." Alaska crossed her arms. "You and Isaac can go to the chateau. I won't let my brother step foot near Andersonville."

She leaned back against the cave's wall. Shadows devoured her face, and, in the darkness, her jawline morphed into sharper angles like a warrior's deadly blade.

Griffin tromped toward us with eyes only for Kyra. He stopped right in front of her, cupped her face in his hands, and leaned over to whisper in her ear.

Kyra nodded, and I was forced to watch their lips meld together without a blink. Her body immediately softened under his kiss. When he pulled away, her eyes were alight with honey amber again. As much as I hated Griffin, I was grateful for his ability to keep her grounded.

"Grab your stuff, Jay." She slapped his bare chest. "We're flying on Ashes to Elana. Now."

He nodded.

Alaska stood, swaying. "No, I'll teleport you. Just give me an hour."

Griffin held up a hand, but before he snuck in a word, Alaska rose on her tiptoes in his face. "Don't you even dare say no. You don't get to make my decisions for me. I can take you one at a time."

I met Kyra's golden eyes, full of spunk, and let myself become immersed in them for the last time. Before I had a chance to say a word, Alaska grabbed the emerald from her brother's hand and touched Kyra's shoulder. They disappeared in a flash, leaving a whirl of wind in their wake.

Gone. What happened to waiting?

"What the fuck?" Griffin and I said at the same time.

Instead of his eyes lasering into mine, he burst out laughing. With all the madness surrounding our every move, I couldn't help but smile with him and finally succumbed to laughter too. He leaned on the cave wall and wiped a tear from his eye.

"Fuckin' women, am I right?"

I grunted and inhaled deeply, trying to center myself again.

"Thank you," he managed to croak out.

I leaned forward, shocked, "What did you just say?"

"Thank you." He stuck out his hand to shake. "For finding me to save Alaska, for taking care of Kyra when I was *detained* with Elana last month, for being there for her and having her back."

Speechless, I shook his hand.

"By the way," Griffin quieted. "I sent a mass message to the Dravians, so they know you're in charge of my village if anything happens to Alaska or me. Our kind already admires you. Look." Griffin gestured smoothly, showing me that the knots of Mystiers were watching us, with eyes on me, awaiting my next move.

He was right. I could lead more than Vayuians.

"I need you to do me a favor." Griffin looked at his watch.

"Sure you do."

"It's prophesized that on the Teal Moon, I'll…I'll lay down my…I just won't be around anymore." His brows knit together. "When that happens, I need you to promise me to watch over Kyra."

I coughed and kept coughing like an entire stick was lodged in my throat. Griffin pounded my back until it stopped.

"Please promise if I'm not around, you'll take care of her, support her, stay with her, listen to her, and lo…" he grunted, stumbling on his words, "love her…always."

My heart slammed against my ribs. What the Flames was I supposed to say to that? Did I want Kyra by my side? Obviously. I'd always protect her within my abilities. But she'd be a shell of a soul if anything happened to Griffin. I couldn't let anything hurt her, even if that meant doing my part to keep Griffin alive. For now, I had two choices: ease his concern by agreeing *or* give him a reason to stay alive.

I backed up. "Sorry, man. I'll always care for her, but Kyra isn't mine to watch over. Plus, I've connected with someone. She's as fine as Flames."

Griffin's entire body turned as rock solid as a statue. "You're kidding me, right?"

"No, you've met her, and don't think of stealing my woman."

"Why have I wasted my breath. You're such an asshole," he growled. "Who is it?"

18

KYRA

After my feet hit solid ground again, I gripped my bag closer to protect the two remaining vials of lava. "What the Flames, Alaska! You didn't listen to me at all. I said we'd ride Ashes."

"Too bad. You're here already." Then she collapsed, coughing and spurting blood from her lips onto my shoe.

I froze as she slid a finger through it, cutting the red in half, and said, "Well…fuck."

"It'll be okay. I'll heal you again."

"You can't. We're in The Crooked Chateau," she said softly and gestured to the electrical wires lining the ceiling of the dark room we sat in. "Can't you feel it? Our Magik is gone."

"Then how are you able to teleport in here?"

She fumbled with the emerald around her neck. "This gem isn't natural."

Natural. My ᑖsμwi Magik wasn't natural either. But now I knew that Isaac enticed it somehow. The touch of his skin or inhalation of shared breath was like a drug to the spirit claiming my soul. I wasn't sure if I'd be able to summon it without him near. Using all my concentration, I focused on my Circles and envisioned the gray rings. Yet, when I actually needed to harness that energy, it failed me.

We were hunched in a corner with unfinished walls, maybe a basement. As I peeked over Alaska's shoulder, my legs scratched against a gritty cement floor. Under dim lights were several rows of metal cages. Someone sneezed, and another person cried softly. Who else was here? Wait, were people in those cages? It smelled worse than death. In the middle of the room stood two metal science lab tables with an electric chair between them. Not a good sign.

Rage coursed through my veins. This must be the wretched place Elana had controlled Jay and, by the looks of it, the same place she held the prisoners.

"Is this The Cavity?" I whispered and checked if Elana's hoverchair lurked nearby.

Alaska leaned against the wall, closing her eyes.

"No, Alaska. Stay awake."

"I lied to you all. Tell Jay I lied to him, and he can hate me if he wants." A soft, weak smile rose on her cheeks as her head drooped to the side. A little trail of blood oozed from her nose.

"What? No, you tell him yourself." I shook her shoulders gently. "Alaska, open your eyes.

She chuckled softly, then coughed again. "Maybe…maybe it's better this way. I was trying to bring Paola back, but now, I can go to her."

In horror, I sat back on my heels. Jay would never be okay again if something happened to his little sister, especially after he had just lost Gemm. Maybe if I distracted Alaska enough, she'd keep talking and stay awake.

Coaxing her, I rubbed her wrists with hard pressure and said sarcastically, "Alaska, you'd never lie. You're the sweetest person I've ever met."

She half-chuckled again. "I lied to…to bring you here. I was never going to bring Jadox too."

I couldn't linger on her deceit. There would be time to hash it out when she was healthy, safe, and able to yell again.

"And I lied about the emerald…and my plan." Her voice sounded drunk. "But now, it doesn't matter. I'll see Paola soon."

A gnawing need for answers gutted me like a hatchet to my stomach, and guilt dissected me for wanting to ask her for more answers when she was weak. "Alaska, open your eyes."

Her hands went limp at her side, and I softly slapped her cheeks.

"Shit! Come on. Damn it, wake up!"

"Is someone there?" an unfamiliar male voice, smooth as silk, projected from near the cages.

I rolled my lips and sucked my body as close to the wall as possible. The only natural sunlight came from the sole window across the room, nowhere near us.

"Who's there?" he repeated, and this time, footsteps clunked against the cement floor. Closer. Closer.

Kyra? Are you here? I can feel you nearby.

Caspian's unexpectantly clear voice through our Link surprised me, but I responded quickly.

I'm coming to help you, Caspian.

His relief flooded through our mental bond, and I wanted to reach out and hug him.

"Maybe you need *my* help," the male voice said.

I hadn't said anything about help out loud. How did the man here know what to say?

From the shadows, Caspian stepped under the flickering light. What was he doing here? Surprised, I looked up to meet my brother's eyes and immediately plastered myself further against the wall. His gaze was hollow and petrifying. When he smiled, it was as if his face didn't belong to him anymore. Fuck! The ₵sμwi Magik had stolen my brother. I stood slowly and shielded Alaska's crumpled body.

"You need my help," he said—deadpan.

"What do you mean?" I said carefully, assessing the spirit's every move.

The way he swayed on his feet and shoved his thumbs in his pockets didn't resemble my brother. When had my curse started affecting him so severely?

"You need my help to heal your friend," he nodded behind me, his voice not his own.

I blocked him quickly, and a wave of confusion washed over his features.

"Why are you waiting?" he said, "Your friend is going to die."

"No, she'll be fine."

"Maybe with my help." His brows knitted. "Move over."

I studied him intently, wishing to the goddess above I had access to my flames. "First, tell me our nephew's name."

Only a moment of hesitation flashed across his face until he ran a hand through his brown hair and said, "Come on, now, puppet, she won't last long."

"Puppet?" I shoved his chest hard, making space between him and Alaska. "Get away from her."

The moment my hands touched him, the obsidian eyes flickered to blue, then back again. He shook his head, then glanced around as though he wasn't sure of his location. Was it my touch that had snapped him out of it? I shoved him again.

Right when we made contact, his eyes turned royal blue. This time, I held onto his elbows tight and felt the rush of ₾sµwi storming inside him, devouring him completely. I knew what I had to do. Latching onto him hard, I embraced our Link, welcomed the ₾sµwi in, and commanded the power to leave my brother. It resisted. The darkness wanted to devour Caspian, but there was no chance I'd let that happen today. Or ever.

"Ky, what are you doing? You're hurting my arms." Caspian tried to wiggle out from my grip. "Wait, how did you get here?"

I clutched harder, accepting all the darkness into my Circle where it belonged. Power charged through me, and Caspian's power of the ocean was also now at my disposal. What I had felt before was only half of the strength. Now, I completely understood. I needed the ₾sµwi like I needed air. It felt like a living ball of forceful energy coiled in my chest, ready to be used.

Finally, I released him and stared into Caspian's blue eyes. This time, it felt different. I had more control of the ᏣsμWi inside me. I was growing with it, and we were learning about each other.

I turned away from my brother and checked my tattoos. Not four, but five gray Circles looped together, the beginning of the end.

My time left was limited. In fact, I might only have a few seconds left. The darkness was about to absorb me completely.

Swiftly, I turned, laid a hand on Alaska's shoulder, and focused on the unnatural. *"Terra angakok. Terra angakok."*

Alaska's eyes flew open, and she sat upright. "Kyra?" She patted down her chest. "No, no, no, I was *so* close. Paola was waiting for me."

"I healed you." I staggered back when Alaska swung at me.

"You shouldn't have." Alaska stood as if she hadn't been close to her last breath moments ago. "I feel weird, wrong. What did you do to me?"

"I saved your life."

Suddenly, a pounding headache throbbed at my temples. The dark power swirling within me threatened to break free, pushing against my skin like my bones couldn't contain it. I wasn't sure how much longer I could keep it coiled tight, but I acted like it was all okay.

"I don't remember the last few hours, Ky. But now that you're here, help me save Brent." Caspian traced his long scar.

"But all the prisoners need us too. We have to pick between one man or hundreds of innocent lives."

"You can't expect me to sit back and let him be murdered," Caspian said.

"What other choice do we have? Elana will probably be nearby if we find him, and she'll try that crazy plan to replace Brent with you. I won't risk losing you, not again."

Suddenly, my stomach warped into a braided mess of nausea, and I held back the urge to vomit, further coating the disgusting floor with more fluids. A voice echoed in my ear, whispering secrets in an ancient language that I wanted to pay attention to. Instead, I shut them out. The ᏣsμWi called to me.

"*No*!" I yelled, silencing the beckoning. It was getting too forceful, coercing me into the darkness.

"Shh," Caspian took my wrists. "The guards will hear us."

More silent, luscious promises egged me to listen. Resisting the pull felt like someone had taken a chainsaw to my temple. I bent in half, my body shaking while desperately fighting the darkness.

Caspian's hand rubbed my back.

"I'll be fine." I swallowed the lie. "Let's make a deal: I'll help you find Brent if you help me get a piece of both demons."

"A piece?"

"Yeah, it's the first part of a spell that'll change them back to nymphs. I think they'll be able to defeat Elana once they're turned back into their original form."

"How do you know the spell will work?"

"We succeeded with Oniskel. She's a wind nymph again."

Caspian gawked at me for a moment before clamping his mouth shut again. "Come on, I'll show you where they're at."

We walked through the dark basement to the sole window.

Caspian rubbed his scar again, then pulled the window open. "Do you remember the story I told you about a siren caught in a fishing net?" He climbed out of the window up to the street level.

"Yes, we all have scars, some visible and some not."

He reached the side of the building as if to scale the sleek orange metal spikes curved out at odd angles like flames.

"Um, what are you doing?" I asked.

"Follow me." He started climbing like it was a rock wall.

"There's no way I can go up there."

"Don't be ridiculous, Ky. Come on."

"I'm scared of heights, Caspian."

"I know. I'll distract you." He nodded his chin toward the sky. "Have you changed your narrative about your scars yet?"

"My *narrative*? Are you a psychologist?"

"Haha. Very funny." He rose higher, leaving me trembling below.

"Caspian, spit it out. What are you asking?"

"It was never your fault that the waves took me."

"I know it wasn't my fault. I never fully blamed myself. That doesn't mean my scars are healed."

"Then what are your biggest fears? Because it's definitely not heights," he grunted and rose higher.

When I craned my neck, his dark hair contrasted against the bright sky. How many guards surrounded this building? Would a soldier spot us in broad daylight?

I bit the inside of my cheek and stared up at the third-floor window, then the fourth. My hands shook.

"I want an answer, Ky. What are you still holding onto?"

My arms burned as I climbed higher and higher, facing my fears. "I never should've hated all men. I blamed all my problems on them because a few caused me pain." I paused, getting a better grip and repositioning my foot where it was slippery, terrified to look down. "But, when I think about it, I don't think that was the main issue."

Caspian groaned above, rising higher, panting.

"I think even if every man had been a perfect angel to me growing up, I still would've held resentment toward someone for your disappearance."

Before I finished, he reached the fourth floor and toppled inside. When he disappeared, my heart rate tripled. What was on the other side? Who was waiting for us?

I quickened my pace, shaking more and more until I finally reached the high window ledge. Anxiety clawed at my throat at the sight of the room.

Caspian pointed to a corner near a fireplace where Surh-Sig lay, chained and sleeping, covered in soot. Next to her was a bubbling hot tub holding a sleeping Moroka.

"What do we do?" I whispered.

Caspian put a single finger to his lips and tiptoed, gesturing for me to circle behind Moroka. He may have seen snippets of my memories when we Linked, but I took this time and opened up to him fully to show him more because the darkness might overwhelm me soon.

I need to tell you something, Caspian. When I was younger, my fake dad caught my boyfriend and me in bed.

Moroka stirred slightly, and I held my breath, frozen in place. I wasn't sure how I'd get a piece of her with only this small knife, but I didn't want to dwell on it, so I continued my story.

He killed Tyrique in my bed, right in front of me.

Caspian's eyes widened, and he stopped his momentum toward Surh-Sig. I could feel the distraught battle in his soul of how to comfort me. Instead of allowing him to, I finished my story.

He took pictures of me next to Tyrique's body. He said that if I told anyone about the murder, he'd plaster the pictures everywhere. And he said I couldn't touch another boy as long as I lived in that house, or I'd have the same fate.

Fake dad didn't deserve my tears, but they pooled behind my eyes. I wouldn't cry for him, but I'd let myself cry for the angry Kyra who had spat on his body, wishing I could wrap her in a hug and let her know it was okay to slip into darkness. I held back a sob for the memory of so many years, pushing down the pain and faking smiles at Hallie and Mom.

If I had only released my shadows, screaming them into the night air, I probably never would've made the wish to have a world without human males. Instead of shaming myself, I was suddenly hungry for the darkness itching under my skin. My hair stood on end to be in the same place where fake dad took his last breath.

"I'm sorry, Ky," Caspian whispered, "I'm glad you told me."

Moroka snapped awake at the sound of his voice. Her movements splashed against the surface, showing a rope bound around her wrists.

"Sister, you're here," she hissed, pleased to see me. Surh-Sig rolled over, her hollow eyes focused on me.

Caspian hesitantly scanned me up and down. "Why is she calling you sister?"

I grinned, caught between my brother of blood and my sisters of spirit. The darkness within was eclipsing everything and ready to burst. Maybe I was viewing the lesson all wrong. Maybe demons were superior to nymphs. Maybe all Ordull women needed to leave and join their counterparts in the Abyss. Lodesa would be better off with only Mystiers.

The corner of the Unetlo Book containing the spell poked out of the bag. If I threw it into the hot tub, all the ink would smear into illegible scribbles. Maybe there was no need for the transformation spell at all. For the first time, I truly understood Elana's need for vengeance against those who did her wrong. Maybe we were two of a kind. Famished with the chance to encompass who I was truly meant to be, I gripped the knife tighter.

Now that Caspian knew about the spell, he'd expect me to slice off a piece of Moroka and break Surh-Sig's bones. But they were me, and I was them. We were one of the same darkness. I'd free them instead.

19

KYRA

I whipped my knife out, pointing it directly at Caspian's face.

"Ky, what are you doing?" His blue eyes grew to the size of saucers.

Unique eyes. Eyes of power. Eyes meant for me to take. Maybe I could have my name written in legends: The Eye Carver. Ordulls and Mystiers alike would tell stories around their campfires of the ways I wedged my blade behind hundreds of eye sockets and popped out each and every eye to hold fresh in my hands. What would I do with my collection? Keep them in jars like sweet Oniskel kept her spiders, swallow blood like Moroka or wear them as decorative cloaks of flesh like Surh-Sig?

"I need your eye, Little Puppet." I licked my lips and pranced forward.

"Stop playing games. We need to hurry before Elana shows up."

Surh-Sig hissed, "That stupid Elana isn't the one you should be afraid of."

I glanced at the binds tying my sister to the chimney. Adrenaline flooded my body as I searched the shadows of the room. Did this puppet do this to my sister? I tore the pin out of my hair and pointed it at the wretched man with the ugly scar down one side of his face.

He deserved another just like it on the opposite cheek, but first, I wanted to steal his eye.

"Hold still," I commanded. "Should I use the knife or this pin?"

He backed up. "Ky?"

The aqua shade of his iris was captivating, and inspiration hit. Each eyeball I collected could serve as a bead for my hair. I'd push a needle through the middle, letting fluid drain slowly, then thread strands of my hair through to the other side. How many eyes would fit? How heavy would it be to hold? Were Ordull or Mystier eyes better? There was only one way to find out.

I lunged forward, knife out, slashing at his cheeks. He dodged, yelling nonsense. My sisters laughed and clapped with joy. Moroka's cackle was music to my ears. They taunted him as he leaped from side to side. I barely missed him with each swipe.

"Ky, stop! It's me!"

"Hop, boy."

"Bounce, boy."

"Skip, boy."

The crazed way his eyes dilated and showed such an array of emotions in such a short amount of time was fascinating. I'd have to find a spell to maintain its ability to do that once detached from his useless brain. Would his veins gush blood when I gutted it from his skull? Anticipation spiked my powers.

"He's a weak one." I smiled, relishing in his fear that made me stronger. "My new puppet."

"Guess I'll have to change them back to nymphs myself," he said.

From the corner of my eye, Surh-Sig leaned forward, tugging on her chain. "What did you just say, boy?"

Puppet flipped a dusty table over to use as a shield. "We can turn you both back to nymphs, but tell her to stop attacking me."

Moroka hissed in disbelief, but Surh-Sig yelled, "Wait!"

Little Puppet plastered himself against the wall, his gaze darting to the open window. He held the table in front of him. I dropped my blade, letting it clatter to the floor, and smiled.

"I'll be gentle, Puppet. Ready?"

"Ky, I know you're in there. Come back," he whispered.

I summoned Magik as the wind tore in from outside and ripped the table from his hands. His chest pumped fast, and I heard every fast thump of his heartbeat.

Surh-Sig struggled against her binds. "Wait, sister, we should hear him out. I want to be a nymph again."

"No."

"Very well, cut me free first, so I can help you."

In one swift swing, I slashed my knife through her cuffs. Surh-Sig rose on her skeletal frame. The pieces of flesh over her back fell as she floated toward our prey.

With a twitch of my head, I called vines to me. They flew in the window and wrapped around the worthless boy. He pushed and writhed against them until one tied around his ankles. He fell to the ground, stiff as a pencil, and landed on his side.

"Ky! You don't know what you're doing. Think of Landon."

A head of blond curls overtook my sights for a moment, followed by a sweet smile—a face I once knew. I growled and shook the illusion away.

"What color are the Landon Puppet's eyes? I need to create a pattern for my hair beads." I kneeled, hairpin in hand, and hovered it over his face. "I think I'll do lighter shades up top and darker colored eyes on the bottom. Maybe you'll be my eye specialist after we get you an eye patch, of course."

Heart pumping hard with giddiness, I clutched his chin with one hand. His ancestor had trapped my sisters for years, and someone needed to pay for this crime.

My hand was steady as the pin lowered closer and closer to his eye. He squeezed it shut and tried to turn away again, his muscles straining against the vines.

"Look at me, Puppet." I stabbed it down, but he shook his head back and forth so fast that I rammed the end into his nose.

"Ky! Stop." He kept his eyes shut and shook his head back and forth faster and faster. I jabbed his cheek. The air. His forehead. The air. His nose.

"Aah! Hold still!" Desperation consumed me wholly. "Surh-Sig, hold him down!"

She snarled and moved toward me, bones clattering together. When she crouched down, my dear sister snatched my blade from the ground and cut him loose.

In a single breath, she cracked her arm in half at the elbow with an agonizing roar and handed the piece of her over to him.

"What are you doin'?" I yelled and lunged at her.

I pinned Surh-Sig underneath me, straddling her. Puppet stared at me for only a moment, then grabbed a bag from the ground.

"Change me back to a nymph!" Surh-Sig yelled.

"I can't yet. I need a sacrifice from *her* true love first."

Surh-Sig growled, and I smiled. "See, beloved sister, you helped him for no reason. I have no one who loves me."

He jumped to the window and scrambled out of sight. Before I could lurch toward him, Surh-Sig's legs cradled me in a cage of bones.

"Let me go!"

"He could turn us back!" Surh-Sig yelled. "We could be as we once were."

"Lies!" Moroka angrily squealed from the hot tub.

"I was never a nymph! There's nothing to turn me back into," I hissed. "This is who I am!" I was a deadly nightmare, and I welcomed it.

Pushing hard against her hold, I split her bones apart at her ankle. Her foot skittered across the floor, separate from the rest of her bony form.

I grabbed my hairpin and pointed it at my deceiving sister. "I'll be back to take care of you. Stay here!"

Fire roared from my fingertips. The afternoon breeze lifted me from the ground and carried me out of the window. Bright blues and puffy cotton balls in the sky made me giggle. Once upon a time, I think I used to know a Blondie who loved the sky and stars.

My daydream ceased when I caught sight of the puppet struggling amid a bush along the street. He pulled at a backpack zipper while mumbling obscenities under his breath.

A high-pitched screech shook the air and stole my breath. Perfect. My massive red beast zig-zagged between the skyscrapers. Her giant scaled wings stretched wide, flapping, then angled to help dive low. I was running out of time.

I flicked my wrist, making the winds gust me toward him. Meeting my glare, he chaotically tugged and ripped at the bag. Suddenly, a soft whisper sounded in my head.

Ky, it'll be okay. Griffin's almost here. Just hold on.

I pushed the voice away and charged. The terror written in his eyes spiked me with excitement. Soon, that eye would be dangling from my hair. Mine. Mine. Mine. The word swelled in my chest, wringing at my heart like a decayed memory, but I shoved that sensation away.

The jugosaur flew closer.

"Come here, Puppet." My feet hit the ground, and I charged—fire, earth, wind, and water all waiting at my beck and call.

Little Puppet glanced up at the electric wires umbrellaing The Crooked Chateau, then blocked his face with his arm. The sun reflected off his watch and sent a beam into the sky. The jugosaur shrieked again and changed direction, plummeting straight toward us. For the first time, I noticed two small riders on her back. Irrelevant. This time, nothing would stand in my way.

Ky, take a breath. I know you're in there. Don't be scared. Griffin's here. He's here.

"Enough!" I yelled, smashing Puppet against the building's wall with a slam of wind.

Not wasting another chance, I screamed at the top of my lungs and hovered my pin over his face. His eyes grew fuller with horror. I lifted his eyelid and shoved the curved pin around the back of his eye. He let out a spine-chilling scream. It was glorious. His other eye cried fiercely, and his face turned bright red. Panting, he froze like a statue. I used the curved pin like a spoon. He screamed and screamed.

In one quick pull, I yanked the hairpin out. Pop! His blue eye rolled into my hand. The squishy, slimy ball rolled in my palm, and I reveled in it. Mine. Mine. Mine.

He dropped to the ground, one hand clutching his empty eye socket. I was done with him and what he could offer me. Where could I find a needle to pierce a hole through the middle? More importantly, who would I conquer next?

A loud thump sounded behind me as the jugosaur landed.

"Kyra!" a deep voice shouted, followed by two sets of fast footsteps.

I glanced up, prepared to use my Magik. Instead, I locked onto deep brown eyes, layered with years of loneliness and speckled in shades of exotic soil. The ultimate eye. Mine. Mine. Mine.

I tilted my head, memorized every hint of forest lingering in his gaze, then raised my pin at him, ready to strike.

"Kyra!" He grabbed both my arms in his strong hands. "Kyra, fight the darkness. Come back to me."

I bit my lip. "Why do you suppose people have two eyes when one will suffice?"

His eyes roamed over my face. "Kiss me, Kyra. I'm here."

"I'd rather not. Give me your eye."

"Hurry, Petal, before it gets worse," he said.

"I need a spoon this time." I made a hook gesture with her finger.

He gripped both my shoulders. "Okay, I'll get you a spoon. Just kiss me first."

20

JADOX

Mayhem. And complete madness. Pandemonium couldn't adequately describe the scene in front of me. At the center of it all, Kyra stood blissfully calm and unaware of the havoc she had caused. The wickedness in her face was more unsettling than before, as if the emptiness inside had its own depth and weight. She smiled, blind to the building on fire to her left, deaf to the roaring wind plastering Caspian to the wall and his screams, and immune to Ashes' terrified shrieks. I needed to try to heal Caspian, but Kyra snickered between us, mumbling nonsense. When her shirt lifted. Through her shirt, five gray tattoos glowed fiercely. It felt like infinite strength coiled through her.

"Shit, shit, shit, shit."

From afar, I caught a whiff of saltwater headed our way like a fuckin' tsunami. Another impending obstacle. Fantastic.

"Griffin!" Caspian's voice cracked in pain. "I have a piece of Surh-Sig. We need your sacrifice."

Movement caught my attention above, in a high window of The Crooked Chateau. To my horror, Surh-Sig floated out of the window toward us, missing half an arm and a foot. Her other bones rattled against each other when the stinging wind ripped the remaining chunks of flesh off her back. My heart slammed, and sweat dripped down my neck. The eeriness of seeing a demon in broad daylight turned reality upside down.

"Fuck!" Nilson finally clamped his jaw shut and rushed toward Surh-Sig with his hands raised.

I couldn't worry about him right now.

"Kyra, look at me," I said.

Her deadly gaze sent a shudder down my spine as they lasered through my soul. "We have met before, haven't we, Puppet?" She stepped forward, and I held my ground, despite every voice within shouting at me to run.

"Yes, Petal. Now, give me a quick kiss, and I'll explain it all." I sucked in a deep breath and kept my voice soft and in control.

"Okay, first, give me my payment." She tilted her head to the side and licked her lips. "Your eye, please." Kyra held out something in her hand. Caspian's eye.

Bile rose up my throat, but I swallowed it back down. I'd seen much worse before, but the fact that Kyra did it with her own hands felt so wrong. If she ever snapped out of the Ꞓsμwi insanity, she'd never forgive herself for hurting her brother.

Kyra stepped forward again with purpose. Her hands shot out a blast of flames aimed straight at my face. Ashes roared between us, blocking the heat from touching me.

Kyra grinned and snapped her fingers. Ashes immediately fell asleep on the pavement, looking as if she were simply basking in the beam of sunlight. How did she do that? Stupid dark Magik.

Kyra lunged at me again, hurling fire. The heat increased in speed through the air. I commanded soil to rise between us, forming a wall.

On the other side, Kyra growled. She punched a hole through it with more flames. Through the smoke, she glared with those onyx eyes made from nightmares. My entire body, head to toe, tensed. Her Ꞓsμwi Magik was too strong. The only way to calm her down was to convert Surh-Sig into our ally.

"Okay, Petal. Come here." I held my hands behind my back. "It's a deal. Take my eye for a kiss."

"Such a pleasant puppet."

Slowly, I inched toward Caspian and cast him a glance. I nodded at the pack that hopefully held the vials. He fumbled with the skeleton foot in his lap.

"See," Kyra hissed and strutted forward, her hips swaying with each movement. "That wasn't so hard."

My heart broke for her. Whatever war she was waging internally must be ripping her to shreds. I knew somewhere, deep down, Kyra was battling to overcome the ₡sμwi. She just needed some help.

Kyra moved toward me with a smirk. Her raging fire ceased. I closed the distance between us. Finally, we stood toe to toe. Kyra raised a knife in one hand, but before she could pounce, I clutched her wrist, controlled the weapon, and brought her lips to mine. She tasted of stale wine and maggot cheese, yet that didn't stop her from roving her tongue over mine. I held her tight, pressing my lips to hers. But, this time, her body never softened. She pulled away roughly, and those terrifying soulless eyes glared at me still.

"Shit!" My hand tightened around her wrist. "Caspian! Ready?"

"Let me go!" Kyra squirmed, and fire blazed hot under her skin, scorching my hand with instant blisters.

A scream scratched my throat raw. I grabbed her blade. Dropped to my knees. Hovered the sharp knife over my hand for the second time. My mind wrestled my body. Humans weren't meant to inflict self-harm. In the army, we knew that pain and risks were part of the sacrifice, but it was still against nature to torture our bodies.

"Come on!" Caspian urged me on. "Do it!"

Sunlight sparkled off the sharp edge, and I tried to push away the memory of how badly it hurt the last time I chopped off my finger. I had a choice, but when it came to my love, there wasn't any chance I'd abandon her.

I spread my fingers. My heart beat frantically. I rose the knife higher. Sucked in a breath. My body went rigid. Dizziness took over as I stared at my fingers, then swiped the knife down fast and hard. But before it could make impact, a gust of wind bulldozed me to the side. My back hit the street hard. The wind was knocked out of me, and I clutched my chest.

"Try this!" Nilson screamed from across the street. His own hand was bleeding, and his finger flew through the air to Caspian.

Caspian caught Nilson's severed finger, then finally laid it next to the bone foot. The world spun. He read from the open page of the Unetlo Book. It wasn't going to work. The wrong person gave a sacrifice. And what if only Kyra could perform the ritual?

Caspian tipped the vial of lava over the skeleton foot. But just as the first drop was about to land, a cyclone wind tore it out of his hands, and the vial cracked over the curb. The lava flowed onto the pavement near the sewer.

"Noooo..." I shouted.

What would we do now? Kyra crawled fast toward her brother, lunacy in her expression. From behind, I pinned her to the ground, her strength fading. She scratched at my face, but her fire didn't burn me.

"Use the third vial!" I shouted over to Caspian.

He reached into the bag, bit off the topper, and quickly poured the remaining lava on top of Surh-Sig's bone and my finger. He chanted quietly, and the street fell silent.

Not one bird chirped. Not one breath could be heard.

The ground tremored silently. I crushed Kyra to me, protecting her from the possible quake. But the ground didn't split. Rather, thousands of tulips sprang up, over five feet tall, followed by a round of orchids, then cherry blossoms. A forest of titanic flowers bloomed in front of my eyes. From deep within, my Circle pumped with awe.

"Sleep, child," said an old voice.

Kyra's body immediately went slack under me. I held her even tighter, mind racing at how I'd fight off another threat and protect Kyra's unconscious form at the same time.

Then a wrinkled hand, covered in henna, reached through the flowers' stems. Her light pink skin reminded me of soft petals in springtime sprinkled with freckles. She drifted to Nilson on the curb and hovered over his bleeding finger. From her touch, his injury was stitched and sealed shut as a nub.

"Thank you," Nilson whispered and leaned against a building wall, panting.

How did the spell even work? Nilson wasn't her true love.

A face resembling perfect porcelain gazed at me and glided over. She was cloaked in long leaves draped down her back, and flowers were twisted into a long black braid.

"Surh-Sig?"

"Yes," she said with a smile and bowed her head. "Thank you, Jadox Griffin, for all you have done for Draven and our kind while I have been...away."

Her beauty captured all my words, and they stayed lodged in my throat. She was the nymph of earth, my kind—our protector. We were safe now. A deep longing to touch her vibrated through me. As if she knew, she smiled again and stroked a finger against my cheek. Warmth, extra strength, and power catapulted into my chest, shocking my system.

"You've done well, Jadox. It's almost over—you're near the end."

So many questions lingered on the tip of my tongue. Did she mean my life was near the end? I swallowed and pushed out babbled words, "Is it...is it destined that I would sacrifice my life for Kyra on the Teal Moon?"

"Nothing is truly fated. You will have a choice."

My chest cramped tight. "But will it save her? Will the darkness leave her if I die?"

"It is not my story to write."

She ran a soft hand through my hair, almost like Gemm did when I was a boy. For some reason, I even saw flecks of Gemm's brown color in Surh-Sig's knowing eyes like they were one and the same.

Caspian pushed through the tall stems, holding a hand over his eye.

"Is she okay?" He stooped next to Kyra's sleeping body and hovered a hand over her head but seemed afraid to touch her.

"She's alive...for now." Surh-Sig frowned and glanced around at the mess on the abandoned street. "You need to find a safe place to hide. Elana and Moroka are nearby. And I can feel Oniskel calling me. I must go to my sister."

Her sister....

My sister....

"Do you know where Alaska is?" I asked.

Surh-Sig plucked a single flower out of her hair and tucked it behind my ear. "Sometimes, when we are lost, the only way to be found is to keep roaming through the maze."

Apparently, Surh-Sig spoke in riddles like Gemm too.

I sighed and glanced down at Kyra—so small and sweet when she slept. My heart jerked with love at the very sight of her. Nilson joined us and looked as if he were about to scoop her into his arms, but he froze, then backed away. He pressed his lips together and stared at the orange chateau building glowing brightly under the sun.

"Surh-Sig is right. Let's get inside," Nilson said. "We're too exposed, and I'm surprised the Ordull army hasn't shown up."

Surh-Sig waved a hand over both Caspian and Nilson. Caspian's open wounds closed shut, but his eye would forever be missing. Nilson's shoulders relaxed as the wave of healing power ran over his other injuries.

Caspian lifted his backpack and nodded ahead. "I know a place to hide. Narelle sent me a message with the address of a safe house. We can come back for the prisoners after we get help."

"I need to go to Oniskel now." Surh-Sig's voice sounded like a poem in itself.

"Will you come back?" I had the urge to follow her to the end of the earth.

"Yes, and hopefully, Oniskel will join me. We still need to revert Moroka."

We watched Surh-Sig wake Ashes and mount her back. The further they flew, the shorter the flowers became until the Magikal plants vanished completely. They rose and soared away.

Kyra stirred, mumbling under her breath. "Jay?"

"I'm here, Kyra."

She looked up and gasped, scanning Caspian's face. "Oh my goddess, oh my goddess, I did that, didn't I? No, no, no. I'm so sorry." She dipped her head down. "I'm so sorry."

Caspian crossed his arms. He stared down the road where trash rolled in front of a dumpster, then trudged away.

She trembled slightly, but at least her skin was still fiery hot. "I can't do this anymore, Jay."

Her tears flowed freely. She was never one to cry so openly. Seeing her break down shattered my heart into shards of glass sharper than diamonds. I was failing her. This darkness was rotting her from the inside out, devouring the woman I adored.

"We're almost done. Surh-Sig is an earth nymph again. You did it." I tried to keep my voice light, disguising the heaviness clamping down.

Her eyes turned red, and she didn't bother wiping her cheeks. "No, I can't keep fighting it. The Ȼsµwi Magik has won. It's implanted so deep in here," she squeaked out through sobs, pointing to her chest. "It's just who I am."

"Kyra, we can defeat it." My words sped out as my mind spiraled. "That spell should turn you into a nymph too. You must be the fire nymph. It's the only one left. All we need is more lava from the volcano and…, and I can sacrifice another finger."

Kyra looked at my hand with a confused look. "Wait, what was the sacrifice?"

Nilson uncrossed his arms and held up the hand that had a stub.

Her hand covered her mouth in shock. "How?"

Nilson shrugged, trying to keep his eyes off her. But I could tell. He loved her too, and it was real. Maybe we aren't destined for one soul mate in our lives. It was like Gemm advised me years ago, *"You choose someone and work hard to make it work. No two people are fated to live a happily ever after."* Kyra had chosen me, and I'd fight for us, no matter what challenges stood in our way, even if a piece of her heart always belonged to a Vayuian.

She stared at Nilson's face, then searched mine. "Jay, I need to go. This has gotten out of hand."

My breathing quickened. "What? What do you mean *go?*"

"I can't let this *thing* inside me hurt you or Caspian or…Isaac or anyone again."

I couldn't breathe, so instead, I just stared.

"Kyra, your place is where I am." I took her hands.

"It's okay, Jay. I've already asked so much of you." Her sniffles stopped. "I'll do it myself. It's okay."

"Do what?" I pulled her closer. "You're scaring me, Kyra."

"You don't think *I'm* scared, Jay? I'm a monster."

"No, no, you're…my roots…my—"

She put up a hand. "Don't. There's no other choice but to go."

I stood, outraged, ready to fight the fuckin' weight bearing down on my chest. "So where will you go? To Brent's? Nope, he left you as a child! To Caspian's place? Is Cydon your home? No, you took out his eye!"

"Jay—" Her sobbing started again.

"Where's your home, Kyra? Is it in Gemm's den? Nope because she's dead! Landon can't take care of you. He's too young! Where will you go, Kyra? Where?"

"You're angry." She nodded and stood on shaky legs.

My chest heaved up and down as I pinned her with my stare. "I'm not angry, Kyra. I'm devastated. If you leave, I have no purpose."

She slid forward and buried her forehead in my chest. "I'll stay until Elana is dead. Then I need to go. I'm not like the other demons. Since I can't be converted back to something that I never was."

"You're not a demon, Petal."

"My soul is sick; it's eating me alive from the inside. Do you want that for me? Do you want me at war with myself every day?"

"No." Hot tears streamed from the corner of my eyes, and I wrapped my arms around her back, crushing her to my chest. "No, Divinities, no."

"Then you'll have to let me go."

An entire century passed in one moment as I sucked in the courage to respond, "Okay." I choked out the two syllables that would utterly destroy me.

"And you have to make me one last promise."

"Petal, please." My tears fell atop her golden hair.

"If I get too out of control and lose myself completely…if I don't remember this conversation or hurt someone else I love…you have to kill me."

I pushed her away, my entire body shaking. "Stop it."

She stepped forward, one hand reaching to my heart. It felt like a claw was digging through my chest, breaking my ribs apart and prying my heart from its cavity.

"Don't say that again. No, Kyra, you can't ask me to do that."

"Jay, I have to be able to count on you." Her face turned more determined, and her red-rimmed, honey eyes lingered on mine. "Maybe if you shatter the Elidi Ruby to pieces, that might work. Yes…" She nodded. "I can feel it. That'll work."

Memories poured onto me like raindrops. Holding her hand for the first time. Helping her steal outfits from Alaska's closet. The way her eyes lit up when she had returned Landon from the Abyss. The way she led me through tunnels and caves without an ounce of hesitation. Her snarky jokes. How was I supposed to go on without her in my life?

"Promise me." She rose on her tiptoes and kissed my chin. "Please, Jay. I trust you more than I trust myself right now."

I squeezed my eyes shut and inhaled deeply, catching a whiff of her hair. "I promise."

What I wouldn't tell her was that if that were to ever happen, it'd be the second to last thing I'd ever do. Because my next move would be to ram a dagger straight through my own chest.

21

KYRA

Scritch, scritch. Click, click.

Bizarre mechanical sounds caught my attention from a high window. Something dark flew out toward us. Then another. A third.

"Watch out!" I pointed up.

All three men whipped around, already in a fighting stance. Wind encompassed Isaac, water beaded at Caspian's fingertips, and Jay stretched his hands toward the distant forest line.

But it was too late. The dark objects were giant electrical nets. They dropped and wrapped around each of the men, encompassing them completely. All evidence of their powers disappeared.

"Run!" Jay yelled at me as he flopped inside the net that slowly lifted him off the ground. "Run, Kyra!"

Their nets rose, floating toward the window as if tethered by an invisible cord. Isaac's face turned red from trying to rip his netting apart. Caspian sat in the middle of his, already defeated and out of breath. And Jay's muscles strained as he clutched the netting and shook it fiercely back and forth.

"Get out of here!" Jay yelled.

"I'm not leaving you." Fire burst from my hands, and I chucked flame after flame at the open window.

"Stupid girl." Elana stuck her head out the window; a devil's face infected with corruption scowled at me.

Three of the Mystier necklaces hung around her neck, leaving me to wonder where Alaska was with the emerald.

I cast one more pathetic flame at Elana, hoping to set her alight, but it disintegrated halfway, its orange sparks fading. Marching footsteps approached from around the corners of the other downtown buildings. The Ordull army emerged, glaring, with guns pointed at me.

"Let them go!" I roared at Elana.

She laughed and taunted me, "Now, why would I do that?" With a quick wave, all three men in the nets soared through a window out of view. "Climb up and chat, child."

I braced, waiting for a net to spring out and capture me too, but nothing happened. For once, I didn't want to rush into action without thinking. I glared up at the window, contemplating my options. I needed to rescue Jay, Isaac, and Caspian before anything else happened. But how? Where was Alaska when I needed her? I picked up the broken vial container with its sharp edges. A possible weapon.

"Are you coming, child?" Elana rested her elbow on the window frame and grinned. "Or will you save yourself and abandon all the males in your life? Again."

I stepped toward the front staircase, and a group of soldiers made a half-circle around me.

"Good girl."

As I scaled the chateau's front stoop, I had an overbearing feeling of being watched. I turned toward the street. There was nothing. No one.

"Hurry up, Golden One." One soldier nudged her long gun against my back.

The soldier was wrong about calling me the Golden One. I was cursed from the inside out and didn't deserve any special title. Maybe another Mystier would've been strong enough to resist the darkness. But not me.

We stepped inside the main lobby. Memories flashed back to the ball—the day I found out that Elana had wiped Jay's memories—the same day I found out my little brother was still alive.

The ₵sµwi surged stronger as we climbed a spiral staircase to the second floor. Up to the third. Up. Elana must die tonight because I couldn't hold out against the darkness much longer. Even if I didn't have much time left, I'd still go down swinging. No one had the right to capture prisoners and lock them in a basement for experiments, sentence Mystiers to the electric chair, or steal Jay's memory and countless other unforgivable crimes.

You need to run, Ky.

No, Cas, don't ask me to do that.

It's too late.

I'm not leaving you three.

There's no way to free us.

There was no point in arguing. If anything, I needed to apologize to my brother for torturing him. My heart hurt thinking of how much pain he had felt when I ripped out his eye.

Stop beating yourself up, Ky. It's fine.

It's not fine. I can feel your rage. How could you say that?

It wasn't really you *hurting me.*

I'm so sorry, Caspian.

You're really not going to leave?

No.

Once I turned Moroka back into a water nymph, we would have extra help. All I needed was a piece of her. My legs burned from the stairs on the fourth floor, and my chest rose and fell harder.

"This way." One soldier led me down the hall to a closed door.

I hovered my hand over the knob, unsure of the scene that awaited me on the other side. Had Elana already hurt one of them? I still had the chance to try and run. Instead, I turned the handle and walked inside.

The chimney crackled with fire this time, and the smell of chlorine hit my nostrils from the bubbling tub holding Moroka. I scanned the room. Jay, Isaac, and Caspian weren't there. My breath hitched in a sudden panic.

"Where are they?"

"Don't you have other questions first?" Elana gestured to the contraption that I had failed to process until now.

She sat on her hoverchair with a tube inserted into her wrist. The cord extended over into the shadows. She tugged it a bit and moved someone into the light. Caspian. Her tube was hooked to his wrist. Elana had strapped Caspian to a different hoverboard. The sleek metal reminded me of something. I gasped, recognizing it. Caspian sat on an electric chair.

Are you hurt?

I asked Caspian through our bond.

He shook his head slowly, but I wasn't sure if he was lying.

"Let him go!" I screamed my fury.

"I think not. I will keep him for a while since Caspian was so kind as to replace your father."

A groaning sound came from the shadows, and a silhouette moved on the ground. I pushed through the soldiers and fell to my knees. Brent rolled over, barely alive, his face ashen, sucked dry of life. My father clutched his stomach in pain and gaped at me, eyes void of spark.

My heart rammed harder. I was losing too much. The soldiers pulled me away from my moaning father, back to the spot where the sunset created a spotlight on the floor.

"Listen to me carefully, child." Elana leaned forward, making hers and Caspian's hoverboards move. "I will only offer this once. We can be a team, and you can be my second in command. We will create a new colony of Golden Ones. I recently learned Isaac also has enhancements. Moroka has finally agreed to bestow my entire line with powers unlike anyone has ever imagined. Elidians will finally rule, and all of our children and their children will be blessed with the Blood Maiden's gifts. My legacy will blossom, and you can be next to me to witness our greatness."

I'd never agree, but I had to get her to keep talking. I moved closer to Moroka and hid the glass piece behind my back.

"Which one are you so gracious to give me? Jay or Isaac?"

Elana smiled and rubbed her thumb along the three necklaces. "Good question. We're going to play a little game, child."

I inched toward Moroka again slowly, the floor creaking under my feet. She lapped up the blood tears that trickled down her cheeks.

"See those two doors?" Elana pointed to the wall where two doors lay on either side.

I hadn't noticed them before since they blended into the wall, but I nodded.

"The Dravian soldier is behind one door, and the Vayuian is behind the other. Whichever you open will be your mate. You can get started tomorrow. We need to hurry."

"If I agree...." I paused for a moment, unsure whether to move closer to the doors or toward Moroka. "...Then you have to promise no harm will come to them."

"Of course, child, I need them strong and sturdy for...you know."

"And I want you to free all the prisoners from the basement."

"No." She frowned. "We're done negotiating. Now pick."

My jaw tightened. I stared at both doors. No noise came from behind either. If I was still Linked with either of them, then I'd know who was where.

Cas? Do you know?

Does it matter, Ky? You loved them both once. Could you hand either of them over to her?

My chest constricted. If I were a saint, I'd have a different answer.

Tell me, Caspian.

They put Griffin on the left. But, Ky...

I lunged for the left and hovered my hand over the door. Something felt wrong, off. It didn't matter. Waiting wasn't an option. I twisted the handle, my heart beating wildly, and swung open the door. My stomach dropped. Isaac stared up at me on his knees, bound and gagged by electrical wires.

"Great choice." Elana laughed. "Isaac will get you pregnant, hopefully with twins, and I'll take the Draven man to my bed tonight."

Isaac's eyes widened in horror, and he shook his head back and forth, grunting a warning into his gag. Just then, green gas oozed out of his hands. I backed up. Unnatural. The electric wires couldn't contain his unnatural Magik, just like my Link with Caspian. I opened the other door. Jay knelt with bruises on his face and fresh scratches near his throat.

"I'm going to kill her." Pulling the gag out of his mouth, I whispered, "Remember what you promised."

"Kyra, no!" Jay tried to rise, but his ankles were bound. "Don't breathe it in!"

It was the very last thing I wanted to do. Fear cycloned through me with such fierceness I could barely breathe, but I sucked in a deep inhale of Isaac's toxins and filled my lungs with the delicious elixir. Time ticked down. Flames sparked at my fingertips, then disintegrated. I needed more fuel. What was unnatural? The depths of Bukti Volcano! I summoned its lava to my palm. The second it appeared, I threw my power at Elana. She needed to burn, scar, and scream. But her necklaces protected her with an invisible shield, and the lava bounced off.

"Stop her!" Elana yelled.

The soldiers exchanged hesitant glances, worried about approaching me as I summoned more lava out of thin air. Jay shouted for me to leave, to run, but I tuned him out. I jumped to Moroka, still tied tight, and collected her tears in the curved piece of glass.

"Stop her!" Elana yelled.

The room darkened. The soldiers started to advance, but I screamed, "Back off!"

I juggled lava in one hand and the bottle of tears in the other. Deep within, my heart wrestled with the monster trying to claim me. I glanced from Jay to Isaac; all I needed was a sacrifice. Someone had to make a sacrifice of love.

At that moment, a bird soared outside, catching my attention. The faint outline of the Teal Moon taunted me. It felt like my heart had stopped.

"*No*," I whispered.

How was it the Teal Moon already? My very breath left my lungs. A tightness attacked my chest. We never should've come here. I never should've tried to save anyone. Nothing was worth losing the love of my life. Nothing.

Ky, it's okay. I'll be the sacrifice.

Caspian's words through our Link stopped me short.

Just...remember me...and our good times.

Caspian reached down to the voltage nozzle on his electric chair.

"Don't you dare. I just got you back."

His smile made him look younger as he whispered, "You were always a good sister, but this is the only way. I must cut off her life source, or you'll never win."

"Caspian! *No*!"

"Goodbye, Ky. Take care of Dad."

Caspian flipped the switch. His neck flailed back. He twitched and convulsed, breaking my heart with every movement.

A sharp sensation stabbed my core, and I bent in half. Each deadly jerk of his body made my bones shudder. Our Link was splitting. I held on. Unwilling to let go.

It'll be okay, Ky. Tell Narelle I love her.

He slumped over. Still. Deathly still.

Each of my ragged breaths felt like a dagger in my chest.

"No!" Elana screamed and pulled the tube out of her wrist. "What have you done?"

I stared at Caspian. Shocked. Frozen. Impossible. My knees buckled. A whimpering sounded like a lost animal puffed from my lips. Swaying, my side rammed into the side of the wall. The bottle of tears almost slipped from my clammy hands.

"Kyra..." Someone far off yet so close was saying something. Something important.

"You ruined everything!" Elana hollered.

"Kyra, finish the spell," someone said. "Don't waste his death."

Death? Impossible. Frozen, I stared at my little brother.

"Kyra. Hurry!" Jay. It was Jay who was telling me to do something.

What did I have to do? Why was I there? There must be some mistake. My brother wasn't dead. He couldn't be. He died when I was five. He had left me once before. Caspian wouldn't leave me again. My little brother.

A scream tore my throat apart, and I darted to him, ready to shake him awake.

"Kyra! The lava in your hand. Do it, Kyra!"

With my whole body shaking and my heart hammering, I glanced at my hands. What was I holding? A bottle of blood? No, Moroka's tears.

"Seize her!"

"Kyra!" A man yelled. "Come on, Kyra, come back. Think of Landon!"

Visions exploded in my mind of the innocent boy who relied on me to make his world safe again. I needed to convert Moroka. In a daze, I stood over Caspian's sleeping body. He was only sleeping. Sleeping. He'd wake up. I poured my handful of lava and the bottle of crimson tears onto his brown hair at the same time. The ancient spell whispered through my soul like a long-lost lullaby. I chanted softly, tears rolling down my cheeks. But that didn't make any sense. There was no reason to cry. He was fine. Caspian was okay. There was no other option.

The hot lava trickled down Caspian's face and into his empty eye socket. I choked on a sob and fell to my knees before him. I grabbed Caspian's legs and shook them.

"Wake up!"

"Seize her!"

"Wake up, please." I tried to talk to him through the Link, urging him to wake up, but there was only silence.

Rough hands groped at me from all angles, and a tangled cord wrapped around my neck. Electricity surged through me, and I fell to my side, shaking.

"Kyra!" Jay yelled.

"Avanido muati," I whispered feebly.

A soldier draped a heavy net on top of me. It twisted me until it cocooned me like a wrapped blanket.

In the corner of the room, a bright blue light projected onto the ceiling. Too exhausted to care, I met Jay's eyes across the room.

"It's the Teal Moon, it's the Teal Moon," I repeated again and again. "I didn't know it was the Teal Moon. Caspian is gone."

His face twisted in agony. He was speechless.

A mermaid's tale flapped in the hot tub, sending water onto the floor. A face made of legends, covered in seashells, surfaced. The nymph's thick blonde hair was twisted in a braid sprinkled in the sand, and Moroka's eyes were bluer than even Caspian's.

"Please, please defeat her," I croaked, barely able to speak. "Please, kill Elana and get this over with."

"We don't kill." Her voice held the language of dolphins and sea turtles. "We only give gifts."

"Then give the gift of stopping Elana's tyranny!" Jay yelled.

"We only bless."

"You can't be serious right now. After…after Caspian gave up his —" I choked on a sob.

"It must be you, Golden One."

"I'm not Golden!" I screamed and looked anywhere but at Caspian's hunched form. "Fuck this! You were worth more to me as a demon."

Elana took the ruby from her hoverchair and connected it to a wire. The wrapped around me and hung me from my waist.

"There, now you are trapped by your own gem." Her smile rose, but I didn't care. "Just as I trapped the others eighty years ago." She turned to Moroka. "And, instead of changing you back to a demon, I'll just kill you."

Elana readjusted her crystal and pearl necklaces and spoke to her soldiers, but I was barely listening. Caspian was dead. Gemm had been right about her prophecy. A man who loved me would lay down his life on the Teal Moon. Why did the sacrifice have to his life, though? This wasn't fair. Blood-red sunset clouds shifted in the sky.

Was it an omen of what more was to come or a way to mourn what I had already lost?

"Let's go," Elana directed the soldiers to drag Jay out of the room. "Time to play together."

I couldn't look at Jay. She'd take him to her bed tonight, and I could not stop it. It didn't matter that my great-grandmother was a hundred years old because she lived in the body of a thirty-five-year-old. She'd use all her powers against him to get her way. Jay was her new sex slave.

I squeezed my eyes shut, unwilling to think. "Please, don't leave me here with my brother," I choked out.

Elana's smile was evident in her words. "I think this is the perfect punishment for trying to act out against me. Plus, you can spend quality time with your father before he passes. It seems like you two have more in common than you might realize. Good night, child. Sleep well."

22

KYRA

A chill entered through the crooked window, but I didn't care because nothing mattered anymore, and if my heart stopped beating right now, it would be a gift to end all this torture. Wires dug into my skin, and Elana was currently fucking Jay somewhere in this goddess-forsaken prison riding him and moaning and touching his skin. The agony that ripped through me at the image was almost pleasant compared to the anguish that beat against my soul when I looked at Caspian's body below me.

Misery gutted me like a crow slashing its claws at a slithering snake and devouring it in the seductive night. The pounding in my head was my only sense of still being alive because hints of ghosts and crumbs of slaughter wrapped themselves around my neck in a chain of pure ugliness and squeezed tight. He was dead, so the ceiling should cave in on me, and the spiderwebs hanging from the wall could be my noose.

Dead.

Dead. Gone. Hollow. *Erased.*

The night was silent as the hours ticked by. All of Andersonville was undoubtedly asleep, except for the screams repeating in my head. Phantom silhouettes loomed like violent shadows on the crooked wall, haunting me with the impossible shape of my brother. The culprit teased me with Elana's words ringing in my ears like a nonstop bell, but how could any of this be real, and what was the point?

Ugly suffocation. No air. Sickness from my head to my toes withered my soul and left me completely distraught with all-encompassing desolation that crushed my lungs. Regret spilled into my mouth, drowning me. Good. Die. Die. Just make it all stop.

Please, please, please take me too because I couldn't deal with the memories that turned sour in my mouth and the harsh plea grasping at my spirit to scratch my neck to shreds until nothing was left of me. Dead. Gone. Dead. And gone.

"Kyra…."

Please. If anyone cared about me, just stomp on my skull or slice me to pieces with a menacing blade because I couldn't go on anymore—there was no use fighting back when he was taken.

Taken. Taken. Taken.

"*Fuck*!" I screamed and wrestled against the cords trapping me.

"Kyra, take a deep breath," Brent croaked out the words through wheezes. He was somewhere in the shadows, below the net entangling me.

But why bother? The malicious moonlight shone through the window, but if the sun never rose again, maybe that was for the best. I should never have converted Moroka but let her eat me alive and drain my blood because her teeth in my neck would be the needed release to end all this turmoil. It was my fault. Mine. Always.

I started it all when I wished the males away and made so many people perish. No matter how many times I shook my head to erase the memories, all I saw were Hallie dead, Gemm dead, and Caspian dead. Who knows how many others would be in pain in this war, too? And then the person I needed to protect was being used this very moment with the devil's hands on his chest and Elana's hair falling over his shoulders and fucking him and…I couldn't breathe…couldn't breathe…please, help me leave this place. This world.

A massacre of sharpness curled around my tattoos and sucked out my source of life, and I still couldn't breathe, couldn't…. I peered at

Caspian again. Unmoving. Stone-still. A murderous orchestra strummed a poisonous tune in my head, warping me with acute sorrow that made no sense and twisted into a poem of loss that would be forgotten because no one is truly remembered because nothing matters, so why bother?

The sobs finally stopped. No more tears were left in my body to fall. Air whistled through the cracks in the walls.

Threats of eternal emptiness loomed over my soul like an eerie slaughterhouse that held weapons stored for slashing and striking to kill.

Creaking bedsprings echoed in my ears, and terrorizing images flashed in my mind. I wished I could take away all his panic, and why won't my heart stop racing? If only I knew the last time I kissed Jay was our last time, I would've savored it and never let him go, keeping him in a safe place forever so no evil would ever hurt those I love. Instead, rotten vultures came and abducted everything I needed and wanted, but why, why, why….

Elana was stealing our chance, stealing our future to spend the next fifty Luna Festivals together. My heart felt like it had been physically torn in half. Our future was ripped away, and I wanted to fight, but everything was numb and pointless.

My body was shaking. I just wanted to fade away fast and never look back. I wanted to forget the sliver of hope in my pocket to return the rest of the males, to free the prisoners, to live a life with my family, but a bruised heart that was streaked with loneliness was not meant to endure this much.

If only the Ꮯsμwi would overtake me now, swallow me whole, then I'd never need to remember this type of aching again. An ache that resonated so deeply and caged me in purgatory, which I felt deep in my bones.

Couldn't breathe…

Everything was collapsing around me. There was no escaping, and I wanted to tear out my nasty hair, punch a wall, and carve out my own eyes, this time to beg for forgiveness, but he was no longer here to talk to.

Brent coughed weakly and groaned. I couldn't help my father either, so he'd die right in front of me too, and I'd have to watch the final breath leave his chest as his glassy eyes stared at the ceiling. Maybe if Brent died and stayed in the shadows, I'd be saved from the torment of staring at him all night too.

Ravens crowed a deep promise of doom in the shade outside the window. A clouded future without Caspian or Jay stole any ounce of happiness straight from my chest. I'd heard Caspian's voice and Jay's heartbeat for the last time. They had both been taken, so why did anything matter?

I wasn't able to endure this life anymore. Weak. My chest clamped so tight that I swore I was having a heart attack, panic crushing me from the inside out in a sweet release.

Kill me, I wanted to call out, "Just kill me now," because Jay wasn't here, and Caspian wasn't here, and I'd be alone.

"You're not alone. I'm here."

Brent.

Was I talking out loud? I didn't even know because nothing made sense. I hated the world, despised Elana, and needed it all to go away because if she was raping Jay and sliding onto his body again and again, I wouldn't be able to bear it.

"Alone." After all, more tears must have been possible because they stung my cheeks, hot and real.

"Kyra, shh, my baby girl, breathe," Brent said softly, repeating it over and over like a lullaby. "Shh, breathe."

"Please, please, please," I whispered from within the hanging net for who knew how long until everything slipped into darkness, and sleep gulped me down whole.

Hopefully, for the last time.

23

KYRA

I awoke, exhausted and sore, in the same room of The Crooked Chateau. I was still cloaked in darkness, yet the sunrise was imminent from the birds' songs outside. My foot was numb from cramped in the electrical netting, my lips were chapped, and my stomach rumbled. If someone didn't let me down soon, I'd piss all over myself.

I looked down from my high position, tangled in the cocoon. Caspian's body remained untouched, unmoved. I sighed deeply and scanned the shadows. Brent lay in the same spot as last night, near the quiet fireplace, his chest rising and falling slowly. Still alive.

I didn't even remember when and how Moroka left the hot tub. Did the soldiers haul her away last night? Could water nymphs survive on land?

Then again, I didn't recall Isaac leaving either. Was he waiting for me in bed somewhere? He was my new designated mate, after all, unless I managed to free us. How did Isaac feel about our forced circumstance? I might have loved Isaac once, but he didn't fully have my heart.

"Kyra," Brent mumbled. "Kyra."

"I'm here."

He grunted and rolled over onto his back, his arms limp at his side. "My son—"

"Is dead," I finished.

"...Was a hero," he corrected.

"What good was his sacrifice? Elana's alive. Jay is with her. Moroka left us."

"We've all got an inner beast. The water nymph has been trapped in hers for eighty years. Give her some time."

"We don't have time!"

"You're hanging from the ceiling. Until I find the strength to stand, all we have is time."

A shudder ripped through me at the thought of Elana's victorious grin and the pain of facing Jay again. Did she hurt him? Tears bloomed behind my lids again, but I no longer had the luxury of grieving. Elana's troops would charge in here and rope me to Isaac's bed any moment now.

Brent dragged his body passed Caspian, closer to the table in the room. A thin trail of blood followed him, streaking a line across the floor where the first morning rays beamed through the window. At this point, I wished I could erase all traces of Magik from my body—natural or not. If I was able to heal my father, he'd be able to stand, but no energy surged through my Circles.

"Tell me...why did you wish all males away?" Brent asked. "Was it because I erased your memories of me? Had you started to gain some of them back?" My father's earnest face surprised me. "Did you wish men away because you hated me?"

His question felt genuine, and his admission of stealing my memory was painfully blunt, so I simply said, "No."

He grappled with the leg of the table and pulled himself to his side weakly. "Then why? Did someone hurt you?"

"Yes, once, it seemed like all men had hurt me. My band manager, my ex-boyfriend, the man I *thought* was my father...."

Early pastel light shone through the window as a welcome to a fresh day, but I wanted to stay lost in the shadows. Brent winced as he rose to his knees, swaying slightly. His knuckles were white as he clutched the tabletop.

"I'm sorry they hurt you, Kyra, and I'm sorry I had to leave when you were so young."

"I understand why. But, how...how could you erase my memory?"

"I only took bits and pieces."

"The pieces of you. Pieces that would've given me hope."

His face contorted into an expression I couldn't place. "If you knew I was handing myself over to Elana to protect you, you'd hunt her down until you found me. I wanted you to live a happy, normal life with your mother and brother." He staggered to a stand, knees shaking. "That was one blessing of the deal I made, that you both didn't know about Magik until later than most Mystiers."

Witnessing my father rise, despite all the years Elana had stolen from him and the memories and pride he lost by that witch's hand, made a twinge of energy spark my Circles.

"Everyone makes mistakes, Kyra. Maybe I should've let you remember me, but asking 'what if' is pointless, don't you think?" Hunched over, he leaned against the top of the table, out of breath, his skin ashen white. "I chose between sacrificing myself or letting Elana have you or Caspian. Either way, she would've caused me pain. I'd rather suffer than let you."

I sniffed back a tear. "Is this the time you give me some lame enlightened speech about never giving up, seeing the light, or forgiving everyone from my past?"

He smiled and took an unsteady step toward me, dragging the table like a cane. The legs scratched loudly against the floor.

"No, baby girl. I don't need to give you a speech."

I wished I could reach my nose to wipe it. "And why is that?"

"Because you already have the answers you need."

I pressed my lips together and watched him trudge across the empty room at a snail's pace—each wobbly step accompanied by a *screech* of the table's leg. Step. *Screech*. Step. *Screech*.

Any soldier within a mile's radius would have heard that, but no one came running. Instead, the sun rose higher, the birds chirped louder, and the day continued without Caspian by my side. This was a sunrise Caspian would never see, a date in time he would never experience.

"Why did you pick me over Caspian?" I asked.

He sighed. "Kyra, you're so strong, so fierce, just like your brother. But, since the day you were born, you had this rare light within you, a zest for life and what matters most."

"What matters most?"

"Passion. Your soul sings…so brightly. When you were angry, that rage blazed to the other end of Lodesa." He smiled to himself. "When you cried, your voice could be heard from every corner of our world. You possessed the energy of thousands in one little heart."

I waited, processed, then finally admitted, "I think while I was growing up, I was targeting my anger toward the wrong person."

"Oh, really? And who should you have aimed your daggers at?"

"Myself. I hated *myself* for not loving *myself*." I chuckled humorlessly at the ridiculous irony. "I couldn't accept my resentment, making it seem like men were the villains. Obviously, some of them did horrendous things, but I held onto so much anger." I paused, trying to find the right words. "I didn't allow myself to figure out my feelings but rather let the rage overcome it, so everything worsened. I tried to hide who I was and cover up the mess with a brick wall around my heart."

"It sounds like you wanted to love yourself but hate your shadows. But, baby girl, they're one and the same. We all have a bit of darkness."

"Yeah…we all have a little bit of darkness."

Our eyes locked on one another.

"I've got an idea." Brent limped until he was just under me. "Scream. Let it all out now."

"What? No, you're crazy. They'll hear us."

"It'll help if you scream." He braced his side against the edge of the table. "You can't stomp or punch me or break something up there, but if you hold onto that anger, it'll be a poison inside that will consume you."

"I don't have the energy to scream."

"Yes, you do."

Brent sucked in a deep breath and yelled at the top of his lungs. The deep sound bounced off the walls as if every jugosaur bellowed together. Every vein in his neck bulged, threatening to snap. When his strained face turned red, and his voice finally gave out, he slumped in half onto the table, chest heaving.

I gaped, unsure if he had officially lost his mind.

"Come on," he smiled gently, "join me."

"No."

"Yes."

"It's pointless."

"Trust me. You used to trust me when you held onto my pinky with your whole hand."

"Brent—"

"Can you call me 'Dad' just once, as you used to before my body gives out?"

I snorted. "Right, you'll be just another person to leave me."

"Kyra, release it. Give me the pain; let it out."

"If I do it once, will you stop asking?"

"Sure." He smiled, "I'm about to die anyways. A dead man can't talk."

I sucked in a breath, glanced at the brightness through the window, and let out an explosive scream. I roared into the emptiness consuming me. My body tensed. It scratched my throat. My temples pulsed. My chest constricted. Just when I was about to run out of air, my Circles tingled, and the net shredded apart. I dropped with a thump to the hard floor.

Panting, I rose to my knees. I was free, but not really. Grief overwhelmed me. I was about to lose my father next. And I wasn't strong enough to prevent it.

Brent shoved the table over and said, "Here, baby girl, use this," then he sat on the floor, unable to hold himself up without it.

I kicked the table leg. It snapped apart. The table topped to the side. My knuckles clenched around the wood like a bat. With a scream, I beat the table again and again until a giant dent formed in the side. I screamed and hit. Screamed and struck. Screamed and destroyed. Wood splintered. The splinters dug into my palm. Sweat dripped. Wood flew through the room. I screamed more and thrashed. The battered table absorbed the rest of my pain.

I whimpered and dropped to my knees. "Dad, I don't want to hold onto this anymore."

"Come here, baby," I'll take it all for you.

I went to him.

Brent cradled me to his chest. My tears soaked his shirt. How freeing it was, letting go at last.

Eventually, Brent laughed softly as he petted my hair. "You've got some pipes, Kyra."

I made a strangled sound, stuck between a laugh and a cry, then said, "Yeah, you wouldn't know since you missed *all* of my shows."

He laughed deep from his belly, and I joined in like a lost lunatic, both of us holding each other tight. "I'm sorry, baby girl, but I'm not sure I'll be able to see your next show either."

"I don't want to lose you too."

Even if the others were gone, I was still here. Alive. Powerful. I'd save my father. Five gray Circles scorched my skin. I swallowed and met his eyes.

He nodded knowingly, a sly smirk forming on the edge of his mouth as he said, "There's my girl."

I needed all my strength, all my power. Nothing could belong to the Link anymore, severed or not. I had to solve my problems on my own. If Caspian currently floated in the Abyss, I decided to send one last message with our Link and let him go.

Goodbye, Caspian.

The responding silence was deafening, but I imagined the breeze taking my words to the sea so he could hear them.

I climbed and stood on the tipsy table, then pulled down the Elidi Ruby, still wrapped up in the cords. So much mysterious power was harnessed in such a little gem. What else was it capable of? Maybe it couldn't confine me like Elana had assumed because I wasn't truly the fire nymph that they had all expected me to be.

What was the meaning of the fifth Circle if there were four elements? How had I not considered that before? Maybe I didn't have to be who they wanted me to be. Maybe I was someone different: an angel of the night or the nymph of shadows. I'd be boundless if I stopped fighting myself and gave the cursed Magik free reign.

There was no reason to be afraid of what lingered within me because, with acceptance, I'd be able to conquer the dangers of the ₾sμwi, too, until I was my own master. Darkness and all, I'd accept myself, step by step, one day at a time, even if it took an eternity.

With that thought, all five Circles shot with a fierce bolt of energy. Newfound power washed through me, and I welcomed it, closing my eyes and receiving the ₾sμwi Magik meant for my soul. I laid a hand on my dad's shoulder and slowly chanted the healing spell, *"Terra angakok. Terra angakok."*

Memories of the first time Jay used the spell gave me extra strength. Even when he wasn't here, Jay fueled me.

"Terra angakok. Terra angakok." My voice grew louder and louder, and the sun's rays warmed my skin from the window.

Brent grunted and gasped. I snapped my eyes open and met my dad's gaze, alight with hope. His hands roamed his body as the color returned to his face. "You did it, baby girl. I knew you could. Thank you."

"What are daughters for?" I nudged his side, but he was as solid as a brick. Immovable.

"Now, let me repay you." Brent eased into my mind.

His enhancement was stronger than any other I had encountered. The fireplace, hot tub, and table were in shambles. All fell away. In their place, snippets of the past rolled like a vintage video.

A boy around age ten, with messy brown hair and eyes the color of the sea, laughs and splashes in the waves with a young girl who looks awfully like Narelle. My brother.

. . .

My heart twisted in gratitude that Brent showed me glimpses of Caspian's childhood. Then it switched.

Caspian, as a teen, obtaining his blue Möbius Circle and feeling the powers of the sea for the first time. The pride and joy exuding from him are as radiant as the sun flowing through me, as if I am there myself. A few years flip by, and Caspian tests his ability to hold his breath for long durations. He surfaces with excitement as Narelle shows him a stopwatch. Caspian stands taller and broader, with a long scar down the side of his face. He is in front of a crowded room. He bows his head slightly as the group erupts in cheers. Their leader.

The memories disappeared as quickly as they came, and I staggered back. My brother. He had served Cydon well, keeping them protected, and was loved by many. Just like I had loved him all those years without knowing he was safe and then had the gift of spending just a bit more time with him.

"Thank you for showing me his memories."

"Of course, Kyra. When we have more time, I'll show you more." Brent cracked his knuckles. "There's one memory he gave me that will have you rolling on the floor with laughter."

"He gave you those?"

"Yes, baby girl. I don't take what's not given to me...anymore."

I wouldn't let Caspian's sacrifice be in vain. After all, with all the elements swirling through me, coated with a hint of heaviness and darkness, I might be more powerful than I gave myself credit for.

I stood, letting out a huge sigh, then stared into the water of the hot tub. My reflection peered back at me with amber eyes, thick brows, and a hopeful expression. A different Kyra lived in that face compared to the Ordull who had stolen money from a band manager, the woman who had watched Hallie die, and the confused girl who had kissed Isaac longingly. I was no longer the same person who had feared cave demons or believed a life without males was preferable.

"Dad?"

"Yes, baby girl?"

"Have you looked inside my mind before?"

"Only when Elana demanded it when we were under the sea in Cydon."

"What did you see?"

He picked up the leg of the table I had used as a bat and handed it over. "Fierceness."

"This could come in handy."

He nodded, shoulders back, seemingly a foot taller than before. My father looked just like Caspian. I had lost a brother but gained a father. And I loved him. I loved males and wanted them in this world. More importantly, I was willing to let the darkness within show all the shapes of my shadows to destroy Elana. And in case I failed, Jay had already promised to end my life for the greater good.

"Come on, Dad, let's go save Jay."

For better or worse, this ended today. I knew what I had to do.

24

JADOX

Morning light shone through the window, illuminating my luxurious bed and the silk sheets covering my bottom half. It was too bad that I was cuffed and unable to escape. Spread on the floor, mounds of pillows served as cushions for the man slaves that women were currently riding. Up and down, up and down.

I was going to be sick. Hours of wondering passed last night about how exactly Elana planned to lift herself atop me when she didn't have legs to support herself. Thank the goddess above that I hadn't found out. Yet.

When I risked glancing at the men, only one had his eyes open, the sole guy enjoying the view of the Ordull bouncing on him.

At least, last night, I had been blessed with the darkness that shadowed their movements. However, that didn't save me from the women's moans and the sounds of bodies slapping together repeatedly. One of the chained prisoners was already on his sixth woman since midnight. A soldier would force the man slave to swallow another pill. Once one woman was satisfied, she'd leave, and another would take her place.

I strained against the electric wires binding my wrists above my head for the hundredth time. *Pop*. Ah, fuck! My shoulder dislocated from its socket, shooting pain down my arm. I refrained from screaming so as not to draw attention to myself. Instead, I bit my lip—hard. The taste of fresh blood wasn't enough to distract me.

I tried to ignore the pain and sniffed the breeze to try and catch any fresh whiff of Kyra's presence. Nothing. Was she still tied in that net? I prayed she had managed to escape and run far away from here. But the wish was pointless because she'd never leave me.

The door opened, and three armed female soldiers pulled a tall, naked man into the room. They each held a thick cord attached to his neck like a leash. How many men did Elana have as prisoners? When the leading guard shifted, a blond bun that haunted my nightmares came into view. They had brought in Isaac Nilson. Of course.

Nilson shuffled forward, barely able to take a full step with the electrical cords strapped around his ankles. His eyes widened at the sight of the couples, his face paling before fury took over his features.

My heartbeat went into overdrive as I tried to study Nilson's face for any proof he had slept with Kyra last night. The tightness in my chest at the agonizing thought of her being forced to do anything she didn't want to coiled so tight that it felt like bricks laid on my sternum. At least with him, she'd be safer than with other men. I could rely on Nilson for that much since I knew he cared. But why would Elana bring him in *here*? Then it occurred to me: the bitch wanted me to watch them together.

Fuck, no! Fuck this. This must be payback. Elana was probably still furious that she couldn't get me hard last night, no matter what she attempted with her hands and mouth or any kind of pill they shoved down my throat.

I pulled my good arm against the wires, hoping my wrist would slip through. I yanked. Heaved. Useless.

"Griffin?"

"Shh, they'll shock you." I looked up, wishing Nilson had pants on or that I wasn't splayed, completely vulnerable in front of him.

"I don't care if they shock me," Nilson growled.

"You two, shut up!" A soldier clicked a button, and Nilson's head snapped back momentarily. He toppled to the side and rammed into the bedpost.

"Fuck!" he yelled.

"I said shut up!" She pushed a button again, and Nilson fell to his knees. His body twitched, but he fought against the electricity surging through him. His veins bulged through his neck.

I locked on his gaze, not wanting him to endure the pain alone. When his spasms stopped, I silently asked the only question that mattered, hoping he'd understand.

Nilson simply shook his head and mouthed, "*no.*" So, he hadn't seen Kyra last night. Why? Was Elana torturing her at this very moment?

Suddenly, a woman on the floor screamed in ecstasy as she climaxed on her recent *purchase*. My jaw clenched, and Nilson's brows furrowed into a straight line.

"Come on." A soldier tugged Nilson.

The soldiers yanked Nilson to a pile of pillows by the window, directly in my eyesight, then tied his wrists above his head. Yup, the bitch was planning for me to watch them together. Fuck her! Fuck everything.

There was only one positive in this situation. Well, two. The first was that Elana wasn't currently in the room, and the second was she had stupidly left the two necklaces with a guard in the corner. The pearls hung from her belt loop, and the crystal reflected in the sunlight. I caught Nilson staring at them too. The wheels in his head were obviously turning as he started to scan for the exits.

But it was useless. I had spent hours trying to escape these cords. My stomach rumbled with hunger. When would we get breakfast? The men tied up all looked healthy and nourished, so at least Elana wasn't starving her toys.

"Hey, babe." Nilson dialed up his charm to full force with the sudden change in his tone. "I saw you peeking…come here."

A young woman blushed and lifted her eyes from focusing on the man beneath her.

"You like what you see, hmm?" Nilson smiled, but I knew it was fake. "Untie me, and we'll have some fun."

The closest two women slowed their momentum atop their partner.

Nilson clicked his tongue. "I can please you better than that guy."

Goddess, I hated him. Yet, I couldn't help but smile at his trick when I noticed the one woman stop her movements and lift herself off her partner. She crawled to Nilson, breasts swaying, her eyes excited.

She started to straddle Nilson, and I sucked in a breath. He wouldn't go through with it, would he? If I couldn't change our fate, Kyra needed Nilson as hers. She needed one person to trust.

"Nilson! Stop."

"Don't worry, man. She needs me. Come on, doll, come a little closer." He licked his lips.

Then, in a quick movement, Nilson wrapped his legs around the woman's neck and strangled her between his knees. She wrestled and pushed against him. She tapped at his leg wildly, eyes bulging.

"Let her go!" A soldier pushed a button, sending an obvious wave of electricity through Nilson.

Nilson twitched violently and screamed in forced bursts, "Give me…the crystal…I'll let…her go!"

"No!"

"I'll…fuckin…kill her," Nilson screamed. "Give me…the crystal!"

The woman's face gradually turned blue.

Adrenaline shot through my body, and I tugged against my restraints. My Circle sparked to life. But the Magik within wasn't strong enough to overpower the electricity. I heaved against the wires around my wrists again, needing to help.

"Give me the crystal!" Nilson bellowed, his face turning red.

I glanced at the door. We didn't have long. The distinct scent of sweat grew from the chateau's hallway.

"Turn up the voltage on him!" one soldier yelled.

"I can't! Elana gave us strict orders to keep him alive." She dropped the remote and ran to Nilson, about to smash him over the head.

He spun around, grabbed the crystal from her belt loop, and tugged. When it fell into his hands, Nilson immediately released the Ordull woman. She clutched at her neck. Whimpering, she scampered across the floor, grasped all her clothes, and stomped out of the room, slamming the door behind her.

I glanced back at Nilson, and he was already free. No wires or cords. The crystal glowed brilliantly in his hands, matching the blueish-white tattoo pulsing with energy in his torso.

"On your knees!" a soldier yelled and pointed a rare gun at him.

Nilson ignored her and jogged to me, unfortunately, still ass-bare nude. Footsteps thundered from the hallway.

"Leave me! Go save Kyra."

"No, she needs you," Nilson said calmly, untying the complicated knot at my wrists. "Shit, I can't loosen it."

"Back away from the prisoner!" The soldier's hands shook, her finger hovering over the trigger.

"She won't need me if she has you. Please, take care of her," I begged.

The scent of the incoming soldiers grew even stronger.

"You're her everything." Nilson placed the sharp edge of the crystal against the cord and mumbled to himself. The gem sliced through, freeing me immediately. "Yes! Come on, man!" Nilson lunged over the couple. I glanced at my clothes across the room.

A gunshot fired, cementing my decision. Well, naked fugitives made for a better story around the campfire someday.

"Tell Elana to go fuck herself!" Nilson roared to a soldier and jumped out the window.

I gasped. The door opened, and Elana glided into the room on her hoverchair, wearing only a silk robe that covered her amputation site.

"Griffin, jump!" Nilson yelled from outside.

Without time to check what lay below, I leaped into the air. The fall stole my breath until I landed atop a flying venti. My injured shoulder spasmed with pain.

"Good girl, Tawoli," Isaac hooted happily as he straddled the beast, still nude like me. I shook my head and tried to resituate. A pair of naked refugees.

"Holy shit, man, this crystal has insane new powers I've never felt before." The excitement in his voice was contagious.

We sped away.

"Wait! We need to go back and get Kyra!"

"No, we don't."

I was about to strangle Nilson the same way he choked that Ordull. "Yes, we do! I'll never leave her."

"Calm down, Griffin—look." He pointed to the tree line, just to the side of The Crooked Chateau, where two small figures stood under an oak. "They must have just gotten out."

They both shielded their eyes from the sun as they watched us lower. From the high window, Elana barked orders. She still had the Cydon Pearl at her disposal. We didn't have any time for reunions. As Tawoli galloped to the ground, Kyra's eyes widened at the sight of us both naked. Her father laughed and cringed at the same time, then hopped on Tawoli's back.

"What happened?" Kyra ran closer.

"Your boyfriend and I were getting to know each other during strip poker. Will you take a first-class seat or economy, my lady?" Nilson's arrogant smile was evident in his words.

"Uh, Jay?" She reached up, and I lifted her with one quick swing.

The pain in my shoulder sliced sharply, and I hissed. Awkwardly, so damn awkwardly. Kyra scooted between her father and me just before Tawoli cantered into the forest. Once we were hidden by the budding trees, the venti rose again, carrying us into the sky.

"Where are we going?" Kyra yelled into the wind.

"A safe house Caspian told me about," Nilson responded and directed Tawoli with each turn.

Hopefully, no one in Elana's army would track us. Kyra's body radiated tension, so I was reluctant to hold on too firmly. When she brushed her finger softly over my wrist, a thousand pounds eased off the burden I'd been holding. She was probably wondering if Elana was successful in her attempts last night. And I knew she was hurting from losing her brother. Who knew what else Kyra had endured overnight?

For now, I was just glad she was safe. Her hair smelled like leaves the higher we flew. Relief flooded my core, and I finally healed my shoulder with a silent healing chant.

"You okay?" she whispered over her shoulder.

"I am now."

"Did…" She pressed her back against my chest. "Did Elana…did she force you?"

"No, Petal. My body doesn't want anyone but you."

She sighed and laced her fingers through mine. "Are you okay?"

"I will be as long as you are."

She turned halfway, the wind blowing her hair wildly. Her perfect lips grazed my beard softly. We had to get off this venti as quickly as fuckin possible because the love exuding from her soul was making my cock hard, and her father was right in front of us. Disastrous.

After conjuring the ugliest images possible to calm my boner, we finally landed on a street I'd never been to on the outskirts of Andersonville. Tawoli slowed to a trot and stopped in front of a rundown apartment complex. How many safe houses were the Aurum Orbis Society responsible for? Nilson slid off and covered his crotch with both hands.

"Uh, Kyra, do you mind knocking on the door?" Nilson nodded forward.

"We don't have to." Brent planted his feet on the ground. "I used my power to inform the leader of our arrival and asked her to bring some clothes."

"Who's the leader?" Kyra asked.

"Narelle Arno."

"Shit," Kyra mumbled under her breath. "Does she know?"

"No." Brent shook his head. "I'll tell her. He was my son, I'll tell her."

The door opened a sliver, and Narelle threw us blankets. "So, is this when I get a great story about the lack of clothes?"

"Not a story worth telling."

"I'm so glad you're finally here!" Narelle opened the door further. "Wait, there's four of you. Only four. Where's Caspian?"

Brent moved toward her, and Kyra's eyes widened. She shook her head and backed into the side of the house.

"No," Narelle whispered, sagging down to the ground. "No!"

Brent caught her and held her tightly. "You all go inside."

I guided Kyra through the door, trying to block out the anguished cries from Caspian's wife trailing behind. On any other day, when I had more energy, I would've tried to help ease her pain, but Kyra was my priority. Too tired to scope out the details of the house, I marched through without a care. Now that we were safe, my brain turned to mush, and my senses were foggy—except for my smell.

I followed the scent of cinnamon into a full kitchen and collapsed onto a chair. The heaviness of a dozen pairs of eyes was on me, but I was too tired and too hungry to care. Someone's hands pushed a slice of bread to my lips. Only then did I notice my eyes were closed, and my head was leaning against the wall. The last few hours and days crashed into me like a tsunami, and I let my body relax.

"Can someone please bring him clothes? His size is extra-large," Kyra said, then sat on my lap.

My hands found her waist as she fed me pieces of cinnamon bread. My jaw could barely chew. Something plastic poked at my lips.

"Open, Jay," Kyra said softly amid the group's chatter. "It's a straw."

I sucked in the water, and the icy cold liquid tasted like a dream.

"That's it, Jay. Keep drinking."

The voices of the society members went in and out of focus, and I only caught bits and pieces as I kept my eyes shut.

"Two hundred soldiers…against thirty…."

"Five of us have Magik…."

"They have electric rods and tasers…."

"Doesn't matter, the prisoners need us…."

"Did you hear? Caspian is dead…."

Everyone gasped.

Kyra's body tensed against my chest. I needed to comfort her and make sure she was eating and drinking too, but something deep within convinced me to let her be the strong one this time. My body was at its limit, and only one Circle gave me powers.

"Jay, I'm going to dress you." Kyra's soft hand rested on my cheek, pulling fabric over my head. She threaded my tired arms through the sleeves and rolled the shirt over my chest as if I were a helpless infant. And I let her take care of me.

For a moment, my eyes popped open, and I snapped a mental photo of the group congregating in the kitchen. They all wore stolen army uniforms of spandex material that could camouflage into any surrounding.

Kyra pushed more bread between my lips, and I absentmindedly chewed. The gnawing sensation in my stomach finally ceased after sipping another glass of water. Strength slowly returned, and it helped that the scent of Kyra's hair was just below my nose, fueling me with energy for the upcoming battle.

Of course, we had to go back to free the prisoners. And Elana needed to be stopped. Frustration laced my veins that we had sacrificed so much to convert the nymphs back to their original form, and all three of them abandoned us to fight this battle alone.

The group continued chatting, and now that my head felt clearer, it was obvious that Nilson was leading the pack. I kept my eyes closed to steal any extra moments of needed rest. Chewed. Drank. Breathed. Listened. Repeated. Chewed. Drank. Breathed. Listened.

"Three demons are nymphs again…."

"More Ordull women in Andersonville have been reported missing…."

"What time will we attack…."

"We can call more ventus…."

"What about the Golden One as a decoy?"

My eyes snapped open again, and I would've bolted upright if Kyra weren't still sitting on my lap.

"No," Nilson commanded the group. "We're not using anyone to lure Elana out. Let's stick to Caspian's original plan: free the prisoners and stay alive. Our goal isn't to kill Elana but to get everyone out safely."

"We don't have Alaska anymore to teleport them to safety."

I glanced at my watch out of habit to check for a message from my sister, forgetting Elana had stripped me of that when she undressed me. The phantom feeling of Elana's hands on my skin made me gag. Kyra didn't need to know the details of Elana's ferocious attempts last night.

My lips were still dry, so I sucked down more water from the cup she held in front of me, locking onto her honey gaze. If anyone would keep me grounded, it was Kyra.

"You still need pants."

Even when the world was crashing around us and shattering to pieces, we could still find joy in a shared moment. Neither of us was able to hold back the onslaught of emotions attacking us; the only thing we could do was laugh. Our chests rumbled together in a fit of laughter behind the scenes of a revolutionary group planning to attack the president's headquarters.

Nilson clapped once. The sound echoed off the fridge and bounced off the stove. "Alright, team, you know the plan. You have thirty minutes to tie your life in a neat little bow, then meet at the back door."

I didn't have to ask Kyra if she planned to join them, already knowing the answer in my gut.

"I love you, Jay." She kissed my chin and nuzzled into my chest again.

"I love you more, Kyra."

"No matter what?" she asked.

I kissed her nose. "No matter what. Tonight, after the battle, I'll hold you in bed, and you can make a joke at my expense about how awesomely I fought this battle without pants."

"Yes, the naked ninja." She smiled, lighting up the room.

If this was the last smile I ever saw, it was worth it. The passion of our flame burned stronger than I could've ever imagined. Now, it was time to find some goddess-damned pants. After that, everything would be okay. It had to be.

We'd both return from this stronger than before.

25

KYRA

The sun warmed my neck. Apparently, we held the element of surprise if we attacked The Crooked Chateau during daylight.

A large hand wrapped around my waist. I jumped and jerked around.

"Woah, it's just me," Jay whispered. "Take a deep breath, Petal."

I tried, but each breath came in short little spurts as I wrung my hands. Our group of thirty was divided into five teams, each Mystier among us guiding a group of Ordulls. They were all insane to assume my gray Circles would protect a bunch of soldiers when the ₾sμwi might take hold at any time. Separating from Jay was not my first choice, but Isaac had won that vote.

"Kyra, breathe." Jay folded his hands over mine. "You can do this."

I was momentarily distracted by the Vayu Crystal reflecting the bright sunlight. The necklace fit between the curves of Isaac's chest. For only a moment, my nerves disappeared at his ridiculousness for heading into a battle shirtless. Isaac always knew how to make me laugh, yet I didn't even have the chance to say goodbye—just in case. He turned away to lead his team down a shadowed alley. He was my past, and we'd move on separately.

Narelle and Brent used silent gestures to command their groups in different directions. However, they all headed to the same destination —The Cavity. Even though their goal was to free the prisoners in the basement, the only thing on my mind was killing Elana.

"Just...give me one second." I bit my fingernail and spat it out, then another, until the corners were raw and bleeding.

"Kyra, you don't have to go."

"I do." I inhaled deeply, memorizing Jay's brown eyes. If his pupils were dilated, I must look like a wreck. "I'll be okay. It'll all be okay."

Jay tied a knot on the makeshift twine that served as a new chain for the Elidi Ruby hanging from my neck. "You have choices here, and no one is making you do this."

"We can't miss all the fun." I forced a fake smile when my voice rose an octave. "Ready? Or do I need to force you into battle?"

He kissed my forehead. "Ready when you are."

I gulped and watched the women load their guns. They counted on not having to use their weapons and, instead, relying on my powers to keep them safe. How many of them had families waiting? Or how many of these women had lost a male in their life because of my wish? Most likely, all of them. And yet, they were all volunteering to help us free Mystiers from captivity.

"I know Isaac had said for us to split up, but can we...can we stick together?" I hid my shaking hands behind my back.

"I wouldn't have it any other way."

Slowly, I pulled out the music pod he gifted me and slid it into his pocket, saying, "I made a playlist on here for you to remember me by, just in case." Then kissed his lips, just once. I wanted a thousand more, but something in my gut said we'd run our full course. Time was up.

Jay's brows furrowed. "Don't you dare, Petal."

I hadn't told Jay my plan, but even without a Link binding us, he read my mind. There was no easy way to say goodbye to him since I needed to keep his hopes up.

"Or we can listen to it in bed together tonight." I patted his chest. "But you better make me a milkshake. I'll deserve one after this."

"Sounds perfect," he said, not even trying to hide the tremor in his voice.

"You lead. I'll be at the back."

His face flipped to commanding mode. "Alright, soldiers. Step lightly and keep up."

My tattoos tingled in anticipation as I jogged at the end of our group's single-file line. As the capital of Lodesa, Andersonville was once vibrant and full of commuters on hoverboards, no matter the time of day. Now, the buildings were covered in graffiti, trash lined the curbs, and only the beeping sound of an automatic *walk* sign at a traffic light proved that people had once claimed these streets.

A cat jumped out of a nearby dumpster, and I clutched my racing heart. I wished time would speed up and fast-forward to tomorrow so this whole day was over. My boots crunched over the shattered glass. For a moment, I had half a mind to turn and flee. What if Elana knew we were coming? What if she caught Jay again? What if she killed me before I had the chance to kill her? What if the ₵sµwi controlled me?

I rammed straight into the soldier in front of me, my chest colliding with her back.

"Ouch, sorry," I whispered.

The unnatural stillness of the city racked my spine with panic. An enemy might be lurking around the next corner. Red spots flared in my vision, and a sudden overwhelming sense of dread crashed into me like a wave. How was I supposed to kill Elana? My fingers tapped a beat on my thigh, and I tried to focus on the rhythm.

"Hey! Golden One, let's go," a soldier whispered, then she turned and ran after the others.

We were already at the back entrance of The Crooked Chateau. How long had we been jogging?

"Calm the fuck down, Kyra," I whispered to myself and sprinted after them.

My shoulders tightened, and I wiped my clammy hands on my pants. Hopefully, the tightness in my chest would stop soon.

The city was silent. That didn't stop me from feeling eyes trained on me from the high windows of the skyscrapers caging us. I glanced up and only saw wisps of white clouds.

Ahead, Jay slid open a basement window and waved everyone inside. This was too easy. The window should've been locked. Guards would've noticed us by now—in broad daylight. Cameras moved back and forth on the building. Something wasn't right.

Stepping forward, I caught Jay's eye from afar. That was when I knew for sure he was already aware of the threat looming over us. Of course, he'd notice. He was a soldier through and through. Jay nodded toward the window, giving me the answer I needed. Shit. We'd be safer underground in Elana's domain than out here as targets.

A whizzing sound soared past my ear. I leaped back. A ball of wires parachuted mid-air into a net and wrapped around the woman in front of me. She screamed.

I pulled the knife out and tried to slash through it. The cords were too thick. Another hiss sound flew down and barely missed me. I was out of time.

"I'm sorry," I whispered.

She screeched something unintelligible. When I looked back, the net rose and floated like a bubble into a high window. Shouts escalated, and officers gave orders to their units.

"Come on. Get in!" Jay pushed the first few women down through the window.

A gunshot. One of our soldiers collapsed. Blood leaked out of her side. My breath caught in my throat.

Another whoosh sounded behind me. And another. They were getting closer each time.

"Go!" I yelled to Jay. "Go!"

"Not without you. Hurry!"

A net latched onto my heel, and I fell forward onto the pavement. Gravel stuck to my skin, and scratches burned my arms. I kicked the tangled net away. Sprawled on my stomach, I got to my knees and crawled. Faster. Faster. Another whizzing sound behind me sent my heart spiraling out of control. The window was too far away. They'd capture me before I even entered the damn building.

Suddenly, strong hands lifted me and dragged me the rest of the way. Jay. Thank the goddess.

Angry yells intensified, then footsteps thundered like a stampede. We'd be trapped and surrounded.

Mid-run, I stepped on a rock sideways, and my foot twisted. Pain sliced through my ankle. Jay caught me as I went down, hauling most of my weight. I silently chanted the healing spell to myself, but nothing changed.

Gunfire exploded. Defeating booms. I scrambled chaotically.

Ten more feet to go.

Sweat pooled on my back. Something crashed behind me.

Seven more feet.

My heart slammed in my chest.

Three more feet.

I was limping. Out of breath.

Jay shoved me through the window, and I fell into the basement, landing on my side with a *thud*.

The rest of our team quickly barricaded the window shut with a hoverboard, table, and boxes. The room darkened, but I didn't need much light to remember the layout. One flickering light in the middle shone a weak spotlight on the electric chair in the middle of the space. Surrounding it were three layers of metal cages stacked atop one another. But it was too quiet. There were no sniffles, hacking coughs, or pleas.

"I can't heal you in here." Jay lifted me to my feet again. "Can you walk?"

"Yeah, I'm fine."

He didn't wait for assurance this time. "Hurry, everyone! Use your tools and free as many prisoners as you can. We only have a minute or two."

We were down two teammates already. There was no way we'd have time to free hundreds of prisoners. Maybe if we started with the youngest ones first. No, there was no time to guess their ages.

Outside, a gunshot blasted, tearing a hole through the barrier.

I hobbled in pain to the first cage. Empty. Shuffled to the next.

Empty. Panic set in. I glanced at the rest of the aisle. All the cage doors were already open. Where were they? Eerie squeaks haunted me as some swung on their hinges. I froze. Our team stared at us for directions, eyes wide and fingers fidgeting on their weapons.

"Jay..." I whispered.

"I know, they're all gone."

He paced each row of cages, then commanded some of our teammates, "You three, find more items to barricade that window. The thicker, the better. You two, see if there are any other exits."

The last part didn't make sense. Jay had been a prisoner down here and knew where all the exits were. I met his gaze. He nodded quickly, telling me that giving the soldiers a task was better than doing nothing.

"Maybe Isaac's group already freed them all," I said uncertainly. Beads of sweat formed on my lip.

The banging escalated from outside the barricade. My head was all over the place. This was it. I'd have to use my ₾sµwi to keep the rest of my team safe. Each time the ₾sµwi was used, it grew stronger.

A soft whimper sound cried to my left. "Did you hear that?"

Jay sniffed the air, but there was no way he'd be able to detect anything other than the rotten stench of human feces and piss.

The sound came again. I limped over to the corner, pain radiating up my shin. A little girl, maybe eight years old and filthy, was crouched in the corner.

"Over here, Jay!" I shook the door, but it was locked. Hands trembling, I pulled out my knife.

She scrambled back, blinking rapidly, tears dragging lines through the dirt on her cheeks.

"It's okay. I'll get you out."

The knife was too big and didn't fit the hole. Panting, Jay joined my side and reached into my hair, "Try this," he said. "Hurry up."

I bent the metal clamp straight like I'd done with a paperclip and inserted the end. After a few tries, the lock clicked open. "Come on. Hurry."

The girl shut her eyes and shook her head back and forth. Her knuckles turned white from gripping the back of the cage.

"I'm not going to hurt you. Come on. We have to hurry." I reached in and had to pry her from the corner.

Once she was out, she lunged into Jay's arms, burying her head in his chest. Maybe she was afraid of women after Elana's experiments. The chaotic ruckus by the window was like a fresh shot of pure adrenaline. We had to leave. Now.

I tried to rise on my tiptoes to peek into the higher cages to look for others, but my ankle screamed in response. "Do you think there are any others?"

Jay nervously glanced at the window. "I don't know, but we can't stay."

The little girl pointed to the wall and whispered, "Behind there."

"Someone's behind the wall?" I limped over and groped the wall up and down.

"Griffin!" A soldier ran to our side. "We found a tunnel."

"There wasn't a tunnel here before." He pressed the little girl closer to his chest.

"Well, there's one now. Come on. We don't have much time."

I felt a dip in the wall and pushed a fist through. Without knowing what I had touched, the wall opened like a door. At least fifty more cages sat in a small room filled with prisoners.

"No!" Jay and I locked eyes at the same time. Dumbfounded.

"No, no, no, no." My hands formed a steeple by my lips. "What are we gonna do? We don't have time!"

"You." Jay repositioned the girl in his arms and pointed to two soldiers. "Open all the cages on the left and lead them out. Carry them if you have to!"

"You two do the right side. Hurry!"

More pounding slammed against the barricade.

I put pressure on my foot and sucked in a silent breath. Broken. Based on the pain level, I had no doubt it had to be broken.

"Kyra?"

"Just go, Jay!" I didn't even turn around but waved him off. "Get her out of here!"

The sounds of Jay rushing away toward the tunnel sent my nerves into overdrive. I fumbled my hairpin into lock after lock. In a daze, I helped prisoners out of their cages. Half were unable to walk. There was no way we'd be able to free them all.

Running out of time. Hands shaking. Head pounding. I had to block out the whimpers of the caged prisoners further down the line. We wouldn't get to all of them. Next to me, the soldiers swore and shook their cage doors, barely making progress picking the locks.

"Come on!" Jay ran back and waved for us to follow. "We have to go."

"I can't leave them!"

"You have to."

"No, Jay!" My voice broke as I rammed the pin into another lock.

He darted over, crouched, and bent two prisoners over his shoulders. He jogged away, heaving them both to safety.

The other soldiers looked at the barricade, slowly collapsing, and helped the last few prisoners to the tunnel. Thank the goddess.

Finally, I was alone. I stared at the electric chair in the middle of the basement. It was the same technology that had killed Caspian.

Pounding and thrashing sounds hit a crescendo behind the barricade. The soldiers were close to breaking through. A beam of sunlight burst through. The enemy would be here in mere moments. Now that my team was out of the way, my five gray Circles all sprang to life under my command. It felt like I carried the strength of midnight in my pocket. My veins flooded with the promise of death.

I glared at the barricade crumbling in front of me. Another piece cracked off the hoverboard and fell. One hand poked through, holding a gun. It aimed straight at me. I rose both my hands and summoned the power within. There was no need to hide my wicked intent this time. It was finally my chance to see what my shadows were capable of.

"Kyra!" Jay spoke from behind. "Hurry."

No. He was supposed to leave.

The gun's aim changed to Jay. It fired. I stopped the bullet in a heartbeat, changed its direction, and commanded it back to its owner. Blood gushed from her hand. She screamed and dropped the gun. I tilted my head and smiled. A voice deep within sang like a siren to me, calling up my powers to a level I'd never experienced. My darkness was ready to be used, rising from the deep. Just as I was about to launch the energy toward our attackers, I heard his voice again.

"Kyra!"

I pivoted fast to see Jay's confused face. The fire at my fingertips shot out without warning and set the electric chair ablaze. The entire thing exploded before my eyes. The pressure threw me back against the wall. I dropped to the floor. Screams pierced the air from outside. Raging flames ignited and spread across the floor and up the walls. Smoke consumed the basement in moments.

"Kyra!" Jay dodged the blazing inferno and darted to my side.

In a trance, I stared up, hypnotized by the puppet. The voice deep inside me laughed in wonder, humming a victory song.

"Kyra! Reach out to me."

A hand waved through the thick wall of smoke. Whose hand?

"Where are you?" The voice sounded so far like from another life. "Grab ahold of me!"

I did. When the hand lifted me, shooting pain seared through my ankle, but he yanked me forward and swung me over his shoulder. He dodged crackling fire. I giggled. I loved fire. But not as much as I loved shadows.

Somewhere, far, far away, a hard hand smacked my back. "Kyra! Stay awake. Stay awake!"

Then the entire room caved in on itself. He ran forward, away from the tumbling walls. The room fell to ruins. And it was all my doing. Success. A slithering smile crept up my cheeks again.

Loud breathing sounds and hard stomps echoed in the darkness as my ribs poked into the man's shoulders again and again.

Thump, thump.

He wheezed.

Thump, thump.

He coughed.

Thump, thump.

We reached the opening where the rocks and dirt turned to grass, and sunlight warmed my face.

Puppet coughed, then stopped. "We got separated from the others when the tunnel collapsed, so it's only us two."

My delicious puppet kept speaking, saying something about teammates and soldiers. I could only focus on the hundreds of thump-thump sounds nearby. At first, I thought they were footsteps. Nope. There were heartbeats. Hundreds of heartbeats, and they were close, begging to be heard.

"Kyra. I need you with me."

Puppet's scrumptious lips pressed onto mine and the haunted heartbeats faded away. He tasted of a smoky garden when fresh vegetables had been burnt to crisps. I sighed and leaned into his mouth. The sound of white water in the distance was as meditative as Jay's tongue playing games with mine.

Jay. My Jay.

My heart tightened with relief. He was okay.

I pulled away and studied Jay's face, then skipped over all the questions rushing through my mind to land on the most important one.

He turned me toward the forest scene. Bits and pieces of the last few minutes formed half a puzzle in my mind, including the members of our team getting separated from us. Were they with the prisoners?

The tunnel led us out of the city. We stood at the border of Andersonville, inside the tree line. Fire roared and erupted from the top of The Crooked Chateau in the distance and chased after us. It spread quickly from building to building, devouring the city unnaturally, to the forest line where we stood.

Something or someone was encouraging the vitality of that fire, and it sure wasn't me.

The sound of the rushing river that served as the city's limits caught my attention. It divided the skyscrapers and towering trees on the other side. To our right, the raging water cascaded over a deadly waterfall. But that wasn't what I was staring at.

By the river, Elana sat on her hoverchair, holding two wires. One was tied directly to a plank in the river, keeping it from floating away. The other cord was tied around the person's neck who sat atop the plank.

Alaska.

26

KYRA

The sound of a crackling, massive fire prowled after us like a live predator. Its flames darted outward from the center of the city. Red and orange bounded from rooftop to rooftop, destroying everything in their path. The growing fire's absolute strength tore down Andersonville, street by street. The beastly flames roared with the heart of a lion, rolling to the river in a grand ball of death.

"Surprise!" Elana tugged the wire connected to Alaska's neck. "I was expecting you a little earlier."

"Alaska!" Jay started toward his sister, but I grabbed his shirt.

"Dehano huc! Dehano huc!" I chanted silently to the fire, needing the fury roaring in the city to be at my fingertips.

My Circles resisted my call for flames. They wanted something else, but I refused to use the ₾sµwi with Alaska's life teetering on edge.

"Let Alaska go!" I growled.

The tiny raft rocked violently in the river. Alaska gripped the sides of the plank firmly.

"What do you want?" Jay shouted next.

"For my name to be written in legends!" Elana shrieked madly.

"But you took away my life source, so this useless body is already deteriorating…." When she motioned down her handicapped form, she yanked Alaska's leash. "And last night. *This* boy was useless last night and couldn't seal my legacy." Her veins pulsed in her forehead. "But you won't win, child. And neither will the nymphs. They think they can pick and choose who is worthy…I was only a child when they mutilated my entire future! So I made my own path."

"I understand your anger." I stepped forward slowly with a racing pulse. "The nymphs were wrong. They should've given you a chance when you were a child."

Elana's features froze, listening for once.

"Even though they feared the darkness inside you, if they had gifted you with an extra power, even a small one, none of *this* would've happened." I spread my arms out wide at the raging fire growing hotter. "I also know darkness, Elana. You don't have to be this way. I know what it's like."

"So, you think we're the same?" Her lips twitched, and her nostrils flared.

"It depends on what you decide to do next."

"Are you done with your little speech?" Elana touched the pearl around her neck.

Her vicious smile communicated a thousand deadly promises as she released the rope tying Alaska to the bank. The rapids quickly rocked Alaska off the plank, and she flew into the white water. The current dragged her toward the edge of the waterfall.

"Alaska!" Jay leaped toward the bank.

Alaska's head bobbed at the surface. Above. Below. Her shoulder crashed into a boulder mid-stream. She screamed out.

It was time to push my limits. I'd have to accept becoming a murderer. I forced a bundle of fire straight at Elana's hateful face. Her hoverchair swerved to the right, dodging it. My flames exploded against a tree behind her. More smoke encompassed us like a tomb, blocking my view of Jay and Alaska further down the bank.

Hyperalert, I glared at Elana's heinous gaze. Her movements were scarily calm, focused, and precise. Elana possessed a century of practiced Magik. She twirled her finger, and a monumental cyclone of water rose from the river.

But she didn't have my spirit. I was the warrior. I'd kill her and end all of this. Defend my people. Confront the villain. Withstand her evil.

I set my jaw and balled my fists. Putting all my weight on my good ankle, I stood as solidly as possible and cast a wall of fire in front of me.

I braced myself for impact, anticipating the worst. The water thrashed against my barrier. Elana's face was twisted. With her final push, her water shattered my shield and burst through. It pummeled me, soaking me head to toe. My back crashed against the ground.

Ignoring the pain, arms shaking, I pushed myself up. No matter how often she knocked me down, I'd get up. Every. Single. Time.

A whimpering sound caught my attention from the tunnel entrance. The little girl Jay had saved sat exposed at the opening. Shit. Elana's gaze followed mine and whipped to the girl. She smiled and sucked more water from the river, even more than before. It hurtled toward the girl.

My heart stopped. Time slowed. My tattoos begged to be used. Maybe I was strong enough to control my shadows this time.

Every muscle clenched tight. With mud underfoot, wind whipping my face, and fire crackling from all directions, I jumped in front of the water, careening toward the girl. I felt them. I sensed all the elements. They were all a part of me. Fire. Earth. Wind. Water.

I spread my arms out wide like wings. The water smacked into my front full force, but I didn't waver this time. I held my ground. Unmovable. Unstoppable.

Elana's jaw dropped, and she yelled, "Impossible!" Full of rage, she chucked more bullets of water at me, again and again.

My tattoos scorched and burned. I felt the warning deep within, drumming, accelerating with each moment. There was no going back this time if I used them. For the first time, that realization felt okay. I accepted myself–all of me–shadow and light.

"*Digati impetu! Digati impetu!*" I yelled.

Gray, smoky shadows oozed out of my fingertips and crept into the air. It divided each water rocket from Elana straight through the middle and sent them to the ground like raindrops.

I laughed in awe, power taking the wheel. Fluttering tickled my chest, and my cheeks warmed. I could do this! The drumming in my bones quickened.

"You wretched girl!" Elana rubbed her hands together, then flung sharp icicle spears at me.

Heart pounding, faster, even faster.

Two spears. Three. Fuck! They lodged into the ground beside me. The flames crawled closer, pressing Elana and me together. The whites of her eyes were tinted with popping red veins.

"Kyra!" Jay hollered from within the thick smoke.

Elana's gaze shifted to the direction of his voice, and she licked her lips. The song drumming in my head rose to a peak, the fastest tempo possible, ready to explode and shatter the melody. Ancient spells lingered on my tongue, and cursed Magik gushed through my veins. I'd never let her hurt Jay.

The shadows that jutted out of my hands hardened into a hooked, tangible sword. I hunched forward under the surprising weight of it. Sunlight glittered off the sharp blade. Golden gems on the handle winked like stars in approval.

I raised it above my head and charged. The five Circles pulsed like a chaotic drum.

"Elana!"

She turned away from Jay and met my eyes. She had Brent's eyes. My eyes.

I swung.

The ȼsμwi claimed me fully. I roared.

Elana's eyes widened.

The edge of the shadow blade hit her neck.

It sliced through her throat, and blood spurted everywhere. Her head rolled to the ground down the riverbank. Her body collapsed over the hoverchair into a heap in the mud. All the water under her control fell in a single beat.

I stared at her decapitated body.

Fire crackled.

I stared at the sword in my hands.

Mine.

Fire crackled louder.

I stared into the thick smoke, where a tall silhouette ran forward.

Mine.

"Kyra!" he bellowed wildly.

I smiled and growled, "Mine."

Fire boomed.

I moved toward my attacker, each footstep a drumbeat deep in my soul. I was ready to burn Puppet's heart to ashes. I'd take his land down and smash it to pieces. There was no way to defeat me because I'd break them all. Every crown was mine. The legacy was mine. Immortality would also be mine.

Raising the sword over my head, I zeroed in on his massive bulk jogging toward me. He stepped through the fog, dripping wet. The green tattoo on his stomach gleamed brightly. He had dark brown hair made to crumble hearts, deep brown eyes I'd carve out with a blade, and nine fingers I'd smash to pieces.

I whirled the sword straight down to his stomach.

He pivoted, hands lifted in surrender. "No, no, please, Kyra. It's just me."

His devastating brown eyes flickered between my eyes, then down to the gem around my neck.

I rose my sword again but paused.

Thump, thump.

Thump, thump.

His heartbeat felt like my own. Why?

"Petal. Don't do this." He backed away a step, but the puppet didn't have much space to hide.

"Petal?" My chest seized curiously. "Do you know me?" I lowered my sword.

Desperation lined his eyes. They were almost darker than the smoke enveloping us. "Yes, I promise. Fight the darkness, and come back to me."

My Circles gripped my core loudly in protest. "I like the darkness. This is who I am!" A tear fell from the corner of my eye, but I wasn't sure why.

Who was this man looking at me like I was his very sun?

"Kiss me, Kyra."

I lifted the sword halfway, but he grabbed my wrists and held them down. I had so many other ways I could demolish him, but the drumming in my head struck so fiercely, a beat meant for another soul—a rhythm I couldn't ignore.

Gently, his lips brushed mine. My grip on the sword loosened, and I fought the urge to wrap my fingers behind his neck. His tongue expertly wound against mine, making my blood boil. What was this feeling? My heart slammed as I pushed him away.

"Who are you?" I asked softly.

The look on his face ruined me. But I didn't notice that the man now had my sword in his grasp. Instead of raising it to me, he placed the sharp blade against his neck.

I gasped, reached forward to stop him, then froze.

"Kyra, remember who you are." He pushed the blade against his neck, making a tiny trail of blood trickle down. "Remember yourself."

I gasped at his injury. "Jay! Stop it! You're bleeding."

"Thank, goddess."

When Jay lowered the strange, curled sword, everything connected —the blood speckled on my arms, and the smell of copper stung my nostrils. My heart seized solidly. Then, I'd always be a danger to him and those I loved. I remembered everything this time.

"The little girl is by the caves. I need you to take her somewhere safe," I said quickly.

Alaska was already by her side when I glanced over at the little girl. Good, they were both okay.

"We'll take her to a safe house together," Jay said.

"I can't come with you. Elana is dead, so my job is done." Without another thought, I yanked the ruby necklace off my neck and placed it on the ground. "Destroy it. Now!"

"No!" Jay held the mystery sword behind his back.

Fire embers rained down on us from the crackling branches above.

"I'm not strong enough to control the darkness. If you don't destroy it, I'll keep trying to hurt someone." I dropped to my knees in front of him. "You promised me!"

"*No.*" His tears fell from the corner of his eye. "No, I won't do it."

But the fact that he was crying showed me that he already knew what he had to do.

"Jay, I'll become like Elana, or worse."

"You're stronger each time. You came back faster than before," he whispered so softly.

"We can't risk it. The ₾sμwi Magik will wreck all of Lodesa. Please." I reached up and placed my ruby in his hands. "Please strike through the center and shatter it. I trust you."

He took the ruby. Acceptance lingered in his eyes. A sob attacked him, and he dropped to his knees by my side. Jay's head drooped, and his chest moved up and down fiercely. It was the first time I noticed the savage drumbeat in my heart had gone silent.

Peace.

"I can't live without you." Jay rested his forehead against mine.

"Yes, you can. Draven needs their leader, and you love your people." I wouldn't cry in front of him. I had to be strong. "Do me a favor and give Chocolate one more kiss for me."

He half-laughed, half-choked on a sob and hugged me. "I need more time."

"We don't have time, Jay. I can feel the darkness creeping back again." It felt like I was swallowing rocks. "I'm sorry I'm not stronger to fight it."

Jay lifted my chin. "Don't you ever apologize for your strength, Kyra. You are my roots…." He kissed my cheek. "Gnarled, twisted, and rough…." He kissed my chin. "My very source of life."

"My very source of life," I repeated and kissed his lips. One last time. And my heart completely broke.

Backing away on my knees, I dropped to sit cross-legged in the mud and gazed up at the man holding my life in his palm. Nothing could stop this now. The furious red and orange flames still roaring behind Jay made him look godly. My everything.

He set the ruby on the flat surface of a rock, raising the silver blade above it.

I locked onto his eyes as he shed more tears.

I nodded and held my breath.

Jay screamed an agonizing battle cry that ripped my heart's remains to shreds and rammed the blade's point straight into the ruby.

Pain pulsed through my body. I collapsed to my side. My shoulder crashed against the rock. Time stopped.

The power of a thousand suns scorched me, and an inhuman scream ripped apart my throat. Smoke exploded from my fingertips, completely out of control. The pressure tore me apart, snapping my neck back. Then...only darkness.

27

JADOX

Gone. She was gone. I sank to the ground, staring at her lifeless form sprawled in the mud. I did this. Everything was done and over. Gemm was dead. Elana was dead. Kyra was dead.

I lifted Kyra's sword to my wrist. Pressed the blade against my skin. Slashed it open. Blood seeped out. So much more than I expected. Alaska would take care of our Dravians. My vision turned hazy.

A flicker of movement caught my eye by the riverbank. The sun played tricks on me as a misty silhouette rose from Elana's body and hovered mid-air. What the fuck? The transparent woman glittered like gold and resembled Kyra and Elana, but her features weren't an exact mirror of either. When she glided closer to me, I noticed the glitter was embers of fire crackling and forming her shifting shape like a fluid flame.

The fire nymph.

I gasped as more blood flowed from my forearms, staining the dirt crimson. If this was the true fire nymph in front of me, then who was Kyra? What had I done?

28

KYRA

I opened my eyes to a pristine music store full of drums. The shop felt both familiar and foreign at the same time. Impossibly bright white light shone through the windows, making the cymbals almost blinding. The metal stands sparkled as if newly cleaned, but I couldn't smell any chemicals. In fact, no one seemed to be working here at all. Sheet music plastered the walls, hung at different angles, and rustled gently, but no breeze swept in from the open window. Weird. I picked up a drumstick atop the snare but couldn't feel the wood in my fingers.

"What the?" I said, then thumped the phantom drumstick against the tom-tom. No sound.

A shadow moved by the window like a ghost.

"Hello?" My voice echoed loudly. Maybe this sound was the only thing these walls had heard for a century.

I moved toward the window, but nothing greeted my ears. No birds chirping, not even a hoverboard zoomed by. Yet, a second shadow in the shape of a person moved, just on the other side of a veil outside, separating us.

I reached for the window, but something held me back.

"Who's out there? Can you hear me?"

The silhouette on the other side of the veil of light turned, clearly forming the profile of a person's pointy nose and round chin. As I was about to step closer to the window to see who was out there, a voice spoke from behind the counter.

"I wouldn't do that if I were you."

I turned to meet the eyes of an older woman who could've been any age between fifty and seventy. When she smiled, her bright eyes reminded me of the liquid gold that oozed between the cracks of Bukti Volcano. She wiped down the cash register, but the cloth didn't make a sound as her hand swept back and forth.

"If you go through that window, there's no coming back," she said calmly and draped the cloth over her petite shoulder.

I walked toward her, though it felt like I was ice skating or defying gravity altogether. "Why can't I come back? Who's on the other side of the veil? Where are we? Who are you? Where's Jay?"

"Always asking questions, firecracker." She grabbed a pair of scissors and ripped through a box, pulling out a pile of sheet music. "Help me hang these, will you?"

"I...uh..." I swept the walls for a clock, but there was none.

"Don't worry, it won't take long." She smiled and handed me a stack.

Another silhouette joined the others outside. For some reason, some sensation begged me to hurry as if once the light was blocked by these shadow people, I'd run out of time. But why was I here?

I stared at the top sheet of paper the store clerk had handed me. The entire stack was duplicates of the same song. It was a song I had written roughly ten years ago in high school.

I dropped the pile, and the pages fluttered in the non-breeze. "What's going on? Where did you get those? No one has ever seen that song."

More shadow people arrived on the other side of the veil. The more who came, the more light was blocked from their smoky frames. I needed them to leave before everything was draped in darkness. But I also wanted to hear my song. If I couldn't see the drums, how was I supposed to read the music that I wrote? Playing in the dark was too hard. I'd make too many mistakes or play the wrong beat. The light from outside was my only chance to finish the song.

Those people had to move. They had to get away from the window.

"Kyra." The old woman suddenly stood right in front of me, and it was like looking in the mirror at my future. This older version of me stared at me with her fiery eyes.

"I need to go through the window and tell those people to go home," I said.

"They don't have a home."

"Why not?"

"You took them from their homes."

"No, I didn't. I don't even know them."

She picked up the top sheet of the song I had written and stuffed it into a crumpled ball in my palm. "They want you to bring them back."

"I don't know what you're talking about." I looked over at the corner holding a dozen bass drums. "Something's not right. I don't feel good." I swayed. "I'm not supposed to be here."

"Where are you supposed to be?"

I paused, staring at the drumstick in my hand that I couldn't feel between my fingers. "Not here." My heart raced or slowed. I wasn't sure. I pressed a hand to my chest but couldn't feel a heartbeat. "Jay. I'm supposed to be with Jay. Let me go back to him."

"I thought you wanted to leave him behind." She smiled and started hanging sheet music.

"What? No, I…" I tore the paper out from between her fingers. "Tell me what's going on."

"I can't do that," she sighed. "You have to figure it out on your own, firecracker."

That nickname. It throbbed a pulse in my temple. "What did you just call me?"

"Firecracker…" This time when she said it, her voice wasn't an old lady's but was deep and rough, sounding an awful lot like Brent's.

"Is this a dream?"

"No."

"Where am I?"

"The in-between. I've been here for decades."

"I need to leave."

"I'll help you." The woman smiled, but her voice deepened again. "But first, you have to ask the right question."

I stared at her long brown hair, the same shade as Caspian's, and her skin complexion, the same color as Brent's. Suddenly, I knew her. Without ever seeing her before, I knew this was my grandma, Elana's daughter.

She winked, and fire shot from her eyes like laser beams, setting the sheet music aflame.

"Woah, how did you do that?" Realization struck like a perfect chord in a symphony. "Wait, it's you. *You* are the fire nymph."

"Yes." She put the fire out and said, "Now, ask me what you truly want to know."

"Who am I?"

Grandma nodded—it felt strange and right at the same time to consider her as that. "You already know. Read your lyrics out loud to me."

Outside, more people blocked the light shining into the store. Another drum was devoured by shadows.

"I don't have time—"

Grandma lowered her chin. "Now."

You torture my soul that could've shined so bright,
Behind the mask of this minnow is a deadly shark.
You've swallowed me whole and stolen all my light,
But no matter what you do, I'll find my violent spark.
So watch your damn back, cuz one day I'll ignite,
And not one single man will keep me trapped in the dark.

A tear slid down my cheek. I wiped it away but felt no hot liquid on my finger. It came away dry. I wrote that song when I was another person—full of bitterness and anger toward men.

Suddenly, I knew all the shadows trying to get through the veil of light were the males I had wished away. They were stuck here, wanting to return home, just like me.

"You have choices, firecracker. You can go through that veil and live an immortal life as the *shadow nymph,* or you can go back and live for an unknown amount of time."

A tightness curled around my chest, but at the same time, I felt feather-light. I was a shadow nymph. I had never wanted immortality like Elana or for my name to be written in legends.

"No matter which I pick, there will be a price either way, won't there?" I whispered.

Grandma nodded. "There always is."

"I don't want to live in fear anymore." The bodies on the other side of the veil started smacking against the thin barrier, sending rippling waves around them. "I want to learn to fully love a man, to be myself with him. These males here shouldn't have had to suffer because of my past fears. I want to return them to their homes. I want males in our world again. There must be thousands more males like Jay, those who know how to find the light. I want a life with Jay."

"What if only you or the males can go back?"

"Then it has to be them. Caspian once told me that one life isn't as valuable as thousands."

Grandma tilted her head. "He's a smart one, but it's hard to agree. You are my treasure, firecracker."

I looked out the window. The vague shape of a man's cheek scrunched against the veil as the mob behind him pushed him flat against the invisible wall. They were all someone's treasure, too.

"I'll stay to save them." I checked for a clock again. "How do I return the males?"

"Are you sure, Kyra? If you stay here, things may not be easy. You'd take my place in bestowing enhancements to the strongest lineage of each Mystier tribe. Some will worship you, and some will grow to hate you. If you stay here, you'll watch Jadox Griffin grow old without you.

I nodded, wishing there could be another way. Grandma ushered me to the nearest drum set and set the phantom sticks in my hand.

"Just play. You'll feel the ancient spell, then your Magik will return some of the males."

"Some?"

She nodded, her lips drawn in.

A little boy's small hand pressed against the veil, and this time, his finger poked through. Sounds whooshed through the opening, attacking my ears. A thousand pleas of fathers begging to be reunited with their families scraped against my skull.

"The light is almost gone!"

Grandma moved my hand for me as I gaped in shock as more agonizing cries jabbed my heart.

Boyfriends, sons, uncles, neighbors, bosses, sons, grandfathers, brothers, and nephews all begged for relief from the Abyss I had trapped them in. Panic set in, and my hands froze over the drum. What would I play?

Grandma's eyes turned wild as the hole grew larger and a little boy's whole arm stuck through. "Kyra, remember, there's a price to pay for each choice. Not every male will return."

"I have to save who I can. Grandma? What is the meaning of my fifth Circle? There are four elements. Why do we all have five?"

"Deep down, you already know the answer to that. The world may be created from earth, wind, fire, and water. But each one has something extra, a special ingredient."

"Our spirit," I whispered to myself.

She nodded. "And your spirit thrives on music. You are a nymph. Now, play your song, Kyra girl."

I tapped my left stick against the drum, then the right. There was no sound.

"Grandma, what if the ₾sμwi won't let me save them?"

Shadows crept along the store floor until they gobbled Grandma's feet. She floated in front of me, half a body, yet still held a smile.

"My sweet girl, you're not cursed. You are the roots, holding everyone together."

My breath hitched, and my heart stopped. Before I could ask her anything else, the darkness ingested her completely.

"Kyra," a deep voice penetrated the darkness outside the window. "Kyra."

Jay was calling for me, but his voice was weak. He needed me. But I couldn't return. He'd have to find a way without me. I wished our Link was back for one final moment.

I love you, Jay.

"No! Kyra. Stay. Please, stay!"

I banged one stick against the drum. This time it made a soft *thud*, barely audible. There was no holding back anymore. I only had a sliver of light left from outside. If I returned Landon and Wes, I'd be able to save some of the others too. I slammed the sticks in a slow, steady rhythm, and the sounds eventually grew louder the more I believed. I chanted the ancient spell that had worked once before.

My rhythm quickened. *Thud, thud. Thud, thud.*

"Reditus atsutsa. Reditus atsutsa," I said, the spell to the same beat as my drumming.

The sliver of light grew larger, and the pack of shadows on the other side of the veil was thinner, but a sharp pain tore open my stomach. Wincing, I checked my tattoos, four grays, one gold.

"I love you, Petal." Jay's voice was so far off, so quiet. "I'll see you on the other side."

I looked back at the window, but Grandma's words urged me to keep playing. I dug down deep within and beat harder. I pounded the drumsticks fiercer and faster than my own erratic heartbeat. *Thud, thud. Thud, thud.*

"Reditus atsutsa. Reditus atsutsa."

An intense sting shot through my Circles. Now, only three gray tattoos. Two gold. More light beamed through the window. One of the faces that was pushed against the veil disappeared.

Thud, thud. Thud, thud.

It felt like a razor blade was being taken to my tattoos. Only two gray tattoos. Three Golden. I was changing.

"Reditus atsutsa! Reditus atsutsa!"

I squinted, almost having to shield my eyes from the brighter light.

The cries from the hole grew softer and further away. I struck the drums with all my might. Sweat trickled down my neck.

Thud. Thud. Thud, thud.

A painful tear shredded my muscles, and I almost bent in half but gritted my teeth and hammered on. Harder. Faster. Out of breath.

"Reditus atsutsa! Reditus atsutsa!"

One gray tattoo remained, and the other four were golden.

Boom, boom, boom, boom.

So much light radiated through the window that I squeezed my eyes shut.

"Kyra, I know you can hear me from wherever you are. I'm coming. Wait for me." This time, I understood Jay's words and what they meant. He was dying.

"No! Jay, keep fighting!" I slammed my drumsticks, blasting out all the harnessed pain trapped inside. My arms lifted and crashed down fiercely. With a last mighty strike, I screamed at the top of my lungs and battered the sticks so hard that it tore open the drum.

Panting, only the feeling of peace engulfed me. I opened my eyes. The music store was gone. Tilting my head, I tried to make sense of what was in front of me. Moroka splashed in the river, sending giant rings of water into the trees to put out the forest fire. Wait...was I back?

My fingers were curled in mud.

"I'm back," I whispered.

Ahead, a dozen boys, ranging from toddlers to maybe twelve, stood nearby. The three nymphs hovered over them. Surh-Sig and Oniskel's faces were a mix of relief and despair. I wasn't supposed to return.

"Thank you," a little boy said as he rushed forward and wrapped his arms around my neck in a hug.

"Jay, where's Jay?" I softly slid the boy off me and bolted to my feet.

A terrible pain shot through my ankle as I hobbled through the crowd and crunched over the shattered ruby. The group of boys parted, revealing Alaska kneeling next to Jay. He was slumped against a tree trunk. Red paint covered his forearms and clothes, and a pool lay by his legs on the grass. His shoulders sagged, and his head hung to the side. Why was he sleeping?

"Jay?"

Why was there so much paint? No, maybe he wasn't painting. Why would he be painting in the forest? Was he eating cranberries? Why? I pushed away the thoughts trying to ambush me. Then, I heard Alaska's soft whimpers and saw her slack expression. I stopped.

"Oh, goddess, no, no." I couldn't breathe.

"He's gone." Her hand moved away from his wrist, where giant gashes still poured out blood.

A complete numbness overtook my body, and dizziness crashed into me. My heart rammed inside my throat, and my limbs turned to lead.

Everything. Shut. Down.

I stared at Jay's pained frozen expression.

My breaths turned shallow, and I dragged my hands through my hair, gripping it tightly between my fingers.

"No...no. Wake him up."

"Kyra, he's gone." Alaska's eyes were red, and her lips pinched together.

I shook my head slowly and staggered forward. With each step, my knees weakened, and my chest hitched. I dropped to the ground by his side and cried uncontrollably.

"Wake up!" I shook his side.

"Kyra, stop." Alaska placed one hand over his face softly.

"I'll heal him." I took his bloodied hands into mine and chanted, *"Terra angakok. Terra angakok."*

Nothing happened.

"Why isn't it working?" I rolled down my shorts and saw five golden tattoos. No gray. No Ꮳsµwi left.

Tears fell down my cheeks, and Alaska reached over, but I pushed her away. "You're a Griffin! You must have healing powers in you somewhere. Help me heal him!" I wailed.

"I can't," Alaska whispered and stood, moving away. "This can't be happening. Not him, not my brother too," she kept whispering to herself.

"Jay, no." I pressed my face to his chest. "Please."

Surh-Sig and Oniskel flew over quietly and rested a hand on each of my shoulders.

"You can save him. You're nymphs!"

"You are too."

"No! I don't want to be. I chose to bring the boys back, to stay in the Abyss." My entire body turned numb. "I didn't want *this*! I can't live here without him!"

"To bring him back...." They shook their heads. "We'd need a sacrifice and all four gems, but we only have three." Surh-Sig held up parts of the crushed ruby and the pearl.

Next to her, Alaska frowned and rubbed the emerald hanging around her neck. "These gems aren't special. I tried to bring Paola back, and it didn't work, so you can have it." She handed over the Draven Emerald and walked away without another word, destroyed in every way.

Pressure built in my chest, and my heart physically hurt. I wrapped my arms around my knees and rocked back and forth. I didn't know what to look at or what to do. It felt like my chest was caving in, and all words escaped me.

A loud *squish* sounded from the mud behind us.

"Hurry, come here," Surh-Sig said, but I had such little energy it took everything I had to turn around.

Two strong hands lifted me out of the mud and pulled me away from Jay. I wanted to kick and scream, but nothing came out. Tears soaked my face.

"Pay attention. According to the legend, you four can only do this once, love."

I whipped my head around to see Isaac's gray eyes and the Vayu Crystal around his neck. The fourth gem. My heart sang with hope, but had too much time passed? Jay hadn't moved. Isaac scooped me into his arms when I tumbled over from my broken foot. He followed the nymphs to the riverside to meet Moroka. Isaac set me down and handed over the crystal. I vowed silently to repay him at some point.

"Are you all sure about this?" Oniskel met each of their eyes. "If you're sure, then this is it."

Moroka and Oniskel glanced at me, then nodded. "We owe her."

"What…what do…what do you mean this is it?" I sniffed.

They ignored me and said at the same time, "Yes, we're ready."

"Hurry, sisters," Sur-Sig said as she handed the gems to their respective owners. "We must all say this spell together, *Cupi geyiu,* on the count of three."

I squeezed the sharp ruby piece in my palm and swallowed hard.

"One." Oniskel smiled and nodded to her sisters.

"Two." Moroka splashed her fin once behind her.

"Three." Surh-Sig squeezed my other hand and inhaled deeply.

"Cupi geyiu," we chanted. *"Cupi geyiu. Cupi geyiu."*

A throbbing prick quickly turned into a scorching ache in my abdominals. My Circles pinched, burned, singed, and tightened. I strained to stay upright as my legs trembled and the sky shook. I held my breath and leaned in, muttering please under my breath. Each of the nymph's faces started to shine. I held still. Hope fluttered deep in my belly, and adrenaline spiked through my veins.

The strongest sense of calm washed over me. I was flooded with a floating sensation like all my burdens had been removed. I was finally willing to believe everything would be alright.

"Kyra?"

Jay's voice.

Goosebumps slid along the back of my neck. My hand covered my mouth as I turned around, noticing every shift of the blades of grass, every sound of a butterfly's wing, and the weak smirk on Jay's face as he reached his arms out to me.

"Jay!"

Time slowed down, and everything felt different than before. I ran, or wobbled, as fast as possible to him. He was okay. He was alive. The spell worked!

"Come here, Petal." He stretched out his arms, clean and healed. There was not a speck of blood near him.

"Are you okay? How do you feel? What hurts? Do you need something?" With shaking hands, I dropped to his side and felt his cheeks, neck, and ears. He was here. Alive. Safe. "Are you sure it's you?" Tears streaked down my face again. "You're here."

"I'm here." He wrapped me in a tight embrace. "And you're here."

I never wanted to pull away, but Isaac cleared his throat behind us. Turning, I fell into Isaac's arms and hugged him, whispering, "Thank you, thank you, thank you."

Isaac steadied me as I swayed. He chuckled and pried me off him. "Quit being so handsy, woman."

"Wait, where are the nymphs?" I looked at the riverbank.

Isaac shook his head. "They're gone, Kyra."

"Where did they go?" But, somehow, I already knew.

"All the nymphs are gone, as well as the four gems. That was the sacrifice for healing someone at such a…significant level."

"How do you know that?" I asked.

With a sly grin and a fake accent, Isaac cast his arms out wide and said, "I'm the librarian, love. Haven't you learned anything by now?"

Despite everything, I snorted and tried to hide my smile.

"It's okay, Kyra," Jay said. "I bet they knew what they were doing."

I checked my tattoos. There weren't five anymore, just one. It wasn't gold or gray. The only Circle that remained was red.

I was no longer the Cursed One.

No longer the Golden One.

No longer immortal.

Nor a nymph. The spell must've changed it all.

Just an Elidian with fire Magik, but even that didn't matter as long as I had Jay.

29

JADOX

My Kyra was back. When I had shattered the ruby, she died. I had killed her. Her pulse and breathing had stopped. Yet, now, she stood above me like a fierce angel. My heart rammed inside my chest.

Mud stuck to my clothes. Nilson lowered his hand to me, and I accepted it. He pulled me up from the ground, and a silent conversation passed between us—one that Kyra never needed to know about. We loved her, but Nilson was officially moving on to a different future.

Next to him, Kyra was patting her stomach as if in disbelief.

“Kyra, what’s wrong?” I asked.

“Four tattoos are gone.”

I needed to stay strong for her now and be her rock. So much had happened over the last few minutes, days, that she needed time to process. My sole purpose was to keep it together for her sake. I’d try to give her whatever she needed, whether it was answers, a bath, or lassoing the fuckin’ moon.

One bright red Circle remained on her stomach. I traced it with my finger and blew out a deep breath.

“The ₾sµwi power is gone, and I can’t feel any connection to water, air, or earth anymore." She perked her head to the forest. "Actually, I can't hear the same as before, either."

Quickly, she limped around the base of the tree, once, twice, three times, looking for something–maybe the sword welded from darkness, but it had disappeared. The shattered pieces of the ruby in the mud were also gone.

"Stop limping around, Petal." I grabbed her waist. "Let me heal you."

I hovered my hand over her ankle. Nothing happened.

"Terra angakok," I said aloud.

Nothing.

"Hm, that's weird."

"Maybe we just need to rest," Kyra said as she studied the rising smoke from the trees.

Most of the flames had been put out by Moroka earlier, but the charred trees still looked like death. I cast my hand out and commanded the soil to move. It did. At least I still had some Magik at my disposal.

Something tapped my shoulder. I turned. Alaska sat atop a gorula with the Unetlo Book in her hand. I was so glad I had caught her in the river before Elana's plan sent my sister over the deadly cascade. In fact, I was grateful Elana was dead and gone forever. Forever. For eternity. And it seemed like Kyra wouldn't be a nymph after all. So many emotions and thoughts bombarded me.

Wait, I hadn't smelled Alaska's arrival. I'd recognize the animal's scent from a mile away any other day. Things were different. My Magik had changed, somehow.

Alaska slid off the beast's back and wrapped her arms around me, almost knocking me over. She squeezed so tightly that I was afraid she'd never let go.

"You're alive?" Alaska pulled back and abruptly slapped me across the face. "How dare you try and leave me?"

My cheek stung as I swept her in for another hug. "I'm sorry."

"You better be! You owe me for your whole life, which will be at least sixty more years." Alaska pointed in my face with the intensity of a warrior. "Don't you *ever* do something like that again."

"Deal." I sighed and brought my sister closer.

I had been an idiot to try and end it all, but the thought of going on without Kyra was unfathomable. Maybe she had sacrificed her immortality and endless powers to save me. Now, she stood beside me, alive and mine. With a love that ran so deep, I knew everything would eventually be okay.

Alaska tossed the Unetlo Book to Nilson, who opened it and said, "It's empty."

"I know." Alaska peeked over his shoulder. "Every spell written in there has been erased."

"Maybe that book belonged to the nymphs. When they left, they must've taken everything they created with them."

"Like my enhancement?" Alaska's nose scrunched up. "That would explain why I couldn't teleport here."

Kyra leaned against me in exhaustion. "Isaac, try your poisonous gas thing."

I stiffened. "I don't think that's a good idea."

"I'll give you space." Nilson jogged to the river and stood ankle-deep. The breeze shifted directions, but no toxic mist came from his fingers. His face tightened, and his lips moved silently.

"Well, that's a relief," I mumbled.

When he jogged back over, his s-watch pinged.

Kyra's gaze whipped to my watch. "Have you heard from my father?"

Nilson's brows pulled together. "Yeah, he and Narelle are with all the free prisoners in a warehouse on the other side of Andersonville. They lost four Ordulls during the rescue mission, which is a surprisingly low number, and…." His lips twitched at the corner.

"What's that look for?" Kyra tried to sneak a peek at the message.

Nilson covered it up with his hand and turned away. "Nothing, but just to let you know, Landon is fine too. Dez…" He cleared his throat and met my eye for just a moment.

At that moment, I knew Nilson would move on, and I didn't have to worry about him trying to steal my Kyra back.

"Dez has Wes and Landon at my old place in Vayu. She said rumors were already spreading about Elana's death and that newscasters who haven't been on the air for weeks were about to broadcast an emergency announcement about some of the males returning."

"Some?" Kyra sucked in a disappointed breath. "Grandma did say only *some* of the males...."

"How about you sit down." I guided her to a large rock that wasn't caked in mud or ashes.

Nilson pushed buttons on his watch and projected a news channel into the air. On camera, a woman was smiling with glistening eyes as three boys surrounded her. "As you probably know, *some* males have returned. Thousands of reports have flooded our team within the last few minutes of sons and nephews returning to us." She pulled the three boys in close, all shorter than her shoulder. "We are grateful and all in shock, but it's important to know that every report has been of a child. No male over age twelve has been recorded to return." She paused and looked at the camera. "There are numerous speculations about why they have returned, if witches were involved and if the adult males will ever come back to us. We are here to support those of you who are still awaiting your husbands, fathers, and loved ones."

Kyra grabbed my hand. "I only saved *some*."

My jaw dropped. "Wait, did *you* do this?"

She nodded. "I tried, Jay. I tried to bring them all back." Then her head rested against my chest. "I don't think I'll have another chance. What if those women wait forever, hoping for their person to return? That's not fair."

Nilson turned off the news feed, listening to our conversation. "You could make a public statement."

My muscles tensed around Kyra, wanting to protect her from any backlash against the Ordulls who would blame her. It was her face, after all, that Elana had plastered across Lodesa, marking her as a felon not to be trusted.

"Why would anyone believe me?" Kyra whispered.

"You'd have the Aurum Orbis Society's support and mine too."

She tapped her fingers on her leg in a nervous beat. "Why would *your* support mean anything to their people?"

Nilson gulped, then slowly pushed another button on his watch. He scrolled through image after image of people in Vuldow holding signs up that read, *Isaac Nilson for President,* and *Nilson has my vote,* and *The man with air will truly care.*

I rolled my eyes at the last sign.

Kyra rubbed her forehead. "What...when did all of *that* happen?"

"Apparently, Gemm, Landon, and Wes had a secret mission of their own while we were away on our adventures. My son was campaigning for me. Since he has both Mystier and Ordull blood, the people are listening to him."

"Well, maybe Wes should be president then." Kyra half-laughed, but her eyes looked exhausted.

"Maybe in a decade or two—" Nilson rubbed a hand over his beard.

"This is overwhelming. We've been through a lot," I interrupted. "How about we get back to the group, find a doctor for your ankle, and sleep for a few days." I scooped Kyra into my arms, and she wrapped her hands around my neck.

"Only if I get a mountain of pillows."

"Of course, you always hog the bed anyways." I lifted her onto the gorula's back and climbed behind her.

When I reached a hand toward Nilson, he shook his head, "You two go ahead. I called a venti to come to pick us up. The little girl's name is Sarisha, and she's from Vayu, so I need to take her home."

"Are you sure?" Kyra's voice was so soft and tired that I couldn't help but smile.

"Yeah, you're in good hands. Griffin will protect you; he's a good man." Nilson nodded to me.

Alaska smiled and lifted the girl into her arms. Words didn't need to be spoken between my sister and me. Everything would heal between us...eventually.

Nilson smacked the gorula's backside, and it ran off in fluid gallops, all six sets of knuckles pushing off the ground.

I held Kyra close, inhaling her scent. The strong aroma always around her had disappeared, but maybe a normal sense of smell wouldn't be the worst thing in this life to have. I smiled and tugged her closer. We passed by The Crooked Chateau, where women were already scaling the outside and ripping down the electrical cords. I couldn't figure out if they were Ordulls or Mystiers—or maybe both—working together. Since the streets were quiet and calm, I wondered what had happened to the rest of Elana's army, if they had fled or surrendered.

A little boy ran out into the road, chasing another and giggling. Our gorula stopped just short of trampling them, then licked one's face from chin to forehead. The boy's eyes widened into saucers, then he stroked the creature's golden fur.

"This is what it'll be like from now on," Kyra whispered, half-asleep. "Our two worlds combined. If Isaac is the new president, he'll make sure everyone coexists, whether they possess Magik or not."

I nodded, hoping she was right, but all of this was too much information, too soon. All I needed was to make sure Kyra got a doctor's attention.

"There'll be a lot of changes he'll have to implement to make that work, but he can do it," she said proudly. "Didn't you hear?" She yawned. "He's the librarian...Isaac knows everything."

I chuckled and nestled her even closer. The gorula raced by hoverboard racks, past abandoned grocery stores and empty clubs with broken doors and cracked windows. It'd take time to rebuild the cities from Elana's destruction. At least we knew where citizens had been hiding recently—Vuldow. Hopefully, with Elana dead and no more demons roaming with dark Magik, we will have the chance for a peaceful future. I tried to imagine a rebuilt Draven village without a shield making us invisible to the rest of the world. It was a nice thought.

At this point, I only wanted to lay in a bed with Kyra and curl into her back, sheltering her from the outside world.

But maybe my Petal didn't need protection, either. She was the one who saved *me, after all.*

The gorula stopped in front of a tall skyscraper with a bent-in door. I scooted off its back and gathered Kyra in my arms again. She didn't even argue or resist but looked up at me with complete adoration in her eyes.

"Remember..." Her sleepy eyes fluttered. "A mountain of pillows."

I smiled and kissed her forehead.

When we entered the safe house, Brent was pacing the front lobby of what seemed to be an apartment complex. When he saw his daughter, his hands pressed into a steeple and his shoulders completely relaxed. I nodded silently, hoping he understood how tired she was. He returned the gesture and led me past groups of people chatting quietly to an elevator. When the doors closed, he peeked at her sleeping face.

"Is she okay?" Brent whispered.

"She needs a cast for a broken foot. Can you find a doctor, sir?"

He nodded quickly. "You can't heal her?"

"No." I studied his face, which was so like Caspian's. "Have you been able to manipulate anyone's mind or read anyone's thoughts?"

Brent shook his head.

"I think all our enhancements are gone, sir."

His jaw dropped.

"I don't think things will be the same anymore."

He nodded slowly, processing. "What happened out there? Is Elana truly dead?"

"Yes," I whispered, my arms tiring from holding her weight. "And the nymphs are all gone."

"Gone?" His gaze darted to Kyra's again. "But Kyra was supposed to be the fire nymph. Shouldn't she be gone too?"

I remembered my vision of a woman rising from Elana's dead body. But if my guess was correct. It wasn't something Brent needed to know yet.

"I don't think Kyra was the fire nymph, but a different kind. I haven't been able to ask her yet."

We stood in silence as the buttons in the elevator brightened to level ten, then eleven, then twelve. It reminded me of the first day I met Kyra when she was fleeing from her band manager at the club–the night that changed my life and the world. If I had known then all that was to follow, would I have stuck with her?

Definitely.

A tiny snore escaped Kyra, and as I watched her sleep, I felt Brent's eyes trained on me.

"You love her." It wasn't a question.

I swallowed. "With all my heart, sir."

"You're a good man, Jadox."

"I'm not so sure about that."

He patted my back softly. "Well, you have my blessing…just in case you get any *ideas*."

A thousand thoughts rushed through my mind, and my sole tattoo singed my core, but I was too tired to process it all.

"I'm sorry about Caspian," I said.

"Thank you." He nodded. "I heard you lost your grandma."

"Yes, I guess they both gave the ultimate sacrifice."

The elevator stopped on level twenty. Brent led me down a long hallway to a door. He slid a key through and held it open.

"All the prisoners from The Cavity are in this building, eating, showering, and recovering. You won't miss anything vital while you rest. Here's some water, and I'll find a doctor for Kyra. But now, just sleep, son."

A warmth spread through my chest. *Son.* No one had called me that since I lost my parents.

Brent nodded and closed the door. The apartment must have once belonged to a musician because there were four guitars, piles of vintage records, and a small sound booth in the corner. Of course, this would be Kyra's space for temporary sanctuary. She shifted in my trembling arms, and I had to grasp her tighter, so I didn't drop her from pure fatigue.

I nudged the bedroom door open and laid her on a giant white comforter. Her hair pooled around her like a puddle, and it was the first time I realized it was no longer gold but brown like Caspian's had been. The Golden One was gone. Just like the cursed Magik was gone. Thank the goddess above. I laid down and draped my arm over her side.

Then I closed my eyes and was ready to fade into a sleep full of dreams about my Kyra, my love, my roots.

30

KYRA

We were finally back home. The crutches dug into my armpits as I surveyed the remains of Draven's village. The gardens toppled with overgrown weeds, and the stone pathways leading to each den were knocked out of place. Jay swished his hand through the air, and a dozen roses bloomed on the nearest bush. He always made everything in my life more beautiful.

My gaze climbed the tall ladders up to the treehouses where many wooden planks were cracked or dangling off the side. But my attention was snagged downward as Jay sighed and lowered in front of me on one knee. My heart fluttered. Was he going to— Would he— No, he wouldn't do that only one week after we both halfway died. Jay gently held the cast wrapped around my foot and wiped the dirt off its side.

He slowly picked up one of Chocolate's adorable puppies and handed it to me. Apparently, she had made a new friend during our adventures. I snuggled the pup's soft fur to my cheek as it wiggled and licked my face. Jay grinned up at me and reached into his back pocket. I held my breath, and my heart cartwheeled again. He pulled out a protein bar and ripped open the package. As he rose agonizingly slow, his eyes never left mine.

"You are..." I grumbled. "You are...."

"Famished." He grabbed the bar and split it in two, then shoved his half in his cheeks, puffing them out like an adorable chipmunk.

"Don't eat too much. Alaska and I are making a four-course meal for dinner later."

He sighed. "I'm glad she came back."

"Me too." I patted his back. "Give her some time to process everything."

"She better not try to move in with us, though." He leaned in for a kiss. "No matter how much I love my sister, I want you all to myself. Maybe you'd be a better snack than this."

I lifted the base of one of my Draven-made crutches, created from strong branches with flowers twining around them, and playfully swatted it behind Jay's knees.

"Hey!" He laughed and blocked my next attack. "Don't you make me break your other foot."

I swung at him again. "You wouldn't dare!"

"Oh, I would do anything to keep you stuck in my bed for months. It'd be a good excuse to take full advantage of every opportunity." He twisted me against his chest, sending both crutches to the ground.

Our chests rose and fell quickly, but I could no longer hear his heartbeat like before. That was something I'd miss. The liquid desire in his eyes, turning my bones to lava, would have to suffice.

The moment was abruptly ruined by a pack of gorulas swinging into the clearing above, all grunting in harmony. Jay gathered my crutches and helped me hobble back into place. We'd make our home here, but it'd be different. Since both Mystiers and Ordulls resisted the idea of raising invisible shields again, this Magik within Draven, the flowers, trees, and lakes would now be exposed to all of Lodesa.

"We will keep rebuilding," he whispered. "The Dravians who want to return will still have a home here."

"Can we put a fountain there? Right in the middle of the clearing? As a memorial for those we lost." I pictured a mixture of all the elements in a marble structure and the names of those we lost inscribed on the side, including Hallie, Zeph, Paola, Gemm, and, of course, Caspian.

My brother wouldn't ever see his precious Cydon rebuilt. At least Narelle had Brent's help to take care of their people and encourage them back to the sea.

After my speech at the press conference last week in Andersonville, I needed rest. Especially since word got out that I'd killed Lodesa's president. A knot formed in my chest, but it didn't linger long. Watching my speech on replay was an out-of-body experience. Only a few citizens still viewed Elana as a hero, idolizing her as Syvonne Stirk, a woman of the people, so that didn't mean I was completely safe from attacks. Maybe Jay was right; I needed some time in bed with him as a distraction. Things wouldn't be happily-ever-after for at least a few months, but we were on the right path.

Only time would tell how the rest of Lodesa would cope after they processed my news that the adult Ordull males were truly gone forever. No nymphs, spell books, demons, gems, or cursed Magik were left capable of returning them. Only the four basic elements of Magik remained: fire, earth, wind, and water. Hopefully, Isaac's charming speech about being grateful the male children had returned would keep the peace for a while. We'd address that later, but for now, I needed to focus on one person.

Landon.

My nephew ran up to me with Chocolate at his heels. When I crouched down, he threw himself against my chest, surprising me since he hadn't ever liked being touched. I pressed a finger to my lips, then pointed to his forehead, asking him permission. He nodded with a smile, so I planted a wet kiss just below his blond curls.

This little guy was the last connection I had to my previous life. Since I returned thousands of males his age, he wouldn't have to grow up in a confusing world of only Mystiers as I had feared. Landon had the chance to go to school among both Ordull and Mystiers. The next generation's future was an unknown for us all—but it was full of hope.

He signed with a gesture I wasn't aware of and then pointed to

Gemm's old den. I expected to see Alaska with a basket of ingredients for our upcoming dinner, but Dezlian stood in the doorframe, waving. She deserved the world on a silver platter for taking care of Landon and Wes during the last few weeks of chaos.

Jay laced his fingers through mine as he led me to the old den. I squeezed his hand in reassurance since it was the first time he'd been here since Gemm passed away.

"Nice speech last week." Dezlian stepped forward and tossed Chocolate a treat from her pocket. "But you look prettier in person than on camera."

"Uh, I'll take that as a compliment, and I only made that speech because Isaac asked me to."

"Thank you, though. He's got a challenging road ahead of him, and I appreciate you taking some of the responsibility off his shoulders." Dezlian crossed her arms and leaned against the side of the den.

We all had a rough road ahead to deal with all the grief and plan for a new future. Once things settled more, I had every intention of signing up for therapy with a professional. It wouldn't be fair to dump every feeling on Jadox about losing mom, Hallie, and Caspian. He'd always be my rock and be there to listen, but what I'd been through was extensive. There was finally some safety and time to fully process. Hopefully, those I cared about also found a way to cope.

"Is Isaac okay?" I studied the look on Dezlian's face, curious that her cheeks flushed at the mention of him.

"Oh yeah, he loves how involved Wes is with campaigning. Everyone loves that kid."

"Brother," Landon said and pointed to the pictures of Wes on his keychain. "Brother."

My heart clamped tight. Landon had spent so much time with Wes recently, and now they'd have to be separated. I hated the thought of snatching him away from comfort during this time of unknowns. Even though I knew we weren't blood-related, I was still the only caregiver in Landon's life. I understood nothing about raising a nine-year-old, but we'd figure it out together with Jay by my side.

"Hey, buddy, can you play fetch with Chocolate for a few

minutes?" Dezlian avoided my eyes. "I have something I need to talk to your aunt about."

Was she about to bring up her obvious crush on Isaac right in front of Jay? How devastatingly awkward would that be? My body tensed, and I gulped down my nerves. It wasn't a conversation we needed to have. Dezlian and Isaac were both single and free to choose whomever they wanted. I had no right to have any opinion on it whatsoever.

"Kyra, I want to ask if I can start the process to be a foster parent to Landon," Dezlian said.

My knees buckled, but Jay caught me and said, "Woah, I got you, Petal."

I glanced across the clearing at my nephew, spinning in circles around Chocolate, then cleared my throat. "Um, you want to foster Landon? You barely know him."

"I know y'all have known each other since he was born, but we formed a special bond, and I can't imagine leaving here without him. I know we haven't been together for long, but Landon has taken over my heart. I can send a venti from Vayu for you to visit him whenever you want."

She rambled on about activities and conversations they had together during my time away, but I tuned her out, concerned only about what was best for Landon.

Dezlian's rambling quickened. "I know you'd miss him, but I just thought…since you're not his *real* aunt, wait, that's not what I meant. I shouldn't have said it like that…but me and Landon…his sweet soul…." A tear slid down her cheek, and she wiped it away nervously. "I'm sorry, I'm trying to convince you, but I'm being rude. Let me start over."

Utterly shocked, I silently met Jay's eyes and asked him his opinion. After he nodded, I exhaled slowly, wondering what Landon's life would be like in the city of wind and skyscrapers.

"Can we have a day or two to talk it over? You're free to stay in Draven while we discuss it."

Her face brightened immediately. "Yes, of course. I'll go get his favorite toys for you and his backpack." She turned on her heels. "And his toothbrush, I'll have to find a new one actually because he used the last one to brush Chocolate's teeth and—"

"Dezlian," I cut her off. "Go ahead and stay with him like you have been until we decide. There's no need to transition him again in the meantime."

She clapped her hands together happily and skipped inside the den.

A flock of ventus soared high, blending in with the puffy white clouds. It was strange to think that nothing Magikal would be kept secret anymore. We were all united now.

I turned to Jay and shook my head. "That was *not* what I was expecting Dezlian to say. Fostering Landon, I mean…wow…that's a huge step."

"How do you feel about it? Did you want to adopt him yourself?" Jay asked.

"I have no idea." I leaned against his chest, and he wrapped his arms around my back as I replied, "I haven't had time to consider the future. Everything has been about surviving the next minute, the next hour, the next day."

"Well, I know *my* future."

I craned my neck and gazed into the dark eyes that held all my tomorrows. "Um, excuse me, Jay…where *exactly* do you think your hands are going?" A welcomed shiver rippled over my body, creating goosebumps as his hands moved under my shirt and up my back.

His skin against mine felt like home. It didn't matter if we lived in Draven, Elidi, or Andersonville. If we had each other, I'd be happy.

The base of my crutches sunk into the mushy grass. "Ugh, these things suck!" I tried to chuck them far away but barely managed a few feet. Power singed through my Circle, and I shot flames out of my fingers fast and hard.

One of Jay's brows rose to his hairline. "Are you about done with your temper tantrum?"

I stood like a flamingo and groaned, "Ugh, I guess you'll have to carry me up."

"Oh, Petal." He kneeled in front of me for the second time that day, stealing my breath away. But he swiftly rotated to give me access to his back. "Someday, you'll be the death of me."

"Shut up, soldier. You already died. Technically, you've died twice since I met you, so you never will again." I wiggled on top of him like a drunk sloth, clinging on pathetically. There was no other option but to dry-hump his back as I shimmied higher.

A laugh burst from deep in his belly as he patiently waited. "Are you okay back there?"

"Just go," I grumbled, but a smile still lifted my cheeks. "If we want to keep one of Chocolate's puppies, we won't be able to live in a treehouse. Maybe a den like Gemm's would be better and safer long term."

"Are puppies the only future you're thinking about?"

I grinned, but he couldn't see. "I'm not answering that, soldier."

He carried me passed the spot where I had played drums around the campfire at the Luna Festival, through the clearing he had taught me basic Magik, and to the base of the ladder of his childhood treehouse. When he started climbing, I tightened my grip around his strong muscles.

"Hey, Kyra?"

"Hey, Jay?" I licked behind his ear, and he stilled.

"If you want me to accidentally drop you, try that again."

"You'd never drop me." I kissed the back of his neck and swirled my tongue behind his ear again.

Jay groaned, deep, carnal, and raw. His entire back tensed, but his pace quickened.

"Are you ready to tell me what happened after I shattered the ruby?"

"Does the change of topic mean you want me to stop this?" I giggled and blew a soft breath onto his neck. Little goosebumps rose, and I could feel how much he was struggling to concentrate.

"I need to know the whole story, Petal. What happened when you blacked out?"

"The spirit of my grandma was there."

"Elana?"

"No, Elana was my great-grandmother. Her daughter was there. She was the fire nymph all along, and Elana had taken control of her powers when she cast her under the spell that sucked out her life energy."

"So…you were never the fire nymph..."

I gave him a moment of relief from my teasing lips as he gripped the top rung of the ladder and reached the treehouse platform. Jay flattened straight on the floor on his stomach, and I started massaging his muscles, appreciating the bulk beneath me.

"Mm, that feels good." His guttural groan stroked my tattoo awake.

It had been too long since we had sex, and whether I had a broken ankle or not, I refused to wait another day. My hands rolled his shirt up, and his entire back was on display. I dug my thumbs into either side of his spine and rubbed all the way up and down. Delicious. All I needed was oils to make his skin a bit more slippery.

Mid-groan, he asked, "If you weren't ever…" his words came out in spurts when I pushed into his muscles deeply. "Supposed to be…ugh… the fire nymph…then what exactly were you meant to be?"

"I don't know. I think I could be something different, something stronger and unprecedented. Maybe I'm just like Elana."

"You were…never like Elana." I knew his brows were knitted together in concentration without seeing his face. No matter how much he enjoyed this massage, he latched onto my every word. "You didn't want power…ugh, that's the spot…you didn't want immortality."

"I only want you. Forever and always," I whispered.

"Forever?" He paused. "You mean it?"

My hands stopped. "Roll over, Jay."

"Is that a command, Petal?"

"Now."

I lifted my ass a bit so he could turn onto his back without crushing me or my new cast. When he rolled, his long, hard bulge under his pants twitched with need. Jay folded both hands behind his head, giving me the perfect view. Jay's shirt stayed bunched up high, revealing his perfect chest. I sighed at the jagged *MINE* scar scratched into the skin on his upper pec. My fingers traced the letters slowly.

"Maybe I should let you tattoo me…anything you want to write on my body," I said.

He frowned. "I'll never do anything to hurt you, Kyra."

"It'd only be fair, though."

Jay stopped my hand and pulled my fingers to his lips. That simple tug pulled my whole body forward over the top of him. I swept my lips over his. If wishes were made of his kisses, then I'd never need anything else again. I was *his* completely.

As if reading my mind, Jay whispered, "What you branded on me is true, Kyra. I'm yours."

"Prove it." I kissed him like it was our first kiss, our last kiss, our forever kiss.

Instead of grabbing my waist like I expected, Jay stretched his arm to the side of the treehouse. His body squirmed bit by bit, inching us to the corner.

I finally came up for air and laughed, "Jay, what the Flames are you doing?"

His brown eyes were locked on mine, full of a whole new kind of intensity. "Kyra…."

"What? What's wrong?" I sat up, heart hammering.

Just as I was about to check behind me, a beam of sunlight reflected off something small in his hand. A gold ring with a red diamond in the middle.

"Jay…" I gaped at him, confused by the confident smile plastered over his stupidly perfect face.

"Link your life with mine, Kyra. Link your soul, your mind, and your heart with me. Be mine."

No song or drum could compare to the fiery beat of my heart as it danced for him. He slid the ring on my finger, but my eyes never left his. I used to spend all my nights on stage, in the background, wondering how to run away from all men. That whole time, without realizing it, I was waiting for Jay; now, he was mine. If I had never loved him, maybe I'd still be faking smile after smile, doing my best to survive another day. But he brought me back to life when I was almost too far gone. He had a way of helping me forgive my past, so now, I'd return the favor. Together, we'd be there for one another and let each other heal over time. I'd kiss his scars until they were coated with love.

The devotion in Jay's eyes was truer than the very air in my lungs, the breeze through my hair, and the fire in my soul. People say nothing lasts forever, but with the passion aflame in his gaze, I knew I had made the right choice. I'd rather live for only a few more moments with him, just like this, than an eternity without Jay.

"Yes, Jay. I'm already your roots. I'll be yours, and you'll be mine."

THE END

EPILOGUE

ISAAC

One year later

Sunlight reflected off Vayu's skyscrapers, casting Magikal blue beams across the festival downtown. We were celebrating one year since the return of the young males. The oldest Ordull male would turn fourteen next week. At this point, most Ordulls had accepted that the adult males would never come home.

Before the festivities required my attention, I had to find Dez. Every desperate breath I sucked in was at breaking point, unable to wait a moment longer. Too many weeks had passed since I realized my feelings for Dez.

My tattoo tickled my core in anticipation of her lips on mine. My heartbeat whirled like a speeding windmill, circling faster and faster. Where was she? If I had to wait until tonight for this conversation, my head might explode.

Little boys and girls giggled in the street as they cut in front of me and ran in their festival costumes. They depicted a perfect picture of our combined worlds in their cute gorula, jugosaur, cat, and horse masks, all chasing each other. It brought back memories of a younger Wes. Right now, he was probably discussing politics with the Minister of Topell or playing video games with Landon. If Dez returned my feelings, they might be brothers someday.

"Look, Timmy!" said a little girl with venti wings strapped to her back. "It's President Nilson!"

The group rushed over, hopping at my waist and asking questions all at once.

"What are you doing here?"

"Have you ridden the Ferris wheel?"

"My mommy has a crush on you! She has a picture of your face on our ceiling."

"Show us some air Magik!"

"Did you actually know the Golden One?"

I smiled at their questions and rustled the hair of a boy who reminded me of myself as a child. Gray eyes sparked with wonder and curiosity. With a quick flick of my wrist, I summoned wind to lift a foam ball from a game cart stationed on the street. My wind carried the ball across the stand into the basket for an impossible score.

"Hey!" the vendor yelled. "That's cheating!" Once he caught my face, he blanched. "Oh, sorry, Mr. President. Here, have this stuffed animal for Wes." He reached up, pulled down a green hydraco, eyed the children surrounding me, and yanked down six more. "Actually, here, you all can have one."

They all cheered and grabbed their favorite, then ran off to the booth that was selling tickets for the rides.

I surveyed the decorations and banners with my face painted on the blue ribbons. Not my best image, but better than a mug shot. At least, that was what Dez had said when she had created them. My heart skipped a beat as I picked up my pace. Where was Dez? Maybe by the ceremony stage? Or she could still be setting up the target range and signing up participants for the competition.

A premature firecracker exploded, and a little girl shrieked and ran behind a sign. It read *Vayu's Library,* pointing to the center of our city. Of course, Dez would be in our mutual sanctuary, away from the chaos. Guessing what plot she might be writing today gave me fresh goosebumps that spread over my arms. I loved to listen to her talk about her passion for hours. Dez was a mastermind at developing characters and giving them obstacles that made each of her readers sit on the edge of their seats. My Circle throbbed with the need to see her. Goddess, I needed that woman. I'd been an idiot for taking this long to figure it out.

The crystal steps ascending to the library's front door gave me flashbacks of the similar-stoned gem I used to wear around my neck. That adventure with Kyra felt like a lifetime ago. At least I received occasional updates from Alaska that Kyra was still safe, and none of the angry citizens who still blamed her for not returning the rest of the males had laid a hand on her. As far as the rumors went, she and Griffin had some big announcement for their village after today's festival's events concluded. Maybe they'd set a date for their wedding. I smiled at what life had in store for Kyra's future. She only deserved the best.

When I pushed the heavy library doors open, the intoxicating scent of old books wafted through the air, full of nostalgia and adventure. In the front lobby, a table of books was displayed professionally. Behind it, Dez unpacked another box, stacking the books into a neat pile.

She looked up and met my eyes. My heart fucking flipped, and I inhaled a much-needed breath. Dez completely consumed me, not just because of her giving spirit and how she helped take care of Wes, but her insane patience for me and my new leadership role. The woman could handle anything. When things got tough, she always knew the answer.

"Phew, these are heavy." She smiled brighter than the sun. "Help me?"

She captivated me, even when she talked to herself while unpacking and whispered her endless "to-do" list. Every word I needed to say to her lingered on the tip of my tongue, but nothing would come out. I stumbled over my feet as I darted to her side and silently lifted the last box onto the table.

Did she know how I felt, or would we always stay in the friend zone? Was I meant to live a life alone? Wes would always make me happy, but this woman defined "devastating" in a whole new way. If I didn't have her by my side day after day, the pure devastation would rip me apart. I no longer had time to waste. It was now or never. Dez had to know how madly in love I was with her. Finally, I opened my pathetic mouth to confess it all, but she started talking.

"It's been a whirlwind. I can't believe I wrote three whole books in a year. Which one is your favorite?" She wagged a playful finger at her name in the author position on the cover. She was my hero, who wrote my personal story over three books, changing some details to disguise it as fiction. "Let me guess…was it the first one?" She laughed, melting my heart. "Naw, you always depicted yourself as a villain in that first novel, so that couldn't be your favorite."

Words failed me. Again. No clever comebacks or teases shot out because Dez had the ability to destroy any rational thought in my little brain. I knocked my knuckles against the table and stared at the book's cover, which showcased a ripped blond model with a high bun holding the coolest sword I'd ever seen.

"Oh, the second book must be your favorite. When you got the girl?"

She was referring to Kyra; all I could do was shake my head like an idiot. I hadn't gotten the girl I was meant for —yet. Leaning towards Dez, I accidentally tipped over the top few books.

Dez smiled and restacked the pile. "The third book must be your favorite. That's when everything changed for you."

Dez rose on her tiptoes and hovered her lips an inch from mine, closer than she had risked in the last year. I gulped and absolutely froze. Did she know what she was doing to me? Fuck.

"Maybe the fourth will be *my* favorite," she whispered. "A new beginning…I could title it *The President Prince*."

When she backed away, my sanity returned, and I shook my head and took a steadying breath. "That's a terrible name for a book." I licked my lips. "Is the hero a president or a prince?"

"Who do you want to be?" She bent to pick up another box of exclusive special-edition books that all had a sticker *signed by the author* on the front.

I seized the opportunity and pulled the gift for her from my pocket. Before she turned around, I quickly fixed its crumpled shape and held it in my shaking hand.

"Hey, Isaac, when you—" Her head tilted to the side. "What's that?

I chewed the inside of my cheek and placed the origami folded like a pinwheel into her palm. "It's for…it's for you…from me…I made it…myself."

"If you have time to make this, then maybe the presidency is too easy." She laughed and inspected the detailed curved edged. "Wait, there's something written on the flaps."

I nodded and ran a hand through my hair.

"Isaac?" She squinted and lifted the paper to her eyes. "What does it say?"

I swore my heart was about to explode out of my goddess-damned chest. I felt like a teenager at prom. "It says, 'Can I kiss you?'"

I stood still, waiting, wondering, wishing on every cloud that she'd say yes. Her face snapped up to mine, and a thousand expressions rolled over her features. Her perfect lips parted just a tad, and her gaze dropped to my mouth. What was she thinking? Did she want this?

"Isaac?" Her shoulders rose and fell harder with each breath, and she laid one hand on my chest.

I grabbed her free hand. "You've been everything to me, Dez. When our world fell apart, everyone was in panic mode. Through the disorganization of our new laws and the merging of our cities, you stood by me every step of the way."

Somehow, the woman of my dreams hadn't backed away from me yet. I still had her attention. Dez's eyes widened, and her jaw dropped slightly, encouraging me to continue. So, naturally, I kept rambling.

"You make the most delicious chocolate brownies, and Wes loves doing puzzles with you. Every time you laugh, it gives my soul the air I need to live. I want to be the reason that you smile each day."

A slow tear slid from the corner of her eye, and she squeezed my hand softly.

"I don't just want to kiss you, Dez. I want to wake up to you each morning and pretend I can cook eggs the way you like them. I want to visit this library each Saturday and huddle by the back fireplace in the restricted section where no one can bother us. I want to get four cats with you and yell at each other about who feeds them."

She laughed and wrapped her hands behind my neck, nodding along with each thing I listed.

Unable to stop, I said, "I want your fourth book to be *our* story and the life we make together."

More tears freely streamed down her face.

Before another word escaped, Dez pressed her lips to mine. She tasted of syrup, and summertime flowed into one. I held her close and pressed her body to mine, knowing I'd never been happier than this exact moment. We kissed slowly as if we both understood we had decades ahead of us to explore each other more thoroughly.

After what could've been seconds, minutes, or days, she pulled away, her eyes dark with desire. "You took too long." She shoved my chest playfully.

"What?" I scooped her closer, unwilling for our bodies to separate.

"I've been waiting for you to say that since the day we met."

My cheeks started hurting from smiling so big. "Well, how can I make it up to you?"

Her cheeks flushed as her eyes went to the door labeled, *restricted section.*

My heart rate doubled again as she tugged my hand and walked me across the lobby. Her heels made quick *click-clack* sounds against the floor, echoing up to the high ceilings. But there was no one else but me to hear them since the rest of the town was outside at the festival.

I hovered a hand over the doorknob and paused, looking her straight in the eye. "You ready to plot out book four?"

She bit her lip. "I'm about to wipe that arrogant smirk off your face, my sweet. Book four is erotica."

My entire body shuddered at her confidence, and I opened the door to our new beginning.

ABOUT CASSIE SWINDON

Cassie's next writing idea includes fairy-tale retellings. She's very interested in turning the tables to show stories with gender reversal from other perspectives. Of course, she finds the best place for brainstorming ends up being in the shower or while trying to fall asleep, which isn't convenient in the least for taking notes. In her spare time, she collects bookmarks, stickers, washi tape, and cats.

Check out free short stories as prequels to my upcoming works in progress and also sign up for my newsletter here: https://cassieswindon.com/

facebook.com/cassie.swindon.3
twitter.com/CassieSwindon
instagram.com/cassie_swindon_author
bookbub.com/profile/cassie-swindon
amazon.com/stores/author/B091N72414
goodreads.com/cassieswindonauthor
tiktok.com/@cassieswindon

CHARACTERS

Alaska Griffin - Jadox's little sister. Enhancement- teleportation. From Draven.

Brent Elidi – Kyra's biological father. Enhancement- mind control/manipulation.

Brynn - hydraco creature based in Cydon.

Caspian Arno - Kyra's biological brother and Brent's son. Enhancement- holding breath for extra duration (AKA Caldo). From Cydon.

Chocolate - Jadox's brown lab based in Draven.

Elana Elidi - Kyra's great-grandmother. Only member in the leadership tribe without an enhancement.

Gemm Griffin – Jadox's grandmother. Enhancement- prophecies. From Draven.

Hallie Kozelski - Kyra's step-sister. Ordull. From Andersonville.

Isaac Nilson - Librarian and leader of Vayu. Enhancement- eyesight and weather.

Jadox Griffin - Past soldier for the Ordull army. From Draven. Enhancement- smell and healing.

Kyra Kozelski/Kyra Elidi - the Golden One. Enhancement- hearing and knowing ancient spells.

Landon Kozelski - Hallie's son. Ordull.

Moroka - The Blood Maiden/water nymph. Harnessed by the pearl.

Narelle - Caspian's wife from Cydon.

Paola Perez - Alaska's Ordull girlfriend/soldier in the army. From Andersonville.

Rajitha - Isaac's Ordull ex-girlfriend and Wes's mother.

Surh-Sig - The Skin Scraper/earth nymph. Harnessed by the emerald.

Syvonne Stirk - President of Lodesa (truly Elana Elidi).

Tawoli - venti creature based in Vayu.

Wes - Isaac's (and Rajitha's) son - hybrid. From Vayu.

Zeph - Isaac's Mystier ex-girlfriend. From Vayu.

CREATURES

Gorula – (Goldie) A mammal with six long arms that end in sharp claws and fur that ranges from peach to gold, beige, brown, and tan. Five feet tall and 400 pounds of mostly muscle. Omnivore. Likes to dig in the dirt and swing from trees like a monkey. Usually lives in/near Draven. If a Mystier accepts a gift from a Dyad, there is/will be a price to pay.

Hydraco - (Brynn) Swimming creature that looks like a crocodile with a seahorse tail. Greenish in color with scales and all-white eyes. Estimated to be over 2,000 pounds each. Territorial- like to bite. Usually stays near Cydon's underwater castle unless pulling a chariot.

Jugosaur - (Ashes) Flying dragon-like with peacock feathers as eyelashes. Usually red or orange and usually breathe fire. Rare overall and live in volcanic settings. Stands over two stories tall. Lays eggs in a massive nest and are very protective. Usually stays in The Land of Nothing or on Bukti Volcano.

Venti/Ventus - (Tawoli) Flying creature. A mixture of an eagle and a horse. Beak mouth. Omnivore. Covered in feathers of white, beige, powder blue, or gray. Nine-hundred pounds. Twelve-foot wingspan on average. Gallops on four legs with hooves or flies. Usually lives in/near Vayu.

For drawings of the four fantastical beasts, check their images at www.cassieswindon.com

DEMONS

Moroka - An immortal demon called The Blood Maiden by legend. She is a mermaidesque figure without legs, whose lower half never healed. She was banished to the ocean by the pearl. The most ruthless of the sisters, she sucks the blood from her victims as her nourishment. Always cries never-ending crimson tears.

Oniskel - She is the Soul Sucker by legend. Tall and slender woman with red hair down to her ankles. Gold butterfly wings attach to her back, with the ability to float. She wears a transparent/golden silk toga. Honey drips out of her mouth, and spiders endlessly crawl out as she speaks. She sucks souls out of mortals as her nourishment. Oniskel was banished to a mountaintop by the crystal.

Surh-Sig - An immortal demon called The Skin Scraper by legend. She is a skeleton-like figure who drapes herself with an assortment of others' skin. Surh-Sig has disfigured bones as hands with crooked fingers, obsidian eyes, sharp fangs, and a slimy, long tongue. She is known for also eating mortals' skin for her nourishment. She was banished to The Forbidden Caves by the emerald.

MYSTIER TRIBES

The locations of the village tribes are named after the most powerful ancestors in their tribe. Before The Fall, about 80 years ago, there were over 50 Mystier clans. Now only four remain.

Cydon - Cydians possess water power. With training, they control elements involving water, ponds, rivers, lakes, oceans, waves. Their Circle tattoo is a blue/green/aqua swirl. The strongest family of this element, blessed with enhancements, is debatable.

Draven - This village is on the northeastern coast, full of dens and treehouses deep in the forest. Dravians possess earth power. With training, they control and manipulate elements such as soil, rocks, plants. Their Circle tattoo is a green/brown swirl. The strongest family of this element, blessed with enhancements, are the Griffins.

Elidi - Elidians possess firepower and are wild at heart. With training, they control elements involving heat, flames. Their Circle tattoo is a red/orange swirl. Mystiers with this Magik originate from The Land of Nothing.

Vayu - This Mystier city is on the Northwestern coast, with a population ten times that of the other villages. Vayu's skyscrapers look as if they are floating when viewed from across the ravine that separates the city from the Ordull world. Vayuians possess air power. With training, they control elements involving wind and oxygen. Their Circle tattoo is a white/blue/gray swirl. The strongest family of this element, blessed with enhancements, are the Nilsons.

LOCATIONS

Andersonville - the capital city of Lodesa (where Kyra grew up).

Aurella Fortress - an ancient, crumbling castle on the edge of Vayu's border.

Bukti Volcano - In the Land of Nothing. Home of Ashes creature.

Crooked Chateau - originally an art museum and community center with a ballroom, which has a shifting purpose as the novel progresses.

Forbidden Caves - on Draven's border, which is the setting for many legends.

Galudi Lighthouse - originally a port for Lodesa to trade with other countries, haunted by ghosts from The Fall.

Lodesa - the country.

Vuldow - The Shadow Land in the south is miles of a dystopian-like terrain, not due to a nuclear bombing that the Ordulls assume, but because of the massacre during The Fall eighty-two years ago that wiped out hundreds of cities.

See the full epic map at the beginning of this book or online at www.cassieswindon.com

Necklaces

All four elemental necklaces have the power for enhanced protection and power when used.

Crystal – necklace from Vayu that bound Oniskel to the top of a mountain peak.

Emerald – necklace from Draven that bound Surh-Sig to the forbidden caves. Helps Alaska teleport more than one person at a time.

Pearl – necklace from Cydon that bound Moroka to the depths of the sea.

Ruby – necklace from Elidi that burns when touched by someone without a protective spell.

UNETLO BOOK

The strongest and oldest spell book belonging to the Mystier race, residing in the Vayuian Library from year 05G-present day. Spells are listed alphabetically.

Atuyasdodi promitto - I vow to Link to you

Aurum shiyo - ridding of a curse/dark Magik

Avanido muati - revert the demon beings back to their original nymph form

Ayasdi sospit- protect a loved one

Cupi geyiu - ultimate sacrifice

Dehano huc - come

Digati impetu - attack

Hostia donadagohvi - let go

Ines meocha - obey

Memi anvadis - return one's memory

Monile volare - levitate

Opus amare - open love

Reditus atsutsa - return to me

Tenebris agvnig - summoning of darkness

Terra angakok - heal

Tohiyus elawe - leave

Uyetsgi waklo - wake/rise

Vand zalit - release

Venereae ostaguyelu - protection against pregnancy and STDs

Yelas secar - sever/cut

ENHANCEMENTS

Healing - Jadox
Hearing - Kyra
Holding breath - Caspian
Mind control - Brent
Prophecies - Gemm
Scent - Jadox
Sight - Isaac
Spells - Kyra
Teleportation - Alaska
Weather - Isaac

GOLDEN CHAINS

Cassie Swindon

New Adult Romantic Suspense

BREAK THE STONE

CASSIE SWINDON

CHAPTER ONE

Raelyn Bell

S*HOULD I SEARCH UP there or not?*

Raelyn Bell stared up at the forbidden barn loft. Her truck's keys clanked against the ladder as she hovered one hand over the rung. The sweet scent of straw wafted through the autumn air.

I have to look. Maybe there'll be something of Ma's up there.

Bear placed his fluffy golden paws on the ladder, his sharp barks echoing throughout the barn.

"Okay, Bear, I'll go. But if Pa catches us, I'm blaming you." She pointed a finger right at his big brown eyes.

Raelyn's cowboy boots scuffed against the ladder. The higher she climbed, the whiter her knuckles turned from clenching the rungs so tightly. Once at the top, she stood alone in the abandoned loft. The emptiness around her felt familiar, paralleling all her current relationships.

While she looked around at the deserted space, Raelyn lost any hope of finding anything of Ma's. She sighed and poked her head over the side of the platform. Bear's rear wiggled back and forth on the ground, his whining bringing a faint grin to Raelyn's face.

"Don't worry, boy. You're not missing anything. There's only dust up here." He barked and danced in a circle below.

As she turned, the toe of her boot caught on one of the slats of the floor, and she fell straight to her knees. The strap of her satchel rolled off her shoulder, spilling her journal onto the cracked beams. Mid-groan, she glimpsed the sunlight shimmering through the rafters, reflecting off something metal in the back corner. Raelyn crawled closer. A latch protruded from a warped, wooden door. The door whispered her name, its secrets creeping over her like a cold chill. Her pulse quickened. She jiggled the rusty handle.

Stuck.

Raelyn gripped it harder and yanked. "Hun?" Pa hollered from below.

Raelyn jumped at the sound of his deep voice. After stumbling, she started to hurry down to see what her father needed.

Wait! What about what I want?

Raelyn chose to ignore him for the first time since…ever…and moved back to the door. She accidentally kicked her journal. It soared over the side and landed on the barn floor with a splat.

Crap!

Raelyn held her breath for a beat, praying Pa hadn't heard it, and peeked between the wooden slats of the wall.

Thud. Thud. Thud.

Under the oak tree, Pa swung an axe down hard, splitting each log with one swift blow. Heart pounding at the thought of getting caught, Raelyn turned and pulled on the latch again.

Nothing.

She gritted her teeth and rammed into the door hard with her shoulder but fell back onto her side. Glancing around, Raelyn spotted her canoe paddle hanging on the wall. A soft grunt escaped her lips as she leaned off the side of the loft and pulled up the paddle.

Wedging the tip between the door and frame, she tightened her fists and pushed with all of her 110 pounds.

The door jerked open, sending her flying through the opening and tearing through a spider's silky web and into a tiny room beyond. The chopping sound of the axe stopped.

"Raelyn?" Pa's boots stomped and cast a bear-sized shadow on the floor. The man, others called William Bell, stood below with his broad stature filling the barn.

Raelyn hunkered down in the back corner of the secret space, struggling to quiet her panting.

Please don't look up.

Pa ran his hand through his thick, wavy hair. Bear sat right next to her journal, tongue hanging from his mouth. Raelyn silently dropped her forehead into her palm.

Pa squatted, picking up her journal. His strong hands made her journal look so small as he laid it on a barrel. "Where'd she go, boy?"

Why does Pa suddenly care?

Pa turned quickly and jogged back to the farmhouse, dialing his phone on the way.

See. He gives up easily and forgets about me.

Once his footsteps faded, Raelyn looked around. Behind a pile of dusty crates was a large trunk.

In her way rested a canvas picture of Ma standing among a line of a dozen young women who were all covered from head to toe in hijabs. Ma wore her typical journalist attire, her work ID badge reflecting the desert sun, showing her name Joanna Bell. The other women looked defeated and exhausted, but Ma's sapphire eyes hinted of hope—like she possessed a secret. Raelyn flipped it over, revealing the year 2004. Twelve years ago. She moved the canvas and walked over to the large chest. Scratches and dents marred every corner of the worn, wooden trunk. It was sealed with a rusty lock.

What's inside? Something of Ma's? Treasure? A skeleton?

When she kneeled in front of the chest, her jeans brushed dust away from a small metal oval. She bent down and rubbed harder, revealing a name:

Joanna Rae Bell

Raelyn froze.

Finally! I knew I'd find something!

She placed both hands on the top and blew out a big breath. Dust flooded the air like the faded memories swirling in her mind. Picnics by the lake, baking cupcakes, and planting strawberry seeds—all with the mother she had lost years ago.

Raelyn pulled on the lock, but it didn't budge.

Pa's axe!

She descended fast, staying out of view of the farmhouse windows, and snuck around the side of the barn. The heaviness of the axe felt familiar from all the times she helped Pa around the yard. She lugged it back up the ladder as Bear watched the spectacle unfold. Raelyn raised it high above her head. Before swinging down, she peeked through the wooden slats again to check for Pa. She crashed the axe hard onto the lock, making her bounce back a bit. It didn't even make a dent. Bear barked.

Raelyn whispered, "You're right, Bear. The wood." She slammed the axe into the side of the trunk, creating a quick crack at the bottom. A hard grunt escaped her lips as she pounded the axe one more time, turning the split into a hole just big enough to fit her thin wrist through. Kneeling, she reached in and felt blindly.

There are way too many papers in here.

Raelyn tugged on a stack and pulled out a bundle of her parent's wedding pictures wrapped with a rubber band. At the bottom of the pile, a thicker parchment stuck out. Raelyn cocked her head to the side, turning it over.

What is this a map of?

There were a bunch of handwritten symbols.

At the bottom, written in cursive, was one word: Zohaib.

Squinting, she read small numbers, potentially a serial number or USB code: 35.1415N and 79.0080W.

Raelyn snapped a picture of it with her phone. "Raelyn!"

She shoved the map into her pocket and hurried down the ladder. A sharp piece of wood sliced into her fingertip, making her gasp, but she held in any signs of discomfort—as usual.

When she landed with a soft thump, Bear circled her heels. She crouched and kissed his forehead. "Don't you tell a soul."

His adorable growl brought a smile to her lips.

Pa strode around the corner of the barn. "There you are. I was worried."

Worried? No, Pa's never worried.

His scent radiated fresh wood. Pa always smelled of the forest. If someone ever mentioned the word hunting, the comfortable memory of his scent whirled through her mind. Raelyn looked up at him, her neck uncomfortably angled to meet his gaze.

"Don't disappear on me like that," he said softly.

Raelyn turned toward the log pile so he wouldn't see her eye roll.

Like he cares...

By her boot, a dandelion sprouted up from the hard-packed clay, tough despite all the odds stacked against it.

Raelyn scrunched her nose. "So, did you catch any fish earlier?" "Trout. It's in the fridge. You're still making dinner?"

"As always."

After an awkward silence, Pa rubbed his back and stretched. "I feel old." "Guess you're falling apart before you even turn forty."

Their conversation was longer than any of their interactions over the last week. She smiled and playfully pushed his sturdy shoulders. "Come on, Pa. You used to chop wood for hours."

"I'll just fix myself with some duct tape," Pa grunted. "Remind me what it feels like to be seventeen?"

His green eyes went vacant like he had gone back in time. What was he thinking about? Probably Ma. She used to bring him lemonade whenever he worked outside for too long and then sit on top of the pile of wood, flirting in that gross way parents should never do.

He scratched his chestnut beard, which was peppered with hints of gray. Raelyn looked nothing like Pa, with her thin frame and high cheekbones. His emerald eyes didn't match her amber ones, either.

She twisted the heel of her boot and dropped her gaze to the ground. "Uh, so do you need anything?"

"Well, during my fishing trip, only one paddle was in the boat. Have you seen the other one?"

She wiped the sweat off her brow and forced herself not to look to the loft. "Um. I'll look for it."

"Thanks." His callused hand pulled out a rolled-up newspaper from his back pocket. A page flipped from the warm breeze. The date in bold on top read,

September 23

The anniversary of the last time I saw Ma...so long ago.

Pa handed it over. "Can you check for any listings looking for handyman work? I could pick up some extra cash on the weekends."

He began chopping again, slamming the axe down strong. Raelyn's fingers grazed the nearby tire swing that her parents used to push her on—a reminder of a different time when family laughter rang like a constant melody. Neglected for years, its only remaining purpose was to tether them to the past.

Some days, her memories with Ma felt like wounds from a dagger—not a thin slice that barely grazed the surface, but a deep cut that could pierce her entire soul.

Raelyn leaned against the barrel and skimmed through her journal, landing on her book wish list, full of stories about desert worlds and handsome heroes. She plucked a pen from her messy bun and placed it on a fresh page until gold ink bled.

My soul split between the options ahead
Searching for a clue of what beliefs to shed

"Hey, Bear. What rhymes with 'shed'?" She tapped the pen to her round chin. "I wish Ma wasn't dead."

Bear nudged her leg softly, always knowing what she needed. Raelyn tightened the plaid shirt snugly around her waist. She drew in a deep breath before she could lose the nerve and fabricated a lie. "Pa, I have a project for class. I need to bring in a family heirloom."

"Use your grandma's little mirror."

Does he know about the trunk or not?

"Actually, I was hoping I could bring in something of Ma's. The project is about connecting with our ancestors, and I thought you might have something you could lend me."

His eyes hardened and flickered to the loft for a moment. "Got rid of all your ma's stuff years ago. Plus, you don't need Ma. You have me."

No. I don't have either of you.

Raelyn identified with the red leaf falling down from their oak tree, completely at the mercy of the wind—and alone.

As Pa turned, with each stride he stepped away, he grew more distant from her heart.

She swallowed her nerves and raised her voice as she followed him across the yard. "You gave away everything?"

He marched into the house.

The scent of burning wood from the fireplace filled the air.

She stared at the compass hanging from his belt loop. "You still have the compass Ma gave you."

He squared his jaw. "That's different."

Raelyn pulled the crinkled map from her pocket. "What about this map?

Was it Ma's?"

Pa hustled forward and tried to swipe it from her grip. "What is it a map of?"

"Nothing. Just a souvenir."

"Can I keep it?" She pressed the map to her chest. "No."

Raelyn raised her voice. "Why?" "Give it here."

She reluctantly laid it in his hand. "Are you lying about–?"

Before she could finish, Pa ripped the map into pieces, marched to the brick fireplace, and chucked them inside. The paper turned brown, curling under the fierce heat.

Her heart pounded. “Why did you do that?”

Pa didn’t look at her. “I love you.”

Raelyn looked out the window at the barn.

I need to see what else is in Ma’s trunk.

www.ingramcontent.com/pod-product-compliance
Lightning Source LLC
Chambersburg PA
CBHW060544310726
48982CB00009B/1368/J

* 9 7 8 1 7 3 7 3 4 6 9 4 4 *